GUINEVERE

A Medieval Romance

Lavinia Collins

First published in Great Britain and the US in three volumes on Kindle by Not So Noble Books and The Book Folks, 2014. This paperback edition published in 2015 by The Book Folks.

Copyright © Lavinia Collins, 2014

The moral right of the author has been asserted.

All characters and events in this publication relate to figures already in the public domain, in the imagination of people the world over who marvel at and revel in this timeless legend.

All rights reserved.
This publication may not, in any part, be reproduced, uploaded to or stored in a retrieval system, or transmitted in any form or any means, without the express permission of the publisher, nor otherwise be circulated in any form or binding or cover other than the existing one without tacit agreement to the same conditions on behalf of the subsequent purchaser.

Typeset in Garamond
Design by Steve French
Printed by CreateSpace

Available from Amazon.com and other retail outlets

Published by
The Book Folks
106 Huxley Rd
London E10 5QY
thebookfolks.com

For my own Kay
Lover, Inspiration, Friend

Part I
The Warrior Queen

Chapter One

The soft light filtered between my flickering eyelashes, the lovely golden rays dappling through the green spring leaves blinking and dancing. I could smell the grass beneath me, feel it on the bare skin at the base of my back, hear my heart beating in my ears, still fast. I had the adrenaline of the hunt still rushing in my blood, and I was thinking of the men coming home from war, the same bright victory in their veins. I was lost in the same daydream I dreamed every day, back then. *It will be soon,* I told myself, *it will be soon.* The air around me smelled of the coming summer, and the breeze on my face was light and lovely as a kiss. Contentment, deep and soft, was upon me.

"Guinevere! Guinevere!"

I sat up at the sound of my own name. One of my ladies was running towards me through the clearing, her dress torn from running through the woods. Through the thin silk tiny streams of blood, soft, white flesh showed. She must have been in a hurry, to run out here in her dress. I stood as she came towards me, pushing the thick, coarse red curls of my hair back from my face, running my fingers through them and twisting them back out of my way, tying them fast, and then I took up my bow.

"What is it? Why are you out here?"

I knew something was wrong. Badly wrong.

She shook her head, gasping in breath, leaning down on her knees. I put a hand on her shoulder and shushed her until she had gathered herself.

At last she steadied her breathing, and then she glanced up at me, and in those glassy eyes, brimming with the tears she had been choking back so long, I saw already the answer that she would give.

"The war... the war is lost."

The great hall of Carhais was empty when I entered it. This was not so unusual. My father's feasting-hall had lain empty these past two years and more, since Carhais had emptied out its armies onto the battlefields of Britain, across the sea. The last time it had been full, we had been sending our men – and our boys – off to war, my three brothers among them. And the man to whom I had been promised in marriage. I had been meant to become his wife that summer, and instead I stood at the gates of Carhais with the other women, the children, the old and the weak, and my father, and watched the men ride away to war, with my mother at their head. I had taken my brothers' place; hunting, overseeing the organisation of what little of the household remained, and Carhais' defences. That had been easy. I had been schooled for it all my life. It had not been easy watching the news of each new loss reach my father.

When there had been someone to scold me for it, I would not have come into the great hall in my hunting leathers, but my mother was gone, and there was no one left who cared. For the enormous formal hall she would have had me in a dress of silk, a circlet of gold about my head, but today I came straight from the forest. My fine clothes were sold for iron and horses, and there was no one left to note that I strode in without fanfare, without a bow to anyone. No one to be a *proper* princess for. No one who cared how I looked, or if I could sing, or read in Latin. What mattered now was that I was useful, that I could count the dwindling stores; that I could hunt. That was how I spent most of my days now; hunting in the forest. There was little else to do, and those of us left behind needed to eat.

Or, I thought it was empty. A black shadow on the dais, on my father's throne, unfolded itself as he lifted his head from its droop of despair.

"Guinevere..." He breathed my name, and shook his head. I let the lady at my arm slip from my grasp, ran forward and knelt before him, taking up his hands in mine.

"Father..."

He put a hand on my head in the same fatherly benediction that I had experienced there since I was a child, but this time it was trembling. *No*, I thought. But he was already speaking.

"Guinevere, they're all dead. Your brothers are dead, our allies are dead." He drew a breath in that rattled him at the core.

"What happened, father?" I turned my face up to him, and he cupped my chin in his soft, aged hand. I was glad in that moment – deeply deeply glad – that my father was too old to fight. My mother had not been. And she was not here.

"No one thought Arthur capable of it, but he came, that child, with his army of brutes. They wiped us out. The way they tell it, he would not have done until all his enemies were dead. All those he could lay his hands on. Barely one in ten left alive. He's returned to his court at Camelot. Like father like son – his father Uther was a brute, too. The men from our lands who made it back alive are... few.

Mainly deserters who fled. Carhais will turn them away; this castle is no place for cowards."

"And...?" The name I wished to speak stuck in my throat, and my father nodded, and pressed his lips together. The man among them I was pledged to marry was dead, and he had been sweet and kind. I had hoped he would come back to me. He had been my safety. Marriage to him would have meant I could stay in my own home. Now, all of sudden, I was a defeated princess, heir to a proud and ancient kingdom, with no brothers. I felt the dread gathering around me. Some awful foreign man would come to claim me. I would be taken from my home.

"He, too, Guinevere. He was brave, at the front, and so he died first." I choked back the tears, then, for the first time. I hated to cry, I hated to seem weak. I would not mourn. I would carry on. Gather my fighting women, and the few men who were left, and defend my lands. When I had three brothers older than me, it had not mattered much to whom I would be given, but now whoever had me would have Carhais, and Brittany with it. If I wanted to stay in my home, if I wanted to keep possession of myself now, I would have to fight for it.

"It may yet be for the best, Guinevere." He drew in a deep breath, and gently turned my face up towards him to look him in the eyes. Those old eyes, the wrinkles drooping sad at the sides, the deep lines of care. I knew what was coming. "Arthur has sent messengers. They wish to bring you back to Camelot. To be his bride."

"No!" I jumped back, and I was on my feet before I realised what I had done, the anger pumping hot through my veins. I had not thought it would be so soon. I had not thought it would be *him*. I was not ready to leave my own lands, nor was I prepared to go into the hands of the boy-king Arthur, the savage who had slaughtered my people. *Never.* I was shouting already. "Father, he's a brute. He's a *child*. No. I won't do it."

I had not even thought to fear it. What could have convinced my father that the only way was to send me to *him*? I had been betrothed to a man, and everyone said that Arthur was nothing more than a boy, and a foreign conqueror besides. I didn't want a boy. I wanted a man, and I wanted one of my own people. I wanted someone who would stand by my side and fight for Brittany's independence from Arthur, not for it to be handed over to him, and me with it. I thought at least I would be married to a prince from our own side. I could not imagine my father would agree to this if there were any other choice. The losses had been that heavy, then. But I would not go. I would not marry Arthur. I had not given up.

"Guinevere..." My name fell like a sigh from his lips and it clutched me in the pit of my stomach. He did not have to say the words, I knew there was no other way, not really. We could not refuse Arthur, and I could not refuse my sad, old father. He had lost everyone else. *Perhaps, since I am not a parent, I cannot know the desire to have a child in slavery, rather than dead.* I inclined my head in a nod. Arthur had conquered Britain, and if we wanted the remains of Carhais to stay alive, we did not have a choice. *I* did not have a choice.

My father took me by the hand and led me through the empty halls of our home. Before, this emptiness was expectant, tingling with the possibility of our people about to return from war. And the return of one man I already knew I would never speak of again, could never speak of again. Especially if I was to wed Arthur, to keep myself alive for my father's sake, and to keep the people of my lands from his ravaging wars. My father led me up to his tower and into the room that I had not been into since I was a child. Before my first bleeding, I was allowed in there all of the time. After that, my mother always said, *a woman's blood is too potent.* I didn't know why, or what she meant, but I knew she was right. She was afraid that I was not ready, that the old magic of that room was too much for a new-made woman. Not too much for a girl, not for a child, but once my age had come she was afraid. She had always avoided that room herself. And my father, my father the witch, would laugh indulgently at my superstitious but magicless mother, who had not a drop of Otherworld blood in her veins. Still, he did not let me in, and I knew there was some wondrous secret within, for I had felt it, in my blood. I knew myself to be my father's daughter.

The room was as I remembered it, the shelves stuffed with leather-bound books, and animal parts in jars, and drying herbs – that acrid smell of plants with secrets. Plants I remembered the names of, and the uses. But these things were small and whispering nothings compared to the table. Gorgeous dark wood, smooth, smelling of the ancient powers of the woodlands, the Round Table of Carhais. Fashioned by my ancestors, the witches. Before I even stepped in the room I could feel its powerful presence.

As I did when I was young, I climbed onto the table and lay on my back across its breadth. It always smelled the same. That lovely, intense smell of old wood. Of old magic.

"Last wishes, Guinevere. Last wishes."

I closed my eyes, I breathed in deep of the air of my home. I would come back here.

I wish for Arthur's death.

"I'm sending the table to Arthur, Guinevere," my father said softly, after a long pause.

I sat up.

"No, *no*, father. It belongs here, in Carhais. Not with *him*."

"Guinevere, I am an old man. You may yet have a son. The Round Table belongs with you." He took my hands. His hands were dry as parchment and trembling. I wanted to beg him again not to send me, but I knew that this was as hard for him as it would be for me. I was the heir to Carhais now the others were all dead, and I had to act to protect my people. I didn't want it, I could hardly bear it, but I would have to do it. For him. For them. "Just keep it close by you. Don't forget your old father. Don't forget your ancient blood."

I kissed his wrinkled forehead.

Last wishes. The last day of my life as a free woman.

I was loaded onto the boat along with the Round Table and three of my ladies, Marie, Christine and Margery. I was not supposed to take my hunting gear, my bow and arrows, my sword, but I hid them among the rest of my things, the fine dresses of silk, the books and jewels. What was left of them. Almost everything had been sold, as the war went on, but I had at least saved all my books. I had to leave behind my fighting women, and I had to go dressed like the kind of princess Arthur desired. No longer with the trappings of a celtic warrior princess – the iron and leather and sweat – I felt vulnerable and naked. Arthur did not want a warrior queen. I was bought and sold, and if my people were going to be safe, Arthur had to get what he wanted.

The journey was long, and the sea made me sick. I had never wanted to leave Brittany. The air was cold when I stepped off at Dover. The wind blew right through the pale green silk – chosen by my women to emphasise my porcelain skin, my dark red hair – and I felt my skin turn to goosebumps already. The country was as hostile to me as I was to it. I had never had to be a thing of beauty before. It was enough to be strong, enough to be swift and deft. But I had to, now. For my people. For my father back in Carhais. I wondered how young this *boy king* was; he could not have been such a child to tear through Britain as he had done, but I knew he was younger than me. I hoped he would be small and weak, and that I might be able to bully him into sending me back home. But those were not the tales that came back to us at Carhais.

I could see far away the party of knights approaching. Hardly a greeting for a new queen. But then I had heard that this was what Arthur was like – not so much like the French kings with their showy courts and fine things, but a killer with a small war-band of knights, swift and violent. I steeled myself for it. I could be a good queen. I would bide my time. I would have my revenge on him for killing my people, for leaving my father alone, without a wife or sons. For, after all of that, demanding me from him.

They came closer fast, a band of five of them. I could not tell which one was Arthur. Some of them were dressed for war, in platemail from the neck down. Hostile, unwelcoming. Perhaps he had not even come himself, but had sent his servants to collect me, like cargo. I did not like the look of a band of heavily armoured men coming to fetch me. I supposed the land was still recovering from its wars. In that case, I should have liked better to come armed myself.

The knight at the front of the party jumped deftly from his horse. He was not armed, but dressed in a beautiful surcoat of black and gold, though he had a sword at his side. Handsome, dark features, tall and broad, with an easy smile. A flicker inside me betrayed my hope that this was Arthur.

"Do I have the honour of addressing the lady Guinevere?"

I and my ladies curtsied. It rankled with me. In my country, as a princess, I bowed like a man, and only to my father. Margery had come to me from Logrys, Arthur's country, and instructed me on their customs. She, too, was sorry to return to them.

"Lady Guinevere, I am Sir Kay, King Arthur's Seneschal," he took his horse by the bridle, "may I help you onto a horse?"

Arthur had sent his *Seneschal* to collect me. Oh, we had one of those in Carhais, but we were not so grand about it. We called ours the keeper of the household. Arthur had sent his *housekeeper* to collect me, as though I were a sack of corn that needed to be checked for quality before it was accepted. Sure enough this man was the keeper of the whole of Britain, but I did not think much of it, nonetheless.

I strode forward, and took the bridle from him. I was aware of his eyes flicker across the taut silk of my dress, glancing for a second where my nipples, hard from the cold, were just visible. I was not afraid. I had been looked at like that many times before. As he reached forward to try to help me onto the horse, I grasped the saddle and swung myself up, pulling my dress up to my knees to sit astride it like a man. I hated that dress. Too thin for Britain's cold, too small, since it had been a long time since I had been required to wear such a thing, and I had grown taller, more muscular since, though Arthur's war had made me thinner.

"Do you think we do not have horses in Carhais, Sir Kay?"

He laughed. I noticed that, behind him, a knight dressed in green armour with thick stubble, and wild orange-brown hair did not laugh with the others. His face was heavily freckled, and scarred. From the look of him, he was one of King Lot's sons. It was King Lot who began the war we all lost so badly against Arthur, my king and captor. Another half-prisoner, then, brought here to be another one of Arthur's servants. Another old enemy. He noticed me looking at him and met my gaze. His grey eyes were steady and cold. I did not sense an ally there. I felt a cold shiver at the base of my spine, and I wished that I had more about me that made me feel safe.

Three of the other knights took my ladies on the back of their horses, and Sir Kay leapt up behind the knight on the remaining horse, and we turned away from Dover, and I turned my back on the sea, and my home beyond it, as though it were nothing at all to me. Nothing at all.

The ride to Arthur's new-made court, the city of Camelot, felt unbearably long, even though it took less than a day. I could feel my heart heavy within me, heavy and slow with the thought of my home receding farther and farther away behind me. The land we rode through was ravaged and bare. In the villages we passed though, the people cowered from the knights, lowering their grubby faces and retreating into the shadows of their doorways, as the huge men with shining armour on themselves and on their horses thundered by. This is not how it had been in Carhais. I had walked barefoot through the woodlands to the villages nearby and no one had known who I was. I had listened in on the conversations of my father's subjects, smelled their food cooking, seen them crying. Perhaps if Arthur had walked among his people he would not be such a warlike king; perhaps he would be gentle and prudent instead, like my own father, who would rather have sent his daughter to a stranger, and a brute, and a conqueror, with no more protection than an enchanted table, than risk his people's lives.

I was glad to be ahead of the rest of the party – my horse was strong and fast, and bearing less of a load than the others was happy to prance ahead. I could see the landscape opening before me, softer and less wild than my own country, but full of deep, lush-looking woodlands and wide, proud hilltops. Perhaps I could be happy here in my time alone, as long as I was far from the war-hollowed villages or Arthur's brutish court. If I could ride through the land, smelling the earth and the warm, homely scent of the horse beneath me. He was a handsome horse, the one I was riding, a bay with a glossy mane and velvety nostrils. I had left my own dear horse at home. I tried to put these thoughts from my mind. If I were to have any chance of happiness I had to be resolved to my new life, and try to forget about the past. My childhood stubbornness still lingered with me, determined to go home, but another part of me – I supposed what I had inherited from my father – knew I needed to be practical. That I might never go home.

The smell of spring was strong in the air, and the gentle breeze that lifted my hair lightly off my forehead was soothing. It was when the sky began to redden at the edges, when the first edge of the sun dipped below the horizon and threw its fire onto the underside of the clouds above it, that I first saw Camelot. Black and sharp against the horizon, high on a broad hill, I could count eight round turreted towers reaching up high into the sky, and around them the castle walls. Silk banners whose colours I could not see fluttered in silhouette in the breeze above it. It was everything I had refused to believe it would be. The boy king's city was a thing of beauty with its delicate towers fluttering with flags and banners, but also a siege weapon – oh, I could see that, too, from where I was, already. Word of Camelot had come to Carhais years ago when it had been the mighty fortress of the warlord Uther Pendragon, the man they said was Arthur's father, and people had associated its name with a shiver of the spine. I had imagined iron, and steel. The smell of blood. It looked a different place from that, now. Welcoming, though I only saw it black against the red sky, and far-off, with its fluttering banners. It was a place of celebration. Of course it was. Arthur had the victory. It was as though all the joy in the world had poured out of Carhais, and into this place. Of course it had. Joy followed victory. The sight of that city, my future home, black against the setting sun, filled me with a tentative, fluttering hope, but it also filled me with dread.

Chapter Two

By the time our party rode through Camelot's gates and arrived in its great courtyard, night was almost fallen, and at the edges of the sky I could see the little white stars peeping out, and the ghost of the moon in a sky that was still indigo with night. *This is the last moon I will see as a free woman*, I thought. I slid down off my horse and handed Sir Kay the reins. Our hands brushed as I passed them and our eyes met, but this time I saw that I had been mistaken in what I had seen in him before. The look he gave me was not one of lust – as I had thought before – but something more complex, softer. A look of kind interest, but also of strange affinity, as though he knew me already, and as he brushed past me to take the horse by the nose and lead it away I felt a power that I recognised, and I understood that Kay was one of the Otherworld, and he had seen it in me too. My father had told me that I would meet others like us at Arthur's court, and this giant of a man – for Kay stood head and shoulders above me, and I was tall for a woman – left some strange vibration in the air that was at once unexpected and deeply familiar to me. I felt I would be pleased to have him around.

The other knights had not introduced themselves. Lot's son had jumped down from his horse, leaving Margery stranded on the back of the charger, clinging on to the saddle, unable to get down, terrified and unable to ride or jump down safely from a horse so large. I made to walk to her and help her down, and Kay put a gentle hand on my arm to hold me back. I felt it then for sure; the warmth of knowing, of the same Otherworld blood in our veins. I wished harder that it was he, not Arthur, that I would wed. One of my own. What would a man with no magic in his blood do with my father's Round Table?

"Gawain, help her down," Kay scolded patiently. Now I had a name for Lot's son, and it was the one whose reputation on the battlefield had already reached me. The second of them, I thought. I wondered if the other sons, too, were at Arthur's court. He strode back over and plucked Margery down from the saddle, his hands around her waist, and placed her lightly on the floor. He didn't look at her or say anything, and he disappeared down a stone hallway into the night.

"Don't mind Gawain," Kay said, his gaze following where Gawain had gone, his tone distracted for a moment, before he turned to me. "He is not usually so uncourteous. His mother blames him for bringing his brothers to Arthur's court. She thinks he should have stayed in Lothian. She's worried that all his brothers will follow him here. They probably will." Kay turned back with a smile, less serious, and I was glad. "He usually wouldn't pass up a chance to put his hands on a fair lady, such as your Margery."

Kay gave Margery a gentle little nod of a bow, and she seemed to relax. He had an easy charm about him; another gift from the Otherworld, I supposed.

The knight Kay had shared his horse with trotted over. He was a large man, muscle-bound like an ox. I could see it in the way he moved, with an easy, muscular grace. He had a tanned, handsome face and a ready smile, and his golden hair was scruffy from the ride. He looked like an overgrown boy, flushed with excitement, and eager to get off to some game or other. I wondered if he were Kay's squire. He jumped down from the horse and handed the reins to Kay.

"Sir Kay, I hope you don't mind taking the horses." He turned to me and inclined his head. "My lady, Princess Guinevere."

I inclined my head in return, and the knight strode away. Marie and Christine had been helped from their mounts and were looking anxiously to me, uneasy about what we should do. I did not know either. It was not my country. They were not even speaking my native language. My head hurt already from the effort of speaking it, of understanding, and I just wanted to go to sleep. I had no idea what I was meant to do, did not know the customs of the court. No one had offered to show us to any rooms or offered us any refreshment. The man who had demanded me as his bride had not even come to greet me. The wedding was due to take place the next day, but what would be done with us until then was unclear. And I was prepared to protect myself. Beneath my silk dress I had concealed a small but highly effective dagger, in case the need might call for it. I was not so young and naive that I had not thought that some trick at my expense might be played. I had to submit to a lawful marriage, but not to anything else.

"Sir Ector, my father, will take you to your chambers, my ladies," Kay said, leading the horses away, all together. And they were calm for him, of course, and quieted their whinnying when he put his hand gently on their flank. *Otherworld.* How could I have not seen it at once?

A knight, older than the others, the one who had shared his horse with Christine, came over. He had a kind face, and I could see instantly the family resemblance to Kay. This must be his father. He led us up to a set of rooms perfumed with spices and oils I had never smelled before, and decked in silks. Our Breton court in Carhais was more of a gathering of warriors, and I had silks only because they were gifts from courtiers coming to pledge their faith to my father. We did not value such things. Our rooms smelled of leather and straw. Our riches were in the arts of medicine, of poetry. We valued our ancient blood; we did not gather such things. I had never seen riches like this. How could this warrior king have also such a rich and decadent court already? I suppose it was the plenty of victory. The beds were heaped with rich coverlets and more candles than I could count at a glance filled the room with a soft, enticing light. The value of the luxuries in my room could have bought my father's court. And now Arthur had bought me. Perhaps he had sent my father silks from the east, and gold and candles. But my father would have no use for them; these were not our ways.

Sir Ector bowed goodnight as he made to leave.

"My lord King Arthur sends his greetings to the beautiful Princess Guinevere and wishes you to have as a gift for your wedding tomorrow the dress and the jewels laid out upon the bed for you. He asks that you forgive his absence."

And he shut the door.

The dress on the bed – he obviously had thought me too much of a savage to have fine clothes of my own – was nonetheless beautiful. Marie gasped as she lifted its soft fabric in her tiny bird-like hands and gently laid it against her cheek. It was a deep emerald green. It would be a beautiful colour for me. I could see as I looked at it that Margery was only being kind when she told me the dress that she had chosen for my being brought here – the finest of my dresses – was as fine as the dresses women wore in Logrys. No. It was old, and plain, the silk thin but coarse. I brushed my fingers lightly against the fabric of the dress that had been left for me. It was like a whisper, like a kiss. I sighed. *Arthur sends gifts, but will not see me himself. I am truly something he has bought, a token of a distant kingdom.* Otherwise he would care if his wife-to-be were beautiful or clever. He could have bought a cripple or a simpleton; he didn't seem to care. I suppose it was not really me that he wanted; it was Brittany, and the table, and the last knights of Carhais who would gather for him now in Camelot, now that he had me.

The jewels sparkled with gold in the candlelight, a gold net set with emeralds for my hair, and thick gold bangles, and a necklace set with an emerald the size of Marie's little fist and hundreds of tiny diamonds. I supposed that, compared to these, what I had brought with me could hardly have been called jewels. I had gold – my gold circlet, the circlet of my ancient people, and a bangle of beaten gold that had been my mother's, made to be worn high on the arm, no good for cold Britain, but nothing set with jewels like this. I would be covered in gems when I went to my marriage tomorrow. No one would see me. They would see a thousand dazzling gems and I would be a display of the riches and grandeur of the great King Arthur's court. Or perhaps he was worried I would be plain. I knew I was not plain, at least. I had seen many of the women of Logrys and found them plainer, smaller, quieter than our own Breton women, many of whom like me were touched with fire, red in the hair and the soul, passionate and quick with life. What would Arthur make of me? I knew what I made of him already.

Chapter Three

I did not sleep during the night. Instead I listened to my heart fluttering in my chest, trapped under my skin, under the useless hushing of my ribs. I didn't know what I was afraid of, or even if I was afraid. I wasn't afraid of what I knew would come after the wedding, like other girls I had known were, though I knew all about it. I had heard other women talking about it, and even seen it once as a child when I walked past a half-closed door and peeped in to see one of my brothers on top of a girl from the village. It had not looked so bad as it sounded when I'd heard it described. Besides, I was not going to let Arthur touch me. He was not going to think he was just going to demand me here and throw me down beneath him like a whore. No, I was not worried about *that*, because it was not going to happen. Perhaps if it had been a man like Kay, as I had wished when they had come to collect me, then I could have borne it, to have his hands on me, but not a man who hid from me, and who in turn tried to hide *me* beneath silks, and jewels.

I was anxious, though, that I had not seen yet the man I was to marry. Only his knights. Of them all, only Gawain was what I had expected; rough and quiet, with the ungentle hands of a killer. Sir Kay had been kind, and Ector. But what would Arthur be like? He was not a man who had been born and raised to his throne, so he would not be a spoiled fop, but he was a man who had killed for it, who had slaughtered his rivals for it, including my father's own men, and done so relentlessly to get it, so he would not be a gentle man, a civilized man. Not that there had been so many of those at my father's court, but we were wild people in a different way. Woodland hunters, proud fighters, but not warmongers, not battle-generals. We didn't ride around on armoured horses, terrorising the peasants as Arthur's men seemed to do. My father had sent our people because my mother's people had owed King Lot allegiance, not because he was interested in wars. And now the war was over, and he found himself on the losing side. The knights of Carhais who would now come to Arthur were the last of my father's forces, and though Carhais would be safe, it would also be empty. The glory of Carhais was all gone from it, seeping out into the big, bloody sponge that was Arthur's Logrys, and the bloody beating heart at the centre, Camelot.

I must have slept, because Margery gently woke me with a hand on my shoulder. It was full light already, so late, but my head throbbed with an insistent weariness, that of a night of broken sleep. I think I had dreamed of home, and the dappled light of the forest, watching the leaves dance in the breeze, chasing a doe through the woodlands.

Marie and Christine came in with a bath and began to fill it with steaming water, and then lavender and rose oils. So Arthur even knew how he wanted me to *smell*. I slid out of bed, and out of my nightdress and into the water. It was too hot, and my pale skin blushed deep red at the heat of it, but I didn't care. It felt as though it was burning the journey away, my past life away, preparing me to be the queen I was now going to have to be. Margery brushed out my hair with soft strokes as I lay soaking, and when I got out, wet and pink like a newborn, plaited it into the style the women wore in Logrys – not loose how I had always had it, but plaited into two thick ropes that she wound together into a bun at the base of my neck and pinned in place with the jewelled pins and net of gold that had been left by the husband I would acquire today. She placed the delicate golden circlet I had brought from home, made to look like an ivy-strand twining around, on my thick, red curls. The dress Arthur had chosen fitted well, its sleeves long and close down to the wrist where they ended with a point that reached almost to the knuckle of my middle finger, its bodice tight and embroidered all over with little gold leaves of ivy. He must have known the traditions of my father's people. I was pleased with that, and with the swish and flow of the silk skirt around my legs. It was a well-made dress, truly. But, it was the dress of a princess, who stood still and was looked at. If I had wanted to run in it, I could not have done. When I was dressed in the green silk dress, and the emerald jewellery, they brought me before the mirror. I had been told, always, that I was beautiful, but all the young marriageable daughters of lords were told this every day, and I was not interested in being beautiful, so I had shrugged at it, and turned away, bored. I had been expecting the fairness of my youth, and the brightness of my hair, but dressed as I was I looked like the queen I was about to become. It was a fierce beauty I saw looking back at me, grand and aloof. I looked proud and cold, and I was pleased with it. I did not want this boy king to think that he had a defeated princess in his grasp. I was still strong, and proud even if my father's people were defeated and gone.

Sir Ector came to fetch me to Arthur, when it was time that we were wed.

"My Lady Guinevere." He took my hand and kissed it lightly. His manner was fatherly, and I was glad to see him. "You have the beauty of a true queen."

"Thank you, Sir Ector." I dipped in a slight curtsey.

"And your ladies, they are lovely little stars beside your radiant sun."

The three ladies bobbed in thanks. It seemed to be all talk at Camelot. Perhaps I would get used to all of these little politenesses, or perhaps they would stop once people had got used to me. I could not say I liked them; they seemed artificial to me. My ladies were dressed in matching gowns of pale blue that I had had brought over with us, all embroidered in silver with little flowers. It best suited Christine, whose dark hair, ice-blue eyes and pale skin made her seem every bit the fairy-woman in her dress. There would be many eyes on her, too, this day, although she was the oldest of us.

Sir Ector offered me his steady arm and I took it, and he guided me down the stairs of the tower, and out across the open courtyard of Camelot's keep, to its small chapel. I ought to have had my own father there, but I knew why he did not come. He was too old to leave his home. To old to suffer the final grief of watching me be handed away. Outside the chapel stood a man dressed in a plain black habit whom I would have mistaken for a monk, were his shaven head and face not patterned with the ugly bruise-blue of woad in beautiful swirls and whorls like the depths of the sea. He measured me with black, beady eyes. I suppressed a shiver down my spine and turned my gaze away.

Inside, the chapel was decked with red roses, and white roses, and white wildflowers all through. But these paled beside the gilded decorations within, pictures of the god of the Christians emblazoned in gold all around; or rather, not their god, but the man who reminded me of our Hanged God, but who I knew was not, but who hung there all the same, made in gold and on a gold cross. I think, like the Hanged God, he too had come back from the dead. So I was to be wed in the sight of Arthur's gods, not my own. I don't know why I should have expected anything else. Arthur's strange Hanged God would be my god now, too.

Everything in that chapel was red and gold and white, shining and overwhelming, so bright and ornate that it took me a while to notice that the chapel was filled with the lords and ladies of Logrys, men and women in ceremonial dress for my wedding, and some knights too, in their armour. I noticed Gawain in his, sat beside a woman with the same russet hair, who had a beautiful, gentle face, and clever, darting blue eyes that caught me with a swift look of appraisal as our gazes met. And in all this, I could scarcely see the golden-haired boy king waiting for me at the altar. All I knew of him was his name, that he had conquered all of Britain and that he was a few years my junior. But I was old for a bride at nineteen; his war had made me so. As I walked down the aisle with my ladies I realised with a sting of betrayal that he had been among the knights that had come to meet me at Dover. *He had wanted to look at me, to check I wasn't ugly or old; he wanted to decide if he liked the look of me before he agreed we should wed.* That was the action of a child, a selfish child who wanted only what was good for himself. I felt my cheeks burn with anger. If I had not the thought of my father and my country in the back of my mind, I would have slapped him in the face, right there.

As I reached him at the altar and my ladies and Sir Ector stood back, Arthur took my hand and kissed it lightly. He had the smug, laughing face of a boy who had got everything he wanted. He was big and strong, clearly, but looked young, barely a man. I would have guessed seventeen years of age at most, from the look of him. Probably younger. Truly, a boy king.

"My apologies for yesterday, Lady Guinevere," he said, quietly, as he turned from me to face the altar.

I gave only a small nod. I had to be obedient, I did not have to be kind.

The words of the ceremony were unfamiliar, and they rushed by me without my comprehending them. There was nothing about the sun, the moon, the stars, the cycles of the earth; it was all about this strange God of his. I said what I was bidden to say, and when Arthur took me in his arms to kiss me as his bride it was with all of the impetuous passion of a young man, new with women. But still I could feel his formidable strength as he held me to him. I was in the arms of a conqueror. I could not have slipped away.

There was more of the ceremony – we drank from a libation cup together, and ate a small piece of bread. I did not follow the meaning, but I hoped it was a ceremony about husbands and wives sharing their meat and wine. We had something like the same, and I would have liked to feel that our ways were not so utterly strange.

As Arthur led me by the hand out of the chapel, the lords and ladies around us cheered and clapped, and threw flower petals over us. I liked their cool soft kisses against the bare skin of my neck and the top of my chest. I closed my eyes against them, for a moment. As we walked out, Arthur leant down and spoke softly in my ear,

"I am pleased to have you as my wife, my Lady Guinevere. I hope you are pleased, as well."

I gave only a little nod. He would not have more from me until he had deserved it.

He slid an arm around my waist and again I felt how strong he was. Even in that light touch I felt it, the power that was held back. He had earned his throne with war, for sure, and at least this man, who was my king now, was not a king who needed others to fight for him. But it was possessive, too. He put his arm around me as though I were already his. As though he owned me. But then again, I supposed that he did. In the eyes of his law and his god, I was his possession now.

He led me to Camelot's great feasting hall. This was more familiar to me than the chapel, though grander than the one I knew from home. There was a long table on a raised dais at one end, where Arthur and I would sit with those he favoured, and down the hall long trestle tables for the other lords, ladies and knights. The high-ceilinged hall was hung with tapestries, embroidered in dark green, red and gold, with scenes of hunting a white hart, or knights riding through the forest. There was a wonderful savoury smell of some kind of meat stew that reminded my stomach that I had not eaten properly since news came to my father's kingdom of a lost war.

Arthur pointed to the high table. "My lady, I will put your Round Table there, so that I and my knights may feast around it as equals. I won this kingdom with war, and in war, a king is no different from a knight. These knights are my brothers and my friends, and it is an honour to me that you bring me this table where we might eat as equals with them."

He shouted an order, and servants spilled out from the shadows to take away the high table, and brought from behind us through the crowd at the main door of the hall – it was the only place where it would fit – my father's enchanted Round Table. I felt sick inside once more. It wasn't an eating table, to be smeared with wine and mead and meat grease. It was a sacred table. I closed my eyes for a moment, and breathed in and out slowly. He was using it for what was sacred to him – his fellowship of knights, his war-band. I had to try, to try to understand his ways, their ways. There was, after all, no going back.

The servants set down the Round Table and threw over it a rich tablecloth of crimson embroidered with Arthur's heraldry, the twisting, roaring dragon of the Pendragon line, bright in gold, and around the border, a little gold row of ivy leaves. Glorious enough for a king and a queen, that simple wood table, when it was thrown over with that. If only its magic could fill the empty seats they were placing around it with the men that had been lost as Arthur forged this glorious new kingdom of Britain from its heart, Logrys, outwards, swallowing up the kingdoms like the dragon swallows its prey. No hesitation. No mercy. A beast has no need for mercy.

When the table was ready, Arthur led me down through the hall and we sat side by side. He had spoken of equality, but our chairs were gilded and larger than the others, and we had crimson velvet cushions beneath us. Sat round with his men, but still a king. The crown on his head was the crown of his father, Uther Pendragon, who had ruled Logrys before him. It was a war-king's crown, truly. Made of gold, yes, but wrought with the sharp shapes of crosses and set boldly with sapphires, it looked proud and brave. It shone bright against his golden hair, but it did not look gaudy. It was thick-made and strong set. I no longer wore the slender wreath of ivy leaves brought from my home that I had worn into the chapel. My head was bare – the priest had lifted the little circlet off me when we wed.

Now approached Arthur's mother, the Queen Igraine of Cornwall. She was a beautiful woman, still, though she looked as though she must be nearly forty years of age. Long, dark, glossy brown hair flowed down her back, pulled back simply at the front. On it had been a crown like Arthur's but smaller, the crosses slimmer and more delicate, the gold hammered thinner, and set with little sapphires at the centre of each cross. Now she held that crown in her hands. She moved with grace and around her eyes were the soft lines of kind smiles and gentle wisdom. If Arthur had a mother like the Lady Igraine, then perhaps, perhaps I could be happy. Though I remembered she had not raised him. The Lady Igraine placed the crown gently on my head, and kissed my cheek. I felt the weight of it, pressing down on me.

"You make a lovely queen, Guinevere," she said, and leaning down as if to help me adjust the crown on my head she whispered in my ear, "It will get easier, my dear."

She had known it, too. She had been married twice to men whom she did not know, who had desired her and chosen her and to whom she had been given. I hoped that she was right. I hoped that she would stay at court. I also hoped that my discomfort was visible to no one else but her. I did not want to show any weakness. She slid into the seat beside me, with a warm smile. I supposed I ought to take some comfort in the fact that Arthur had such a woman as his mother.

The woad-faced man in the black cowl and habit sat beside Arthur, at his left hand side. His dark eyes were on me, I could feel them. I had not seen him sit down; he must have slipped in there, like a shadow. I tried to ignore him. Approaching the table came Sir Kay and Sir Ector, who greeted us both warmly. Arthur smiled a deep, warm smile like his mother's as he greeted Sir Kay, his Seneschal and, as he told me then, his foster-brother. I thought it strange that Arthur had been fostered with one of his father's subjects, but I was glad that they would be there, in places of high honour and close by me, because of it. After them came a pale, slender woman with dark hair pinned back at the front, but loose and free behind, shining in the candlelight in a cascade that fell all the way down her back. She was robed in dark blue, sewn all over with little dark sapphires so she appeared to be covered in a dress made of dark, glossy scales. Her face was pale as porcelain with high cheekbones and thin, arched eyebrows, a tight, thoughtful mouth and watchful grey eyes. Like the man beside Arthur, her skin was decorated with the blue woad of the druids, all over her pale face in delicate swirls like the growth of vines, and down the deep neck of her dress. Her hands, too, were patterned with it, and I suspected she was painted like this all over. She walked up to Arthur and bent down to kiss his cheek. Her gestures were affectionate, but her look was absent. He kissed her other cheek and gave her the kind smile of his affection.

"Guinevere, this is my sister Morgan, wife of King Uriens."

She turned to me with a respectful nod, which I reciprocated, but she looked at me as if she did not see me, and while Arthur looked on her with kindness, she did not seem to see him either, and the grey eyes remained hollow, as though they were looking at something else far away. She sat beside her mother Igraine, whom she also did not seem to see. From what I knew, it was only the mother they shared, and Uther Pendragon had killed her father in order to have the Lady Igraine for himself.

After her came the russet-haired woman I had seen sitting beside Gawain in the chapel. I would not have called her beautiful now that I saw her close before me, but she had all the look about her of a noble queen, a broad proud face, striking and attractive, with a few pale freckles. On her head she wore a crown of dark gold, formed in spikes. She must still rule Lothian as Lot's widowed queen. She seemed strong and brave enough to do so. I wondered why Arthur had not wanted her as a wife, but I supposed she was almost ten years older than I was, and she had many sons already. She came forward to greet Arthur and I noticed that though she kissed his cheek, he did not return the kiss as he had done with Morgan, but seemed to shy back from her. She did a curt little curtesy towards me.

"My lady Queen Guinevere, I am Morgawse, who was King Lot's wife, sister to King Arthur and mother to Aggravain, Gawain, Gaheris, Gareth and Mordred."

Well, that explained well enough why Arthur did not marry Lot's queen. And she was older than the other sister. Another half-sister of his. I gave her a little nod and she sat beside her sister Morgan with Gawain and another one who was clearly her son, and older than Gawain. It must have been Aggravain. His name, too, had come to Carhais. Lot's widow. My father would have known her pain, a widower himself from Arthur's wars. Perhaps I should ask Arthur to send her over the sea to keep my father company. She was gentle of expression and good-looking, far more comely than her grim sister Morgan. She had a ready laugh, which I had heard already, tinkling like a bell, and something about her movements made her seem as though she were about to dance. I liked her already.

The fifth knight who had ridden with us from Dover came up and was introduced to us, a quiet, slender youth with a serious demeanour and dark sandy-coloured hair, named Sir Perceval. More came, more names that swirled in my head – Pedivere, Bors, Uriens, Accolon, Urry, Tristan – until I could no longer remember who was who. I would, I supposed, have all the time in the world to learn.

When all were seated, Arthur stood with his goblet of wine in his hand – a golden goblet, studded with jewels, but old and worn, too, with the hands of many kings of Logrys – and announced, "Lords and Ladies of Britain, I invite you to feast with me and my new wife, Queen Guinevere."

Queen Guinevere. I was already becoming someone else. I had been just Guinevere all my life until now. I supposed there had been those who had called me princess, but not in my own land, not in my own castle. And later tonight I would become yet another woman, or I was supposed to. A wife, in every sense of the word. I wrapped my hand tight around the stem of my golden cup, which was full almost to the brim with wine. I did not intend to change.

There was a loud cheer and a thundering as the people in the hall thumped their cups against the tables and stamped their feet in celebration. I could feel my heart racing within me. I knew no one in the room, really. I was their queen, but we were strangers to one another. I stared deep into my own goblet of wine and in the dark red liquid saw the shadow of my own reflection, red hair, white face, gold crown, and then I drank.

Chapter Four

Arthur stood and the room of cheering, singing, drinking, eating people fell silent in an instant. I had eaten little, though I had been hungry, and the wine was soft and strong in my head, and I was beginning to feel pleasantly dizzy. I had not drunk much, and yet I felt it. I had wanted my strength and my wits about me for what I knew was coming next, but I had let my nerves and the wine cloud within me, and I felt the edge of danger in it, how it was blurring through me. I had wanted the food, which had been delicious, but my anxious stomach had clenched shut after a few bites of bread, a few morsels of the succulent beef stew we had been served. I had managed some sweet cake, but not much. The Lady Igraine had given me a sympathetic smile.

"My lady Queen and I will now retire from the feast," Arthur declared, and I saw him smile, pleased with himself. There was great cheering at this, too. I knew what this meant. I rose slowly and took the hand he offered me. His hand was steady, confident. I wanted mine to be the same, or better, tense and defiant, but it was neither. I could feel myself trembling.

As he led me down the hall and from the room he smiled and called to some of his men and they laughed back. He was loved here, by his people. That was some comfort. He did not say anything to me as he led me across the courtyard to the north tower that housed his rooms, nor did I try to speak. There were servants there to open the heavy wooden doors to the tower for us, and he led me up the narrow spiral staircase within. A war-king's rooms as well. Easy to defend. Camelot was no show-court made for pageantry and display, it was a siege-fortress and the king inhabited the heart of it. The first room off the stairs looked to be a council chamber, although filled with artefacts that suggested the woad-faced man spent his days there – an astrolabe, a row of jars of herbs (or poisons) on a wooden shelf – and we carried on up. The second appeared to be a room for entertainment, bare but for scatterings of crimson velvet cushions and a lute resting in the corner. I had not heard the music of a lute in a long time. All of our musicians had traded their lutes for swords and gone to war. I don't know if any had returned.

Finally, we came to a bedchamber. Inside, candles were burning ready for us, and I could see a brass jug of wine, two cups, a silver plate piled with the fruits of Logrys – strawberries, apples and pears – standing on a table beneath the window, and the bed. *The bed.* I felt my body tense at the sight of it.

Arthur shut the heavy wooden doors behind us, and drew across an iron bolt. He still had not spoken to me. I would not speak first. If he wanted me, he had to at last be brave, not the kind of man – the kind of boy – who would come and peer at me in secret.

I could not even run, now, for I had nowhere to go. He had me in his kingdom, and I was just another prize of his conquest. He lifted the heavy crown off his head and set it beside the jug and silver cups on the table. He poured into both glasses, drank from one, and offered me the other. I took it, and drank until it was all gone. My resolve to stay sharp had dissolved away as the moment was finally upon me, and I remembered Christine saying to me this morning, *the more you drink, the less it hurts.* But I was still resolved to resist. He set his drink down and bent to unlace his boots, taking them off and placing them at the end of his bed; then he unbuttoned and shrugged off the crimson and gold brocade surcoat he had worn all day and set that on an empty chair beside the table. I could see the strength in his shoulders as he moved to take it off, through his shirt. I stood frozen, feeling the bolted door's presence at my back, waiting.

Arthur turned to me with a kind smile, but I was still wary. "My lady Queen." He offered me his hand. I did not reach out to take it, but crossed my arms over my chest. I could feel my heart hammering already. The wine had not helped; if anything it had made it worse. I could feel sweat on the palms of my hands, my feet, between my breasts, bound tight together in the silk bodice of the dress. *He is still a stranger to me.*

He sighed when he saw I would not take it.

"Are you upset that I did not reveal myself to you yesterday?" I said nothing, turning my face up defiantly towards his. He sighed again. "Do you know why it was you I wanted?" He did not wait for an answer. "My advisor Merlin told me that you were of the blood of the Irish Witch-Queen Maev; powerful, magical blood." He sighed again, softer this time. His gaze on me was earnest, gentle, but it was still that of a king. His tone was patient, but it was the patience of a man who knew there was no other way but that he would eventually get what he wanted. In the light of the candles, his hair was flecked with gold, and in his thin shirt I could see the powerful muscles of his shoulders and arms. I could see beneath that sweet, young face, the body of what was already a hardened warrior. But his face – it was that of a boy, lost. If I had not been so angry, if he had not been the conqueror who had demanded me from my home, I might have put my hand against his cheek, in comfort, but I did not. I would not. "I have... I have a bad destiny, Guinevere. I did not know who my parents were, and – the child Mordred, the youngest child of my sister Morgawse – he is *mine*, Guinevere." His voice cracked slightly as he spoke, and he hesitated to see if I would react. I did not. "I didn't know, I didn't know she was my sister, but Merlin tells me that God has cursed me for it. That is why I need you, your powerful magic blood, the blood of the Witch-Queen Maev. I needed to know that you were truly the blood of the Otherworld. Kay, my foster brother, he can tell, and I wanted him to see you, and tell me if what they said about you was true. But you can tell, I know. I saw you notice it in him, too." He tried a wary smile, but I remained still. He would have *nothing* from me, if I did not wish it. Not even a smile. "When I saw you I was pleased, so pleased... you're beautiful, and..." he took a wary step closer, "we will make a son. I will be safe from my evil destiny. Guinevere..." He moved towards me, as if carried by his own imploring words. Perhaps he thought his painful honesty would sway me, but he had not been honest with me yesterday. I did not move away. There was only a foot or so between me and the door, and I wanted that space for when I might finally need it. He reached out a hand and gently touched my cheek. It was more gentleness that I had thought a man of his size was capable of. I felt a sudden rush of heat of my face that I had not expected, and I was resistant to it. I had come resolved, and I would not be swayed. "Was Queen Maev as beautiful as you?"

"Maev was a Warrior-Queen, who commanded an army of thousands, who subdued in battle the hero they called the Hound of the Ulstermen. The blood she spilled carved valleys in the land. She had four consorts and eight sons. She rode into battle, and men talk of her tearing down lines of her enemies with her sword. They don't say much about her beauty," I replied, coldly. Maev of Cruachan had been my father's grandmother, and I knew I had her blood in my veins. I did not have to give in to anything.

Arthur took another step towards me and reached out to lift the crown off my head. I felt my skin burn where his hands brushed it, lifting it off, and I was yet unsure if this was revulsion, or the wine, the heat of the fire, or something else. He walked back away from me and set it down beside his own, and took another sip of his wine.

Mine was still in my hand. I tipped it up for the dregs, and set it down on the floor beside me. I could feel the nervous tingling all over my body, the tension in the air between us. Neither knew what the other would do next. He walked back over to me. His eyes still had all the excited eagerness of a boy, but I was not so eager for him as he was for me, and I kept my face still, and cold.

"Guinevere, I think you and I together can make this kingdom great. I know we are strangers, but..." He reached out his hand and laid it gently against my waist, then slowly slid it upwards, to stroke my breast. I caught him by the wrist, hard. "Guinevere..." He was firmer this time, and though he did not move his hand any further, he did not lift it away. I could feel the power in his arm under my grip. He could have pushed me away. He did not sound as patient as he had before. I knew it would wear thin fast. "Believe me I have been warned that brides can be nervous."

"You are but a boy, Arthur." He was shocked by my sharpness, and clearly he had not noticed as I had that he was younger than me. He thought himself all grown. The hint of an arrogant smile chased across his lips.

"But I have had more lovers than you, my Lady Guinevere." He slid his arm around my waist, lifting it easily from my grip as I had suspected he could, pulling me up tight against him; the other he buried in my hair, winding his fingers in it, turning my face up towards him. I could feel the power of his body, his strength, all the way around me, and although in my mind I was resolved, resolved to resist until I had forgiven him and his people the loss of my own, to my frustration something in my body was responding, against my will. I did not like *him* yet, but despite myself I liked the feel of his strong arm around me, his hand rough in my hair, and it only made me angrier. I did not want to like it. "Unless there is something your father should have told me." His eyes gazed right into mine. I could not tell if he felt himself to be being playful. Our faces were close, close enough that I could see the fine shadow of gold stubble against his chin catch in the firelight. I felt the touch of his breath against my lips. I was not repulsed as I thought I would be by the feel of him this close to me, our bodies pressing together, and the desire to refuse was leaving me, my desire to resist weaker than I had expected, but I was stubborn by nature, and I had come decided to resist.

"Oh no, my lord," I hissed, "I am *intact.*"

"Well, then." He leaned just a little closer, and I felt our noses brush. I felt my heart beat faster, my breath come quicker. I felt my body preparing to fight. "I do not think you will find me disappointing, despite my youth. I know what I am doing."

He kissed me roughly, his hand on the back of my neck pulling me closer against him. I had been kissed before, in Carhais by the man I was supposed to marry, just once before he left, under a plum tree in the orchard. I could not honestly have said that I liked it much; it had been wet and clumsy and playful, a children's game, nothing more, though he had been older, then, than Arthur was now. Nothing like this. This rough kiss was leading me somewhere. I felt his fingers at the back of my neck, growing soft now, almost tender and felt myself weaken, just a little, at their touch. No. If I relented I could not go home. I tried to push him off, and for a moment it caught him by surprise, but he pushed back and we slammed against the bolted door. A little gasp of pain escaped me. I could feel, against my thigh, that he was hard.

We were both breathing fast, and rough, pressed tight against each other, up against the door. I was sure he must have been able to feel my heart, pounding in my chest. He had not loosened his grip on me, but I could see that his gaze on me was soft.

"Guinevere... this is how it has to be. We are married, you are my Queen. I don't wish to force you –"

"Perhaps you could not. Perhaps I would kill you," I whispered, cold and threatening. But I no longer felt it. I was no longer sure I meant what I said. He smelled of the stables, clean straw and the homely scent of horses, his strength about me was almost overwhelming. I could feel my lips were hot from his kiss, and tingling, wanting more despite myself. The closeness of his body against mine was clouding my thoughts.

He laughed a soft, little laugh.

"I chose well, looking for one like Maev, then. But, Guinevere, this has to be," he whispered. "Please."

I said nothing. He leaned down to kiss me again, this time softly at first, and then when I did not push him away a second time, harder. I felt my mouth open under his, the instinct within me that I had denied waking through me. I had never been kissed like this by a man before, had never imagined it would be matched in me by my own desire. Arthur's passion was rough, but it was also compelling. His hands were in my hair, unwinding the tight plaits, throwing the pins to the floor where they fell with a soft tinkle. I felt my heavy curls fall about my shoulders as he leant to kiss my neck. I felt my knees weaken a little, and I knew it was not the wine. I did not have to know him, or love him, to *enjoy* him. I had heard the women of my father's court say that enough when they thought that I was not listening. I could not pretend I did not like the feeling of his strength. I was beginning to wonder if my stubborn resolve to go home wasn't childish. This must have been what it was to give up childhood and become a woman.

Arthur unlaced my outerdress at the back and pushed it up fast, and pulled it over my head. One of the sleeves tore, but he did not seem to notice. He pulled me to him once more and kissed me again, his hands searching the undershift for laces, a way in, found instead my breasts and there he brushed my nipples gently through the thin fabric, and I felt a tingling go through me; a desire to be free from the underdress. My body responded, pressing back against him, and he made a low noise of excitement when he felt me yielding, just a little. He pulled his own shirt off, and his breeches. He had a young man's haste. I reached out, unconsciously, to touch the bare skin so suddenly before me, irresistible. I had seen a man before, but if I were honest with myself no man as fine as him. Old men, my brothers when I was a child; we were not prudish about our bodies in Carhais. But still I had never before felt what I did now, at the sight of Arthur naked before me; a flutter of something enticing and unfamiliar in the pit of my stomach. I let my fingertips trail softly over the muscles of his chest, down across his stomach. I could feel the blood high in my cheeks, and his eyes on my face, and I knew he was excited by the sight of me, looking at him.

He reached for me again, fired with desire, his kisses more insistent. This time found the laces of the underdress, deftly undid them, and pushed it off my shoulders. It fell to the ground around my feet, and I stepped out of it. He took a step back then, and looked at me, for a moment, naked in the candlelight. From his lips escaped a tiny groan of pleasure and lust before he grasped me by the hips and threw me down on the bed. I felt my heart thud, and I was not sure it was fear. It was new, and dangerous, but exciting. I stretched out under him as he climbed onto me. His hands were all over me, strong, but gentle, yet demanding. I felt a delicious haze of it spread up around me, through me, and I was lost in it. My body responded with its instinct, following the heat of his touch. His kisses were hot and strong, first on my mouth, then neck, then my breasts and nipples and down my body until he found that place that made me cry out sharply, but quiet, with pleasure, and surprise. I felt at the centre of a hot, bright swirl of heady sensations, deliciously lost, and my body seemed to know what I wanted better than I did. At last, he entered me, his face hot against my neck, one hand tangled in my hair, the other at the small of my back holding me tight against him as we moved together. He was rough, but he did not hurt me, and I found I liked the feel of his bare skin against my own, his lips agains my neck, at my ear, his powerful movements on top of me. There had been a sharp pain at the start, and I felt the patch of blood beneath me against my leg, but as Arthur groaned deeply, and with satisfaction, into my neck and rolled off me, I thought that it was nothing like I had been warned it would be, by Christine, who had been married and widowed before she had come to me. Unpleasant, but soon over, she had told me.

Arthur turned on his side, propping himself up on his elbow, to face me. He reached out his other hand and gently smoothed the red curls back from my damp brow as I stretched out beside him, feeling the warmth of the wine and the pleasant ache inside me spread through me. He said nothing, and I said nothing, but this was a new kind of saying nothing between us. He leaned over and kissed me once, tenderly. The last candle guttered out as he gathered me into his arms, and we fell asleep.

Chapter Five

When I woke, for a moment I didn't remember where I was. The sunlight winked under my fluttering eyelids, dazzling and lovely, and for a moment I could have been anywhere. I could have been home. But home was gone. *Camelot.* I was in Camelot. And I remembered last night with Arthur. I slowly opened my eyes, and pushed myself up onto my elbows. He was there beside me, and it was real. This was my life now. Last night I had become his queen, and it had not been a dream. It was done now, and I was a wife, and I would not run home. I could not.

I looked at him, still sleeping, with the soft gold touch of the sun glancing and lighting in his golden hair. His rough, masculine features relaxed in sleep, but still those, unmistakably, of a man who had forged his kingdom through war. He was handsome, I supposed. People always said that about their rulers, but Arthur did have a rough, primal charm to his looks that was undeniable. Besides, he had told me that he had had many women before, so I could not have been the only one who thought so. I was not sure, then, if I cared or not. Arthur groaned softly as he woke beside me, sensing my wakefulness, perhaps. With one strong arm he reached for me, rolling onto me, gathering me under him. Still sleepy, he rubbed his face – newly rough with a night's growth of beard – into my neck. I could not suppress a little gasp of surprise as he thrust himself inside me again. It was slower, this time, less hurried, gentler. I was surprised that it already felt familiar, and my body, seeming to know, followed his. His mouth found mine with a deep, slow kiss, the heat of which seemed to mingle with the heat already rising in my body. I ran my hands down his strong arms, feeling, too, our legs brush against each other, his skin hot from sleep against mine. As I felt the breaths come to me quicker, the heat within me spreading, I reached my arms around his broad back and pulled him tighter against me. He gave a deep moan of pleasure at this and sighed against me, rolling aside and gathering me into his arms as he had done the night before. Between my legs I felt the warmth of where he had been, and the slickness that promised something distant of new life. In Arthur's arms I felt small, small and fragile, but safe. I was a tall, strong woman, with my own lean and competent muscles from a lifetime of running and hunting in the woods, but beside Arthur I was little and frail as a bird. His arms and shoulders bore the thick, corded muscles of a short lifetime's training with broadsword and shield, of wearing the heavy armour. He was not sinew but brawn, the blood of conquerors, for sure. Across one side of his chest ran the thin, white line of a scar, running from the centre, above the nipple towards his shoulder. I traced a finger along it as I lay with my head on his shoulder. His eyes followed my finger.

"That one was the gift of the King of the Vale."

"What happened to him?"

He smiled slightly, a little proud, a little pleased with himself. I supposed he had a right to be.

"Well, there is only one King of the Britons now."

"Hmmmm," I agreed, quietly. In that soft, morning light, with Arthur's warm, bare skin against my own and a warm bright soft feeling spreading through my limbs from his touch, I was not sure how I felt. I had not wanted to come, I had not wanted to be wed, but all of a sudden, against every expectation I had had, I felt happy. I spread my hand out in the middle of his chest, feeling the skin, feeling the strength beneath it.

"So I am not so bad, my lady Queen?" Arthur reached out and gently brushed his fingers against my cheek, and I looked up to meet his gentle smile with a small, tentative one of my own.

I rolled on to my front, propping myself up on my forearms to look back, deep into the eyes that – I had not noticed before – were dark steel-grey and serious beyond his years. Thoughtful. *Not the eyes of a brute*, I reproached myself. He also looked less like a boy to me now, more like a man. I supposed that I had seen, in my anger, only what I had expected to see.

"Not *so* bad." I reached out to, gently, tentatively, touch his cheek, and he laid a big hand over mine, drawing me closer with the arm still wrapped around my back, for a soft and tender kiss.

"And I? Was I as like my ancestress the Witch-Queen Maev as you had hoped?" I teased.

Arthur laughed softly with what seemed to me like embarrassment. Perhaps he had not meant to speak of it last night.

"Oh, far less frightening, and far more beautiful."

"That's not *always* what a lady likes to hear, you know." I gave him a playful smile and he wound his fingers deeper into my hair. I liked the feeling of his fingertips pressing my scalp, the power of the hand that wound there. I sighed softly into it. My body still felt hot from having him inside me, and hungry. He pulled my head back, gently, and, rolling back over me as he turned me onto my back, kissed the soft skin under my neck, beneath the ear. I sighed softly with pleasure, and he took one breast in his hand, brushing the nipple lightly until I pressed myself up against him for more and, as I felt the longing in my body for him again, his slid his other hand under my back and, pulling me towards him, entered me again. I wanted it as much as he did now, more even perhaps, and I found myself lost in the lovely whirl of desire. This time I moaned softly as he did and he buried his face in the thick hair at the side of my neck, moving against me as I pressed closer to him. I wrapped a leg around his back and he grasped it by the thigh, holding me faster against him, closer, harder as I felt the pleasure rising within me, the heat in my stomach, then at my heart, at my face. I felt the hot, sweet clench of it at the centre of me and the heat go out of me, suddenly, with a sigh, as Arthur groaned above me, and was still for a moment, breathing hot and fast against my neck, and then slid away. Slowly, I stretched my arms above my head and turned my face, eyes closed, to the sun pouring in at the window, to feel its soft red touch on my closed eyes, and then, opening my eyes, I reached for Arthur and laid my head softly on his chest. I felt sleepy again, but I did not want to sleep. I had not expected to like being with Arthur. I had assumed he would be clumsy or unkind, but I had been wrong. He stroked my hair with one hand, and with his other arm down my back, cradled me close.

"Look at all this fire," he said thoughtfully, running a hand through my hair.

I kissed softly the skin of his chest, where I was resting.

"Did you always know you would be a king?" I asked. I had been raised all my life in the knowledge of who I was – *what* I was – but Arthur had fought for his throne. I wondered if he had had a sense of it, in his blood. I had no idea what it must have been like, not to know who you were.

"Me? No. No. Sir Ector raised me, and his wife. I hoped I would be a knight like my older brother Sir Kay. I never thought I would be here. I'm not sure if I would even say I wanted it. But I found out it was mine. The will of God. I was... I was squiring for Kay in this tournament, but he had forgotten his sword – I think he did it on purpose to annoy me, because Kay never forgets anything *or* misses a chance to play a joke on his friends – so I went to get him one. I didn't want to go all the way home because I knew if I wasn't back in time that stubborn old Kay would fight anyway with just his shield and get himself wounded. People said that there was a sword in the church in the town and I thought I would just borrow that one. There it was, resting in a block of stone in the church. I didn't know then it was covered in writing. I couldn't read then, so it could have been anything – pictures, numbers. I just put my hands on the sword and it flew out. I really *was* a boy then. Thirteen, maybe. Anyway, I took it to Kay, and my father – no, Sir Ector – was so shocked, I didn't understand it. He kept asking Kay how he'd got it, and then everyone else around was shouting and demanding to know where he got it from, and eventually when my witch Merlin, who was not *my* witch then, came out of the crowd and asked him, Kay told everyone I had brought it to him. They made me take it in and out of the block of stone again and again and Merlin told me the stone said "Whoever pulls this sword from this stone is rightwise King of England", and that was me. He told me that Uther Pendragon, the just-dead king, was my father, and the Lady Igraine was my mother." He paused, for a second. "That was the saddest day of my life."

I knew what he meant. I would not tell him, but that was how I had felt, watching my father's castle at Carhais disappear in the distance. On the one hand is the path that is decided for you, that might indeed be a path for greatness, and on the other hand is everything you love, and you never dreamed would change. But everything changes. *Arthur has lost something like you lost.* A father and brother and mother who now have to see him as a king. A self that he thought he was. And gained a heavy destiny. And a bad one. I had not remembered the child until just then. I was not sure how I felt about that, either.

"You have Kay and Ector close, still. And your mother the Lady Igraine seems kind."

"She is kind," he replied. *But she is not my mother*, were his words unspoken. No, Sir Ector's wife had raised him as a child. And I had not met her. She must be dead.

"A man must face his destiny, and his God. A man must face these things, and try to be good."

I pushed myself up, resting my chin on my hands, folded on his chest and looked him in the eye. He had that simple sincerity about him. I could see, now, why the people followed this man, whom I had thought a boy. The serious eyes, the quiet sense of duty. No, last night in my anger I had seen truly only what I had expected. A boy. This morning, I did not doubt that he was a man, grown.

I was about to say something, to try to say something adequate in response to his humble gravity, but he took my face in his hands and kissed me. It was a deep, intense kiss, and when he grazed my bottom lip lightly with his teeth I felt it at the base of my spine. He pulled me on top of him as we kissed, wrapping his arms around me. He seemed to have an endless desire.

"Arthur?" An insistent banging came from the door. Someone tried the latch. It was still bolted. Arthur pulled gently away and released his arms around me, but did not move. A wicked boyish smile played on his lips and he pressed one finger gently to my lips. "Arthur? Arthur?!"

Then, with a splintering crack the door flew open. Arthur leapt from the bed, naked, swiftly out from beneath me, quick as a wildcat, already tensed to fight. I gathered the covers around me, my heart pounding in fear, blushing like a girl. I hated it when I blushed. I was a married women in my husband's bed; I had no reason to be embarrassed. When Arthur saw who it was, he relaxed with a deep laugh, and across his face came the boyish smile that still betrayed his few years.

"For God's *sake*, Kay. The door was *bolted*. We were asleep."

"You were *not* asleep," Kay replied peevishly, trying to prop the door back up in the space he had knocked it from. "How was I to know you hadn't both been murdered in your sleep?"

What he meant was *I was sent to see if she had killed you in your sleep.* Someone had their eye on me. Someone thought I might be dangerous. Last night, I was prepared to be.

Kay was laughing too, now, at his king standing naked before him, who had somehow already got a sword in his hand. *He is still afraid*, I thought. The days of fighting were not long past. That sword must have been beside the bed all night long. I had not even noticed it. The new-finished war must have left its mark on all of them. King Arthur did not sleep so easy in his bed, nor did his knights shrug at a silent, locked bedroom. I had, foolishly, thought that war could have only scarred those who lost in it.

"Don't you know, *Sir Kay*, that is is terribly ill-mannered to burst in on the king and his queen abed?" It was the easy banter of brothers that he spoke to Kay with, his tone light and playful, but still when he noticed Kay's eyes wandering towards the bed where I still lay, holding the sheets around me, Arthur sharply drew shut the bed curtains.

"My liege," Kay replied, with an easy, friendly, mocking tone. "Most apologies. You and my lady the queen are expected at mass in an hour."

"We shall attend."

Kay left, and I could hear Arthur shoving at the door, trying to get it back into place. I shuffled on my knees to the edge of the bed and peered through the curtains.

"*Kay*," Arthur muttered under his breath, indulgently annoyed, shaking his head to himself.

"What is mass, Arthur?" I hoped mass was a meal. I could feel my stomach empty within me.

Arthur froze in the doorway, and turned to look at me thoughtfully for a moment.

"Your people aren't Christians." It wasn't a question. I nodded. I knew what a Christian was. I had seen the monks in brown with their shaven heads, and the nuns dressed in black and white, neat as pages in a manuscript, filing in and out of their big stone temples. I had been inside a chapel before, but not one like Arthur's. Not one where the plain wood cross was made in gold, and bearing the Hanged God. Not one where everything shone with gold. Not one where kings knelt down.

"Mass is... mass is how we pray to God. My God must be your god now." He sighed silently. I could not hear it, but I could see his shoulders fall. "I'm sorry, Guinevere."

I gave a little nod and slipped out from between the curtains, stepping across the room and into his embrace as though it were a habit of many years. That was the way of it. The foreign queen must take the gods of the land.

"It seems to be that you would be better off taking my gods, though, since your god has already cursed you," I pointed out, gently, taking his face in my hands.

Arthur shook his head, kissing my forehead, thoughtfully.

"God isn't like that – God gave me this Kingdom. God doesn't like or dislike people, he just judges each thing that they do, on its own."

Sounds like a funny kind of god.

Chapter Six

Servants came in with bowls of hot water and we washed and dressed in the fresh clothing they brought. Arthur had his splendid red surcoat, with the dragon of his father's house spread in gold across it, and he put on his sword and his crown to go down to the chapel. I wondered if he wanted to look every bit the king, or if he just always wanted to have that sword at his side. I was dressed in red and gold, too, and my hair tied up in a golden net. Arthur placed my crown tenderly on my head and kissed me lightly.

"You look as if you've been queen all your life."

"Queen's blood," I told him, with a smile.

In the chapel, Arthur was solemn again. The youthful play he had shown with Kay evaporated in the sight of his Hanged God, whose name, he told me, was Christ. As he grew older he would no longer be by turns mischievous and solemn. He would grow up, out of the boyish ways as the cares of the realm weighed upon him. I could see that already. And his god. Arthur bent his head in prayer so diligently to the god who had already doomed him. Why not pray to another?

I thought of my own gods as I knelt beside him, my head down. At least people could not see that I did not know the words, or the songs. Then we went up to receive the libation and bread as we had when we wed. None of it made sense to me, and I felt disorientated and alone again suddenly. Out of the safe privacy of Arthur's bedroom I felt a foreigner, lost again, and I longed painfully for home. I didn't remember half of the names I had learned last night, and Arthur was a different man when we were not alone. Once again I felt unsure if this place with its strange rituals could be my home, but then I remembered the Lady Igraine leaning close to me and whispering *It will get easier.* I supposed it would. I saw her, in the chapel, and we exchanged a friendly smile. I could not bear, somehow, to meet eyes with her daughter Morgawse sitting beside her.

After the mass, Arthur took me by the hand and we led all the assembled lords and ladies out of the chapel. Standing at the entrance was the witch Merlin, and I felt his black eyes pierce me to the bone, strip me down to my muscles and sinews and a shiver ran through me. I did not trust the man.

As we processed out into the light, Merlin took Arthur aside and they began to speak in hushed tones, leaning together in the shadow of the chapel. Merlin liked to stand close to that building, but I had already noticed that he would never go in.

I turned as I felt a light touch on my arm. Beside me stood Sir Ector, smiling, squinting against the morning sun.

"My lovely queen." He bowed a little, then placed a hand in mine and fixed me with an earnest look. He seemed nervous, drawing me aside to ask me quietly, "My lady... I trust, I trust my Lord Arthur was kind?"

I knew what he meant. I nodded.

"He was kind, sir."

Ector sighed with visible relief. "He is a kind boy – ah, a kind king, a kind man, a good man – I was sure he would only be so. Just, young men can be foolish, when passions... and a lady as beautiful as yourself –"

I nodded again, and he smiled. I could see he had worried over it. I was glad he had asked. I was glad that this warm, avuncular man who had nothing to do with me, to whom I was nothing but a foreign princess, cared. I was pleased, also, that Arthur had been raised by such a man. Already I was finding it hard to hold on to the hard stone of hate that I had carried with me from Carhais. It was being worn smooth, turning to sand, running through my fingers. Ector pressed a fatherly kiss against my cheek and walked over to join Arthur and Merlin. If Ector was not afraid of the witch, perhaps I need not be either.

From the church behind me came Arthur's sister Morgan. Her face was blue as Merlin's with woad, but she could pass into that place. She was wearing the same shining dark gown of deep blue and sapphire and as the light caught it, she looked half-dragon. But she was not. Only Arthur fought under the banners of the dragon. Her father had been another, some duke of an outlying kingdom. She gave me a cold look as she passed by, but said nothing, and I was not sure if the cold look was *at* me, or past me.

Watching her go, I did not notice that Arthur had come back to my side. He slid an arm around my waist and drew me to his side. "I'm sorry I left you on your own." He spoke, soft and deep, into my ear, letting his lips brush against it. I felt the hot, pleasant prickle of the intimacy of it at the base of my spine. But the words that came next chilled it from me. "Merlin has had news from Rome. The Emperor is not pleased there is a King of all Britain."

I felt a sinking in the pit of my stomach. *Not already.*

"There might be more war," I said, softly.

"There might. But not any day soon. And now is not the time to think about it."

He gave me an easy smile, but he was wary. I was pleased he was wary. It meant that he was a good king, thinking of his people and his borders. Perhaps he did care about those scattered little villages I had seen on the way. As time went on, I felt more sure he might.

Kay sauntered past and flashed us both a knowing smile. Arthur smiled back warmly, and chuckled under his breath. Reminded of the morning in public, I blushed dark red. I was angry with myself for blushing again, and angry for Kay for making me blush. I did not want to appear embarrassed or weak. Arthur had not noticed, but when I caught Kay's eye, I saw he had. He looked a little sorry, but also a little pleased, and slunk off into the shadows with a kind little wink. He was truly a creature of my blood. I had known many boys and men like that growing up. Wicked as sprites, but kind.

Gawain came up then. He bowed to me, brusquely.

"My lady queen." Then to Arthur, "My Lord Arthur."

Arthur smiled at him broadly. I found it strange that Arthur had as much of a big, open smile for the gruff Gawain as he had for the charming Kay. Before Gawain could speak what he meant to, a hunting-horn was blown and we were called to feast again.

"Another feast?" I asked.

"But surely, my lady, you are hungry?" Arthur whispered to me with that wicked, boyish smile. I could not suppress a smile in return.

This time I could taste the food, and I had an appetite for it. There was grilled fish, cooked with mushrooms and onions, a huge roasted boar, potatoes roasted in goose fat, plump game birds, little meat pies, plates piled high with every kind of vegetable, and big, hot sweet pies filled with apples and pears, which were the first thing I knew to ever make Gawain smile. Arthur laughed indulgently as Gawain cheered their arrival. I sat at the Round Table that I had lain on, days before, and wished for Arthur's death, beside Arthur who was now my king and surrounded by his knights. At my side sat the Lady Igraine, but everyone else was a knight at that table, apart from Merlin, who sat on Arthur's other side. I laid my palm flat on the cool wood of the table. I was not yet ready to un-wish my wish, but I was no longer glad I had made it. But the wine was sweet and rich, and soon I had forgotten about it. Arthur and I shared honey-glazed meats and sweet vegetables from one plate, and big chunks of fresh bread, still warm and soft. I did not think I had ever felt so hungry; nor had food tasted so good.

When at last the harpist and the lutist slumped in their seats with sleep and the stars were full out in the clear night, and almost everything was eaten, Arthur stood and called an end to the feast. He took me by the hand and led me away, away from the others, the knights with whom I had to practice little courtesies, anxious not be accidentally offending, and talking sweet but empty pleasantries with the gentle Lady Igraine, and out from the cold beady stare of Merlin. I realised as we left that I was yearning to be alone with him once more.

Arthur did not lead me up to his room, but back to the one where I had stayed on my first night.

"Why do we not go to your chamber?" I asked, as we stood in the doorway. My parents, my whole life, had slept in the same bed at the centre of the castle.

"These are your chambers, my lady. This whole tower is yours. The queen of all of Britain must have her own rooms." He put his hands gently against my hips where he stood behind me, and drew me back against him, pressing his lips lightly against my ear. I could feel myself dizzying with it already. "Besides," he whispered, "I will not leave you lonely."

He stepped into the room, and I moved with him. I heard him shut the door softly behind us, his hands already in my hair, unwinding the plait of it. I felt it fall loose around my shoulders, and his fingers brush down my cheek, across my jaw, down across the flush already rising at my neck, down, lightly, across the soft skin that showed above the neck of my dress. I leaned back against him, unable to suppress a sigh, a sigh of desire for something I was not yet consciously sure that I was longing for. New, still, but all the more wanted because of it. I had not expected myself to grow used to being a married woman so fast. Nor had I thought that I would want my husband so powerfully so soon.

I turned my face back, over my shoulder, towards his, and I felt his other hand brush against my cheek as our mouths met in a kiss, deep and passionate. We were strangers still, really, and yet my body knew what it wanted already; the touch it had known the the night before, and that morning, once again.

"All day, all I have thought about is being alone with you again," Arthur murmured, his fingers slowly drawing apart the lacing at the back of the overdress. Too slow; I could feel the delicious impatience of my body, but I did not give in to it. Not yet. He kissed me again, and I could taste the sweetness of the wine, which this time I had drunk in a tentative happiness, on both our lips. Arthur pulled the overdress down over my shoulders, and I shrugged out of it, letting it fall to the ground and gently kicking it aside. I heard Arthur laugh, low and pleased, and suddenly he pulled me hard back against him, his huge hand spread against my stomach, his lips at my neck. I could feel his body pressed tight against mine, his other hand winding into my hair, pulling gently, and I could not pretend that I did not like it, did not already want his touch.

With the hand in my hair, he turned my face back to his, kissing me, but teasing this time, and his other hand brushed light across my breasts over the thin underdress. I held back, just for the moment, from pressing into his hands for more, but I felt the skin beneath tingling at his touch, longing for the feel of his bare skin against my own again. His fingers went to the lacing again, but he paused there. I could feel my heart fluttering against his hand, the heat of my skin under his touch.

"Tell me you want me," he murmured, kissing me once more, gently pulling on my lip with his teeth, leaning away as I leaned towards him, trying to kiss him deeper. So, that was what he wanted. After my resistance last night, he wanted to feel that he had won me round. I was not sure that he had not, but I was not going to yield a position of even the slightest power if I did not have to.

I said nothing, but gave him a small smile. He smiled back, pleased but not yet entirely satisfied. One hand still tight in my hair, he ran his other hand down my throat, lightly, his fingertips brushing across my skin, tantalising, and I could feel the flush of desire hot all through me as his fingers reached the ties of the underdress again, and he pulled it open a little more, and slid his hand inside. I could not hide my quick breaths of excitement, nor stop the sigh escaping my lips as I felt his thumb brush soft across my nipple, but he stopped there, as I was lost to it, lost to his touch already, gasping for more, and I felt his lips brush my ear again, as he whispered.

"Tell me."

I said nothing still, but I reached behind me and pressed my hand against his breeches where I knew he would be hard already. I heard him groan. I supposed that was enough of an answer for him, for he turned me around in his arms to face him and kissed me with such passionate force that I stumbled back with him, a few steps into the room. A few steps closer to the bed that we were both sure, now, was waiting for us. My fingers fumbled clumsily against the buttons of his surcoat, not yet used to undressing a man, but soon it was done, and when I pulled it open, he shrugged it off, and threw it aside. I lay my hands on his chest, and through his shirt I could feel the heat of his skin beneath. I slid my hands up under it, letting them run over his chest, through the light coarse hair, across the muscle, as I pushed it over his head, and he threw it aside as well, walking us both towards the bed. I heard him kick off his boots. I had slipped out of my shoes already, and through the lovely haze of it all, I could not remember when. He turned me around again in his arms, pulling me back tight against him, and I felt his hands run over me once more, over the underdress, as I turned over my shoulder to kiss him once more. Then, he grasped the front of it in his fist, and pulled, hard. The thin underdress ripped to the ground under the power of his hand, and I felt once more my own smallness and vulnerability in comparison to him. But tonight it was exciting, and pleasantly dangerous, and I was suddenly naked in his hands, feeling them run over me, appreciative and hungry. It was good to be wanted. I had never dreamed I might enjoy it, and yet here I was already losing myself in the pleasure of it. Stubborn all my life, I had never before experienced the pleasure of surrender.

Arthur threw me down lightly on the bed and I heard him pull off his breeches and throw them aside as he climbed on behind me, grasping me hard by the hips and pulling me against him. I cried out as I felt him go inside me; half-surprise, half-relief, as I felt the warmth of it spread through me, the welcome pleasure of closeness with Arthur that was familiar already. I felt his hand run down my back, tangle in my hair, and I sighed with it, feeling the warm sweet light of our being together begin to gather in the centre of me, closing my eyes, stretching out with it, like a cat, letting my hands clutch in the frustrated, gathering enjoyment of it all at the rich silk covers around me. I heard Arthur groan low again in excitement, and though I could not see him, I felt the touch of his eyes on me, and then his other hand run soft and light up the inside of my thigh and brush light again at the place he had found the night before, and I felt the brightness of it rush through me, and through both of us, and I sighed hard with it, feeling it wash through me, hot and bright and wonderful.

We sank down together, and Arthur gathered me against him, and I rested my head against the hot skin of his chest as he wrapped his arms around me and closed his eyes with a murmur of content. As I fell asleep, I wondered if it would always be like this between us, and if it was enough. We did not know each other, really, though I knew his body well enough already, and my own seemed to respond in natural recognition. We were still strangers, this warrior-boy and I. But he was also gentle, and kind, and I was beginning to think that he was also good. In his sleep he gathered me closer, rubbing his face into my thick hair, and in his sleep he murmured my name. *He is beginning to love me already*, I thought in the darkness.

Chapter Seven

Arthur left to go to his prayers in the morning, but it was not a public mass, so I did not have to go. I did not *want* to go and stand beneath the sad gaze of his Hanged Christ. Marie and Christine poured me a hot bath and dropped in it the scented oils they made in Logrys. It wasn't like the clean, clear waters of the river I bathed in at home, where I came out smelling like the fresh grass or the green leaves, but Logrys was cold, and I was glad at least of the hot water. The aromas of lavender and rose from the bath felt mildly intoxicating in my nostrils as I sank back into it. Marie began to comb out my wild, knotted hair. I thought about Arthur, about how much had changed already. It would have been easier if I could have just hated him as a brute, but he was not. It would have been easier if I could have dismissed him as a boy, but I had been so very wrong about that, as well. I did not want to lose the connection I felt with the lands and the people of my home. I did not want to be swallowed by Camelot and become a queen of Logrys. I had given up my gods in public, to take Arthur's gods. I spoke Arthur's language with him and in the court. The only thing I had left to hold on to was my anger, the dim memory of my idea of him as a murderer, a savage, a boy-king battle-mad and cruel, and that was not what I had found here. I thought perhaps it would be easier if I let go of the thoughts of my past, if I would be happier if I tried to become what I was, forget my old land and make Logrys and Britain my new, but I could not bear, yet, to let Brittany or Carhais go.

"How do you find it, my lady?" Marie asked me in the lovely, rich Breton of my home. In a moment, it tantalisingly brought it all back, but also it comforted me. I had not left it all behind. I had my two Breton women, and I could hear the speech of my own people. Truly, the only thing about Logrys that had been as bad as I expected was the awful brutality of its language.

"The bath? Very pleasant." I slid deeper into it, and sighed.

Marie and Christine giggled together; I was surprised that the solemn older woman joined in. I opened one eye and peered at her, where she was sitting at the foot of the bath, sewing, her mouth stern, only betraying her amusement at the edges.

"No, my lady," Marie whispered conspiratorially. "With the King."

I raised an eyebrow and flicked water at Christine with my foot.

"I think it would be treason for me to say anything other than very pleasant," I replied, archly.

"No one here will understand what you say, even if they do overhear us," Marie whispered.

Christine gave the younger woman an indulgent smile.

"I wouldn't be sure, Marie. That Sir Kay has a celtic look about him, and he seems to get everywhere," I said, aloof. I wasn't sure if they were making fun *of* me, or making fun *with* me.

"We heard," Christine replied, with an infuriating little smile. "We heard from the smith's boy who had to get iron for new hinges for the door. What that Sir Kay thought he was doing..."

I splashed her again, less playfully this time, and Christine tightened her little button mouth into a knot, holding back her smiles and laughter. It worried me more than it ought to, the jumpiness of Kay, knocking down the door, and Arthur, carrying his sword by his bed. They were still afraid of something, still wary of finding their friends dead in their beds. It was funny enough to the others, but they had not seen Arthur's face as he reached for his sword. The man still lived in fear of his life.

Marie filled a little stoneware jug with water and pushed me forward gently to pour it over my head. It felt good, hot and cleansing, as though I was making myself new. New for my new home, my new role as a wife. I would begin to belong in this place. I thought that it was perhaps better, too, to have rooms of my own where I could talk with my ladies in Breton, where I would not always be under the eyes of the court. Particularly the eyes of Merlin, who I did not think I would ever trust. Marie brushed my hair again, wet, and plaited it, winding it around and pinning it with the little gold net while it was still damp enough to be tame. I missed wearing it long, and wild, but in Logrys none of the noblewomen did this. Even Marie and Christine wore theirs neatly tied away. I thought I had heard Christine tell Marie that it was only children and prostitutes in Logrys who walked about with their hair entirely loose.

There was a soft knock at the door.

"Find out who it is," I told Christine. She went to the door and opened it a chink. It was the Lady Igraine, so she let her in, and brought her a chair. Marie brought me a silk sheet to wrap myself in to dry as I stepped from the bath. We would never have used anything as expensive as that to dry ourselves at home.

"Queen Igraine." I bobbed my head in a little bow. I spoke slowly, my brain still swimming with Breton, trying to struggle back to my English. I hated switching between the languages, and I was conscious of wanting my English to sound as natural as possible. As much as I wanted to keep my connection to my own home, I also did not want to be obviously foreign here. "Are you well?"

"Bless you, child," she smiled, and I saw the lines of smiling crinkle with much use around her lovely pale grey eyes. "You don't have to call me Queen. I have come to tell you that there is a lady come from Avalon who wants to see you."

"What is Avalon?" I asked, as Marie helped me into a dress of pale lilac silk, sewn with little silver flowers at the sleeves and hems. It was not one I had brought with me. I was not sure if the gift of all these new, rich dresses was a kindness, or a judgement on the clothes of my own people. "A realm like Logrys? Part of Britain? Or a noble house?"

Igraine laughed softly.

"Avalon is... many people call it an island. It is here, in Logrys, on the borders. It's a..." she laughed again, "a place that is hard to describe. Merlin the witch came from there, and my daughter Morgan schooled there a long time, but I have never been."

I thought of the cold faces and blue woad of Morgan and Merlin.

"Is it like the barrow-lands?" I asked.

Igraine shook her head. "I'm sorry, I don't know what those are."

When I thought of Morgan and Merlin I felt sure Avalon would be a place like the barrow-lands, where the Otherworld touched the surface and men and women hovered between death and life, filled with the same trees hung with dead leaves, the same mounds where the barrow-wights lived. Cursed, and beautiful. So Avalon was Logrys' barrow-land. Yes, I thought Morgan and Merlin seemed as if they had come from a dark, strange place, a place between life and death.

Igraine led us down to Arthur's throne-room, where I had not been before. It was smaller than I would have expected, much smaller than the hall, though still grand, with high ceilings and enough room for fifty men, at least, to stand inside. Arthur sat on his throne with the casual easiness of youth, although I knew now he did not feel it. He sat lazily in it, one knee bent and the foot braced against the edge of the seat, opposite elbow on the arm, gazing thoughtfully down at the group just before him. At his side stood Merlin, Kay and Ector, two of whom I was pleased to see. The group before him were all women; most, by their dress I guessed, neat little nuns. All but the one at the front, who stood as I entered with her back to me, but whose white-blonde hair marked her out strikingly from the rest. As she turned on our entrance I could see that her face and hands, too, were threaded with patterns of blue in the form of twisting vines and sharp-petalled flowers. When Arthur saw me, he rose from the throne with a smile.

"There you are, lovely as ever, my queen."

"Are four days enough for 'as ever'?" I replied, teasing. He smiled and ran down the steps in two strides to take my hand and lead me back up. He was excited; I could see it on his face. I wondered what for. For once I could not feel Merlin's gaze on me. When I glanced at him, I could see that his eyes were fixed on the white-haired lady before us.

"Nimue, this is my queen, Guinevere."

The girl – because she was a girl as I looked upon her – she could not have been more than thirteen years of age – curtseyed neatly, and so did the nuns. She wore a lovely dress, pale blue like the sky and, like Morgan's dress, sewn with little gems from its high neck to the waist, making her shimmer in the light. Her gossamer-fine white hair lay on her shoulder in a simple plait, shining in the sun that streamed through the windows. She looked as though she were spun from glass.

"My lady, you are every bit as lovely as they say." Her manners were impeccable, but her voice, too was sincere, and I found myself already warming to the little creature. She was not like Morgan or Merlin; her eyes were light and quick, and she had a ready smile. "I am sorry I am late to pay my respects at your wedding. I come with a gift. It is from the Lady of the Lake, the Lady of Avalon. She brings you an oath, for all your knights, that they might swear to you and to the kingdom to protect and be faithful always."

The girl took from one of the nuns a wooden box, and opened it and held up a scroll of parchment. Arthur took it gratefully, and read it aloud. I noticed that his reading was slow, as though he had learned late. I supposed he had not been born a king. I remembered he had said he could not read the stone his father's sword was set in.

"It is a good oath. We shall all take it tonight, for tonight is Pentecost and at this time the spirit of the Lord is closer to us all, and each man will be truer in his oath."

Nimue nodded in approval.

"There is a second gift."

"Your lady is generous." Arthur replied.

"A hunt. The hunt for the White Hart."

This seemed a gift even more to Arthur's liking, but it was also to mine. I would feel more like myself again astride a horse, and I would enjoy the fresh air in my hair and on my skin.

We gathered in Camelot's great courtyard for the hunt. It was a hot, bright summer's day with a soft breeze. I was glad I had hidden some hunting leathers among my things and I strode down from my tower dressed in those – thick trousers and sturdy brown boots, a jerkin of leather over a thin silk vest, the net gone from my hair and instead it plaited back and tied with a leather string. I had not realised how I had missed my boots until I had them on again; the women of Logrys wore little pretty shoes like slippers, no good for riding a horse. Across my back hung my bows and arrows. Arthur smiled when he saw me.

"Now there is a queen fit for a warrior king." He held me by the hips, looking over me with approval.

"Here is a queen fit to go hunting," I corrected him.

I could hear some voices of those in the background not as pleased at the sight of their queen as Arthur, but I did not care. It was a small group riding out: Arthur, Kay, Ector, Gawain and his brothers, and a couple more I did not recognise. Just Arthur's chief knights, and his wife. The others too, were just dressed in leathers, armoured for light hunting not for fighting. Whatever dangers Arthur sensed, they must be further off than in the forest beside Camelot.

As we rode through the forest, the others spread off, deeper into the forest, looking for the hart. Arthur and I rode on together. I would have been happy to hunt on my own, but I think he wanted to keep me close by. Perhaps he was afraid I would try to run away, but I think it was rather that women did not seem to hunt, or even to ride out, on their own in Logrys. I did not think it could be more dangerous than Carhais, but then our men were different, too. We did not have these armoured giants raised for the battlefield. Perhaps we Bretons would not have let our women ride alone if our men were like these men of Logrys.

"How do you know the Lady of Avalon?" I asked, notching an arrow into my bow. There was nothing to shoot, but I wanted to feel as though I was doing something. I did not see any other game about the forest. Perhaps the lady Nimue had emptied it by magic for the purpose of the enchanted hunt.

"She gave me my sword."

"The one in the stone?"

He laughed.

"Not that old thing. It would have shattered at the first fight. My sword. I keep forgetting the damn name Merlin gave it."

He drew it to show me. The steel was cold and blue, perfectly smooth, so sharp it was impossible to see the edge clearly. I knew the name of the sword. Its name had come to Carhais. People did not forget a sword like that. *Excalibur.* Cutter of steel. I could not have missed that sword. The steel was forged in the Otherworld, the blade smooth at the side and sharp at the edge, the pommel covered in jewels of all colours that glittered in the sunlight. I felt the power coming from it as I stared at it. I was about to reach out and touch it, when Arthur sheathed it.

"It is a good sword, but my witch is always telling me the scabbard has the greater magic."

"What does the scabbard do?"

"The bearer never sheds a drop of blood. But the scabbard was stolen from me."

So there were enemies at home. That was why Arthur slept with Excalibur by his bed, so he would not lose that as well. And that was why he rode beside me, so that I would not be snatched in the woods. I thought a scabbard that saved the wearer from harm seemed much more valuable than any sword. I supposed that was why it was taken.

A pheasant suddenly burst up from a bush, shrieking its harsh cries. I hit it easily with an arrow, and Arthur laughed.

"I had no idea my new queen would be so useful with a weapon."

Arthur obviously had known no Breton women before he had met me.

He jumped off his horse to pick it up, and attached it to his saddle. I thought he would leap back up, but he smiled a little mischievous smile, taking me by the foot and with a little tug I did not expect, pulling me from my horse and and into his arms. My horse did not seem surprised. Perhaps it was used to it. I imagined that this was a trick he had learned playing at boys games with Kay. But he was not playing games now. He let me drop to my feet, and gently pressed me against the tree beside us with a fierce kiss.

"You thought I would be some savage. Well, my lady, look at yourself, dressed as a man, with a bloodlust for pheasants." He laughed, running a hand across my stomach under the jerkin. "All the ladies of Camelot were scandalised to see their queen going about dressed like that." I supposed they did not like to see the bare skin of my arms, the flash of it at my back above the vest. I had thought that women in Logrys were covered from neck to ankle because it was cold here, but it must have been, also, from prudishness. He slid his hand up the back, pulling at the lacing.

I pushed him back, gently.

"Any one of your knights could come riding along."

"Well, I don't think it would bother Gawain; *he's* a brute. And Kay has seen it before."

I laughed unwillingly and gave him a half-hearted shove back. He did not give ground. He kissed me again and pressed himself tight against me. I could feel against my leg that he was hard. The feel of the skin of his hand on my back, bare beneath the shirt, was stirring longing for the touch of more of his skin on mine. He was strong, and insistent, and already I was relenting, when the sound of horses' hooves tore him away from me. He stood back, looking around, waiting for the man and the horse, but none came. The sound came closer and closer until it seemed too loud to be natural, and then began to recede.

Arthur swung back up onto his horse and drew his sword in a second. He threw down his hunting horn to me.

"Stay here. If anyone you don't know comes, blow twice."

Then he was gone. I slung the horn around my neck and swung back up into the saddle. Arthur had pulled the straps of the jerkin loose and I could not reach to tie them up properly myself. It would have to do. I felt the tingling of frustrated anticipation all over me. I sighed deeply and looked up through the trees. The sun looked as though it was already dipping. Surely we had not been in the forest so long? We had left before midday. I waited for Arthur a while longer, and when it looked as though it was beginning to get dark, I blew the horn twice, but the forest swallowed up the sound. My only choice was to ride.

I took my horse slowly through the woods, looking out for light, or for men on horseback. I did not want to blow the horn again and risk scaring my horse, who was already beginning to seem wary and restive beneath me. I shushed her soothingly and patted her mane. She quietened a little. I tried calling out, for Arthur, Ector and Kay, but I only heard my voice echoing back. Eventually I came to a little clearing where I could see a figure lying by a little pool, asleep. I did not know the man, so I notched an arrow into my bow. I called out. There was no answer. I called again. I felt uneasy. The clearing gave me an awful feeling and in my panic I loosed the bow from the arrow. It hit the man – though I could not yet be sure he was a man since his face lay turned away from me, and he was curled in a lump – who howled with pain so loud I thought the trees shook. I jammed my hands over my ears, but I had to let them go to take the reins of my horse who was rearing and whinnying loud with distress. A harsh, sudden wind blew through the clearing, throwing debris from the ground up into my eyes. When the wind fell away and I opened them, the man was gone, and it was bright and before the pool stood, glorious, white and shining, the hart. It seemed to glow in sunlight that was suddenly bright as noon and it looked at me with an even stare. I was not going to kill the hart; I knew that as I saw it. Its presence seemed to calm my horse and I rode up to it. It let me stroke its soft, velvety muzzle for a moment, and then walked off. I watched it go, and wondered where the others were, if I had seemed to be caught in the dark because of the storm, or if the Otherworld was close to the surface in this wood and reaching out, gently, to warn me and reassure me all at once.

"My lady, you are lost." I turned my horse to see who had spoken behind me, and saw standing there Nimue.

"Who was the man?" I asked.

Nimue shook her head. "It doesn't matter. He was your future. The hart is your future. I am your future."

"What do you mean?"

"And you," she continued, as though she had not heard me, "Guinevere... the White Enchantress. What a name for a creature like you. The White Goddess of love and death. A destroyer of men. A bringer of greatness."

I was shaken. She knew the meaning of my name and she seemed to know the same ancient gods my people knew. But nothing she said made any sense, and she spoke it all in a strange trance, as though she was not really there. I noticed only then that she was dressed in the clothes of a nun. I did not know what she meant, or if she were real, or just another hallucination of the forest.

"Blow your horn again," she said.

I did, and at once I heard the hooves of horses. I expected Arthur, but out from the trees came Gawain. When I looked back to my side, Nimue was gone.

"I thought you were Arthur," Gawain said gruffly.

"How disappointing for you, sir," I replied curtly.

Gawain leant over and took my horse's reins sharply in his hands, snatching them from mine. She whickered in protest. I considered docking one of my arrows. I held my hand. Since Arthur trusted Gawain I would trust him, but only for the moment. Besides, I had my dagger hidden at my side. Gawain drew my horse right up to his and grabbed my saddle at each end with each hand, the reins of both horses still held in the front hand. Like this he was leaning slightly over me, and I bent to lean away.

"You shouldn't be riding about on your own," he said. In his thick, angry voice I couldn't tell if he was scolding or concerned. With the saddle he pulled my horse one step closer to his own, to him. I could smell him. He smelled of sweat, leather and blood. I could see rabbits hanging from his saddle. He had not chased just the noble white beast. I could not lean any further away from him without falling from my horse, and I did not want to lose her. Like this, my own face was just a hand's breadth from his densely freckled one. I could see, standing away from his skin, the rawness of a rough white scar that ran across his jaw. My heart was beating fast inside me and I felt my whole body tense to fight. I would if I had to. Gawain slowly looked me up and down. "Well," he said at last, letting go of my saddle and leaning fully back into his own, handing me back my reins, "you don't look hurt."

And he trotted off. He stopped at the edge of the clearing and turned back to me.

"*My lady*, you should not be riding about on your own."

I had not understood. He meant for me to follow him. I suppose in his own strange way, he felt as though he was acting as my protector. We passed through the trees together in silence until we came to another clearing where Sir Kay, without his horse, was fighting three men on foot. He killed one as we arrived with a swift, hard blow across the neck, and when Gawain jumped from his horse, his own sword drawn, to help him, the other two were swiftly dead. The one Gawain killed died of a hard downward thrust to his head that split his skull. Kay stabbed the other in the stomach, then drew his blade across the man's neck. They were all armoured in the same plain leather as Arthur's knights, but wearing a strange badge of colours I did not recognise. Neither did Gawain or Kay. The men exchanged a few words together, Kay thanking Gawain for his assistance, before Kay swung up behind me on my horse. There was not room behind Gawain, though his horse was larger than my own. Kay put an arm around my waist, and took one side of the reins with the other hand. I did not really want to relinquish control of the horse, but half seemed as much as I could ask for. I was aware of the strength in his touch, too, though it was not the raw strength of Arthur, and beneath that the dark flavour of the Otherworld hung strong about him. I noticed that he and Gawain had come into the forest with their swords, too. Not just equipped for hunting. Neither of them seemed to be surprised that there were men in the woods who would want to attack them.

"Where is Arthur?" he asked Gawain.

Gawain shrugged.

"We can't find him, and he seems to have left his queen behind."

"Where did you leave Arthur?" Kay asked me, his breath hot against my ear.

"I don't know – it seemed as though it was getting dark, and he thought he heard hooves, so he rode off. I blew the horn but he hasn't come."

I felt Kay nod behind me.

"It seemed to me that it was getting dark a while ago, also. What *is* this forest? How long have we been here?"

"It's the fault of that little witch girl," Gawain growled.

We rode on, in silence. I was conscious of my body pressed against Kay's, wary of it, but his touch was light and gentle and I preferred him to Gawain.

Eventually, we broke from the forest, and it was sudden that we were thrust into bright noonday sunlight. I raised a hand and blinked against the brightness after the shade of the forest. There stood Camelot, grey and immovable before us, made in stone. Not like the living trees and living dreams of the forest. At the gates stood Arthur, holding his horse by the reins. When I saw him, I slipped from my saddle, leaving the horse to Kay, and ran into his arms. He gathered me up and kissed me furiously, burying his hands in my hair, holding me close against him. He held my face in his hands and I looked into his deep grey eyes. He had been afraid. He was breathing fast.

"I feared you were lost forever," he said. I shook my head.

"I feared *you* were."

He looked up and smiled, beamed out at Kay and Gawain.

"I thank God you two are both safe. That means we are all back, except Pellinore."

I remembered Pellinore as a kindly older knight who everyone called 'King Pellinore', though he could hardly have been a king anymore.

The little Nimue slipped out from behind Arthur like a ghost and said in her sweet, reedy little voice: "You found your futures in that forest, your destinies. And Pellinore found his. His fate is to look always for the white hart. He will not come back."

Then she was gone.

Chapter Eight

At dinner that evening, the knights all spoke the words of the oath, but the mood was sombre and thoughtful where it ought to have been joyous. They each laid a hand on my father's wishing table and swore to be honest and true to Arthur, and to be protectors of women. Then we sat down around it to eat, though no one seemed very hungry except Gawain, who ate like a man who had been starved. Nimue, who had returned without a word, sat beside Merlin like a white shadow, nibbling at her food neatly, as though she had not just plunged us all into a forest of shadows and futures. I was angry; I wanted to shout. She had done something strange to all of us, and one of us was lost. No one spoke of Pellinore. They were afraid to under the steady gaze of her ice-blue eyes.

I did not ask what Arthur had seen in the forest, because I did not want to tell him what I had seen. I was afraid that the man I had killed at the pool was him, with my evil wish. I think what he saw was not good either, because that night he took me into his arms with a wordless urgency, and had me with the desperate passion of a man who has seen his own end. Afterwards, he lay still and thoughtful, gazing up at the canopy of the bed above. It was red as blood. I wondered if he was thinking of his Hanged Christ, and if this Christ would save him. He wrapped one arm around me, and I laid my head on his shoulder. I laid a hand on his chest and rubbed there, lightly. He looked down from his thoughts at me.

I reached up to touch his cheek. He looked weary and worried. Not like a youth of seventeen. He let me draw him down into a kiss. He looked at me as though he was about to say something, and then did not.

The next morning dawned a bright new day, and Arthur and the others seemed to have forgotten, or at least no longer be unsettled by, the magical hunt. Arthur rolled onto me in the morning with a smile, and at his kiss, and his touch, I slowly forgot the fears of the night and my dreams of the dark forest and the wounded man. By the time he was inside me, I had forgotten, and all I could think of were his muscular hands holding me, deep in my hair, behind my back, him going deeper into me. I sighed with him and as he rolled away, the day before seemed distant and already meaningless.

When I took my bath, Arthur went down to train with the other knights. That became the routine of our days. I saw him again in the evening for a meal, and then he would accompany me back to my rooms. The meals were smaller now that the wedding-guests who had come from the edge of Britain had gone back to their homes: the lady Igraine to her castle in Cornwall; Sir Ector to his lands in the west of the country; Morgawse and her youngest two sons, who I had not met, and one of whom must have been the ill-fated Mordred, to Lothian; Morgan to the lands of her husband Uriens; and many others that I never saw or knew. The Round Table was moved to Arthur's council chamber, so that he could meet with his knights without all of those who ate at the low tables in the great hall overhearing. I was pleased, too, for I wanted to be alone sometimes with the table. It made me feel a little braver, a little stronger than I had before. It was a warm, early summer day when I found the room where it sat empty and walked around it, trailing my fingertips over the smooth wood. I closed my eyes, and thought of home, and it was not painful anymore. Home was a distant, happy memory in Carhais, but it was also here in Camelot, too. Here with Arthur.

I heard my name, softly, and turned around to see he was there. He looked handsome, having just walked in from training at fighting in the yard, a little flushed, his hair ruffled through, his sword by his side, the power of his muscular body visible beneath the light armour. I felt a flutter of daring within me at the sight of him. I stepped towards him and when he opened his mouth to speak again I rested my fingertips lightly against his lips. I felt a strange flutter of nervousness, for I had not yet been daring enough – nor needed to, from his eagerness. I could feel them soften under my touch as he smiled and, sliding an arm around my waist, drew me towards him. With his other hand, I heard him slide the bolt on the door shut behind us. I let my fingers fall away from his lips, and kissed him, soft and tender. I felt him sigh against me, and a yearning for the warm, sweet familiarity of our love grew inside me. I took hold of the buckle of his belt and drew him with me as I stepped back towards the table. I heard him laugh under his breath, soft with excitement. I ran my hands through his hair, feeling the softness of his lips against mine grow into a demanding kiss, full of desire, in response. He pushed me gently up on to the table, and I felt my limbs spread through with a light, tingling excitement as he pushed back the skirts of my dress. I flicked open his belt buckle and heard his sword clatter to the ground. He made a low noise of longing as I leaned back flat against the table, feeling the cool wood against the backs of my hands as I stretched my arms over my head. I closed my eyes, sighing back against the table, against the feel of Arthur's hands running gentle but firm with desire up my legs. I whispered his name and he went into me, with a low groan, and I wrapped my legs around him, holding him closer. He leaned down and I felt his lips brush soft against the sensitive tops of my breasts where they swelled from the neck of my dress. I could hear him murmuring my name. I wound my hands into his hair and I felt myself grow light and bright and sigh with the bliss of our being together. Afterwards, we lay side by side on the table and I told him about my wicked wish, and unwished it out loud, right there, pressing my palms hard into the table. He did not seem upset, or surprised. I still dreamed of my home, but it felt distant now, and I had found something very like happiness with Arthur that I did not think I would have given up to go back to Carhais. Not now.

Just as the last leaves were falling from the trees, and the cool smell of winter filled the air, on the very edge of autumn, Marie reached into the bath and laid a hand on my stomach.

"What do you think?" I asked.

Marie shrugged, and Christine, who knew better about these things and had delivered children in her time, pushed her out the way. She pushed up her sleeve and thrust her own hand in. She made a noise of uncertainty, but she sounded less doubtful than I thought she would have done.

By the time the snows were beginning to fall, a light dusting of white over the land, there was no doubt. There was the definite little swell of a child. I was pleased that it was winter and I was dressed in many layers. I was afraid of losing it, and I did not want anyone to know too soon, except my women, and Arthur. He laid his head gently on the small mound, his ear to my navel, and swore he could hear the sound of a new king on the approach. He wanted a son, but I imagined a little girl, with his lovely grey eyes, who would be wild and wicked as I was when I was small. I could see how happy he was, the smile he could not keep from his face. I was sure he had told Kay, because when I saw Kay, he gave me a new, warm smile. Arthur and I could not keep ourselves from already spending the end of our nights, when we were both warm and sated and sleepy, and all of the candles had been put out, from staring up into the darkness and imagining what the child would be like.

Every nerve of my body felt filled with a wonderful, electric excitement. I could feel the sweet tingle of new life growing in me, and something else I dared not recognise too strongly – a dark sense of promise of the Otherworld.

I decided to go and wish for a healthy child – I would not wish for a son, for truly if Arthur wanted a child like Queen Maev then he would be better with a girl – on the Round Table. The stairs seemed endless, and more tiring than I had ever remembered, though all the other times I had been whisked along by Arthur, half leading, half carrying me to bed, and the child growing inside me made me feel more tired than I wanted to admit. I came to the room, Merlin's room, half-way up. The door was ajar and I could see the repellent witch moving around inside. I moved on, pushing aside my uneasy thoughts of Merlin, up another flight to Arthur's council chamber. It was empty. Good. I bolted the door shut behind me and climbed onto the table, then turned over to lie on my back. I stretched out my arms and felt the wood against the back of my hands, cool, smooth and old. I smelled it all around me. The smell of home. Of comfort, magic and Carhais.

I wish for a healthy child, I thought. I wish for a strong child.

When I went to sit up, I could not move.

I heard the sound of iron scraping on wood, and realised that someone was moving the bolt aside from the outside. My heart fluttered in panic beneath me. I tried to rise again, but I could not move my body; all I could do was open my eyes. I could see the door hanging open, but only the top part of the frame. Then, freezing me to the bone with horror, upside-down above me, leaning over me, the grinning face of Merlin. I tried again and again to move, but it felt as though all the power to move had been drained from my body. I wanted to scream, but there was no breath in my lungs. They too were still. I wondered if I would die. If he would kill me there.

"I'm sorry, my queen," Merlin said, pushing back the black sleeves of his strange habit, revealing white arms, slack-skinned, but tattooed with the blue-green woad. His eyes above me peered wide and black, unnatural and irisless. His teeth unnaturally white against the blue patterns of his face. "I'm sorry, but this is Arthur's destiny."

He laid his hand slightly on my swollen stomach and I felt a pain blossom, hot and sharp, from there, into the core of my being. It was unbearable, and I could not even scream. My blood pounded in my ears, and I could feel a deathly wetness between my legs, making the heavy silk of the dress stick against my skin. Against the rushing and pounding of blood in my ears I heard a voice shouting. Through the pain I forced my eyes open and in the doorway I saw Arthur, his sword drawn in his hand. He swung it at the witch, and the man dissolved into the air as the blade cut through him, and against the cold of his disappearing being, Excalibur shattered into pieces.

Arthur lifted me in his arms and carried me up to his rooms. Through the pain I could barely see; I could barely move. I could feel the life and hope draining out; I could smell the acrid iron scent of blood. Someone stripped the dress from me and lifted me into a bath, but the bath filled with blood and I had to be lifted into a second. Christine was there, and Arthur. Those were the voices I recognised. There might have been others, or I might have imagined them. Dark shapes moved in front of my eyes, and I was limp and weak. I heard the cold, cruel voice of a woman who I could only think of as Queen Maev, though I knew it could not be she, and the little soft voice of the druid Nimue, and the voice of my father, as if from far away, although that in my head was indistinguishable from a voice I could only think of as the voice of the Round Table. It said *I'm sorry, I'm sorry*.

I woke in Arthur's bed when it was, he told me afterwards, days later.

"Was it a dream?" I asked him.

He shook his head. His eyes were red, he had grown a beard that looked to be more than just a few days, and he did not look as if he had slept.

He leaned down and kissed my cheek softly.

"I am glad, at least, that you survived," he said.

I only wept.

Arthur carried me back to my own chambers, and Marie and Christine wrapped me in my bed, while Margery made a cold cloth for my head. I only wanted to sleep again until I was no longer myself. I tried to tell myself that it was just a single child, that I would have many more, but I knew, and I knew Arthur knew from the look on his face when I woke, that the grip of that witch on my stomach had squeezed the life from my womb and closed it shut and we would never have hope of a child. From that day, I never bled again.

Chapter Nine

The days passed and I did not get up from my bed. I listened to the voices changing around me. Margery, Marie and Christine, always familiar. Christine and Marie chatting in Breton when Margery was off running errands. Arthur, Kay and Ector, even Nimue came for me, but for weeks I turned everyone away. I pressed my face into the feather pillow, but my tears were dry and I got no relief there. In the back of my mind, also, was the knowledge that Arthur might put me away. He needed a son. There were many other princesses, all of whom might give him one.

But he kept coming back. Arthur would sit by the side of my bed, and read to me slowly, in his halting English, from a gilded manuscript filled with stories of romance. First I lay still, then I began to rest my head on his leg. He would stroke my hair and tell me what had been happening at court. Another brother of Gawain had arrived, Gaheris, and more knights had flocked to join the men who were now calling themselves the Knights of the Round Table. He told me that the sword he had shattered trying to kill Merlin was not Excalibur, but a fake, swapped with his own, and now he had the true sword back, but Merlin was dead. Nimue had shut him beneath a rock at the edge of the sea. I was glad to hear this.

Then, one evening, Arthur sent my ladies away. They made disappointed noises, hoping to hear more stories and news. He stripped to his shirt and slid into bed beside me, as I lay on my side, wrapping his arms around me and softly kissing my neck. It had been a long time since I felt him this close, and when I felt him there I knew I had missed it.

"We can be whole again, my love," he whispered into my neck. I turned over so that I was lying on my back and rested my hand lightly against his chest. I nodded. He threw the heavy covers off us and rolled onto me, gently drawing me under him.

"You do not want another queen? One who can –"

He hushed me then.

"No. I do not."

His lips found mine, soft but intense, his hands sliding the nightdress up to my waist. I could feel him, hard and ready, against my leg. It reminded me how good, how vivid and alive I felt when our bodies came together. I wanted to feel whole again. But more than that, I wanted to forget, just for a moment, everything else that had happened. Nothing else had worked, but with his hands on me I thought then that, maybe, this might. I pushed his shirt up over his head, and looked at him for a moment in the soft glow of the fire. He still wanted me, he would keep me, he would be kind. He *was* handsome. He pulled away my nightdress as well, and pressed my body all over with hungry kisses. It felt as though his desire was bringing me back to life, and everywhere his lips touched the life in me flowed strong again. My body had missed him, though my mind had been elsewhere and noticed nothing, but there were parts of me that yearned for him and had needed more than him sat at my side. I felt that now, and I felt the pleasure and relief as I pulled him inside me, and once more we were one.

So things went back to how they had been, as if there had never been a child, though Arthur did not visit me every night, anymore, busy as he was with affairs of the realm. I was happy, though, when I did not remember the child, and when I did not remember home. I loved Arthur; I was sure of that by now. I loved his strength and his kindness, and I was happy whenever we were together. As time went by I thought less and less of the child I had imagined we would have. Just when I was beginning to forget the pain of it, just as the winter was breaking into spring, and a new year promised forgetting, and new things, the news came from France.

"King Leodegrance is dead, my liege." The messenger bowed before Arthur's throne.

My stomach did a sickening turn within me. *My father.* I forced myself to keep calm, and still, and stern. I had to show them the face of a queen, not a grieving daughter.

"He was killed by Emperor Lucius, my lord. Lucius says that because tributes have not been payed he will continue to take back his land. King Ban's sons have managed to hold the south of France, but Carhais and Brittany with it are lost."

I pressed my head back into the cool, dark wood of the chair that supported me and closed my eyes. I felt the room spin around me, just for a moment. *So, there is to be more war. And my father is dead.* The last time I saw him, he was putting me and a large wooden table onto a boat. My father. The wooden table where I had been sacrificed to Arthur's destiny by Merlin was the only real reminder of him that I had left. I had left him angry and resentful, though I had said goodbye kindly. He would die without knowing I had found a fragile kind of happiness here at Camelot. I would live the rest of my life without going back to my father and my home, for Carhais would not be quite my home again without him.

Arthur was furious. I could hear it in his voice. Every syllable shook with rage, though he strove to control it. He would not lose Britain's territories overseas. He would not leave his people to be murdered and pillaged by Lucius. He banged his fist on the arm of his throne and the whole dais shook. I heard the messenger scuttle back, but I kept my eyes closed. So, this was the fearsome king who had defeated King Lot in the War with Five Kings.

I thought he would want to be alone that evening, but instead he took me to his own chambers. His love was angry and fierce, but I welcomed it. He tore the dress from me as soon as the door was bolted and threw me down on the bed, casting off his own shirt and opening his breeches, he entered me right away, his hands tight around my thighs, until, with a low groan, he finished. He stood again, when he was done, pulling up his breeches and fastening his belt. His chest was still rising and falling heavily with deep breaths, and I was not sure if it was from his anger, or our union. My hair fell about my shoulders, in my face, long and free, wild, torn loose by the urgency of his lovemaking. I felt fragile, and shaken. I would have liked him to hold me, but he was lost in his thoughts. He poured himself a cup of wine and drank it in one gulp, then poured another. He stood, staring out of the open window. I rolled onto my front on the bed, staring out in the same direction. I liked the feel of the cool breeze from the window against my skin, its freshness.

"Another war," he said, flatly.

"Another," I agreed.

He turned back to me, and, suddenly distracted, smiled at the sight of my hair, tumbling down my back, before my face. He came over and buried his face in the deep red curls, his hands stroking the skin of my back lightly, cool against the air.

"Come with me," he said. I was pleased. I knew how to fight, and I had no desire to wait in an empty castle for news. "The sight of you," he took my face in his hands and kissed me lightly, "will make me brave."

It was not long before the castle was ready to march for war. It had not been long since it fought one. Swords were still sharp, armour not yet rusting. Arthur brought me to his war councils and at first the other knights were reluctant and surprised, but when they saw that I could read the big, brown maps of Europe as well as Arthur's witch had they ceased complaining. These were held in the room with the Round Table. The first time I went there, I knew, would be the worst time. To return. I could see, before the others arrived and Arthur rolled out the maps, faint and dark, the stain of blood in the centre of the table. I laid my hand against it and, again, wished for Arthur's life. Arthur was all I had left. When the maps rolled out and it was gone from my sight I traced for the men around me a line down the spine of Europe, through my father's lost lands, and to its heart, Rome. We could not hope, with our small force, to take back all of the lands we had lost there, but if we struck at Rome, Lucius would have to retreat to protect his own capital city. Logrys had the advantage of being across the sea, so Arthur didn't have to worry about leaving his own capital undefended, and the small size of our army would allow us to slip past the invading forces more easily.

"Besides," Arthur said, "I have friends in France. Sir Ector's brothers and half-brothers, King Ban's sons, have castles there, and I've had word from them that they will join us, and are already prepared."

Sir Ector nodded, returned already from his peaceful lands to ride with his foster-son to war. Arthur would prefer open battle, I knew. I did not think we would survive an open battle. Not from Calais all the way to Rome.

At night Arthur often spoke of fighting, as we lay curled together in the darkness. He wanted it, I think. He wanted to fight again as much as he feared the losses of battle. It was who he was. A warrior-king. He didn't know anything else. It made me wish I was a man and knew only the joy of victory, or the oblivion of defeat, not a woman who had to live on with the weight of loss. But I could go by his side, then my fate would be his fate. I was prepared to not go to Rome a prisoner.

I took Christine, Marie and Margery with me. They all knew the arts of healing to various degrees, and I did not want only the company of men. They had travelled ahead with the main part of Arthur's army and the other assortment of women who provided healing services to the camp. Arthur wanted me with him and his best knights. I was pleased to be not far from his side.

I realised as I swung up into the saddle in the great courtyard of Camelot and glanced back up at its huge grey stone towers, fluttering their silk banners of blue dragon on white, that I felt strongly, for the first time, that this was my home. And I might never see it again. I looked away; there was no use thinking about that now. The smell of leather and horses was welcome and comforting and I leaned down and patted my horse on the neck. Her coat was rough and bristly to the touch; a good horse for war, not a sleek prancing pony. Arthur had had made for me a proper suit of armour, with chainmail leggings, and a steel-plated leather jerkin embossed with the dragon of his house. I did not want a hot, heavy visored helm like the knights wore, so I had a long cap of chainmail that fell as far as my shoulders. Arthur had laughed and said without my hair showing I looked like a fierce little boy riding to his first battle. At my back I had my bow and arrows, though when one of the archers had taken my bow to check it and laughed at it, saying it was a toy, I had taken as well a light spear. I could not lift the kind of steel longsword Arthur and his knights fought with, nor a huge and ugly mace like the one I saw strapped to Gawain's saddle, but I was fast and alert, and confident of my abilities in battle. I was not weighed down as the knights were by platemail, though my horse was armoured like theirs. They must have been a terrifying sight to the enemy, that band of huge men, already hardened by war. To me, they were a comfort.

We set off as one, and as we rode I felt the breeze brush my bare arms and closed my eyes for a moment, smelling the cool, fresh air of Logrys that I was leaving behind. I turned back to Camelot for a moment, and saw it as I had almost a year ago when I had come to be married. It felt like so much longer than that. So much had changed. I felt as though, like a snake, I had lost layers of skin and been made, in no small part by Arthur's love as well as by Camelot, half-new.

We reached Dover by nightfall, but I could not sleep on the ship. It made me feel sick, to be belowdecks, with the rocking of the waves and the guttering of the candles. Arthur slept deeply, dreaming of conquering, but I slipped back up onto the deck in my nightdress. I walked to the edge and stared down into the black waves below. So beautiful. I liked, too, the cool sea air against my skin as it blew through the thin dress. Then I looked up at the stars and saw the night was clear. A swelling moon hung low in the sky and the sight of it made me sigh. It reminded me uncomfortably of the White Goddess. *Love and death.* I did not like that second part. I said a little prayer to the Mother, looking up at the moon, wishing she might turn its cold white face from me, and fumbled around for a piece of food to drop into the sea for the Drowned God.

I found a peach stone on the deck and thought that would have to do. With a whisper of words I dropped it in the sea. Arthur's Hanged Christ hated him, but maybe my gods would protect us. I could not pray to them in Logrys, but perhaps they would take care of us here, and we were going into my country now, where people still believed in them and they were still strong.

"This is better." A deep voice beside me made me jump. Kay was standing just behind me, and I had not noticed him. He held out in his hand a small piece of salted beef. With the other arm he leant lazily against the edge of the ship. I gave a wary smile and took the beef. I wondered if he thought I was looking for something to eat, but I did not want to eat it. I did not want to give it to the god in front of him. His looks were of the Otherworld – black hair, dark, dark, almost black eyes, fair skin, tall and nimble-footed – but that did not mean that he was not a Christian like his brother. I knew enough of the Christians from sitting in the Chapel to know that the Hanged Christ did not take kindly to other gods.

Kay gestured with a little nod of his head towards the sea.

"Go on," he said gently.

I turned from him back towards the sea, and closed my eyes, said the words and dropped in the little piece of beef. When I opened my eyes, Kay was leaning on both elbows against the side of the ship, facing away from the sea, leaning his head back all the way to look up at all the stars. I turned around too, leaning back, looking up. The sound of the waves brushing against the boat at my back was gorgeous. I had missed the sea, sick as riding across it made me. The smell of salt in the air promised change and adventure, even if it did not promise safety, or a return home.

"Do you pray to them when we are at Camelot?" Kay asked at last.

I shook my head.

"For the best, I suppose," he said, thoughtfully. "It's strange, though. Arthur believes in Avalon, in the magical lake there, in his magic sword, in your magic table, in the lands between life and death, but the only god he tolerates is the god of the Christians." He turned round again, to face me, placing one of his hands either side of me on the lip of the deck. The moonlight shone in his eyes, in his dark hair. I felt again a sense of the Otherworld about him, magnetic and familiar. I found myself leaning, just slightly, away from him.

"I hope you are ready for war," he said. I had not expected this. I thought he was about to begin some new game or jape, but he had trapped me there and locked me with his gaze out of concern.

"I am," I replied evenly.

Then he left, walking away across the deck and disappearing into the darkness. I felt strange, unsettled. I was sure I was ready. I was sure I was ready for war.

Chapter Ten

When we arrived at Calais, a huge army was already amassed to meet us. We only had to ride a few miles from the docks to see, stretching across the fields, the huge pavilions of lords, and the small grubby tents of the footsoldiers. Waiting for Arthur and his knights was a small gathering of the largest and finest of the pavilions, raised in the centre of the camp. Inside the one Arthur took for his own was a table set with fruit and wine, and in the corner a bed laid with silks and filled with cushions.

"I did not have this the last time I fought a war," he laughed, picking up a pear, weighing it in his hand. "I slept in the dirt with my men, under trees and in caves, and we ate only what we could find in the forest. The French know how to fight a war in comfort."

This war is going to be different, I thought, with rising panic. What if Arthur doesn't know what to do?

But he did know what to do. A few days later, when at last we rode out to meet with the enemy in the field I saw how he had won his wars as little more than a boy. He was a big man, but on the battlefield he appeared twice the size, lifting the huge longsword over his head as though it were light as a needle, and smashing it down. He and all his knights were platemailed head to foot with visored helms, but I could recognise the way he moved, swift and powerful, on his horse, through the crowds. On the back of his armour, enamelled bright blue, was the dragon of his father, the idea being that the men could recognise their king, but the enemy could not. It worked for Arthur, because he was always at the front of the battle line. I hung back with the other archers. I did not have the strength to fight hand-to-hand with men, but my aim was sure and I was swift to duck and dodge out of the way.

Each night Arthur would ride back from battle, side by side with me, snatch me from my horse and pull me into our pavilion. He was always hot and eager from the fighting, smelling of steel and sweat and blood, full of victory. He would pull the armour from me and toss it aside, and I would help him unbuckle his own huge set of platemail, then he would throw us down on the pillows and have me right away, with the sweat and dirt of battle still on us both, and the smell of leather clinging to my skin. I loved it when he was like that, full of need and hunger, and I cleaved to him those nights and his warm, living body. Every night together was another day alive. Then he would call for a bath and we would sit in the hot, steaming water and feel the day of fighting and death wash slowly away.

The toll was beginning to show. As we slowly moved south, into the lands taken from my father, we lost more and more men. We were not the small force of swift knights I had hoped for; we were a huge army, swelled from Arthur's war-band by the vast armies of King Ban's sons. Moving south like this could only be open war. We were winning, but our men were flesh and blood and died as easily, if not as frequently, as the enemy. Gawain's young squire was killed in battle one day, and he roared like a bear and tore into the enemy lines with his mace, smashing them down as if they were saplings. He only just made it back alive and bore from that day a second scar on his face, down his right cheek. Others were lost, too. The young knights, in their first war. By the time we passed out of Brittany and down towards the south of France, Arthur started to want me by his side in battle, not with the other archers, whose numbers were dwindling and who were often forced to take a vulnerable position out in the open. Beside him in the thick of battle, I could not see what was going on, could not always draw my bow properly. I thought it was a mistake, to be so close by him, but he would not listen.

The fourth day I fought by his side, my spear splintered in one of the enemy, and as he went down his helm fell away and I saw he was just a boy, younger than I was. I stared down at the man I had killed. I could hear the battle continue to rage around me, the smash of iron on wood, and iron on iron. The shrieking of horses. I could still smell the acrid smells of blood, mud and death, but I felt as though it was all happening far away from me. I heard Arthur call my name and I turned to look for him through the thick of the battle. All the knights covered in their armour with their helm-visors down looked the same. He would be facing towards me, so I would not see the dragon on his back. I heard him shout again, and at last saw an armoured man with his arm in the air, and I knew it was him, but it was too late. Something thudded heavily into the centre of my breastplate, sending me flying from my horse and knocking the breath out of me. I hit the soft, muddy ground with a thud that stunned me for a moment, a moment too long to move out of the way of my horse, that reared over me with a screeching whinny. The mail cap had slipped from my head and I curled my arms over my head in inadequate protection as I thought *this is where I die*.

But it was not. Strong arms snatched me up from the ground, onto a horse, as though I weighed nothing. I was dimly aware that I had lost my bow and arrows, although these seemed little now in comparison with my life. A platemailed arm held me tight about the waist on a horse that seemed to be galloping though a brown and grey blur. My head span. I tried to turn my head to see who it was who had saved my life, but all I could see was the iron helm, the visor shut. I sank back against the platemailed chest. I could feel my arms shaking, my hands quivering where they grasped the arm that held me tight; I was afraid to fall again. My vision blurred before me.

The knight leaned closer to speak to me.

"My queen, are you hurt?" The voice was soft and low, *French*. It reminded me, suddenly and painfully, of home. I feared for a second that this might be a knight from the other side, since not all the frenchmen were fighting with Arthur, but his horse before me was draped in colours that I was sure I had seen in Arthur's camp.

"I don't think so."

The knight put his reins in the hand of the arm around me and pulled the leather glove off his other hand. I was afraid again for a moment when he thrust his bare hand up under my breastplate, against my skin, but he drew it out again swiftly to hold it in front of my face. Through my foggy vision I could see that his fingers were red with blood. *My blood.*

"I think you *are* hurt, my lady."

He turned his horse suddenly and I felt a wave of nausea break over me. Now I had seen the blood I could feel my side throbbing. The movement of the horse beneath me was comforting, though, and I thought *he is taking me home*. I was not sure which home I thought he was taking me to. My vision was getting darker and though I tried to hold my eyes open, to look out for Arthur, I could not. The knight pulled me tighter against his iron-clad chest and I could feel the heat of it, warmed by the sun, on my back, and the back of my head as I slumped against him. As I finally drifted off into the darkness I wondered who this man was who had saved my life.

I woke hearing voices around me, hovering below consciousness, not wanting to open my eyes to the harsh light I knew would be beyond my eyelids.

I heard a low, soft voice speak beside me in the gentle accent of the French, the voice of the man who had saved my life.

"How is she?"

Marie answered, and I could feel her press the back of a cool hand on my brow, and gave a little sigh. "The wound isn't from a weapon, thankfully. It looks like the crossbow bolt hit her, shattering the breastplate but not wounding her, and the broken armour cut her when she fell from her horse. It's not deep, and it's clean, so she should be well soon enough."

I struggled to wake fully as I heard the sound of footsteps leaving. I wanted to look at the face of the man who had saved my life, but as I blinked myself to wakefulness, I saw that he had gone, slipped away from me before I could see him, or thank him. Arthur sat beside my bed, the ragged beard of weeks of war making him look haggard, older than his years. Or perhaps it was his eyes in which I could see both anger and weariness. Kay stood in the doorway of the tent, his arms crossed over his chest, looking apprehensive, hovering as if waiting for permission to come in or leave. I felt Marie recede silently from my side.

Arthur put his huge hand on my head and gently stroked back my hair.

"It was a mistake to bring you here," he said softly, but firmly.

"Arthur, I'm alright."

"We should send you home."

"Arthur." I pushed myself up onto my elbows, feeling the wound at my side spasm with pain. He saw it on my face. I wished I knew how to hide it better. I did not *want* to go back to Camelot, to sit and wait in a castle to hear if he was alive or dead, to wait for Emperor Lucius' men to take the castle and kill me, or rape me. I didn't want to wonder what was happening, I wanted to be there in the thick of it. "My place is here with you. I will be whole again soon. My mother rode to war before me, and before her Maev was always at war at the side of her consorts –"

"*Enough.*" Arthur jumped to his feet, his face flushed with sudden anger. "I should remind you that your mother *died* riding to war with King Lot, and you are *not* Queen Maev herself, you are *my* queen." I opened my mouth to protest but he carried on. "For God's sake, Guinevere, I saw you today snatched away, seconds from your death. I was too far away to save you. I thought having you here would make me fight more bravely, but having you here makes me a coward, always watching my back, always looking for you and not the enemy in the battlefield. You're not invincible, Guinevere. None of us are. And you're a *woman*. I should never had brought you here."

"I can fight, you *know* I can fight..." I was angry too, now. I had waited before, waited in my castle like a good girl for the men to come home. They had *not* come home. I wanted to be where I could do something. I wanted to be here where I could die in battle if Arthur did.

"Guinevere – haven't I lost enough men in this? Haven't enough people died? You're not just another knight, you're *my wife* –"

"Arthur, let her rest –" Kay tried to cut in gently, and Arthur rounded on him.

"This is *not your concern*, Kay. She is not *your* wife." Kay fell silent and stepped away and Arthur turned back to me. "My men are fighting and dying out there for me and I can't be the leader I need to be with you here. You are not one of my men. You do not have to fight."

"Arthur –" I tried again.

"*No*. Guinevere, there will be no discussion on this matter. I am your king, and you do as I command." He relented for a second, his shoulders sagging under the weight of his anger, but then he continued. "I've lost enough already. *We've* lost enough. The child, I... I'm not going to lose you as well. Just do as I say." And without waiting for me to reply he left, the tent door flapping behind him from his furious exit. As he left he shouted, "Someone take her back to Britain."

I closed my eyes as hot, angry tears pricked them and lay back against the little bed. I heard Marie move back to my side and felt her lift the sheet to look at the wound beneath my ribs. Kay moved softly to the chair at my side and took my hand, but didn't say anything. There was nothing to be said. I was not foolish enough to think that Arthur would forget his rage.

Chapter Eleven

So the war, for me, was over, and they took me back to Camelot in a palanquin, when I had ridden away on a charger. Christine alone came with me. They needed the other women to heal the injured and tend to the sick. She told me I ought to be glad I was leaving. I was not glad. To sit by and wait when I knew how to fight? But then I thought of the man who had saved my life. I was lucky to be alive. And Arthur might yet live. That man might yet live, and I would see him again, perhaps. Hear the voice. I heard it, at night, when I slept. The soft, French tones close by. I didn't know why I could not get that voice out of my head. It must have been the shock of the injury, or my restless sleep on the journey, because by the time I arrived back in Camelot, I did not dream of it any longer.

It was already full summer when I returned, so the war had been going longer than I thought. When I was healed, it was the height of the summer heat. I lay out in the sun in the little walled garden beneath my rooms. It had bloomed since the spring when we left and all the air in that space smelled headily of roses. I liked to feel the grass at my back and the sunlight against my eyelids. I would lie there in the summer heat and doze, dreaming of return.

One day a messenger came to me to tell me one of Gawain's brothers had arrived at court and I should go out to greet him. I stood and brushed the grass and petals off the dress I wore, plain blue silk and simple. I had sold my finest dresses and the richest jewels to the lands on the borders in return for grain and fruits. With many of the men away, the fields were falling fallow and there was not always enough food in Camelot for every mouth.

Out in the courtyard stood Morgawse. She was dressed finely enough, with a gold circlet in her russet hair, braided up into a thick twist of plait at the nape of her neck. Her broad, freckled face was haughty and proud, and that lent her a certain handsomeness. I had heard men speak of it before, often. It always bristled with me, just a little. I had thought her kind, I knew, when I had first met her, but knowing that Arthur had lain with her I found it hard to like her now. I tried to put the thought from my mind. Beside her stood a boy with her same broad, handsome looks. I thought from the look of him that he was about sixteen.

"My lady queen," Morgawse greeted me formally and kissed me on each cheek. She was friendly and courteous, but I could feel no warmth towards her. "This is my son, Gareth. I've brought him to you to be trained as a knight. There may be need of men in this war," she added with a sigh.

I nodded. Gareth bowed and moved off towards the stables to look at the horses and Morgawse linked an arm into mine and pulled me close.

"Tell me honestly, Guinevere, are you well? Has there been news?" My heart sank within me. Morgawse had lost her king in battle. She knew what I might have to feel, what I might have to suffer. I heard tales of Lothian, of her attempts to rule it with her sons, of the fighting barons calling her a whore, always resisting the rule of a woman.

"I'm well. There has been nothing new. They are doing well, I think. The last I heard, they had reached the south of France, and the Emperor Lucius was in retreat. I pray every day that it will be over soon." I did. I did not pray in the gloomy chapel, though, but beneath the winding arms of the rosebush, to the Hanged God, to the White Goddess, and out there at night, under the stars, to the Mother. There was no one left in Camelot who cared what I did now.

Morgawse stayed a few days, but then had to return to her kingdom. I was bored and lonely, so I decided that I would take some of the instruction of Gareth myself. He was a sweet child, of fourteen he said, though I was not surprised that I thought him older to see the size of his brothers. I had him sit with me in my little walled garden and taught him to read the love poems of Ovid, written into French, and I rode with him around the fields that encircled the castle. We took bows and arrows into the woods to look for game, but they were almost bare and the few rabbits I saw I did not want to shoot, afraid I would kill off the last of them. He was quick to learn, and eager, though I sensed he preferred the only lessons I could not offer him – those in the courtyard with the longsword. The weeks passed and I began to feel as though this boy had been brought to me by the gods in recompense for the child that Merlin had taken. He was gentle and kind, quick to laugh and smile.

One lazy day at the very end of summer, where the sun hung low and orange in the sky, fat against the horizon, I sat against the thick base of the rose vine reading to him in French, and he lay on his stomach, picking at the grass. I could feel the lovely warmth of the early-autumn sun on my face, and I could smell the warm, soft end of summer all around me in the air. Petals fell onto the open book as I read, and their lovely smell reached me too. I picked some of them up and tucked them into my plaited hair. When I stopped reading, Gareth looked up attentively with his lively green eyes.

"Arthur is lucky," he said, with all the innocence of a young boy, "to have a queen as beautiful as you."

I laughed lightly. Perhaps I should have been wary that this day would come. I had seen him as a son, but he had a mother of his own already, and I did not seem so very much older to him as he seemed younger to me.

"There are many more beautiful women than me, Gareth. There is a woman in Ireland called Isolde who is so beautiful that any man who looks on her instantly dies of love."

Gareth picked at the grass more concertedly and replied, sulkily.

"That sounds like she's *too* beautiful."

I laughed again, and shut the book heavily in my lap, closing my eyes and stretching my face up to the sun and breathing the air in deep.

"Will you kiss me?" Gareth asked suddenly.

"Of course," I replied, coming forwards on my hands and knees to place a little kiss on his cheek. He looked disappointed, but said nothing.

He did not ask again, and we continued spending our days together, reading and riding and lying in the garden until it became too cold, and then I would read to him in the library at the back of the chapel. I decided that it would not be sensible to invite him to read with me in my bedchamber. I supposed I had not thought hard enough about the impressionability of a teenage boy when I had decided to give him my attention to keep myself occupied.

We were reading there one day when one of Arthur's messengers came in. There was fear on his face, along with the sweat and dirt of the journey, and my heart raced within me. *Is it Arthur?* I jumped to my feet, the book sliding from my fingers.

"My lady queen," he bowed before me, "Sir Kay has been brought back to Camelot. He is... he is injured."

I took Gareth's hand in mine and pulled him behind me from the library. I think I wanted his hand in mine for my comfort as much as his own, and I wanted him by my side. He made me feel calm, as though I was caring for something. Caring for the boy made me feel that there was one small part of my life that I had some control over.

Out in the courtyard Kay lay on a stretcher of wood. One arm was limp at his side; the other he had curled around his head to keep the sunlight from his eyes. It was not so bright. He must have been feverish. From across the courtyard I could see the yawn of a spear-wound in his side. It looked days old. As I came closer, I could smell it, too.

"Who brought him over?" I demanded. "Why hasn't anyone seen to this?"

The messenger shook his head. "He was far from the camp, my lady. Arthur sent him back to check we still held your father's old castle safely, but when he arrived it was filled again with Lucius' men. Sir Kay and his knights broke into the castle and killed them all, and took it back, but Kay was wounded in the fight. The choice was, take him south to Arthur's camp at Marseilles, or bring him back here, and they thought here was better. There were no healing women with them in Carhais, my lady."

I knelt down beside Kay and pressed my hands gently either side of the wound. Kay groaned, and the wound leaked a foreboding yellow pus.

"Fetch Christine," I said to Gareth, and he swiftly ran away.

"I need men to help me carry him." The messenger nodded and the stretcher-bearers lifted him up again. I led the way up to Arthur's chamber and they laid him down on Arthur's bed. Christine came in with Gareth and she looked at the wound, clicking her tongue softly.

"This is bad," she said in Breton, casting a wary eye on Gareth. She, as I, did not think the boy had to see death already. Kay groaned again. I sat beside him on the bed and took his hand, as he had taken mine. He was feverish and did not seem to know me, and his eyes flickered open then shut. On his skin a grey pallor sat, and as I pressed my hand against his brow I felt the sweat, clammy and cold.

"Help me carry him," I said to Gareth and Christine. Christine nodded, and Gareth looked confused, but he obediently stepped towards the bed. Kay was huge and heavy, and I could barely lift his densely muscled shoulder onto my own. Gareth took the other side, and Christine lifted him by the legs. As we lifted him from the bed, he gave a deep moan of pain. I did not want anyone else to know what we were going to do. Christine had known my thoughts, though, and she led the way down the single flight of stairs to the room of the Round Table. We laid him out upon it, and I climbed on beside, kneeling next to his chest. Christine and Gareth stood back, she solemn, he wide-eyed. I took Kay's face in my hands and leaned close, whispering in my own language, and then his.

"Wish for life, Kay. Wish for life."

Then I lay beside him on the table, one of his arms behind my neck as though in some kind of grim half-dead embrace, and I pressed the backs of my hands against the table, and the back of my head and I wished for Kay's life.

You took one life from me; I want Kay's life in return.

I let the moment fill me, the feeling of power from the lands between life and death, from the Otherworld that I could sense at once, far away, and then close by me, nestled within Kay. When I finally opened my eyes and sat up, a sunset light was filtering through a single window, though I was sure I had lain down, purposely, at midday. The light was the golden orange of new hope, and the red of blood. Christine and Gareth sat in chairs at the edge of the room, talking in hushed whispers. When they saw me sit up they stood. I turned to Kay and pressed my hand against his brow. Still feverish. I lifted up the shirt, and then lifted off the dressing of the wound, to which Christine had applied a poultice. There was no longer a smell of infection, and when I pressed it gently, Kay groaned with pain, but no pus came out. I did not know if it had worked.

We carried him back up to Arthur's bed, and laid him there. I said goodnight to Gareth and Christine. I wanted to stay by Kay's side. Somehow I felt responsible for his wounding. It had been at my father's castle, and he had worried for me in battle. I had not worried for him. I had thought of him, quick and lively and sly, as invincible. Immortal. I drew a chair up to the open window and looked out at the crisp autumn night. The air was cold with coming winter. I forced myself to feel hopeful anyway. The moon was filling out, and I thought of Kay and prayed to the Mother, and then I thought of Arthur and prayed to his Hanged Christ of new life. Someone had to be listening. Perhaps in Arthur's country, Arthur's god would listen.

I must have slept, though I did not remember falling asleep, because I woke with my cheek on my hand in the open window, aching from sleeping in the chair, to the sound of Kay's voice.

"Guinevere?"

I turned. He was sitting up in the bed, his shirt thrown off showing a fair chest, almost hairless and more lightly muscled than Arthur's. I tried not to look. He was twisting around to look at the spear-wound in his side, peeling away the bandage. It had healed fast overnight; the raw wound looked already to be closing, darkening from angry red to purple. He pressed his hand against it warily to test the pain, and seemed pleased. He looked around himself again then, and seemed to notice me for a second time. He was disorientated, like a man waking from a deep sleep. It had been a strong fever I had felt on him.

"I'm in Camelot." He nodded slowly, as he remembered. "I was wounded. I –" He looked up at me again. I could feel the print of my knuckles on my cheek where I had slept, the heavy stickiness of having slept in my clothes. My head ached with tiredness and my eyes still hung heavy and half-closed, but the look he gave me touched me to the core. It was the look of someone who knows their life has been saved. It reminded me that there was a man to whom I owed that look. "You lay with me on the Round Table. I mean, beside me, I... I didn't dream that."

"You didn't."

"And you wished for my life."

"I did."

He nodded slowly, taking it in. I knew how it felt to go suddenly from being sure of one's death, to life. I wondered what he had dreamed on the Round Table. I had not dreamed, but perhaps he had seen things as I lay there and wished for his life.

"I'll have someone fetch you a hot bath," I said, sliding from my chair. As I moved to go past the bed, he darted forward and grabbed my wrist. I saw the pain flicker across his face. I could tell that Kay never made a good invalid; he ignored his pain.

"Guinevere... thank you," he said softly. It was strange to see the imp of a man who I had seen so often with a mischievous smile, dancing lightly through life, with solemnity in his eyes. I took his head in my hands and kissed him softly on the crown of his head, like a blessing, and left.

Chapter Twelve

When Kay was well and whole he was back up to his old tricks again, with Gareth, fighting the boy with one hand, his strong left hand tied behind his back, and then trying to get Gareth to fight back hopping on one leg. I liked to watch them laugh and play together, and in the evenings we all sat together as I read to them, or sometimes Christine would sing. I thought often about Arthur, and the man who had saved my life. Especially when I was alone at night. I would dream of Arthur, dream of him inside me, his body hot on top of me, his mouth against mine in passion, and then I would wake gasping for breath, with the delicious illusion evaporating around me, before it was done. But sometimes I would lie in the dark and think of how he had sent me away. How the last thing he'd said was *Someone take her back to Britain*, as though I were a horse or a suit of armour to be shipped back. I was still angry, but as the days went on into weeks and months and a year was past since I had seen him, my longing was greater than my anger, and I yearned to see him again.

It was on a morning, well into winter, when the air was crisp with frost and the grey walls of the castle, backed by a pale greyish sky, seemed harder and colder in the sharp winter air, that the men began to return. I was watching Gareth and Kay fighting together in the courtyard, with wooden swords and wooden shields. Kay kept trying to trip Gareth, but Gareth was learning fast how to leap out of the way and Kay's old tricks were beginning to lose their effectiveness against him. Their breath steamed in the chill morning air and Christine and I stood close together, wrapped in furs, to watch.

After a while, I went to see the horses. I liked their little snorts and stamping feet, their warm, silent presences. The stables smelled of clean hay, and clean horses. There were few enough left with the men away at war, but mine was there – or the one that had become mine since I was back at Camelot. I took up a brush and began to brush her hair. The action was soothing and I became lost in thought, or rather beyond thought, in the movement of my hand up and down. I did not notice until another horse came to stop beside me that someone else had come into the stable. The horse snorted out a plume of steamy breath into the cold stable beside me and I looked up. A knight was sat upon it, clad in his platemail, but his helm off. Dark hair fell in soft, glossy waves down to his jaw and his face was pale and angular, cheekbones high and nose long and fine. I did not know him, but I felt looking at him as though I recognised him somehow. He swung off his horse, down beside me. I could not speak, I was so surprised. His horse bit hungrily into the hay in its feeder, which was close enough to that of my horse that when he swung down we were so close in the space between the two horses that we were almost touching. I opened my mouth to begin, but I did not know how. He was breathing hard from the ride. I could see the sweat on his face, and on his horse.

After a moment, he spoke through his ragged breaths, and when he spoke I realised why I felt I had seen him before.

"Arthur is returned," he said, in a deep voice, musky with its tones of French.

I ran out into the courtyard, and there he was, face tanned brown from the Mediterranean sun, caked with the dirt and the sweat of riding, dressed in his platemail with his helm thrown from his head. He saw me as I saw him, and jumped from his horse, running over as I ran towards him to catch me up in his arms, lifting me into the air, then down, hard and fast into his embrace and a desperate, hungry kiss. It had been so long, and yet it felt like only yesterday that I had kissed him last. He took me by the hand and half led, half carried me up the winding stairs to his chamber, pushing the winter furs off my shoulders while we were still running up the stairs. He had scarcely closed the door behind him before he was pulling out the lacing at the back of my dress, pulling it away. Both of our hands fumbled on the leather straps of his platemail, hurrying to throw it off. I could feel my heart racing in my chest, and his own heart racing as I laid my hand on his, under his shirt as I lifted it away. His hands left marks of sweat and dirt from the journey on the white cotton of my underdress, but I didn't care and neither did he. He kicked off his boots and breeches and drew me roughly against him, kissing me hard and hungry. The smell of him, sweat and leather, and the feeling of his arms around me, his mouth on mine, was intoxicating after so long. I wanted to put my hands all over him at once, feel his hot skin, the hard muscle underneath, the life beating inside him. I was afraid he would come back tired and weak, but the fighting had made him even stronger. With a deep groan of relief he threw us down on the bed and was inside me before he had finished pulling the underdress over my head, and I moaned loud with the feel of it, and relief to have him with me again, strong and alive. His love was rough and passionate, and he held me tight against him, pressing me close to him as he groaned with pleasure, and I with him, in soft ecstatic sighs, feeling the heat at the centre of myself. He sighed out my name at the end, and fell against me. I wrapped my legs around his back and held his head gently in my hands. At last he had come back to me. Our breaths slowing together, he kissed lightly the skin of my chest, and then up to the soft skin beneath my chin.

"I knew I would not feel I had come home until I was with you again," he murmured. I held his face close and kissed him fiercely. I could not speak. The relief that he was alive and whole, that he was here, returned to me, was too much to take in. I could not believe it was true. "Tonight we must have a feast," he said, rolling gently away, and gathering me up to rest on his chest. I folded my hands together on his chest and balanced my chin on them, looking at him. Seeing him again, it was as though he had never gone. As though he had been in the next room. I did not know how I had survived without him for a whole, long year. More. He rubbed my back thoughtfully. "You could use a feast. You're thin." He could feel my ribs, too close to the surface, through the skin of my back.

"Things have been thin here, while you have been gone."

"I know," he said sadly. "But we have gold from Rome, and things will get better. The men are back, and we can buy everything we need." He stroked my hair lightly. I pressed my head into his hand, relishing the feeling of him, close and real. "But tonight, we must feast and celebrate. The people of Camelot need that."

He rose and called for a bath. They brought us two big iron tubs of steaming water and we slipped into them by the fire. I sank back into mine closing my eyes, though I did not want to close them for too long, in case when I opened them again, Arthur was gone. Arthur scrubbed his skin all over with a sponge in his, turning the clear water to grey. Beneath the dirt his skin still shone brown where the sun had touched it.

I thought again about the man who had saved my life. I felt the guilt clutch at the heart of me that I had not thanked him when I saw him in the stables. I should have said something. I could say it tonight. I should have asked Arthur who he was, but for that moment I wanted to pretend that there had been no war, no change, and only Arthur and I existed in the world.

Arthur had brought back silk and gold from his wars, as well as victory. He presented me with a dress made of lilac silk that left my pale arms bare, and tied around the waist with a little silk cord. It was loose and flowing, fine. I protested it was too cold for winter, and so he fetched my soft grey furs and placed them gently around my shoulders. He had also brought back a golden necklace hung with sapphires from the far east. I did not want to ask how he had got it, but he clipped it around my neck and smiled, so I did too. He offered me the mirror of hammered silver and I peered at myself. I could see, blurrily, that at last I looked like a queen again. Arthur dressed in his father's old red brocade surcoat, sewn with the dragon winding in gold across it. He didn't need anything new. Even in the coat, he looked a fearsome size, his warrior's shape obvious beneath the thick brocade. He looked every bit the conqueror, even before he set his crown on his head. I did not want to wear my heavy crown, so I wore the circlet of golden ivy that I had worn on our wedding day, and it sat nestled among the curls I had woven up into a plaited bun at the nape of my neck. I felt a little better, less fragile, already, at the sight of myself appearing to be strong.

By the time we entered the hall, hand in hand, it was already full. I could see at the high table Nimue, who must have come from Avalon when she heard of Arthur's return, was sat already, and Kay and Gareth and Gawain, and their other brothers, and in the place of honour on Arthur's right sat the man who had saved my life. Our eyes met from the end of the hall, and he bowed his head gently. I felt my heart flutter nervously; I supposed I felt guilty for not thanking him. I wished I had spoken to him in the stables. He was dressed simply in a dark indigo doublet. When Arthur saw him, he grinned warmly.

We sat to eat, and I had not seen so much food in a long time. Arthur's men had brought back game they had hunted on the way, so there was pigeon and pheasant and boar, and bowls piled high with oranges and peaches from the Mediterranean. There were bowls of olives, which I had not seen since I had left home, and only then when the traders from Rome came through Carhais, and fat loaves of bread. I took the cup of wine in my hand and drank. The wine, too, had come from the Mediterranean. I could taste the sun in it. There had not been wine all the time Arthur had been gone, only ale, the bitter taste of which I disliked.

"Have you told your queen the news?" Aggravain cried across the table to Arthur. He was already drunk, whether with wine or the excitement of victory I could not tell. All of the men looked excited, full of their victory. They all suddenly looked like boys.

Arthur turned to me with a smile.

"You're no longer only a queen. You are now also an empress. Empress of Rome."

I smiled, because I knew I must, but my blood ran cold. Arthur the Conqueror had not stopped at taking back the lands that he had already won, but he had marched on Rome. *He could have been killed. They all could have been killed.* And what was it worth, the endless desire for more? The other knights around the table cheered, apart from the man who had saved my life. His eyes met mine, as he hid his face behind a cup of wine, to drink. I felt it go through me like a knife. He had seen into me. No, no, I was imagining it. I looked down into my cup of wine. It was already half-drunk and I had not eaten much that day. I must have been imagining things, and I should be happy. Arthur was back with me, alive and victorious. I had to try to let that overshadow everything else.

"You should have seen it, my lady," Gawain bellowed across the table. His broad face was almost entirely covered in freckles from the sun apart from the white lines of the scars, and he was flushed with wine, already drunk. "By the time we reached Rome, Lucius was cowering in his castle on the Palatine. We rode up to it, the rest of that damned city smoking behind us, and Arthur threw off his helm, and his breastplate and greaves, and his shirt, and scaled the wall of Lucius' palace with his bare hands. When he reached the top and climbed inside, he dragged the bald old man out to the Palatine steps by his grey beard and sliced off his head in front of us all with his sword. You should have seen him, my lady, climbing up the walls of the Palace, all alone, gleaming in the sun. He was *magnificent*. Then we dragged out Lucius' sons and killed them, too. His daughter killed herself, but not before I'd –"

Arthur made a noise of disapproval deep in his throat and Gawain stopped mid sentence, but not before I'd seen the look pass between Arthur and Gawain, or Arthur's glance towards me. My stomach churned and I felt sick. I was glad, then, that I had not been there.

"Then," Gawain picked up his story again, in the same garrulous drunken tone, "we drank Rome dry. We pulled up the barrels of wine from the cellars and feasted in the ruined senate-house. This wine you're drinking is what we brought back from the cellars of Rome. Hail Arthur the Conqueror, King of Britain and Emperor of Rome!" He shouted. The other knights around the table echoed and Arthur gave a modest smile, raising his hand. I thought he ought to have been more than modest. He ought to have been ashamed, if not of himself, then of his men.

"I did what I had to to protect my people. Gawain, you give me too high praise."

"He was like a god. *A god*. Like Mars himself," Gawain persisted. "Those bloody pagans probably thought you *were* Mars. They ran from you like children." Now those sat beside Gawain were trying to shush him. Kay was pushing his cup of wine towards him, hoping he would drink and be quiet. "And *you*." He pointed a wavering finger at the man beside Arthur, the man who had saved me. "I thought all you Frenchmen would be perfumed fools, but you sliced through those Romans like they were made of cloth. This is the beginning of an age of greatness, my friends."

He raised his glass and the knights drank again. Kay cleared his throat to change the subject. For a moment, I was relieved.

"Gareth has come to court, Arthur," he said.

Arthur raised his cup to the boy. "And I am glad to see you," he said. Gareth smiled and inclined his head.

"I should warn you, though," Kay continued, "that he has fallen in love with your wife." Gareth blushed, dark. I gave Kay a cold look, but he did not see me. Gawain slammed his cup down on the table and wine spilled over the rim as he turned to Kay, looking ready for a fight.

"Don't embarrass the boy," I said quietly. Kay did not hear, or did not listen.

"No no," Kay said. "It's true."

"Stop," Gawain growled.

Arthur smiled indulgently and raised a hand for quiet. He turned to Gareth and gently said.

"Perhaps, Gareth, I might offer you a joust for the love of this fair lady?" He turned to the man beside him. "Lancelot, I believe that is how civilised men settle this in the French courts?"

The man, Lancelot, inclined his head in a little nod. So, that was his name. I felt it brush against me, unusual, unfamiliar.

The men laughed and the subject changed, but neither Gawain nor Gareth looked as happy or relaxed as they had before. Kay seemed oblivious, drinking heartily from his cup, and joking with Nimue at his side, who seemed, with her quiet decorum, to be enjoying his japes nonetheless. I caught Gareth's eye and tried to give a sympathetic smile, but he only blushed deeper and looked away.

That night, when it was dark and I lay with my head on his chest, Arthur said, "Have you spoken with Lancelot yet?"

"No. He was the one beside you?"

"Yes. He's the one who picked you up from the battlefield." I made a little noise of agreement. "I have been thinking, you should ask him to be Queen's Champion. They have in France these wonderful pageants with jousts, and women can favour men to fight for them. We should have one here, soon, to celebrate my victories in Rome. I can't fight, because no man would strike his king, so it would be dishonourable for me to fight men who would lose on purpose, but you can have a champion to fight for you, and I think you should ask him. He is one of King Ban's sons, so it would be appropriate."

I agreed, and quickly Arthur fell asleep. I had been tired, and heavy from the heady wine, but after that it took me a long time to get to sleep. I kept thinking of the man Lancelot. I don't know why I felt so unsettled about it. I thought I must feel guilty, still, about not thanking him for saving my life when I saw him in the stables. When I finally did get to sleep, I dreamed oddly, of wandering in the forest, and a helmed man in armour who lifted his visor, and was sometimes Arthur, sometimes this man Lancelot and sometimes nothing more than the hollow, depthless black eyes of the witch Merlin. When I woke, I was covered in an unpleasant film of cold sweat that chilled me in the winter morning.

I sat up in bed to find that Arthur had already gone. I suddenly felt very exposed and alone. I pulled the sheets up around me, but that didn't make me feel any better. I found myself wondering if Arthur had spent his nights alone, thinking of me, while he was on campaign. I hardly thought it likely, the way he would come back from the battlefield every day, blazing with desire. There had been women with the camp. I thought about asking Margery and Marie about it, but the thought that it might have been one of them made me decide not to. There were some things it was better not to know. I was not naive enough to imagine that Arthur had spent more than a year sleeping alone. It made me flush with anger, though I knew I had no right to. I belonged to him in a way that he did not belong to me. *Someone take her back to Britain.* I felt, remembering that, like a belonging, like a discarded sword no good for battle any longer, and sent away. Another sword would do just as well. A man need not take only his wife to bed, especially a king, and a childless king at that. *I have had many more lovers than you.* That came back to me, across the space of time, and now it burned against my skin, the injustice of it. He had discovered other women again, and there was nothing I could do about it. I had no claim over him. This was not like my parent's marriage, formed out of love and made between equals, and though there was love, I knew it was the steady love grown from marriage, not the consuming love of those whose hearts belong only to each other, and I had not come to him as an equal, but as a prisoner bride. I should have thought of it before.

But I had lain alone for a year. I could have, if I had wanted, found another man to fill my bed. Kay. I could have had him, if I had wanted to. I remembered his hand on my wrist, the red autumn sun falling across his face as he lay back in the grass of my walled garden, listening to me read, his dark, handsome looks. I remembered hoping *he* was Arthur when they met me at Dover. I saw the way he looked at me; he would not have denied me if I had wanted him. It would not have been love, though. And I *did* love Arthur. And I was sure he loved me. But I was also sure that that would not have stopped *him*.

No, I should not feel the anger that I did. I washed my face in a basin of cold water, trying to rub away the dreams of the night, and the anger of my thoughts. I looked at the dress of lilac silk, and the horrible thought came to me that it must have belonged to the Emperor Lucius' daughter. I took up instead the dress of blue wool I had worn the day before. It was warmer, and in that dress I would not feel the ghosts of conquered women pressing at my skin. I had hoped, perhaps beyond reason, that when Arthur returned things would go back to how they had been, but in the harsh morning light I knew that they would not. He had tasted battle again, and women. I had heard a soft voice speaking to me in French that I could not forget. Somehow, everything had changed, and I knew, that morning, as I gazed out at the frost on the grass beneath Arthur's window, that my life would never be the same again.

Chapter Thirteen

When I walked out into the courtyard, the knights were sparring with wooden swords. Arthur was among them, and Gawain, Gareth and Kay. Kay and Arthur were laughing, but fighting in earnest, slamming their swords together with resounding cracks that echoed in the yard. They were dressed only in breeches and shirts despite the cold, but both were flushed from fighting. Arthur was easily and obviously the stronger fighter. Likewise, Gawain and Gareth clashed together, though I did not think I had ever seen Gawain be so gentle as he was with his brother. He was letting the boy feel his strength, but only enough to teach him, to prepare him. Arthur saw me, and shouted a greeting, which gave Kay the opportunity to jab him in the ribs. He bent over double, losing his breath, but I could hear that he, like Kay, was laughing. I had not come looking, though, for Arthur. I wished I had worn my furs because the air was biting, but I had only a black wool cloak on. I had not thought of it until now. My mind felt strange and disconnected from my body. I felt half-dazed. I had just about managed to put back in my hair the little circlet of ivy leaves to try to hide the plainness of my clothes. A new-made empress ought to make some effort to look grand.

It took me a while to see him, through the crowd of men fighting – there were many, too, whom I did not recognise that must have come back with Arthur to play court to the man who had liberated Europe from the Romans and now ruled them from Logrys – but then I did. He sat at the other side of the courtyard, one knee drawn up in front of him, his arm resting lazily on it, and clutched in the hand hanging down was one of the peaches Arthur had brought back from the Mediterranean. He was speaking to the man beside him. I wished I was close enough to hear that voice again. He was dressed all in black, and the hilt of his sword flashed at his side as it caught the morning sun. A pale blush spread across his cheeks and he breathed out a little cloud of steam as he spoke, as though he had just retired from the fighting. I wanted to go over, but I could not move. I felt as though my feet had frozen to the spot. I couldn't look away either, though men practising at swordplay moved between us, sometimes obscuring my view. I had no idea why I felt so nervous. He took a lazy bite from the peach and I saw his face crinkle in a laugh. I did not know the man he was speaking to either, or perhaps I just did not take him in. Lancelot wiped the juice of the peach from his lips with the back of his hand before taking another bite.

"Did you come to speak to my half-brother?" I jumped at the voice beside me that I had not expected. I had thought I was standing alone. I blushed to be caught staring, and I felt the quivering of guilt within me, though I did not see why I should be ashamed to look at a man. The voice belonged to Ector, kind Ector, looking down on me with his warm, avuncular smile. He looked tired from battle, and he stood awkwardly, his weight all on the left side, as though he had been injured. I put a hand on his arm.

"Ector, I'm so pleased to have you back." I remembered his question. "Which one is your brother?"

"Lancelot," he said, raising a hand to point. As though he had heard his name from across the yard, Lancelot looked up and our eyes met. For a single moment, I heard my heart beating in my ears, and had a stunning sensation of rushing, or being blown by a fierce wind, and then he looked away. I felt the need to catch my breath, but I could not. Luckily, Ector continued and I did not have to speak. "They say he saved your life on the battlefield. Then there are those things they do not talk about. How he saved Arthur numerous times as well. And many others. Young men are reckless in battle, but he's different, my brother. He sees everything at once, it seems. He's calm. I suppose we're both prudent men, cut from the same mould. But," he took my hand in his with another deep and gentle smile, "I also hear it is you and your medicine-woman Christine I have to thank for my son Kay's life."

"We were all so relieved that his wound healed so fast," I replied.

Ector sighed, looking out at the young men fighting. War had aged Ector, or perhaps I had not looked at him properly before. Perhaps it was the thought that he might have to bury his son that had made his age weigh on him, all of a sudden. His face was deeply lined and weatherbeaten, and grey speckled the hair at his temples. "Young men relish playing at war, and like even better to fight it for real. Old men like me just relish when it's over."

"So do I, Ector." I leaned up and kissed him on the cheek. He laid a hand lightly on my cheek, calloused from years of holding a sword and cold from the frosty air.

"You make a fine empress, my lady," he said, and took his leave, walking back into the crowd. When I looked back over towards Lancelot, he had vanished, as though my presence had scared him away. I felt unaccountably hurt. But I knew where I might find him.

I went round to the stables, stopping to give Gareth a little smile of encouragement as I passed him. He blushed and looked away, but I thought he seemed pleased. I slipped inside, and sure enough he was there. He did not see me, or hear me come in. His back was to me as he brushed his horse, the rough bristles whispering against the horse's flank. He looked as though he was concentrating intensely on the movement, firm and gentle. Through the open stable door came the clacks and shouts of the men practising. I had already waited too long to speak, and I could feel nerves prickling inside me. I had nothing to be nervous about. I would just apologise for not recognising him yesterday, and thank him. Then I would go. I was not shy. This would not be difficult.

"Lancelot?" I spoke the name, but it came out of my throat half strangled with nerves. I hoped he would not try to take my hand, because it was slick with sweat. He turned, and when he saw it was me, he had a look about him as though he had been caught at something. Perhaps I had made him feel as though I disliked him, staying silent so long. I took a little step towards him. "I came to thank you, sir. And to apologise. I did not recognise you when we met yesterday, but I, I will always be grateful to you for saving my life."

Inclined his head in a little bow that he did not look back up from.

"It was nothing, my lady." *Say more, say more.*

I did not know what to say. I did not know what women from France did to be courteous to their men. We Breton women did not grow up with courtesies and formality, and even before coming to Logrys Margery had had to teach the three of us, Marie, Christine and myself, what would be expected. Perhaps I had offended Lancelot. I felt, as I had never done before, unsure of myself. Unsure of my actions. Even when I had been brought to Camelot as a prisoner I had been sure of what to do. But that was, I suppose, because I did not care then whether or not I would be liked.

"Well..." I cringed inside to say it, but it was all that I could say. Lancelot looked up expectantly and his deep blue eyes caught the breath from me as they met mine and my heart fluttered in my chest. *Why am I nervous?* "I will always be grateful to you," I managed to say. I could feel myself blush, my skin hot and red giving me away, and I turned and left before he could see. Why did I feel like such a fool? I was normally gracious, clever and in control, and suddenly I did not know how to thank someone properly. Back out of the stable in the cold air, I turned and leant back against the stable wall, closing my eyes and catching my breath. Then I remembered what Arthur said about asking him to be my champion. Foolish. That was what he would have been expecting, that was what these Frenchmen did. I *had* insulted him.

I ran back inside, but found that he had gone. Slipped away, somehow. The same gift as Kay, I supposed, to be everywhere and nowhere all at once.

Chapter Fourteen

That evening I sent Christine to ask Lancelot to come to my chamber. As I waited for him, I noticed my hands were shaking. *What was wrong with me?* Surely I did not feel so badly about it. Surely I had not done so wrong in the clumsy way I had thanked him. I did not know why I felt so nervous, why I felt as though a line was about to be crossed that I could not go back from. It must have been the strange dream. I must be being irrational. It was only understandable, since Arthur was just back from war. No wonder I was worried. No wonder I felt so afraid. I paced the room, waiting for the knock on the door. At last it came. I opened the door, and there he was, the man who had saved my life. The breath went out of me when I saw him and I could not speak. I could not say what it was about him, about the fact that we were at last alone and I was not looking at him through a crowd, or seeing him without knowing him, or only feeling a strong arm around me, taking me to safety, that froze me to the spot, but it did.

"My lady, Queen Guinevere." He gave a little bow, the candlelight gleaming in his glossy black hair as he did, and I gestured him in and shut the door. My hands were trembling as I shut it, and I leaned against it, for a moment. I breathed in slowly, and out, and turned back to him. He had moved silently into the room to walk to the fire, leaning against the fireplace, looking in. His pale face glowed orange from the flames, his lithe, neat body gently leaning towards the heat. His eyes stared right into the flames. He had come without his armour, and it was the first time I had seen him without it up close. Dressed in just a simple black shirt and black breeches I could see the curves of the muscles beneath. Not huge and powerful like Arthur, but swift and sinewy. *But still strong enough to pluck me from my death as though I were weightless as a flower.* I should not be thinking about that. I should not be comparing him to Arthur. I had to say something. My heart pounded. It felt high in my throat. I could feel my hands sweating.

"Sir Lancelot –" He turned his eyes to mine and the words froze within me. Deep, deep dark blue eyes like the centre of the sea.

"Are you recovered my lady, from your wound?" he asked in his deep, soft voice.

"Quite," I nodded.

He nodded in return. "I am pleased to hear so." The silence stretched on between us, or perhaps it was just a second. He reached forward and took my hand in his. The touch of his skin on mine felt electric, it sent a spark through my body and I could feel myself blushing already. I hated that blush, giving away what I was not sure yet that I knew. "I have thought of you often, my lady."

I looked up to meet his gaze again and as I did my heart quickened even more within me. I could see a slight flush on him, too. Was I imagining it? What was I imagining? My body seemed to know something that my mind yet did not, or did not want to know. *I must just be nervous.* I was not usually nervous. There was a heady, unspeakable potentiality to being alone with him like this that fogged my mind and slowed my tongue.

"I... I wanted to thank you, for saving my life, sir. Arthur – King Arthur, my lord King Arthur – he thought you might like to, to be my champion. I would like you to be my champion."

"It would be an honour," he replied, in the purring French lilt I had already grown to know so well. I wanted to lean in towards him, to close my eyes and listen to him speak, even those few words that he did.

"There is a tournament... there will be a tournament, soon, to celebrate the victory. You should ride for me."

I broke away from his gaze and moved to the bed where I had laid out a cloth-of-gold sleeve to give him, to tie on his helmet. I was glad for a moment to be away from the heat of the fire, from the heat of his gaze, or the heat it was raising in me. I felt clumsy, as if I did not know what I was doing, as if I were moving in a dream. I lifted the soft, cool cloth in my trembling hands and folded it tenderly. I took it back over to him and placed it in his hands. Both of my hands holding the cloth came to rest with it in his upturned palms. Neither of us spoke. I did not think I could have moved if I wanted to. My whole body felt alive with sparks. I did not realise that I had come to stand so close to him until I moved my eyes up to meet his gaze and felt the shock at the centre of myself as they met, so close our noses almost brushed. I could hear his soft breathing and the crackling of the flames. There were many things to say, *Thank you for your valour in fighting, I have thought often of you, too, thank you for your loyalty to my husband*, but already we were beyond words. He leant down, slowly, and pressed his lips on mine with the softest of kisses. I sighed in quiet surrender. Soft, and intoxicating, the touch of a moment, but I felt the soft skin of his lips there still after he had moved away, and, wordlessly, left.

When I was alone I sat heavily on the bed, and slowly lay back. Perhaps this way the way of it, the way of things in southern France.

It was not the way among us Bretons, but we did not have tourneys and champions, courtesy and love-play like the French. Perhaps they always kissed the ladies that they rode for. But that did not explain the way *I* felt. No no, no. That was because he had saved my life. I felt that way because my life was saved. No line had been crossed.

And yet, after that moment, I moved through the days as though I moved in a dream. It was too cold to sit in my walled garden, so the room below my chamber was prepared with cushions and fur rugs and I sat there with my ladies, and sometimes Gareth and Kay, when they were not fighting in the yard, and lute-players came, or we read to one another; but I heard nothing, and saw nothing. Arthur came to me at night, but that too was like a dream, and anyway he came less often, being absorbed with his burgeoning band of knights, and boyish dreams of pageantry and adventure – more battles and more glory. As Arthur prepared the court for its first tournament, it filled with courtiers. I took among my women his sister Morgan, newly widowed from her old husband and visibly relieved, and the druid Nimue, neither of whom I could bring myself to trust entirely on account of their woaded faces, but both of whom I barely noticed by my side anymore, and the young daughters of Arthur's vassal kings, or powerful lords. I could not remember anyone's name.

Every time I walked through the castle, every corner I turned, I expected Lancelot with a mix of fear and anticipation. I did and I did not want to turn and see him there. When I closed my eyes, I saw his face, orange with the firelight, or I heard his voice, soft and close by, as though it was a whisper in my ear, or I felt his lips brush against mine. I did not stop thinking about him. I hoped, when the tourney happened, it would make sense, it would feel resolved, I would feel that I had thanked him enough and I would stop thinking about it.

It felt as though it was an age before the day of Arthur's tourney came, but it had only been a week since I had given Lancelot my golden sleeve. I woke in the morning early and waited restlessly, looking out of the window down at my little walled garden silver with frost, until Marie and Christine came in to help me get ready. They were chattering together in Breton, even the older woman giddy with excitement for the festivities of the day. Margery came in after them, carrying a lacquered box that she laid, with some ceremony, on the table beside the fire. She looked annoyed that her ceremony was largely ignored, and that Marie and Christine were still chattering in a language that she barely understood, and she bustled out, to check on the rest of my newly expanded band of women.

Marie and Christine had brought up for the occasion a dress made of heavy silk brocade in a dark emerald green, embroidered in gold thread with crosses. The symbol of Arthur's god. Still, it was a beautiful dress, and I supposed he had a right to think that I had taken his god into my heart when I sat beside him and spoke the same prayers. It took both Marie and Christine to get the heavy dress over my head, but I was glad of its weight because it would be cold sitting to watch the jousts. The dress had a deep, square neck, and I was pleased to see in the pile of clothing, some white fur, flecked with black. The dress fitted close on the bodice, and on the arms down to the wrists where the sleeves finished with gold hemming. Rich, expensive. It suited me well. There were jewels, too. A gold chain hung with dozens of emeralds shaped like raindrops, and a gold-and-emerald net to hold up my braided hair; the jewels I had worn to be married. No, I had not sold those. My circlet was missing, and when I asked for it, Marie gestured to Margery's box. When I opened it, inside was a circlet of thick gold that looked like two muscular snakes wound together, meeting at the front, their heads nestled side by side, with big, emerald eyes. I lifted it out, lightly and warily, though it looked sturdy and strong. Christine called for Margery, clearly wanting to know about the curious circlet as badly as I did. Margery came up, but not alone. She came with Morgan who took the circlet from me in a businesslike way and settled it on my head. It was a perfect fit. She looked at me, with discerning eyes, grey as Arthur's own, narrowed in consideration. I did not know why I had taken a dislike to her before. She did not have a pretty face, true, nor open, but it was shrewd and intelligent. She was dressed in mourning black in a dress of thick silk, overlaid with a layer of black lace that covered her to the neck. Through the lace I could see that the skin of her chest, too, was painted with woad. Nestled among the lace, black gemstones gleamed when they caught the light.

"Morgan said she had to see it," Margery explained apologetically.

"That crown," Morgan said softly, fixing me with a serious look, "was taken by Arthur from the treasures of Rome. It belonged to the Queen Cleopatra, who was the lover of two Emperors, or... one and a half. She was a fearsome queen, who rode with her people into war. He must have thought it an appropriate gift for you, my lady."

I reached up and touched the cool metal resting on my head. So there were others like Maev, all round the world.

I thanked Morgan and she slipped from the room, silently, as though she had melted.

"You look magnificent, my lady," Christine told me, holding up the hammered silver mirror. I squinted at myself. I could see gold, and the deep fiery red of my hair, the ivory pale skin of my face. I could not see magnificence, but I could see I looked well enough for the tourney.

Chapter Fifteen

By the time I arrived and took my place beside Arthur, it was about to begin. He smiled when he saw me, and as I sat beside him leaned over to me to say, "You look every bit the empress, my lady," and kissed my hand.

"Your sister Morgan told me about the crown."

He nodded, but he was already looking away, at the lines of knights at each end of the jousting field. I had seen jousts before, as a girl, when French knights from the south had come to my father's court. I remembered thinking it ridiculous and savage. I did not think I would like this any more. War was bad enough, without fighting also for fun.

Breath rose in hot clouds from the knights and their horses alike as they waited for their king to begin the proceedings. Arthur and I sat on a raised wooden platform, above the rows of wooden benches that the other noble folk sat on. Across the other side of the field, I could see crowds of the peasant folk standing to watch. I hoped that for them, too, Arthur's return had meant the return of food to the table.

The first pair ran together, and they met right in front of us, lance splintering on shield. Perhaps I would have been able to enjoy it, if I had been sat a little further from the action, but I could see the whites of the horses' eyes, wide open in panic, and hear the grunts of pain from the men knocked from their horses. Arthur was enjoying himself heartily, clapping and cheering each round. As I looked at him, he seemed to me once again every bit the eager young boy, hungry for the fight, not the solemn lord of Europe. I knew, too, that he wished to be out there among them.

Perhaps I also did not enjoy it because I could not rest until my champion came into the field. I could feel my heart the whole time skipping nervously within me. *When would it be him?* I even saw Gareth ride, and be knocked off his horse by his brother Gaheris, barely taking it in, when I knew that a month ago I would have been filled with anxiety for his safety. He took it well, anyway, jumping back up to his feet with a smile, and bowing to Arthur and me.

Then, at the far end of the field, against the grey winter sky I saw the flash of gold. My breath caught within my chest. He was riding against Gawain, first, and knocked him easily from his horse. I felt intensely relieved, more than I should have done. Behind me, I could hear Marie and Christine whispering in Breton about him, though not well enough to make out exactly what they were saying.

He knocked down another, then another. The third man to meet him was Kay. I could tell by the black covering of his horse and the easy, haughty way he sat in his saddle. This was the last round of jousts, and the winner of this would be the winner of the day. Arthur's excitement was palpable as he sat watching beside me. All I felt was dread. When they came together I felt a shock go through me. I saw both men slide from their saddles and thud to the ground. I did not realise that I had cried out and jumped to my feet until I realised that people around were looking at me. Arthur laughed and took my hand.

"It's alright, my love," he soothed. "They're not hurt."

But I did not sit down.

Off their horses and both their lances broken, I could not tell which man was which. They were fighting now with swords, blunted for the match, but steel nonetheless, and sparks flew from the platemail as they struck at once another. One man was a lot faster than the other, and was backing him into a corner. The slower man stumbled back over his own fallen lance and his helm fell off his head and rolled away. I could not see from where I was standing who it was, but the other knight pulled off his own helm and threw it aside. It was Lancelot. I still did not sit down, could not relax, but everyone else was on their feet now, straining to look. Lancelot offered Kay his hand and pulled him back to his feet, and they squared up to begin again. Arthur cheered and clapped as they came together, their swords screeching on one another, but it was clearly not an even match and before long, Kay yielded, throwing his sword to the ground and his hands in the air, as Lancelot had him pinned in a corner. The crowd cheered, and the two men on the field grasped each other in a brotherly embrace and kissed each other heartily on both cheeks. Kay's face radiated delight at a good fight, even though he had lost. Lancelot came towards us, towards me, and bowed before me from below.

"My lady Guinevere," he said as he bowed. His deep voice reached me through the crowd and I closed my eyes for a long second and let it wash over me. I felt light-headed, far from my own body, from Arthur beside me, from everything apart from Lancelot. But I did not feel better. I did not feel resolved. Seeing him fight for me had not undone the nervous knot I felt at the centre of my stomach, nor stilled my fluttering heart. I was *not* content that I saw before me nothing more than a man who had saved my life and would serve me as my champion. The knot was tighter, and I knew now that it would not be undone.

Chapter Sixteen

Before the feast Arthur had set for the evening, I made an excuse to go back to my chambers. I pulled the heavy crown of snakes from my head, and set it down on the table, threw off my furs, poured water into my basin and splashed my face with it. Despite the cold my whole body felt hot, and once I was alone and not striving to control myself, my breaths came fast and ragged. I braced myself against the table, closing my eyes and leaning hard against it, trying to slow down my racing heart, to get myself under control.

After a minute, I felt better. I straightened up, pushed my damp hair back from my face and breathed in, deep and slow. I was not in control of how I felt, but I *was* in control of what I did. I did not know what I *wanted* to do yet, but no one would make me do anything against my wishes, I was sure of that. I could handle this. I felt more and more sure of it as I said it to myself. Certainly, I would not embarrass myself, throwing myself at a man who did not want me. All I could do was wait, and I was good at waiting. With each breath I felt a little more steady. Just a little.

As I was about to leave my chamber to join the feast, Morgan slithered through the door, and shut it behind herself, backing up onto it, so that I could not get past her to get out.

"Morgan," I greeted her, mildly surprised, but not greatly. I wondered what she wanted. I wondered, also, what hopes had brought this new widow back to court. She was young, after all, or young enough to bear children, and her old husband had given her a son, so the new husband would know he was getting a fertile woman. "Are you coming down to eat?"

"You're not wearing the crown."

"It's heavy."

"You should." No 'my lady' when we were alone. I was unsure again whether I trusted her, or liked her. Her keen clever eyes were also beady with a hint of meanness, though I supposed her life must have been cruel. People did not speak often of her father Uther's kindness, and she had been a child of his new wife, not his own. Sent to a nunnery, some said. Sent to Avalon, said others. To look at her druid's woad, I don't know how anyone would have guessed the former.

"I took a lover," she said, suddenly, as though in answer to a question I had not asked. "Many men do it, some women. We should do as they do, our husbands. That is, just as we please."

"I do just as I please," I answered coldly. Morgan would not think I was weak or compliant.

"As does Arthur," she replied with a grin, and slithered away, just as she had come. When I wrenched the door open to look for her in the corridor, ready to grab her by the hair, or strike her, she was gone.

I felt calmer, having resolved to continue as if nothing were different, and I put Morgan's words from my mind as best as I could. It was nothing I had not already thought myself. When I entered the hall, it was already full. I saw the space for me. Of course, I should have known that it would be between Arthur and the man who had fought as my champion. But I had resolved to be calm. I was in control. My resolve wavered as I sat in my place and noticed Lancelot deliberately avoiding my eye. Morgan, I noticed, was already seated directly opposite us on the high table. I reached for my cup of wine, and drank deeply.

Arthur leaned towards me, draping an arm across the back of my chair. Already, I could see, he was becoming bleary with wine. They had been celebrating, clearly, before I had arrived.

"You took off your crown."

"It was heavy."

"Well, you don't need it," he smiled, and kissed me lightly.

They began to bring the food, but my stomach was already tightening; I was already losing my appetite. I could feel the presence of Lancelot beside me, saying nothing, showing nothing. I couldn't tell if he wanted me or hated me.

Arthur chattered happily away, with the other knights about the war, and with me. I smiled and nodded and tried to join in, but my heart wasn't in it. I looked deep into my cup of wine, and saw my eyes reflected back, my face wavering as the wine rippled. Someone filled my glass, and I drank again and again. They were all drinking heavily, too. Gawain was the most drunk, shouting and singing, trying to grab at the serving girls as they went by. It made me angry to see it, but I said nothing. Not Morgan. She wasn't drinking. Even Nimue was, her pale face flushing beneath her white blonde hair. The two of *them* were always talking, accomplices from the Otherworld. As Kay saw me looking he raised his glass, and winked at me, then drank. So did I. My head was filled already with a pleasant, fuzzy warmth, the knot in my stomach untying. I still had not spoken to Lancelot beside me, but he seemed content enough listening to another of Gawain's drawn-out stories of Arthur at war. I could not tell if Lancelot was drinking like the rest of us. I began to feel hungry. The partridge – or maybe it was some other game bird, I didn't know – on the plate before me was sweet, and succulent, glazed with honey and orange or something like that. There were vegetables, roasted with honey and herbs and in the centre of the table, I suddenly noticed, a basket of peaches.

I turned to Lancelot beside me, suddenly feeling brave. As I turned my leg bumped against his under the table. This time I did not feel nervous, I did not feel afraid. I did not blush. I let it rest there, and he did not move. My skin felt as though it was glowing in response to the touch.

"You fought well today," I told him.

He smiled. I did not think I had seen him smile, not at me, before. It was slight and gentle, but it lit up his face. He looked down quickly. He seemed shy. How could a man who fought as he did be shy?

"Thank you, my lady."

I wanted to lean in to that voice, but I could not. I could feel Morgan's dark eyes on the back of my head. He was speaking again, but suddenly I felt dizzy, and sick. Had I eaten too much? Drunk too much? I felt hot, all of a sudden, too hot. The room was spinning around me. I hadn't drunk that much wine. I gazed across at Morgan who, over her cup of water, eyed me with a wicked smile playing across her face. Arthur was laughing hard at something Kay had said, to which Gawain looked angry and Gareth upset. I didn't want to know. They were truly a pack of boys.

I pushed myself up from my seat to leave, bracing myself against the table, though Lancelot was still talking softly. I felt as though I was going to be sick. Arthur turned to me and took my hand.

"My love, where are you going?"

"I don't feel well."

Arthur groaned in disappointment. "We're only beginning. Stay, come on." He pulled me into his lap. "I'm not finished with you for the night."

Some of the men around us laughed and I flushed red, but it was with anger. It suddenly struck me that he was very rude in the way he treated me. When he had returned from Rome and grabbed me in the courtyard, in front of everyone, and on our wedding night when he had offered me the choice of consenting freely or being taken against my will, and *Someone take her back to Britain* and now. I pushed him away and stepped back from him. It was all I could do to hold myself back from slapping him across his face. The room still spun and jolted around me, sickeningly.

"If you are looking for a woman who will go to your bed whenever *you* desire it, *my lord*, I suggest you send for a whore," I spat, turning and striding from the room. Behind me as I left, I heard Gawain say,

"I would strike any woman who spoke to me like that, no matter if she was my queen or not."

I heard Arthur call my name in appeal, but I knew I had to leave. As soon as I left that hot, smoky, room, and stumbled out into the cool night air I felt better. I slumped back against the door-frame of the great hall, feeling the night air's cold touch against my face. My head was still spinning, and when I tried to open my eyes and look up, the stars in the clear winter sky span and blurred together. I could feel my back sliding slowly down the wall, and I turned to try and brace myself against the wall with my arms. If I could push myself up, then I could walk back to my chamber and sleep whatever it was off. Maybe it was Morgan, maybe I was ill, maybe I hadn't eaten enough and had been drinking wine on a nervous, empty stomach. Whatever it was, a sleep would make me well again, I felt sure. But my body felt heavy, my head especially, and I could not find the strength in me to push myself up.

Then, I felt arms around me, lifting me gently to my feet, guiding my arm across strong, broad shoulders and sliding an arm around my waist. I looked up, to see who it was. For a moment my vision was so blurred, all I saw was dark hair and I thought it was Kay, but as I blinked I saw coming into focus the high cheekbones, the deep blue eyes of Lancelot and my breath stopped in my throat. He looked alert, and concerned. Whatever Morgan had put in that cup, he had not drunk it.

"My lady, you are not well."

I shook my head.

Somewhere deep inside me a voice said *This is a bad idea. You are angry with Arthur. You are drunk. He is taking you to your bed. This is a bad idea.* But it was too far away, and my head was too swimming with heat and lights to take it in. I liked the feel of arms around me, gentle, guiding arms that wanted nothing from me, and the cold air outside.

When he took me inside, to the tower that held my rooms, I felt the difference, too. Quiet, not like the busy hall, and cool, empty of other people and fire and smoke and noise. The stairs were hard, and I felt my feet drag every step of the way, but I also felt Lancelot's breath brush against my ear, and I heard his voice, close by my ear, murmuring to me, telling me it wasn't far.

When we reached my chamber, I thought he would leave. He had been nervous to meet my eye in public, but now we were alone it did not seem he was shy at all. He came inside with me, and set me down on the bed. My heavy eyes fluttered closed, and I only opened them again when I felt a cool, wet cloth against my face. I opened them, feeling sharper already, to see he was kneeling over me, on the bed. He was so close. I could smell the already-familiar clean smell of his skin, I could see the pale blue of a vein beneath his chin, only a trace against the thin, soft skin there. I followed the touch of his hand and the cool cloth with my face, relishing it. I sighed in gentle relief at its cool touch, or perhaps it was at having him close by. He was so near, so near. My eyes fluttered closed again as the cool cloth moved away, and I felt fingers, light and deft in my hair, unpinning the gold net, and teasing the curls loose from their braid. I let my fingers reach out lazily, and brush against his arm. Now the opportunity was before me, I could not resist but touch.

"Where are your women?" he whispered by my ear. He was close enough that if I turned my head towards him, we would kiss.

"I don't know," I murmured. He sighed and pressed a cool hand against my brow. I made a little noise of pleasure. Then he moved away, and I felt him pull the shoes from my feet. I wriggled my toes in relief.

Then I felt his hand on my brow again and my eyes fluttered open, suddenly light. I opened them to see him lying beside me, propped up on an elbow. His eyes were full of thoughtful concern.

"What happened to you?" he wondered aloud to himself, quietly. "You ate and drank as we all did. What has made you so ill?"

He noticed my eyes were open and let his hand trail down to stroke my cheek lightly with the backs of his fingers. He sighed very softly again. It seemed, then, he leaned closer, as though drawn by some magnetic force, and if I could have moved I would have drawn him to me. I knew he was going to kiss me again, but then the door flew open and I could hear Marie and Christine chattering away; I could hear their happy voices thick with wine, and Lancelot took his leave of them, and of me, and slipped away. Marie and Christine stripped me off my dress and folded me into the bed. Christine put the back of her hand against my head and clicked her tongue in disapproval.

"She has a terrible fever. Tell the King he should come back tomorrow," she said to Marie.

So Arthur had come for me. To punish me, perhaps, or to collect what he felt he deserved. I rolled over in bed, to press my face against the cool side of the pillow. Arthur would have to wait.

Chapter Seventeen

In the morning, my head throbbed, but the fever was gone. Propped up in bed with pillows, Marie brought me porridge with honey. She did not look well either. Behind her back, Margery made a gesture telling me not to ask as I began to, and Marie looked relieved that I did not. I hoped her weary caste had nothing to do with Gawain.

Arthur came to see me, mid-morning, to see if I was well. He did not mention what I had said to him, and he seemed concerned and kind. Perhaps he had forgotten. He kissed me tenderly and told me he was going out hunting with some of the knights. I nodded, and kissed him goodbye. I was glad he did not want to stay. I still felt weary and fragile, and I was unsure yet whether I was still angry with him, or not.

I felt embarrassed about letting Lancelot rescue me again, and foolish. I was not so sure in the cold light of day that Morgan had put something strange in my cup. Or at least, it appeared not to be my cup alone. Half the castle was groaning with regret. These woad-faced druids never seemed to do anyone that much good.

I dressed in a simple dress of purple wool, and plaited my hair into a simple coil. I did not feel like much adornment today, but I did put the little golden circlet of leaves around my hair.

As I walked down towards the courtyard, I glanced into the room where I usually sat with my ladies. Morgan was sat there alone, with a smug little smile on her face, innocently embroidering a little piece of silk, her white-and-blue hands dextrously guiding needle and silk to and fro. I hurried by, unwilling to speak with her.

Outside in the courtyard, a pale winter sun was already overhead in a clear, frosty sky. It was a beautiful day already. A few of the knights were in the courtyard, though fewer than usual, and those that were there were not fighting, but were brushing their horses, or sharpening their swords. I was afraid that they might remember my shouting, but they did not seem to, greeting me in their usual friendly manner as I went by. I recognised Kay among them, and Gareth, but the others were men I did not know. Kay walked over, leaving his horse snorting steam and stamping against the hard earth of the yard.

Kay whistled through his teeth and shook his head.

"If they all drank like that the day they took Rome, it's a miracle they made it back alive."

I noticed that Gawain was not down in the yard, and smiled, though I still felt a little embarrassed. Kay put a hand on my shoulder.

"Are you feeling better? Arthur said you were ill."

I couldn't tell if he remembered or not, or if I should be embarrassed about what I had done. I nodded.

"Is he out here?" I asked, looking around, but I was not really looking for Arthur.

"He rode out early with my father and Bors, to do some hunting. Best cure for a night of too much wine, he seemed to think."

I did not know who Bors was, but I was getting used to hearing names I did not recognise around my own court.

"You weren't ill, were you?"

I looked back to Kay, sharply, and his mischievous face was suddenly filled with an impish, intense seriousness. I wrinkled my forehead into a frown.

"I was."

"Maybe you thought you were. You know the cup you drank from was not meant for you."

"What do you mean?"

But I did not hear what he meant, because striding across the yard, out from the stables, came Lancelot, and though Kay had begun to speak, somehow I couldn't hear him; it sounded like the rushing of waves on the shore, or the wind. He stopped, when he saw that I was looking away, and followed my gaze. When he saw Lancelot, he made a little 'hmmm' noise, deep in his throat, and if I had been able to, I would have challenged him on it, but I was not.

"You're up – are you well now?" Lancelot asked, breathlessly. After days of him avoiding me, speaking to me as little as possible, I was finding it hard to take in him rushing across the courtyard to speak to me. The little clouds of our breath mingled between us in the cold air, as I stood in silence, suddenly feeling the intensity of my embarrassment rooting me to the spot, stilling my tongue into silence. I wished I had not come down; I wished I had hidden away for a day, at least.

"She's well." Kay spoke for me, and Lancelot nodded brusquely.

"Good," he said, not looking away from me. "I'm glad you are well, my lady."

Kay shifted on his feet beside me; I could feel him getting annoyed, though I did not know why.

"That cup was meant for you," Kay said suddenly, and Lancelot turned to him, confusion written deep on his face. "Morgan prepared that cup *for you*, but before Guinevere arrived you switched them around because you spotted some speck of dirt on hers, and *you thought the Queen ought to have the finer cup*." Kay was labouring the point, but he didn't need to. Lancelot shook his head thoughtfully.

"You told me not to."

"I told you not to," Kay agreed, his voice full of bitter victory.

Why would Morgan want to drug Lancelot? I was not surprised if she desired him for a husband; after all, he was unmarried and handsome, and of an age with her, or thereabouts. Married to that fat old man, she had probably longed for a man like him, but I did not see how plying him with potions to knock him out would have helped her in that endeavour. I toyed with the idea that he might marry one of the women at court. It was not impossible; in fact it was highly likely. Perhaps he had even come back with Arthur to find a wife. All those young and unmarried men and women together in Camelot – spring would be the season for making new marriages, now that the war was over. I did not think I would like it very much, but I could not say exactly why. A woman has no claim over her champion, just as she has no claim over her husband.

Gareth was calling Kay over for a fight, and he shrugged in frustration and left. Neither Lancelot nor I had given what he had to say our full attention, or at least the kind of attention he had wanted. I supposed vaguely that I ought to tell Arthur, rather than running up to my rooms and accosting Morgan with it myself. I was wary, too, of being alone with another druid. Still, I was struck with quite a burning desire to know what she might want with an unconscious Lancelot.

"Are you busy down here now?" I said to Lancelot. Obviously, he had been lost in his thoughts as well, because when I spoke he glanced up with surprise, as though he had been shaken from some reverie. He did not seem all that bothered that whatever drug Morgan had put in my cup had been meant for him. I was a little pleased that he was not thinking of her. Though not pretty, she was proud and beautiful in her own way, and as the King's sister it would not have been a match beneath him.

"No," he replied.

I was struck with an idea, one that might provide me with the opportunity to question Morgan, but not leave me alone with her and nothing more than other women – all of whom I knew I was stronger than – for my protection. I wished that Nimue was somewhere to be found, too. I would put my trust in her magic against Morgan's, since it was she who had shut Merlin beneath the rock. I was still wary of her from the forest, but she seemed to be mostly benign.

"Will you come and read to me? I don't read in French, and I have a book –"

He nodded, and I smiled. It was only half a lie. I did not read as well in French as I did in English or Breton, but I could understand the book well enough. I was surprised that he agreed so readily. Somewhere at the back of my mind, I wondered also if it was an excuse to be alone with him again, but if it was then surely it was innocent. I had decided that it would be, and drugged as I had been, it had been so last night. A sudden flood of memory came over me, of his face close to mine, and the feeling, strong within me, that we had been about to kiss. No, I had imagined it. It had been what I had drunk. I had imagined it, it was in my head, along with everything I felt, and it was under control.

When we came up to the room beneath my chamber, it was empty. Morgan had melted away back into whatever murky shadows she had come from. I felt an unsettling mixture of disappointment and relief. I would have liked to know. Lancelot stood in the doorway, looking around at the piles of cushions and the fur rugs on the floor, wondering where to sit. I went to the corner of the room and found the book. It was a small, leatherbound volume, lettered in gold on the front, a French translation of Ovid. It was a terribly dull book, and rude throughout about women, but now we were here, and there was no witch to confront, I thought I would like very much to lie against the cushions with my eyes closed and listen to him read, if just to hear the sound of his voice. I wondered why he had agreed to come. He could have made any excuse, but he had come.

I walked over and handed him the book. I let our hands brush as I passed it to him. Now I had remembered my resolution to be in control, I could enjoy the tingling sensation the touch of his skin gave mine. I could enjoy being close to him, touching him, and do no wrong.

I settled myself down on a pile of pillows and lay back, closing my eyes.

"Where do you want me to begin?" he asked. I felt him sit down beside me, quite close, but with a decorous space in-between that I felt almost humming with anticipation. I peeped out under an eyelid and watched him settle into place, a pillow behind his back, one knee drawn up to his chest with the book balanced open on it, the other leg stretched out long before him.

"At the start, when the gods create the waters," I replied, closing my eyes properly once more.

He laughed softly. I had not heard the sound before, though I had seen it from across the yard. It was soft and deep, and lovely. I felt it gorgeously all around me.

"You know this book already." I could hear from his voice that he was smiling. What had changed? He had lost whatever it was that had been making him wary of me. Suddenly, it was as though a veil had lifted. Perhaps it was me; perhaps it was that I no longer seemed tense, and anxious.

"I don't remember well," I lied.

"Hmmmm." I heard him flip through the pages of the book. "Since you know the creation so well already, I will read you, hmmm, the story of the gossiping raven. Do you know that one?"

"No," I lied again, settling deeper into the pillows. He knew this book well, then. Arthur did not know any literature, not really. He had proudly told me once that he had read the Bible, though I did not think he could have done because it was written all in Latin and even I did not understand those strange and unfamiliar words.

He began to read. I wasn't listening to the words, and some of them were unfamiliar anyway, the way he said them. We Bretons read the French all wrong, I had been told a hundred times, and I had only ever heard Christine read it to me, awkwardly and in halting stops. On Lancelot's tongue the poetry flowed smooth and low, and though I did not understand it all, I felt it all the way through me. I loved, more than anything, just to listen to his voice. More beautiful still in his own language than in English. I was glad the book I had chosen was so long.

After a while, I heard him ask.

"Are you sleeping?"

I laughed softly. I was not surprised he thought so, since I had been lying still with my eyes shut for so long, and shook my head.

He began to read another tale from the book, but halfway through – just as a woman was changing into a bear – I heard Arthur's voice from the doorway shatter my lovely dream.

"What will my country come to, if you take all my best knights away to read to you?" Arthur laughed from the doorway. I opened my eyes suddenly, and sat up. Unaccountably, I felt as though I had been caught at something I should not be doing. But he did not seem angry about it, nor about the feast the evening before, and I was relieved.

Arthur had come to find Lancelot, to train at fighting with him. He had got used to war, I supposed, and did not know what to do when he wasn't fighting. Lancelot put the book down gently beside me, and followed Arthur as he left. I was sorry to see him go. I was left alone with my thoughts. I closed my eyes and tried to remember the sound of Lancelot's voice.

That night, Arthur came to my chamber. I did not mind, and I was glad he was not angry with me. I was glad, too, of the oblivion of his powerful touch, the all-consuming fierceness of his desire. We did not speak, and he held me fast to him, as though he felt that I might slip through his fingers, and melt away into the night. I realised then that I was glad of his desire, his need for me. It kept me anchored to him. Without it, I was afraid I would float away, like a dandelion seed into the wind. I liked the rough way he held me, and when he was inside me I felt a sense of rightness and belonging, of the wholesomeness of our togetherness. I wanted, in a way, to belong to someone, and I *liked* the urgency of his desire. I wanted it; I wanted him to want me. To have that pressing physical need for me. I could close my eyes and lose myself in the intensity of his desire.

When he blew the candles out, and we lay in the darkness, as we always did, with my head on his chest and his arms around me, he spoke at last.

"Guinevere, I hope that you know how I love you, I hope that you would not think – I hope that you feel I always treat you kindly, and... think of your wishes, as well as my own."

He *did* remember last night. I put my hands beneath my chin and looked up at him in the dark. I couldn't really seem him, just a black shape against the darkness, but I could feel his chest rise and fall under my hands, could hear his breathing close beside me.

"Of course, of course. It was just the drink." There were not words enough, or the right words, for what I really wanted to say. To say, I wanted it and I didn't want it. I needed it, it held us close together. There were only words to say that all was well. He leaned up to kiss me lightly and then sighed with content. His thoughts were simply soothed, and I was glad of it tonight.

"I know things have been different with us, since the war. I have been busy. But the knights coming here from all around will make Camelot, and Logrys, and Britain great. It is something as King I have to do. I have to show them my strength, and the grandness of my court. I know it has been hard. And I have missed you."

I made a noise of agreement, and he kissed my hair.

"It was Morgan, you know, with the drink," he added, after a short quiet. I was shocked. *He knew*. He did not seem too worried about it. "And I know it was meant for Lancelot." *What?* "Oh, she's harmless really. She's just been in love with him since we were children. He was an orphan child, raised on Avalon not far from where she was raised. He used to stay with us, sometimes, when we were all boys together, he Kay and I, and so would Morgan; of course, I didn't know then that she came because she was my sister. Well, she always liked him. Used to follow him around. She and he would have been about fifteen, I suppose, a little older than I was. Well, it turned out that she wasn't a maiden when she married Uriens, and he came to me blustering and complaining about it and I offered him the choice of living with it, or rejecting the King's sister, and he decided that it wasn't so important after all. Anyway, a lot of people said that was Lancelot, though there are others who say it was Kay. Some even say it was Merlin, because he was around often enough. I don't know. But anyway, the other day she came to me, dragging Lancelot with her, demanding that I marry them. I suppose she had been waiting to get free of old Uriens for a long time. I offered him the choice, and he said he thought marriage was well enough for kings, but not for him. He didn't want to leave fighting and adventures to care for a wife. He said he was not the sort of man to take a wife. Well, I doubt if it was either him or Kay, anyway." He shifted under me, gently pulling me closer. He seemed suddenly hesitant. "Kay and he, well, when we were that age they used to sleep in the same bed." That didn't seem that odd to me. Breton boys or girls often shared with relatives if there was not enough room. "Kay seems to have grown out of it, but Lancelot... I don't know." I realised what he meant. "He never took any of the women who came with the camp to Rome to his bed. He's quiet. I'm not surprised he didn't want Morgan, but he doesn't want *any* woman. But he might truly just want a life of fighting. With him, I can't tell." He sighed and kissed my forehead. I could feel he was settling down to sleep. I supposed I ought not to be surprised; many young men were so with one another. I just did not – could not – believe that things were still so with Lancelot. "I'm glad you had him read to you. I was afraid that the two of you did not like one another. I never saw you speak together before. It's good. A queen should show some favour to her champion."

He was already drifting off to sleep. I rolled on to my back, feeling my eyes wide open, pressing against the black. The information rushed around me, but it seemed also to sluice off me, and all I could feel was a sudden acute awareness that the way I loved Arthur was not enough. I suddenly felt very naked, and small and alone. His love was strong and insistent, but it did not fill me to the heart. There was an emptiness in the pit of my stomach that was filled over and over again in the darkness by Lancelot's name. Lancelot didn't want to take a wife. He had not lain with any of the camp women. Arthur, implicitly, had. When I imagined his voice again, it was as though his lips were by my ear, forbidden and velvety. Why had Arthur had to say his name? Saying his name was like calling him into being, between us in the bed. What if Lancelot had refused Morgan not out of love for Kay, but out of love for me? What if his love could make me whole? Arthur was a good man. He was good, and kind, and he loved me the best way he could. There must be something rotten and hollow with me that the love of a good man could not make me whole. I had been happy. I was sure I had been happy. *I want to feel whole.* What had changed? What had become of me for my happiness to evaporate around me like a fog, and leave me with this terrifying sense of my emptiness?

In the darkness, Arthur sleeping beside me, all I could think of was Lancelot.

Chapter Eighteen

When I woke in the morning, all the thoughts of the night before seemed distant, and out of proportion, as though I had dreamed them. Alone in the dark I had allowed myself to half dream, half think something that was not true. Arthur was still sleeping beside me as I woke, and I slipped out of bed to dress. I wanted a hot bath, but if I called for one then I would wake him, and I wanted to run out into the beautiful frosty morning I could see out of my window. As I dressed quietly in a simple wool dress and fur-lined cloak, I thought again of everything Arthur had told me last night. Morgan's desire for Lancelot; I was not surprised, although I did not see why sending him to sleep would help her in that. Lancelot and Kay; though I thought Arthur was seeing something that wasn't there in order to try to understand a man who was not controlled by his desire for women.

And yet all that I could grasp in my mind were his words *I was afraid the two of you did not like each other. A queen should show some favour to her champion.*

He had saved my life, and I intended to do my queenly duty and show favour. Everything else was the half-sleeping mirage of my dreams. He had not *said* anything to me either way. I could not know if it was Kay or Morgan or I that he thought of when he was alone. There was nothing, only the vapourous late-night thoughts. And yet when I turned to go and looked at Arthur, and felt the warmth within me of the love we had shared for years now, I had the sense again that something had changed within me and I was aware it was not enough. I put the thought out of my mind as I slipped from the room and down the stairs.

I was up early enough to smell the baking bread in the courtyard, and the smell of it made me hungry. I was not sure what I had come down for, apart from to feel the cool air against my face, and look at the white winter sun in the morning. Gareth was out there, sharpening his sword. He smiled when he saw me, and I walked over to him.

"That's a fine sword," I told him, lifting it out of his hands. It was heavy for me, and it took me two hands to hold it up when it would have taken Gareth only one. Still, I could feel its steady balance, I could feel that for a man's sword it was light and quick. So Gareth was old enough to own a sword, to be expected to kill. I looked at him, thoughtful. He was beginning to look like a man. The winter and the company of men had brought that on him. His kind, open face had a shadow of stubble across the skin, and across his shoulders, from the training in the yard, the muscles of a man were growing. I touched his cheek lightly with my hand, unable to restrain the motherly impulse, and said, "You're half a man these days, Gareth. I will have to find a knight for you to squire."

"More than half, I hope," he answered, grinning.

I took a step away and swung the sword a little, testing the feel of it in my hand. It had been a long time since I had held a sword. The one made for me that I had tried to smuggle in from Carhais had been lost or stolen on the journey and I missed it. I had not thought it would be impossible to get a woman's sword in Logrys; nor had I thought I would have a need for it. The thought had been half in my mind as I crossed the sea that the only sword I would bear was one against myself. Perhaps if I had had a sword on the battlefield rather than a spear – I pushed the thought away. No sense in re-thinking the moment again and again. The young man's light sword was the closest thing, but I still had trouble lifting it and wielding it as I was used to. Still, it felt good to hold a sword again.

Then, from behind me, a mailed fist grabbed the sword as I lifted it and wrenched it out of my hands. I wheeled around. It was Gawain.

"A sword is not a toy, my lady," he said gruffly. Gareth had jumped to his feet, unsure whose side he was meant to take. I was sure he could see from my face, and Gawain's, that there *would* be a fight.

"I was not playing, *sir*."

I reached for the sword and he stepped back. I felt my face flush with anger and stepped forward for it again. He was holding a sword and dressed all in chainmail, and yet in my anger I did not see that, and as he stepped away, I stepped forward with a hand raised, ready to strike him. Gareth stepped between us.

"It's *my* sword." Gareth reached out his hand for it, and Gawain, not looking away from me with his sullen eyes, handed it back to him.

"Don't give your sword to a woman again," Gawain told him, still not looking from me. I held myself drawn up with trembling rage, but I let him go. I wished I was taller, stronger, bigger. I wished I had my sword. I was angry enough I would have struck him with my bare hand, though it would only have torn against the chainmail. I wanted Gawain to be sorry for all of the things he had said to me. I wanted to force him to respect me, to see that though I was not a man I was brave and strong enough to fight, but I could not. Again, again I felt my powerlessness.

"Is everything well, here?" Lancelot, who to my surprise I had not noticed across the yard, had come over. But he did not speak to me, he spoke to Gareth. He did not meet my look, and he stood warily at a distance from me. *This is because Arthur found us reading together*, I thought. He's wary. He feels guilty. I was surprised, and at the back of my mind, the thought came that he would not feel this if he had not felt, as I had, a secret, illicit thrill at being alone together. But it only stoked my frustration harder, that after that brief moment together the day before, he was ignoring me again. Or perhaps he really did not like me, or he was afraid of Morgan, or he *wanted* Morgan and he didn't want Arthur to have told her and made her jealous. Arthur had only said that he did not want to *marry* Morgan.

Gareth nodded, and Lancelot moved away, back across the yard, and Gawain followed him. I could hear them beginning to fight, not with the wooden practice-swords that the young men like Gareth used, but blunted iron swords that drew sparks from one another and rang out through the courtyard as they met. Gareth looked at me apologetically and went back to sharpening his sword. I sat down beside him, looking out at the fighting.

"Where I grew up," I told him, thoughtfully, as I watched Lancelot and Gawain fight, "women fought and hunted alongside men. I'm still getting used to Logrys."

"You would get hurt," Gareth replied, his tone half-defensive of his brother's actions.

I looked at Lancelot and Gawain. Gareth *was* right; the Breton men fought as the women did, lightly armoured, with bows and light little shortswords, and our warfare had been different, little skirmishes fought in forests, small-scale ambush attacks. Compared to the men I had seen growing up, Arthur's knights were giants all, rippling with muscle from bearing heavy platemail on their backs and the huge two-handed broadswords they fought with in their hands. The lances, too, they took into battle, I could never have lifted. These huge men with their armoured horses and faceless steel helms were *made* for war. No wonder Arthur had defeated my father's forces so easily. In any woodland we Bretons would have won, but in open war I did not see how anyone could have stood against Arthur's knights.

The two men were laying into each other hard, I thought. Perhaps it was because they were alone in the yard, but I felt as though I had not seen any two others fighting like that before. Gawain was giving ground fast. He was taller, broader, but he was also heavier on his feet, slower to block Lancelot's blows, and he was being edged back into a corner. I glanced at Gareth. He had stopped sharpening his sword, and was watching.

"Look at the way he moves," Gareth sighed in admiration. He must have meant Lancelot, because Gawain was shuffling backwards awkwardly. "He's like a cat. Like a lion. I haven't seen a lion, but Gawain saw one in Rome, and I expect a lion is just like Lancelot."

He was right. Lancelot moved like a predator, soft, swift and fluid. Gawain yielded as, backed into a corner, Lancelot knocked the sword from his hands. He raised them over his head in a gesture of surrender. The thought flickered through me that Lancelot might have done that for me. But Gawain did not seem chastened. He laughed, and clapped Lancelot on the back.

Gareth jumped up, snatching up his practice sword and ran over, eager to try his strength against Lancelot. Lancelot smiled indulgently at the boy, and let him fight long enough to feel his opponent's strength, letting him take ground, until more knights began to come out into the yard, and he made an excuse to leave. I watched him go, feeling it burn inside me. He did not glance towards me once.

Chapter Nineteen

That night Arthur called his council. I sat at his side at the Round Table. At first, when I had come to the councils, I had heard men whispering. Obviously, in Lothian women had not played a part in politics while their husbands lived, because it had come mainly from Gawain and his brothers, but they had got used to my presence, and they were not surprised when Nimue replaced Merlin at Arthur's left side. They regarded her woaded face with suspicion, but they listened to her soft little voice with rapt attention the few times she did speak, because her voice was the voice of Avalon, and though they all suspected its power, they also feared it. I noticed that Lancelot sat as far as he could manage from me, across at the other side of table. The frustration burning within me made me determined to get him to speak to me. It wasn't fair for him to be kind and then distant. I hadn't asked him for anything inappropriate and *he* was the one who had kissed *me*.

The knights came in a variety of dress. Among them Gawain and his brothers Aggravain and Gaheris came dressed in armour, apart from their helms, and with their swords at their side; Ector and Bors came in light leather armour and with their swords, but Lancelot and Kay came only in their shirt and breeches. Lancelot had come with his hair wet, as though he had just stepped from the bath. I tried not to picture it. I was getting used to the other faces around the table, too. A quiet, serious man with short sandy-brown hair, cut close to his head, was called Perceval, and I thought I remembered him from the party who had collected me at Dover, and another with fair hair, swept back from his face and a vain look about him was called Lamerocke. He had come in a velvet doublet. There was also a dark little man who moved with funny little quick darting motions who was called Dinadan. These had been with Arthur when he sacked Rome; these had been those who had led parts of his army, who had given their riches and lands and the lives of their people to him. The strongest men in Europe. And yet, all looked nervously on Nimue, who rarely spoke aloud to the group once it was gathered, but if she had something to say, would whisper it in Arthur's ear. I wondered occasionally if Arthur had ever taken her to bed. I could not imagine it. Sometimes, too, Morgan would stand at the back of the room in the shadows, watching. She was not there today, and I was glad. Arthur himself was dressed in light armour, embossed on the front with a brass dragon across the chest and he had Excalibur by his side.

He slept always with that sword at his side. I supposed he was afraid of losing it again, or perhaps he was still afraid for his life.

"I called you all here today because I have had news from Cornwall." He had learned in his time as ruler, the voice of a king. It was steady and strong, and everyone fell quiet to hear it. "My lady mother Igraine has died, may the Lord rest her soul. She has been buried by her people and rests in Tintagel. Tintagel itself has been taken over by one of my vassal-kings Mark. Mark has written begging for a champion to defend him from a *giant*, he says." A few men around the table laughed. I was sure, to them, the man would look like a normal man, but if Kay had come to Carhais looking for war, there were brothers of mine who would have written to other lords to complain of being besieged by a giant. "But I think we could spare someone. I have to be seen to defend my vassal kings; even *Mark*." The men laughed. Clearly, they knew something about Mark that I didn't. "But whoever I send must be able to behave himself." I did not think I imagined the look that Arthur cast on Gawain. "Mark has married Isolde of Ireland, and he is a very jealous man, they say."

"I hear the girl is simple," Kay interjected, with a wicked smile.

I expected Arthur to admonish him, but he just inclined his head in unwilling agreement.

"I heard that she has taken Mark's nephew as her lover," Aggravain suggested. That man always had one piece of gossip or another.

"I heard it was a saracen man," Dinadan said. "A heathen."

Arthur raised a hand for quiet and it fell.

"Nonetheless, we are not here to debate Mark's wife's intelligence or fidelity to her marriage-bed, we are here to decide who we will send to Cornwall."

"Send Lancelot," Kay suggested, flashing a look at him I could not read across the table. "Isolde won't be in any danger from *him*."

Arthur shifted uncomfortably in his seat. Clearly, he had his own ideas about exactly what Kay meant. Was Kay saying it because they were lovers? Or had Lancelot said something to Kay about me? Or about Morgan? The awful thought shimmered past that Kay might want Lancelot out of his way. I glanced at Lancelot; he was sitting back in his chair, fixing Kay with an even look, one knee drawn up to his chest and his arm resting forward on it. He was not giving anything away.

"What about you, Kay? Could you not go?" I asked.

"I'm Seneschal. I have to stay at court." He gave me a knowing little smile. I was not sure what I was supposed to know.

"Lancelot is Queen's Champion," Lamerocke argued, running a hand over his smooth wave of hair, as though he was subconsciously smoothing it into place. "He should stay, too."

"He can go if she lets him go," Kay said pointedly. "He would finish it fastest. If we send someone who fails, or makes a mess of it, then Mark might see it as a sign of weakness, as an opportunity to rise against Arthur."

The voices rose arguing around me, but Lancelot did not look towards me at all. They had gone past arguing about who should go, and the argument had passed to Mark. Gawain was now saying they should send a small garrison of men, set up an outpost in Cornwall to make sure that Mark didn't try anything, and Kay was still arguing for sending a single knight. Dinadan was tapping his fingernails against the table, trying to interject but failing. Lamerocke was blustering on, offended because he thought Kay had suggested that *he* might make a mess of it if he was sent instead of Lancelot. By all accounts I had heard of him, he wouldn't, but I thought Kay *had* said it to antagonise him. Perceval leaned over and whispered something in Lancelot's ear, and Lancelot nodded. I felt as though I was fading away, fading in the face of Lancelot's refusal to look at me, and the shouting rising around me.

Before I knew what I was doing I was on my feet. The room fell silent around me. I felt Nimue's cold blue eyes on me, considering, seeing everything. I felt myself blush lightly as they all turned to me. They were waiting for me to speak.

"If we send more than one knight, Mark might see that as an act of aggression, and ride against us anyway. We send one knight to him, to kill this giant. And we invite Isolde to court."

Arthur nodded, putting his hand tenderly on mine. It was warm and rough with fighting, comforting, familiar. His touch made me feel a little better, a little more centred. I sat slowly back in my chair, feeling embarrassed.

"That seems the best solution. Mark will not cause trouble if his wife is with us. Besides, Isolde ought to come. It is only polite to *my* queen if Mark sends his to court."

I was pleased with what I had improvised. I was curious, anyway, to see this great beauty Isolde.

There was a murmur of agreement around the table.

"As for who we send," Arthur continued, "I will leave that among you. But if someone does not come to me to offer himself as a champion I will choose one of you." Nimue leaned over and whispered in his ear, and he nodded. "You must excuse me." He leaned down to me and whispered, "Wait for me in my room." I nodded, and he left with Nimue. Obviously, she had something in Merlin's old room below us to show him. Some map of the stars that promised more success for him, something in her little whirring astrolabe that portended something or other. Some secret that I would never know.

Gawain and his brothers left right away, then Lamerocke chattering with Dinadan, and then Perceval, with a soft word to Lancelot. Kay lounged in his seat, grinning at me, making no move to leave. Lancelot did not leave either. I was not sure if he wanted to speak to me at last, or if he was afraid to move in case I spoke to him. Or in case Kay said something. Kay was always just saying whatever came into his head.

I cast Kay a wary look, narrowing my eyes at him. If he had something to say, he could go ahead and say it. He had a wicked look about him, tonight.

"Excuse me." Lancelot, seeing the look, or sensing it, stood to leave.

"No!" I protested, the words out of me before I was aware of forming them. "No, I have to speak with you."

"I know what this is about." Kay grinned.

"Oh, you do?" I rounded on him, suddenly fired with anger. I wanted him to go. I wanted him to stop being so smug. I wanted to slap his grinning face. "Do tell us."

"It's about lovestruck little Gareth," Kay teased. "Guinevere needs you to protect her from his loving advances." He made a joking grab at the skirts of my dress and I slapped his hand. He rolled back into his seat, laughing.

"*Get out, Kay*," I shouted, louder than I had intended to. I saw the hurt flicker in his eyes, and the smile dropped off his face. He pushed himself up smartly from his chair and strode out, slamming the door behind him. I winced at the sound. I should not, perhaps, have shouted, but all the patience had drained from me, after all the waiting, and at last *at last* I was alone again with Lancelot. He stood and walked towards the door. I slid out of my chair and darted around the table and into his path.

"Where are you going? I *said* I needed to talk to you."

He turned his face away from me. "Not now," he said softly.

How dare he? Whatever was going on in his head, I was his queen and he would stay if I wanted him to. I crossed my arms over my chest, standing my ground. I was between him and the door. He would speak to me before he left. I didn't want any promises from him, or anything, but he *would* speak with me. I didn't care what about.

"I want you to take Gareth as your squire. He is the right age, and he looks up to you."

Lancelot rubbed his face with his hands, turning away from me, walking a few steps back into the room.

"I don't know why you are being like this with me. First you save my life, then you ignore me, then you agree to read with me, then you ignore me again, and now you're refusing me this. What is *wrong* with you?" I was trying to sound calm, but it was failing. I could feel myself trembling with frustration; I could feel the heat rising up inside me. I tried to hold it back, but I was half-shouting. "Have I *offended* you in some way?"

I stepped forward and put a hand on his shoulder, lightly. He twisted around and grabbed my wrist, holding my hand away. He moved so fast, as though he knew what I had been about to do before I had done it. His eyes were wild and I could see his chest rising and falling fast, but his grip on my wrist was soft, and he left my hand fall away after a moment.

"My lady, you *must* let me go," he insisted.

Once more I stood my ground, crossing my arms in front of me. The candlelight flickered over both of us in the moment of silence.

"Say you'll take Gareth as your squire, and that you will come with me to tell him so tomorrow. Say you won't go to Cornwall."

Lancelot leaned against the back of a chair, as though he was holding himself back from something. Perhaps it was from striking me; I couldn't tell. But I was not afraid; I was too angry for fear. He looked down again, away from me. *Why won't you look at me?* I reached out and took him by the arm.

"Answer me," I demanded.

"Stop *tormenting* me," he shouted suddenly. He looked up at me, pulling his arm from my grip, his eyes flashing with anger, striding two steps away from me across the room. I felt the blood rise in me in response. He would *not* speak to me like that.

"I'm not *tormenting* you, Lancelot. It's a simple enough request. You're *my* champion; you ought to take *my* suggestion," I shouted back. He wouldn't turn back round to face me, but I could see his shoulders rising and falling with his breaths. He was being irrational. I didn't see why he didn't want to listen to me about this. I didn't know why he was so desperate to deny me what I was asking. He might even have done it anyway without my suggestion and I felt as if he was dismissing it just because I had asked. I didn't know what was wrong with him, why he had to be so distant, so opaque.

"That's not what I mean," he growled, low.

No, I knew what he meant. He didn't like me looking for him, calling him to me, asking him to do his *duties* as a champion. I didn't know if he thought he was above it, or if he just wanted time away from *me*. I could feel the anger pulsing within me, sharp now, and red-hot. I didn't want anything other than for him to speak to me, to be close to me. I did not think that was too much for him to concede to me.

"Well I don't *know* what you mean. You're my champion, but you don't want to see me. You *obviously* care about me, but you don't want to talk to me. I'm not asking very much of you, Lancelot. I just want to speak with you sometimes, to see you, to be, to be nearby –"

In less than a second he turned back to me, strode back the distance and caught me in his arms, drawing me close into a kiss that stole my breath and made my heart jump in my chest. It took my mind a moment to catch up with my racing heart, with my body, that reached towards his, and met him, my hands twining in his hair, soft as silk but thick as velvet. *This is truly happening.* He was passionate, but slow; not rough like Arthur, but sensual, his lips soft against mine, and gently opening to a tongue that fluttered against my own. I felt his thumb graze lightly the top of my ear, the side of my face, as he slid his other fingers into my hair. With the other arm, he held me close against him. Every touch against my skin was hot and bright, like fire. I melted into it, into him. I felt the room dissolve around me; the world. I felt no pressing urgency; a passion wakened within me without time, as though time had melted away with the world. He made a sound of pleasure deep within his throat, and lightly lifted me so that I was sat on the edge of the table. He moved his lips to the top of my ear, kissing lightly, and down my neck. I leant my head back, feeling the sweet rush of it, giving a soft moan at his touch. I drew him close again and felt a hand slide slowly up under the skirt of my dress, along my thigh. I felt light-headed, light-bodied, as though I was filled from head to toe with a tingling light. My fingers, it seemed of their own accord, found the lacing on his breeches and pulled free the strings. I sighed towards him. I felt for a wonderful moment the bare skin of his stomach against the inside of my thigh, soft flesh on flesh, as he began to draw me towards him, and I drew him towards me.

Then, suddenly, through the tingling light surrounding me, I heard what could only be boots on the stone steps, coming up the stairs to the room. He heard them at the same time, and jumped away from me, turning his back to me, his fingers quick on the cord of his breeches, and I threw my skirts back down to the ground, jumping from the table, bracing myself back against it, leaning back, the edge of the table digging in hard to the palms of my hands, the wonderful aura of light and unreality that had shrouded us both disappearing around me. I could feel the flush on my skin, and as Arthur pushed open the door, I was still breathing fast, half with panic, half with desire.

He looked between us, and anger flashed across his face. For a moment, I thought this was the end, but then he turned to Lancelot. It must have looked a very different picture to him.

"Lancelot, what's going on?" he said, his voice deep with threat. "What have you been doing to upset my wife?"

Lancelot turned back around, speechless. He did not look at me, and I was glad. Neither of us wanted to shatter the lie, or lose the truth that had at last glimmered between us, like a ghost.

"Cornwall," he said at last, grasping for something that would be suitable, something that Arthur would believe. "I told her, I told her that *I* will go, to be champion for King Mark and defend Cornwall."

I closed my eyes, and felt the blood run cold within me. That was almost as bad as the truth, because now he would be taken from me anyway. Arthur would applaud him for taking the challenge, and he would have to go. I heard Arthur sigh.

"Good. I suppose she wasn't pleased."

Don't talk about me as if I'm not there.

Someone take her back to Britain.

The room span around me, even with my eyes shut. So close, so close. What had I done? What had I *almost* done? But I would have given anything to have been back to the moment before, and taste it again. I could see blue and green spots behind my closed eyes. I had had and lost it all in a moment; it had grown like a star within me and suddenly fallen dark. And I could still feel his lips against mine.

"Guinevere?" I heard Lancelot's voice through the darkness. I wanted to sink towards it; I wanted to feel it all around me. It fell soft against me and I felt the twinge within me again of loss. I could no longer feel my body, no longer feel the wood of the table beneath my hands. I felt myself slip, and felt an arm catch me, pulling me back to my feet. I knew it was Arthur, and somehow that made me want to cry.

"Guinevere, are you alright?" Arthur asked. I nodded, raising a hand to my eyes, shielding out the light.

"I think I'm not quite well. Will you fetch Christine?"

Arthur led me tenderly to sit in one of the chairs and put his hand against my brow. "Of course," he replied, and kissed me lightly on top of my head. To Lancelot he said, "Stay with her."

And he left.

Neither of us spoke. I did not know what held him quiet, but I was trying to hold on to the moment before, to taste it once again before it escaped me. What could we say to one another now, anyway? I felt as though the centre of me had shattered.

Chapter Twenty

Christine and Arthur came back quickly; too fast, it seemed to me, and laid me in my bed. Christine clicked her tongue as she always did, when she felt my brow.

"She's not well, my lord." She said to Arthur. They talked quietly over me for a while until Arthur leaned down and kissed me on the cheek, and left. Christine clicked her tongue again, stroking my hair, sitting beside me on the bed, where I lay face down, burying my face in the pillow.

"You are well enough, aren't you, little one?" she said in Breton. She had not called me *little one* in a long time. She used to call me *little one* when I begged her to read me *lai* as a child. I gave a little groan. She *tsked*. "It won't help you to feel sorry for yourself about it. It will pass." She tucked my hair lovingly behind my ear. "Go to sleep, little one."

When I woke in the morning, the tendrils of a lovely dream still hung around me, a dream filled with soft candlelight, and a voice whispering to me in French. I was sure, in the dream, I could really feel the smooth wood of the Round Table beneath my hands, but it had only been an illusion. Like everything else.

When Christine came in with my breakfast, she came in alone. Usually Marie or Margery was with her with my dress, or just to greet me with the gossip of the day. Christine set my food – I could smell porridge – down and sat down on the side of the bed. I didn't want it.

"How are you, my lady?" she asked, formal and proper once more. I half hoped that she would get onto the bed beside me and call me *little one* again.

I sat up in bed, drawing my knees up towards me.

"Better," I replied. I added, in Breton, "I want you to ask Lancelot to come to me, in my walled garden."

Christine gave me a sharp, motherly look. I did not have the energy to scold her for it, nor the inclination.

"Are you sure that is wise?" she warned. "You don't want to upset yourself again."

"I want to say goodbye before he leaves for Cornwall."

Christine nodded, understanding. She had not known he was leaving, then. She kissed me brusquely on the forehead.

"It will seem better soon."

I nodded. I did't know how she had known, but I was not surprised. Christine had been with me since I was a baby. She was quiet, and good at watching the people around her. I wondered how much she had known, or guessed, too. She passed me the porridge. I didn't feel like eating, but I had a few mouthfuls. It seemed a shame to waste food, when we had been without it for so long. I let Margery finish it, when she bustled in with a light green silk dress sewn with gold around the neck for me to wear.

I was impatient for Christine to be gone so that she could ask him, so I dressed quickly. Margery's fingers fumbled clumsily with my hair and I wanted to slap her bumbling hands, but I held myself back. I didn't care how I looked, I just wanted to get out to the garden. I missed little Marie, who was always so deft and quick. She would have cheered me up. Maybe I could even have told her, and she would not have scolded me. She was the youngest of us, almost five years younger than I was. She would not have dared. When I asked Margery where she was, the dull girl said that she hadn't seen her that morning. I hoped once again that she was not with Gawain.

As soon as I was dressed and ready, I ran down the steps and out into the morning, to wait. I felt my heart fluttering within me. I did not know how it could sustain beating so fast for so long. At last he came to me, as I had asked, in my walled garden. Spring was beginning around me; snowdrops pushed through the earth, white blossom hung on the May tree in the corner, and the air smelled green with new life. But it all seemed fragile and mournful to me, the beginning of something that could never be.

I was glad that he came not dressed in his mail for departure, but in his shirt and breeches, though he had his sword at his side. He hesitated as he entered, near to the little stone archway that led in, as though he was wary of coming close to me, but after a moment he strode towards me. I thought he might take me in his arms, but he held back.

He sighed. "Guinevere... I think that this is for the best."

I closed my eyes, feeling the waves of sorrow, and desperation, rush against me, shaking me right to the heart. I wouldn't give in to them, not yet. I was strong enough for this.

"How is this for the best?" I asked, my voice very small, choked down with the tears I would not cry, looking down away from him. He stepped towards me and took my face in his hands and softly turned me to look him in the eye. I could see that he felt it too, the impossibility of everything. But I didn't care. I didn't care who thought it was wrong, who I hurt; I wanted him to stay. Right then I did not care if people knew, I didn't care what was *proper*. But Lancelot was a man with a castle, lands, people under his care. He was responsible for them. I supposed as the son of a king he must be a vassal-prince under Arthur, with a kingdom of his own to protect. He could not risk their lives for me, if it meant the wrath of Arthur. He stroked my cheek gently with his thumb.

"Think of what just happened, what almost happened. If I stayed we would... you *know* we would. It would not be safe. You know for a queen to take a lover is treason, and that is death."

I pushed him away, feeling the fire of my raging emotions suddenly strong within me.

"*I don't care*. I don't care. I would risk *anything*. But maybe you're not as brave as they say you are."

My voice was soft, but harsh. I knew I had been unkind, and I expected him to bridle against it, to turn to anger in response, but he did not. He stepped towards me again, and took my hand, drawing me closer tenderly, reaching out again to brush my cheek, the hair at the nape of my neck, but lightly, as though he did not trust himself to turn back if he touched more firmly. I felt my skin warm at his touch, and closed my eyes for a moment, into the sensation. There was love in it, and longing. I could feel it against my skin; the promise of a great tenderness I might never know.

"Guinevere, you have to understand, Arthur is my king. I have made vows to him, in the sight of God; he has made me what I am. He is a good king. He is a good *man*. I have already betrayed him in this, I –" He shook his head as words failed him for a moment. "We were boys together, we fought side by side... I owe him loyalty, in everything. I will come back. I will. I just think... For now this is the best."

But you will find someone else. Someone you can have.

"I don't want you to go." It was all I could say, stubborn and petulant like a child. There were not the words within me to say it all, and I could not begin because if I did it would all pour out of me, and

I would cry and scream and someone might come. "See me once, before you go." One memory of him, one night; I thought that might be enough to last me through the years. If I had to say goodbye – and I did not think he would come back loving me still – I wanted that at least.

"Guinevere..."

"No. You don't have to come to me, I'll come to you. I have gone out hunting in the woods before; Arthur won't deny me. No one will suspect. Go up to my room, and take the book of Ovid. Send it to me, when you are ready, and I will find you."

He closed his eyes and leant his forehead against mine. I could feel his soft hair falling against my face, his breath close by.

"I can't," he whispered, but he did not move away.

I took his face in my hands and he opened his eyes.

"Tell me it's not what you want, that you don't love me, and I will not ask you again."

I was the first one to speak the word *love*, and I could see the shock of it go through him, as if I had spoken it into being, given shape to what stood between us. I had not fallen in love with Arthur, it had grown, I had sunk into it; if this was that, it was how I had read it in books, vertiginous and wild and sudden. I did not know if it was love, and I did not think I would know until I had had him, but it felt strong and undeniable and great. I thought it would be a love as great as the universe itself, if he would take the adventure of it with me. He shied back from me, slightly but not entirely. The thought struck me that I *could* choose. I had his face between my hands, and we were here alone. All my life men had chosen for me. I had sent a man I loved to war – a man I had loved as a child, not knowing that love was – and gone willingly to be Arthur's slave, if he had wished it, because all my life I had been told that my body belonged to my father, my brothers, my husband. I had been told my wishes meant nothing. Duty was everything. And if I had taken that boy I had loved as a girl into my bed, there would have been shame, perhaps, and people would have spoken of me as they spoke of Morgan, and perhaps I would not have loved him after all, but I would have known, and my life would not have been in the hands of someone else. I was long past that now, and choices in that were lost to me, but at last again the choice had come to me to seize my destiny in my hands. I was not a woman who could be owned. If Lancelot thought Arthur owned me he was wrong. I did not belong to either of them, to be passed between them. The blood of Maev ran in my veins and I would choose the lover *I* wanted.

I kissed Lancelot hard, feeling him startle, shocked by the fierceness of my kiss. But then I felt him yield and knew the rushing joy of conquest that Arthur must have known time and again. I twined my fingers deep into his hair, holding him fast against me, and slowly, stunned, he wrapped his arms around my back and pulled me to him. I felt light-headed with joy, with new-won pleasure. *I could have whatever I wanted.* His lips against mine were like velvet, soft and heady, giving way to my passion, and they parted with mine, deep and passionate. I felt him shiver, gently, with it.

When at last I sighed away from him, I felt the world all around me had changed, and the scents of spring that had once seemed like the last spring reached me with all their blossoming intensity. The flowers and the sunlight looked brighter, fresher. Lancelot still looked surprised, catching his breath. I felt the thrill of victory within me.

"Send for me," I said. "*I* shall be ready."

I stayed in the garden for a while, feeling the electric excitement and anticipation in the air all around me. When I felt calm, when I felt that I could hide the smile on my face and the thrill in my heart, I went back up to my rooms. When I looked through my books and saw that the little book of Ovid in French was gone, I felt the rush of joy and excitement flutter in me again. I was beginning to feel powerful and bold – giddy. I was free. I could do as I pleased. I had done it, crossed the line, and I was still here. No one would know. It was a heady rush, this feeling of freedom. *This must be what it feels like to be a man, doing always as you please.* No, it wouldn't be this good, because it wouldn't be secret and dangerous.

My body felt full of electric strength, full of the most delicious kind of yearning. I ran to the stables. Kay was there, and he gave me a sullen look, still angry that I had shouted at him. I barely saw him. I took my horse and jumped up onto her bare back, hitching the skirts of my dress above my knees. Kay opened his mouth to protest me riding off without saddle, weapon or accompaniment, but I was already gone. I didn't know where I was going, but I wanted to ride, fast, until I felt all the sensations of it running through me. Out in the fields outside the castle, some of the knights were training and they looked up as I rode past, but no one tried to stop me. I rode into the woods, looking for the light that dappled through the trees, the smells of wood and damp earth and the sound of the silence. I felt the wind tear my hair loose as I rode, and it fell about my shoulders. I breathed in the spring air deep into my lungs. I had not felt this alive in a long time, but now my blood felt new in my veins. I was seeing the green of the trees, I was tasting the breeze. It wrapped around me, the springtime and the potential that glimmered in the air, until that and the wind in my hair, and the thudding of the horse beneath me became one wonderful rush of joy.

When I got back to the stables, it was getting dark. I was flushed from the fresh air, and tired, but ecstatic. I thought I was alone, but as I slid off my horse, I saw Arthur, standing there, looking at me with a curious little smile on his face.
"You look wild," he said. He did not sound displeased. I felt wild. My body felt full of a daring strength, a vivid hunger. We were alone, and dark was falling around. I stepped forward and seized him by the shirt, pulling him into a fierce kiss. He, unexpecting, stumbled back and we fell into the straw. In slow disbelief, his reactions catching up slowly with what he had not expected, he pulled me more firmly onto him as I kissed him hungrily, madly. I felt charged with desire all over my body, and beneath me, I felt him swell in response. This was what it felt like to be him. Powerful, in control. I pulled his breeches open and slid my hand inside. Arthur groaned with pleasure and rolled us over so that he was on top of me, pushing up the skirts of my dress, rough with haste, burying his face in the hair at the nape of my neck. I could hear him breathing hard. He thrust into me then, and we both cried out in wordless pleasure. The straw caught in my loose hair and tangled there as I smelt around me the lovely freshness of it. The pleasure rose fast and urgent in me. I thought of Lancelot, of his lips on my neck, of his hands against my thigh, of the way he had yielded to my kiss. I heard instead of Arthur's ragged breaths at my ear, his soft voice speaking to me in the French I only half-understood. It came hard upon me, and sudden, the white-hot point of ecstasy that spread all though me, as I sighed down into the straw, and Arthur fast after me. We lay there, gasping for breath, and I ran my fingers through his hair, thoughtfully. As the sensations of our love receded around me, I was left with the cold, clammy feeling of guilt. What kind of woman was I, that could lie with one man, thinking of another? Did *everyone* do this? It was too easy. That was what made me feel guilty. Too easy to love two men at once. Because I still loved Arthur, and I had wanted his hands on me for his own sake. He kissed me lovingly, and I felt, awful as it was, the guilt melt away into happiness. Having everything could really be having *everything*, perhaps.

As I was just brushing the straw from the back of my dress and Arthur was rubbing the stalks of straw from his hair, Kay rode in and jumped from his horse. *How did he get everywhere?* Arthur and he exchanged an easy smile and Arthur, excusing himself to meet in council with Nimue and Gawain, gave him a brotherly pat on the shoulder as he walked by.

"Kay..." I began, uneasily. I wasn't sure, really, how sorry I was, because he had been unkind about Gareth, and I knew his well-meaning taunts really upset the boy, so I shied away from apologising directly. He gave a forgiving nod.

"Christine told me you weren't well. I shouldn't have teased you when you were short of patience." His reply was also not quite an apology. *Christine told me.* Hmmm. What had Christine told him? But then I realised he must have ridden out looking for me. He had been worried to see me go. I forgave him a little more, then.

Suddenly he laughed, and leapt towards me. I instinctively jumped back, but I did not have far to go, and he caught me against the wall. I gave a little unconscious laugh in response, but I did not know *why* he was laughing. Then he reached over and pulled a piece of straw from my hair. He gave an arch smile, and lifted an eyebrow at me, still close.

"Hmmmm." He made a little noise – I could not tell whether it was mocking or approving. I batted his hand, holding the stalk of straw, away, but I was smiling. It was a deep and secret smile.

Chapter Twenty-One

I passed the days as I waited for my little book of Ovid to return to me in a kind of luxurious trance. Spring turned to summer around me, and every day seemed full of the promise of news. At first I had hoped it would be soon, but then I thought I would be glad of him sending for me on his return, when this 'giant' was dead, and he was safe and when I had all of these days of tingling anticipation building up around me. And yet, though I dreamed of Lancelot day and night, I went to bed with Arthur, and the excitement of waiting filled me with a fire for him as well. And those nights when I was alone, when Arthur was with his knights, or perhaps with some other woman, in the darkness I would slide my hand between my legs, and think of Lancelot, of his lithe sensuality, his lips soft yet urgent on mine, the moment he had given his will to mine in the garden; and sometimes I thought of Arthur, the feel of his strength around me, the rough urgency of his love.

But word did not come. As summer ripened to its fullness and the big orange sun hung fat and hot in the sky, I still lacked my little book of Ovid. It was a particularly hot summer, and it felt oppressive. I lay in my garden day after day in the shade of my little rose-tree that was drying out, miserably, in the heat, and listened to little Marie read in Breton in her chirping little voice, or Christine in her gentle, motherly voice, or sometimes Kay or Gareth reading in English. I did not like the English so much, but I liked it when the garden was full of people. The noise and the laughter distracted me from my thoughts, which were turning from giddy anticipation to a nervous fear. It went on so long that Marie noticed that my little french Ovid was missing and told Arthur. Arthur had suggested I send to Morgan and ask her to teach me Latin, so that I could read it properly anyway. She had grown up in a convent and, he assured me, would be able to teach me well. I didn't want to let her unsettling presence into my little enchanted summer, and I told him I did not want to. I went, as often as I could, to lie on the Round Table and wish for the return of my book of Ovid, but it did not come.

He had not returned without it, and no word had come of his death. I did not know what it could mean, this awful silence. Arthur, too, missed him and began to complain of his absence. The company of knights was not the same, he said, if one was missing.

"He must have killed that dragon by now," Arthur grumbled.

"Giant," I corrected.

Arthur shrugged his shoulders. "Whatever Mark thinks he saw."

Then the news came. But it did not come to me. It came to Arthur. It had come to him in the morning, and evidently he had been waiting with excitement to announce it when we were gathered to eat in the evening. It was a day when we all eating at the high table in the great hall. It must have been one of the Feasts of the Hanged Christ, but I never paid attention in chapel, which Arthur only asked me to accompany him to once a week. Often, I just stared up at the sad face of Christ, drooping before me on his cross and wondered why people would worship such a miserable god. Also, they kept calling the cross a *tree*, and if it really was meant to be a *tree* then I did not see how Arthur's Christ was any different from my Hanged God in the slightest.

We had eaten a wonderful dinner of fresh fish, and green vegetables, and little soft potatoes in butter that melted in the mouth. I felt happy, festive almost. I remembered that moment clearly. Kay had just handed me a lovely ripe peach and I was just about to lift it to my lips when Arthur lifted a hand for silence. He smiled around at the group of knights, and Nimue and me. I could see he was excited.

"I've had word from Lancelot. He is returning. Tonight." The men all cheered, and Nimue gave a demure little smile. I smiled too, but I knew mine was unsteady. I didn't know how I felt about this. I wanted to see him again, but if he was returning without sending for me with the book, had he rejected me? I had been so sure that he would not. "Wait – there's more." He looked as though he was straining not to shout it out across the room. "He is bringing a woman with him – *a woman who is carrying his child.*"

I heard a roaring silence in my ears. It wasn't true. It couldn't be. And on top of it all *a child*. Whoever that woman was she had what was rightfully mine, twice over. I felt a heavy core of rage grow inside me. I felt something dripping down my arm and looked to see that I had dug my fingers into the peach I was holding, ripping it to pieces.

I stood up slowly, shaking with anger, and held up a hand, automatic, to pat my hair, to check it was in place. I didn't care, but something about the gesture was comforting. Oh, I would go like a queen to this. I thought, perhaps, that I might kill him. I breathed in deeply, and felt the rage inside me cool to a dangerous, heavy calm. Kay reached for my hand, but I excused myself. I felt Arthur's gaze follow me from the room. I could sense his concern. He knew I would be upset about the child, of course. That still hurt. Unconsciously, I pressed a hand to my stomach, feeling what was gone, and holding myself together.

When I was out in the night air I stopped for a moment, to check that I had on me the dagger I always carried. It was there, cool and comforting to the touch. I looked over to the stables. They were dark and quiet. Perhaps he was not back yet. I walked slowly up to my room. Each step was an effort, each moment that I was holding myself under steely control. I would not stand for this. I would not wait and hope and *dream* and be betrayed. That was the worst. The feeling foolish. I had no intention of being taken for a fool.

I hoped to be alone when I got back to my chamber, but when I opened the door it was onto Lancelot, standing framed in the open window, the night sky clear with a moon yawning full beside him. I had not been prepared to see him, I had not had time to gather myself. It all rushed at me. The sight of him, moonlight in the dark hair that I had felt between my fingers, as soft as a kiss, the way he stood, lithe and ready. It made it all rush back to me, unbearably potent, as though his lips had just been on my neck, as though his body had just been pressed against mine, and his voice at my ear, and suddenly I was gasping for breath, my head swimming with the memories. Seeing me like this, Lancelot stepped forward, towards me. The anger of betrayal flared within me, and, slamming the door shut behind me with one hand, drawing the dagger with the other, I jumped back from him.

"*Don't touch me,*" I shouted.

"Guinevere –" He held his arms out towards me in helpless appeal.

"I should never have trusted you. You're a man without honour. It wasn't so very hard for you to break your oaths to Arthur, was it? And you treated me just the same. What is a coward knight with no honour worth? No, *don't touch me.*" He had stepped forward again, only slightly, but I was not going to give my ground. He looked defeated, drained. But I would not melt before his sadness. He had lied to me.

"Please, Guinevere, let me explain."

I did not answer, nor did I move, or lower the dagger, though I did not doubt that if he were serious about defending himself from me he could. He still had his sword at his side, and even if he did not, he could have taken the dagger from me as easily as from a child. Still, shaking with my anger though I was, I felt better with it in my hand.

"Guinevere, *I thought it was you.* Your book. I sent you your book, and I waited for you in my pavilion in the forest. You came to me – or, I thought it was you. It was dark, it was night, and I was *sure* it was you. But, when I woke in the morning, it wasn't. It was once, only once." The distress, the confusion, the utter loss of control he had suffered showed on his face, and my resolve was weakening. I lowered the dagger slightly.

"Why did you have to bring her here?" I demanded, hearing the petulance in my own voice, but I felt I had a right to it.

He shook his head in defeat.

"Her father is one of Arthur's vassal lords. She said she was a *virgin*, before. I didn't have a choice. It was bring her here or start a war. I hoped I would get to you before his messengers, to tell you. Guinevere, I'm so sorry."

"Are you going to marry her?" I asked in a very small voice.

"No, no, of course not." He drew me into his arms and I did not resist, though I still held myself wary. He kissed me, once, lightly on the neck, and I closed my eyes, feeling my resistance slip away. "I only thought of you the whole time I was away. I dreamed of you. I am so sorry, so sorry."

He kissed me again, and I melted into it, feeling again what I had dreamed of so long. He held me close against him, kissing my neck, up, coming to kiss me on the lips, slow and delicious. After a moment, I pushed him gently away.

"No, not now. Come to me tomorrow, and I will make sure we are safe."

Arthur was, I was sure, close behind me, ready to offer me the only kind of comfort he knew.

"Tomorrow?" He sounded shocked, but did not disagree. I suddenly felt that time was short, and if we did not come together soon, then I would miss the chance forever. Already too much had come between us, and my patience was too thin now for prudence.

"Tomorrow," I replied.

Chapter Twenty-Two

The next day I woke as soon as I felt the tickle of the morning sun against my eyelids. I woke with my heart racing with almost unbearable anticipation. I did not know how I would wait until night. Arthur had come to me the night before, full of concern, and himself reminded of the loss of our child. We had fallen together, as we always did, but it had given more comfort to him than to me, and I had lain awake half the night, staring into the thick darkness, my head full of thoughts that would not be still.

I got up while he was still sleeping and sat by the window, looking down at the little garden below. Before tonight would be today, and today Lancelot was bringing Isolde of Cornwall and this Elaine into the city. I had a cold dread lingering in my stomach despite the warmth of the day. Through the open window I could smell the lovely roses and little honeysuckles down in the garden. I could hear the chatter down there, soft and bubbling like a little stream over pebbles, of Marie, Margery and Christine. I wished I was down there with them, not waiting up here for one of them to bring me whatever dress I would have to wear to greet Isolde like a proper queen. The proper *Breton* queens would have greeted others dressed in leathers and armed, like the vassal kings of Britain came before Arthur, but if I did that here, they would know me for a barbarian, a savage. It was more savage and strange, I thought, all those heavy layers of damask and samite, all the strange ceremonial bowing and waving. But Isolde was born in Ireland. Maybe she, too, was the blood of Maev. Maybe there was someone coming into the heart of Camelot who would be like the women I remembered from home. Christine and Marie, too, had changed themselves for Camelot and I often missed the sights of home.

At last, it seemed, though perhaps it had not been so long, because the sun was still fresh and pale in the sky, not yet climbing up towards noon and the midday heat, Arthur woke, and left me with a glancing kiss to make himself ready for the arrival. Marie and Christine hurried in then with some lovely, sweet fruits for me to eat, and clothes for me to wear. The dress was, mercifully, thin summer silk in a light sky-blue and embroidered all over in little silver thread flowers, close down to the wrists and across the bodice, and cut low and square at the neck. The skirt parted in the centre to show the white silk underskirt beneath, and little peeps of it glimpsed through the lacing of the bodice at the front. Marie tied up my hair and wrapped it in the little gold net, pinning it into place. The crown they brought was the crown of snakes and I waved it away. I did not want to look at it again; it seemed like bad luck. I took instead the little circlet of ivy leaves I had come with. Perhaps if Isolde were as I hoped, she would recognise it. In any case, it was the only one I had that was not too heavy.

I squinted into the silver mirror Christine held up before me. I had no idea if I looked right, if I looked queenly enough. I had never really seen another British queen, except Morgawse, and I knew from what people said that the northlands were considered rough and barbaric. Oh, and Morgan, while her old husband had lived; but she had always been dressed like a druid, and I did not think I too ought to paint myself with woad. Besides, there was no right way to look before Elaine. I would rather have come before *her* in my leathers and armed. Meeting her, I was ready to meet an enemy.

When trumpets sounded the arrival of the visitors, I walked down the stairs with Marie and Christine, dressed in the finest dresses they owned, and Margery came to join us from my little public room, still missing its little book of Ovid. She had a little white silk cloth wrapped around her hair, and I wondered if we should do the same. I was dimly annoyed that Margery, who was the one who knew the customs of Logrys as her own, had not come that morning.

At the bottom of the stairs, Kay and Gareth were waiting. Kay took my hand and kissed it lightly. I smiled to see him. At the least, he was always cheerful, and somehow having him by my side made me feel better. It was the comforting sense of the Otherworld about him, which was my feeling, partly, of home, of my father's study and the table. I somehow felt that he would be an ally to me against this woman who came bearing Lancelot's child. I could not have said why. He did a little bow, which was only half-sincere.

"You look lovely, my queen."

Gareth bowed as well and said the same. I laughed.

"You don't have to do that in here, where no one is watching," I replied.

We went out into the courtyard, where Arthur was standing with Gawain, Lamerocke and Dinadan. Perceval would be in the chapel, where he was almost every day. When that man was not fighting, he was praying. I did not think I had ever seen him smile.

I went over to Arthur with the others and he took my hand with a little incline of the head. He was learning fast this new role of a grand king, though I was sure he would not lose the part of him that was a warrior. He knew peace was good, and ceremony and power, but I was sure that something inside him would always yearn for battle.

I turned towards the gates, where I could hear the sound of horses from outside. I felt the nervous flutter in my stomach. I would see, now, the woman who had taken my place. The sun was hot against my face, rising towards its zenith, and I could feel in the heat, sweat gathering in at the base of my back, on my brow. The knights in armour around us shifted uncomfortably, and I suspected Arthur would for once be glad of his ceremonial brocade surcoat, red with his father's dragon sewn in gold, rather than the iron of platemail.

At last the gates came apart. At first I saw only Lancelot, who had slipped away back to his camp last night, so as to arrive with the women he brought, riding on a huge armoured warhorse. Behind him, I could see two lovely white ponies, and flashes of coloured silk on top of them, the two women. He rode without his helm, though he was armoured, and the sight of him again was a wonderful relief to the part of me that felt I had dreamed him in my room last night. He slid from his horse, giving it to Gareth to take to the stables, and came before Arthur and me. Arthur pulled him into a rough embrace and slapped him heartily on the back. They kissed each other on each cheek and embraced again.

"You have been too long away," Arthur told him, and he nodded and smiled.

He turned to me, and kissed my hand with a little bow and a soft, "My lady."

The touch of his hand on mine sent a shock through me that I did not expect. I felt my face flush and my head spin for a moment. He moved away without meeting my eyes, but I felt, as though it was burned into my skin, the touch of his lips on the back of my hand. It was not long, not long now. It would be easier when longing was transformed to secrecy, I felt sure of it. And I needed only to wait until tonight.

He returned to the women on the horses. One of them was already sliding off hers, but awkwardly, one foot caught in a stirrup, making her pony stumble a little. All I could see of her was a flash of pale blonde hair from her bent head, with a little golden coronet on top, and her slender figure dressed in a gauzy dress of light pink silk. She must have been Isolde. The other woman Lancelot went to first and lifted down from her horse. I felt the ugly prickle of jealousy within me, and I knew I could not look on her without hating her. Seeing his hands around her little waist lifting her down from the saddle made me feel sick, feel raw with an anger that was beyond words, and I knew there was nothing I could do. She was small and doe-eyed with soft brown hair wound up at the nape of her neck. She was dressed simply in a green silk dress, and under the hand that rested on her stomach was the unmistakable early swell of a child. Where my features were strong and proud, hers were ladylike and delicate, and where I was lean and lightly muscled I could see the demure little frame of her body move with a perfect grace. *Perfect lady she may be*, I thought, *but she does not look as though she would win if it came to a fight.* This gave me a wicked little thrill.

Isolde came forward towards us first and I was sorry to see nothing of Maev in the girl. She was beautiful, for sure, with big blue eyes like pools, and full pink lips, and soft, full breasts that the draping fabric of her dress made obvious, but it seemed that Kay was right in his estimation of the girl as *simple*. She seemed sweet enough and kind, and curtseyed to Arthur and me, graciously accepting his avowal of her beauty and a kiss on her cheek with a decorous little blush. I was disappointed that the sight of Isolde was not a little glimpse of home, but I was resolved to be kind and I took her hand in both of mine and bid her welcome. Her smile was warm and trusting, her kiss of my cheek dry and papery. I was not sure if her seeming simpleness was just the result of innocence, because up close I could see that despite her shape she was many years younger than I was, perhaps younger even than when I had married Arthur. I was pleased to have her stand beside me. It made me feel stronger as Lancelot approached with Elaine. I could hear people whispering. I could hear Marie and Christine whispering in Breton. I should have liked to have been whispering with them. I heard Marie use the Breton word for 'witch'.

Arthur took Elaine's hand and kissed her on the cheek.

"Camelot is lucky to receive two such rare beauties today," he told her. So Arthur thought her beautiful, too. He grinned past her at Lancelot, and I knew he was not just being courteous. She slipped her hand from Lancelot's and walked over to me, as Lancelot talked with Arthur. I imagined Arthur would soon want to lead him away, and hear all of the stories he had longed to hear, of the fighting and the adventuring, and perhaps also the story of Elaine, though I doubted it was one that Lancelot would be willing to tell. He was not, I suspected, a very good liar.

I took Elaine's hand with a smile I was sure must have seemed brittle and cold, but when I met her eyes – lovely, dark and gentle – I had a sickening sense in the pit of my stomach that I did not think had anything to do with jealousy. *Witch.* It only lasted a moment, but it was an almost unbearable sensation of the darkest place of the Otherworld. It was the smell of death that hung around the barrow-lands. It passed in a moment, the acuteness of the sensation, but the sense of it lingered about me. Surely I could not have imagined it out of irrational hate? The girl seemed benign enough, with her big eyes and sweet little mouth. She was, though, almost a head shorter than me, and tiny as bird, like Marie, so I did not know how Lancelot had mistaken her for me. I was beginning, looking at her, to doubt his excuse. She was nothing like me, and any man would have desired her for her own charms.

I kissed her on the cheek, and she did the same. I moved through the courtesies, detached, my mind elsewhere, as she did the same; we commended each other on our beauty and curtseyed.

I was glad when I could suggest the ladies repair to my little walled garden. Servants had laid out silk rugs and little cushions, and there was already a minstrel with a lute. I would have preferred to lie on the grass and feel its little stalks against my skin, smell its light, fresh smell, and read my Breton books with Christine and Marie, but the greatest ceremony must be given for Isolde of Cornwall I supposed. We did not want to appear rustic or simple.

I invited her to sit beside me, patting the little pink cushion I had reclined beside and she came. I was happy to let Margery chatter with Elaine on the other side of the garden, where I could watch her out of the corner of my eye. I suddenly wished that Kay was with us. He would know. He would be able to feel it, too, and tell me if I had imagined it. I did not know why, if it were truly so, that she was a creature from the depths of the Otherworld, and I had felt it only for a moment.

The lute player began a tune, and a song that I knew well enough about Brutus driving the giants from Britain and giving it his name, and I lay back with a sigh against the cushions, closing my eyes against the bright heat of the sun. I wished I was with the men. I wanted to be hearing about giant-killing and adventure, or hunting in the forest. I did *not* want to be sat in my little walled garden avoiding being polite to Elaine.

I put a hand over my eyes to shield them from the sun, and peered at Isolde. She was watching the lute-player with rapture. Cornwall must have been rich, because her golden coronet was studded with sapphires from the far east, and lots of lovely shimmering pearls, and around her neck hung a long sapphire pendant. She *was* young. Fifteen, sixteen perhaps? Even younger than I had thought her at first. Her skin was pure white and perfect as marble, her light blonde hair glowed in its thick glossy plait that trailed down past her shoulder and rested on one breast in the midday sun. She was lovely, there was no denying that.

"Was your journey pleasant?" I asked her.

She turned to me as though she had been jolted from her thoughts and a slow smile spread across her face. She leaned in close to me, and whispered.

"Very pleasant my lady. And you should know, they say there are but four great lovers in this world, Sir Tristan and myself, and Sir Lancelot and Queen Guinevere."

I pushed myself up onto my elbows, the nerves jangling within me.

"I don't know what you're talking about," I replied, cooly. *What had Lancelot said?* What she was saying was dangerous. I knew Sir Tristan as her own husband's nephew. So what Lamerocke had said had been true. And what Kay said. The girl *was* simple.

"Of course, my lady." Isolde lowered her eyes from mine, but not without giving me a dumb smile of complicity. I had to get her out of court. If she was going to be jabbering to people like an idiot about *lovers* then I could not have her here. It hurt all the more how much I wished it were true.

"Where is Tristan now?" I asked eventually, desperate for any distraction.

She smiled broadly, as though she had been waiting for the question. It was as though dawn had broken across her face, it was so written with joy. The girl was no born liar, lacked any ability to hide her feelings. That shocked me suddenly, that I was looking on her honesty with scorn. I was proud already of my ability to lie, to hide, to be two women at once. This simpleton was a better woman than I, honest in the truth of her feelings. But she would not survive on it, surely. Though the reach of Mark's revenge would never be so broad as that of Arthur, I was sure.

She leaned close again, excited.

"He waits for me at Joyous Guard."

Joyous Guard. That was Lancelot's castle, out on the borderlands to the west. So he was helping her play this dangerous game. But it was no castle for lovers, it was a siege fortress. Perhaps Tristan and Isolde would survive with Lancelot's help. I could not imagine Mark even with all the might of Cornwall being able to fetch them from Joyous Guard.

I nodded, and patted her hand with mine.

"I hope you two will be safe there." I could not help but smile at her. The world was simple to her. Her husband was cruel, so she would run away. And Mark *was* cruel. Or seemed so from what people said. In a jealous rage he had already tried to have her burned at the stake once in a year of marriage, and often he locked her away. Mark must be more than twice her age. I suppose I could not blame her if the young nephew was more to her liking, and if she too desired the right to choose. But she had been rash, and she had been reckless, and she had brought her danger home to me.

"Do you sing, Isolde?" I asked her.

She nodded, shyly.

I wanted to distract her, to stop her talking, and so I asked her to sing for us. The lute player knew the tune she asked for, and she began to sing. Her voice was lovely, soft and low, more complex and mature than I would have expected, full of light and shade, and she sang beautifully. Partly, it was her innocence, as she closed her eyes with the song, but it was also a deep and knowing understanding of the music. Her soft pink lips moved invitingly as she sang and I could see why men found them so attractive. I did not think my angry little red mouth could ever have looked so enticing.

Then, a few minutes into the song, I heard giggling in the corner of the garden. I turned to see Elaine and Margery whispering together. Elaine was laughing and Margery was smiling with her eyes wide. I felt the rage flare within me. Elaine clearly felt she had the right to everything that was mine. I stood and strode over. I expected Isolde to stop singing, but she was lost in the music, and in part I was glad of it. I felt Christine's eyes on me in warning as I went, but I ignored her. I grabbed Elaine by the arm and pulled her to her feet.

She made a pitiful little face of pain that I did not think was entirely sincere. Margery jumped to her feet, too, nervous and wary.

"What amuses you two ladies so?" I asked, my voice bristling with forced courtesy that did not match my actions, my hand still clamped around Elaine's little arm. Margery's mouth flapped open and shut, like a fish's.

"Forgive me," began Elaine, fixing me with her gaze, and there I saw again what I had expected. No innocence there, but a dark pleasure in her gaze, and a malicious knowledge. *Good.* I was ready for a fight, and an innocent opponent was no opponent at all. "I was telling Margery of the love of Sir Lancelot." The girl even managed to force a demure blush. "I know I should not speak in public of such things, but he was so tender. So," she drew her breath in, enjoying herself, "*manful*, I –"

Before I realised what I had done, I slapped her hard across the face. I was not sorry. As my hand made contact, I felt the empty space of the dark Otherworld inside her, and I knew I was right. Margery gasped, but Elaine smiled, a smile just for me, full of perverse victory and wicked delight. She would not smile that way for long. High on her cheekbone, her olive skin was already reddening.

I realised that Isolde had stopped singing, and there was quiet all around us. I let go of Elaine's arm and stepped back. Isolde's mouth hung open, in a big round 'o'. Even her surprise was picture-perfect. I raised a hand to my hair, patting it gently in place, and breathed in slowly.

"I think I will retire to my chamber," I declared.

But I did not go to my chamber. I went to Arthur's room, to fetch Excalibur. I was relieved he was not in his room, but there Excalibur was, beside the bed. I was the only one the guard would let up to this tower alone, so he felt safe leaving it there, and he liked to have it beside him as he slept, afraid always of losing it again. I slid it from its sheath and looked at it. Arthur held it in both hands, as though it weighed as much as all the other broadswords, but I could lift it easily in one. Excalibur had been forged in the Otherworld, and the sword recognised the Otherworld blood in me, yielding its strength to my touch. If I had ever held the false sword, I would have known it for what it was, but I knew this one was true. I slid it back into the scabbard and slipped down the stairs to Arthur's council chamber and the Round Table. I hid the sword behind one of the chairs at the back, where I would know where to find it. Tonight, I would bring Elaine there, and with the sword and table I knew I would have the power to make her give up her secrets. Somehow bringing her, and the child that ought to have been mine, back to the Round Table felt like the right thing to do.

As I went to leave, the door opened, and Lancelot walked in. Caught off guard, not expecting to see me, he looked shaken, but not displeased.

"I'm sorry – I came to –"

"The table?" I asked. He nodded. So he knew its power, too. He shut the door lightly behind him, and my heart jumped within me. *Now? Would it be now?* I had not planned for this; I was not sure that no one would come, and yet to wait another moment and risk the losing of it was too unbearable to think of.

We moved towards each other, both tentative, both filled with a delicate daring. He reached out a hand towards me, and I rushed into his arms, our lips meeting in desperate longing. I felt sparks of light rise inside me, and a wonderful rush of *finally*. I buried my hands in his hair, pulling him closer against me, losing myself in the intoxicating whirl of desire, feeling his hand at the base of my back, holding me tight against him, and the other, lightly brushing against the bare skin at the neck of my dress, then my neck, then down over my dress, his touch even through the fabric filling me with a desperate heat.

The door opened and we parted as suddenly as we had come together. I closed my eyes, cursing again the lost moment, feeling still around me, like a cloud, like a fading dream, the intense heady promise of his touch. The door was heavy, and opened in, so by the time Kay stepped through it, we stood apart, Lancelot leaning against the back of a chair and me, sat perched against the table. Kay fixed me with an odd look as he came in, a look I could not read, and it chased away the warm haze of joy I felt about me, and made me shiver. It was as though he saw into me, and was dismayed at what he found. Arthur came in fast after him, and Gawain and Perceval and Lamerocke and Dinadan. Arthur gave a cry of joy when he saw Lancelot, who he noticed before he noticed me –

"Lancelot! I've been looking for you. Come, join us, we're deciding where to ride out and hunt tomorrow. I'm tired of that same forest."

Lancelot nodded mutely. Arthur saw me then, and smiled. He strode over and kissed me lightly. He did not taste another man on my lips, nor feel the heat inside me, just as he had not seen what Kay had seen in the same room. Perhaps it was because he did not want to see.

"I'm afraid there will be no hunting for you, my love," he told me. "You have to stay and entertain Isolde, until Mark sends to say he wants her back."

I glanced at Lancelot then, who gave a tiny shake of his head. *Arthur was not to know about Tristan, hiding at Joyous Guard.*

"Of course," I replied, leaning up onto my tiptoes to kiss him softly, and before I could catch Kay's eye again I slipped from the room. I hoped they did not notice Excalibur and move it back.

When we dined that night, it was a more elaborate feast than we had ever had – perhaps so that Isolde would go back to Cornwall telling them what great power resided in Camelot – but I barely tasted it. Elaine sat beside Lancelot, and he was ever attentive and kind to her. I knew there was nothing else he could do, but I wished that earlier I had told him what I feared about her. Perhaps he would not have believed me; perhaps he would have thought me mad with jealousy. I knew I was right.

I was sat between Arthur and Kay, though I wished that I had been by Isolde who was on Kay's other side. I felt his eyes on me, and on Lancelot. I would rather have taken the simple girl and her sweet voice and happy smiles. Shrewd Kay saw everything, and now he had seen the truth. The strong wine did not ease my anxieties, though it did stop Arthur from noticing them, as he laughed and joked with Gawain and Lamerocke. Kay was quiet and serious, but no one seemed to notice. I wished, too, that Nimue was at court. She came and went like a cat, suiting only herself. As the sweet cakes came, Kay draped an arm over the back of my chair, and leaned down to whisper in my ear.

"I hope you know what you're doing."

I turned and looked at him with an even stare. He hadn't actually *seen* anything, he didn't *know* anything. He had only his suspicions. But I did want his help.

"She's from the barrows," I told him. He knew what I meant. His lip curled in disdain. He tilted his head towards her.

"That little doe?" he laughed, cruelly. "I hardly think so."

I felt the blood rise in my face. He was the only person who could have helped me.

"If you touch her, you'll see."

"Just a word of friendly warning to your champion, was it, that I caught you at earlier?" he asked with a mean, cynical smile. I gave him a narrow look and turned away, taking up my cup of wine again. If he would not help me, I was capable of helping myself.

I left the feast as soon as the eating was done. I had barely eaten at all, my stomach too full with anticipation, and nervousness. Lancelot had seen my look towards him as I left, and I was sure he would come. Kay had seen it, too, but I did not care. It would be safe enough, to see Lancelot once, and then I could carry the memory the rest of my life at the centre of me, like a hidden jewel. I was sure it would be enough.

Chapter Twenty-Three

But he did not come. Neither did Arthur, though I did not expect that. On feasting days like that he was more likely to stay down in the hall drinking with Gawain and his brothers, and the cheery Dinadan, and Lamerocke – who after wine grew garrulous and even more pompous, but whose long tales Arthur always liked – than to come up to me. If he did come, it would be late, and he would be drunk. I did not really mind. But Lancelot did not come, and that I did mind.

I lay there, listening to the sounds of revelry dying away across the courtyard, and looking out of my window, open to the warm summer air, watching the full moon rise. *Why did he not come?* Had Kay stopped him? What business was this of Kay's, anyway?

I heard noise in the room beside my own, the noise of a woman's voice, and a man's. The room I had given to Elaine, wanting to keep my eye on her. I lay on my bed, still fully dressed, paralysed by the anger pulsing through me, listening to the sounds that filtered through the thick wall. They were unmistakably the sounds of a man and woman *together*. I was shaking with anger when I finally stood, freed from the paralysis of my anger when I heard the sounds suddenly stop, and strode to the door, my head buzzing with every furious accusation I was about to make, but when I got to my door and wrenched it open the sight that I met with was the sight of myself.

There I stood, looking at me, my hair loose around my shoulders, dressed in my bedclothes, a light flush on my cheeks. The deep green eyes were my own, and the dark red lips against the white skin, and yet it was not me. *I* was me. This was the witch. I grabbed the figure of myself by the hair, and saw a sudden flicker, a sudden slip of the mask of my own face, and through the illusion on the skin of my own face, for a second, I saw the blue lines of woad tracing in whorls. *Morgan.* In my grip, the figure of me changed to Elaine, and the hair in my hand from thick red to silky brown, but I did not let go. She began to cry out in pitiful little wails, but I had no pity now I knew who she was. She wriggled and kicked, but hiding her shape had obviously drained the strength from Morgan and it was easy for me to drag her down the stairs, across the courtyard and up to the room with the Round Table. It was the dead of night, by then, but I could hear far away the dim noises of knights still in the great hall. I was glad of that, because I would not run in to them.

When we got to the room, I threw her inside and slammed the door behind us, rushing to Excalibur and drawing it. Elaine backed into the corner of the room, whimpering.

"Please," she begged, "please don't hurt me. I don't know what I have done wrong."

I advanced towards her, the sword drawn and pointing towards that smug swollen belly that she covered with her hand. When she saw I would not be fooled, her face changed to a cruel smile.

"What kind of woman are you, good queen? You have Arthur. Women all over this realm pray every night for a man such as him, and yet you long for another. But you do not love him enough to let him be happy with some other woman, but you must draw Lancelot ever back to you. You desire only to possess him."

"Get on the table." I took another step towards her, and she flinched. I felt Excalibur begin to vibrate in my hands from the Otherworld strength now coming off her like a wave of stench.

She shook her head, stubbornly, but as I moved towards her I could see the patterns of woad showing through on her cheeks, I could see the illusion slipping.

I heard the door open behind me, but I did not give ground. I knew who it would be. Lancelot come to follow the screaming, Lancelot slow to put the pieces of this together, unsuspecting of a trick against himself. But I had seen. I should have warned him, but he probably would not have believed me.

"Guinevere, what are you doing!?" He ran towards me, and moved to take the sword, but I stepped away. "Guinevere, please, let her go – she hasn't done anything wrong – stop!"

He looked at me. I saw confusion flash across his face as he noticed that I was still fully dressed in the blue gown I had worn all day, my hair still braided and pinned.

"Who was with you, just now?" I asked him, with all the effort I could muster to hold it below a shout.

"You," he replied, quietly, sounding unsure.

I took another step towards Elaine with Excalibur, and she had nowhere further back to go. The lines of woad on her face were darkening, her hair beginning to show black beneath the brown; she seemed to grow taller before me. Lancelot looked on in silent shock.

"Get on the table," I insisted.

By the time she stepped up onto it and kneeled, Morgan was in her own form. Unmistakable. Her black hair fell long and loose around her, and her white skin etched with blue glowed eerily in the candlelight where it showed at the open neck of my nightdress. I had not been wrong to smell the barrow-lands about her. But, what had not been illusion was the swell at her stomach. No, that was real enough. Some desperate place hidden away inside me had hoped that was only part of the trick, I stepped towards her, raising Excalibur, but as I did so, with a final grin of triumph she dissipated into dust, as Merlin had done, and dissolved into the night.

I let the sword fall by my side, shaking. The truth was just as bad as the illusion. Lancelot reached towards me, but I pushed him gently away. I could feel the tears gathering in my eyes.

"You thought *she* was me."

"Guinevere..."

I could see he was sad; I could see he was sorry. I could see that he was a victim of this, that he had been an innocent in it all, but I could not bear the thought of him with her. I could not bear it. She had taken my place, twice; she had taken the moment that I had longed for with him, and the child that should have been mine. *How had he not known it was not me?* He should have known. He should have known. We had been so close, and it had slipped through my fingers, unbearably evanescent. He had let it be taken from me, by Morgan. I had lived on this for months, all the time he was away, the promise of him, and Morgan had taken it from me so easily. I did not think I could sustain another missed moment, I didn't think my body could take the hope and then the disappointment again. My heart ached within me. I had betrayed Arthur, if not in the deed than in the desire, I had begun to become someone else, all to have him. I had told myself that it would be worth it; I had told myself that no one would come to harm. And Arthur all the while had given me good, wholesome love, without question. Did I want this? Did I want a love so great that it tore me to pieces? Did I want something that I could not have? Was I supposed to be in this much pain? Better to live with the simple, domestic love Arthur had to offer me, than to throw myself into more and more hurt to have something that threatened to swallow me up. Perhaps I was as much of a fool as Isolde to think that I could live in innocence with it all, to think that it could ever be.

Lancelot stepped towards me, and I put up a hand to stop him. I drew in a slow, quivering breath, stepping further away from him.

"I want you to go," I said.

Part II
A Champion's Duty

Chapter Twenty-Four

I had thought that sending Lancelot from the court would send the whole mess of what had happened away with him. I was wrong. I felt hollowed out; all my hopes had gone with him, everything that had knotted at the centre of me in that exquisite mix of fear and longing, but everything else, everything heavy and complex with regret, had been left behind. I had told myself that I would go back to how I had been. I had told myself that Arthur could be enough to me once more. But I had tasted enough to be unable to forget.

My fingers remembered the feel of Lancelot's hair, the brush of his skin. My lips, his lips. I had thought, too, that sending him from me would spare me the pain of playing what had happened between us over and over again in my head, but I had been wrong about that as well. The moment when he had kissed me first, and we had almost come together, and the moment in the garden with all the blossoms of spring when I had grasped him close, and he had given in to my desire. They were sweet, and bright and painful, and with them, I could not forget the moment he had ridden back into Camelot with Elaine – with *Morgan* – pregnant with his child, and when she had smiled and disappeared, and I was sick with her victory, and I had not had it in me to bear another frustration. I had not had the strength in me, the heart, to hope, and suffer, and have Lancelot snatched from me one more time. I had let him go. I had, in my anger and betrayal and frustration, given up.

By the next morning he had already gone, taking Isolde with him on to Joyous Guard. Arthur complained that he had left so soon and I nodded absently in agreement. Kay's gaze on me now was gentle, and sympathetic, and he sat often with me and Christine in the garden. In turns they read as I lay under the rose tree, staring up at the winking sun through the waving leaves, wishing that none of it had ever happened, and that I would open my eyes, a girl of sixteen again, lying in the woodlands around Carhais, tired from hunting, and watching the big yellow eye of the sun sink slowly towards the horizon with nowhere to be, and no one to please. When Arthur asked why Lancelot had left so soon, I'd told him that he had to take

Elaine back to her father's, and Isolde back to Mark. I wondered vaguely what would happen when Mark eventually sent for his wife, and found that she was long gone.

Some days Kay sat beneath the may tree with a big book open against his knees, his sword lying by his side but forgotten, reading in a lazy, clumsy Breton that Christine had to keep correcting, pointing at the letters on the page and clicking her tongue. It didn't make all that much sense to the ear, and I wondered if Kay could read as well as he said he could – for Arthur when we married had read slow and like a child and they had been raised by the same parents – but it was pleasant enough watching them; and Marie sat beside me, sewing busily with her deft little fingers, and I reclined in the shade, longing for the heat to break and autumn to come, or at least some rain. Some days I lay in the garden alone, reading, or if the heat was not too much, rode out to hunt alone in the forest. I never found my little book of Ovid. Most days we just lay in the garden shade, wishing the time away. The heat only increased the unbearable length of the days and made me feel more weary.

The lazy summer days weighed heavy on me, and every day I could not stop my mind drifting back over the vain hopes that had brought me through winter to this place. The heat of mid-August was becoming unbearably oppressive, or perhaps it was unbearable to think of Lancelot and all that I had done. Worse to think, was all that I had not done. Even now, even after everything, I still felt the longing strong inside me, and I wished that I had not sent him away. In that moment it had been too acute, the sense of loss, for me to see before me everything I almost had, but now that was fading, and I was in too deep to forget him. The nights I lay with Arthur, in the hazy pleasures of our love, I would sometimes forget, but sometimes I would remember more intensely, and only think of Lancelot more. I was back in the place of dreams, where I heard and saw and touched and tasted the world around me in a trance, and only the sight of him once again would break the spell.

Then at last word came, as the summer was ripening into autumn, and some of the leaves in the garden were turning to gold, and then brown. It was evening, and the sun hung on the edge of the horizon, spilling a deep red light into the pale sky above. Nimue came to me, newly returned from the ether from which she came, to tell me that Arthur had called his council, and this time this meant me. More and more these days, Arthur called us all to the Round Table. He liked to be surrounded by his band of knights, but he would always comment sadly on the absence of Lancelot. It had been several months now. I hated it. It was like a knife into me that I was afraid would open up everything I had hidden inside me to everyone in the room. I hated it every time Arthur said his name. I had locked that deep in my core – the loss, the longing, the painful, delicious memories of his touch. I fought always to keep them there, and the sound of his name was enough to shake that core of me, and make me ache.

Fewer and fewer knights came to the council armed, though Gawain always did. In the lazy summer heat they played at swordfighting in shirts and breeches, though Lamerocke and Perceval always dressed formally for council, Perceval in a velvet doublet marked with the cross, and Lamerocke in a brightly coloured surcoat usually decorated with some prancing animal or other, and with a jewel hanging at his throat. Nimue today, when she came to fetch me, was wearing a dress that had an armoured breastplate over the bodice, covering her as far up as her neck. Beneath, pale blue skirts flowed. It was a strange sight, but I wished for such a dress.

When we sat, Arthur looked excited, eager to share the news. In his hand he clutched a letter, written in French. As soon as everyone was seated he jumped to his feet.

"My good knights, I have good news – news that Lancelot will return to us."

There was a murmur of approval around the table and nods. I felt light-headed for a moment, but I could feel beneath my hands spread, palm down, on the table, the cool, comforting wood. I would survive this. It would be nothing to me.

"Though," he held up a hand to quiet the murmuring, "not directly. He has been called to a tournament at Surluse, by its lord Galahalt, and wishes to represent me and my court. He also asks me to send his squire, Gareth. He will then return to court and take up his place here again as I requested." *As I requested.* Arthur, oh Arthur.

Gareth, new-seated at Arthur's council chamber beside his brothers, grinned with excitement. Gawain clapped him heartily on the back in congratulations. No wonder he was excited – his first tournament. It was the beginning of becoming a man; more, of becoming a knight.

"Now," Arthur continued, "I think it is only appropriate that, since Lancelot is the Queen's Champion, that we also send the queen." Suddenly, my heart beat loudly in my ears, drowning out the noise in the room around me. I felt as though I were underwater, hearing from far away, seeing through a film. "Gareth, can you assure me you can get my queen safely to Surluse?"

Gareth assured him heartily. Arthur turned to me with a smile. "Not so far, my lady, from your old home." Then he turned to the others of Lot's sons, Gawain, Aggravain and Gaheris. "You should go, also. It would be good for us to show our might a little."

They all nodded in agreement. I could see that Gawain and his brothers relished the thought of a tournament, and Arthur was wise to send them. If I were Galahalt and I saw those giant brothers ride onto my lands, I would continue to give fealty and tribute to Arthur.

I would have to harden myself for it, to see Lancelot and not be able to speak freely, to touch him, in the sight of those savage brothers. It would have been easier if Arthur were to go, too, then I could at least seek the pleasant forgetting I knew in his arms. If I were there with Arthur, there would be no awful, delicious possibility.

The talk turned to other things, to whom would take what horses and armour to the tournament, but I did not listen. I felt the heavy little knot in the pit of my stomach that I could not untie again, more acutely than before. I wanted to see Lancelot again, and I did not want to see him. I did not want to be close to him, and feel the pull towards him I knew I would feel, but it might fill the hole of yearning within me just to see him again, just to be near. I did not have to speak of it to him, or give into it in myself. I would not feel like a fool again. I would not want him.

Finally, the council ended and the knights began to leave, excited about the prospect of play-fighting in another man's land to prove their might, eager for the chance to please their king. Kay lingered behind and as Arthur took me by the hand to lead me from the room, Kay called him back.

"Arthur, I need to speak with you."

Arthur nodded and, placing a kiss on my cheek, let go of my hand and stood back. I could tell that Kay did not want me there, and I left, but I wanted to know what he was going to say. It felt dangerous that he did not want me there. They were talking already, casually, about the tournament while I was walking out, but I lingered on the other side of the door, waiting for Kay to say what he had been waiting to.

As I pulled the door closed behind me, I heard Kay speak to Arthur in tones of warning that made me glad I had paused to listen, to hang back and hear what I knew was not for me.

"Arthur, reconsider. It is not *wise* to send your wife alone with Lancelot."

Arthur laughed.

"I think you of all people know that I have nothing to fear from Lancelot. They won't be alone anyway – Gawain and all his brothers will be there, too."

There was a steely silence; I could feel it through the wood of the door.

"We're not *boys* anymore, Arthur. I'm serious. He's in love with her; it's obvious. Everyone knows. Even that halfwit Isolde saw it."

He's in love with her. I had not imagined it. It had not just been me. It had been so long since I saw him, and everything had gone wrong. Sometimes I could not help doubting.

"He's her champion. He's just very dutiful. As he is dutiful *to me.*" Arthur's tone invited no disagreement, and I heard the scrape of a chair as though Arthur had got up to leave, and another fast after as though Kay had jumped from his chair.

"Arthur, let me go with them."

Arthur sighed.

"Kay, I need you here. Tournaments abroad are all very well to increase the fame of our court, but they're no good if I lose all my knights to them and someone attacks us here. You said it yourself, Seneschal shouldn't leave the court. Besides, Gareth will be with them."

I moved away, nervous that they would come out and know I had listened. I felt betrayed by Kay in a way that I could not explain. Nothing he had said was a lie, nor had he implicated me in any way, and yet I felt by voicing his concerns to Arthur, he had opened me up to blame. *I have not done anything*, I told myself. It was comforting. *I have not done anything.*

Arthur came to my room soon after I had arrived. I had hoped for some time alone to collect myself, but I knew he would want to be with me the night before I left for Surluse. I could not tell him that I wanted to be alone to gather my strength for another meeting with Lancelot. I hoped that perhaps it would help me forget, but as he took me in his arms, I thought of Lancelot, and his lips soft against mine, his hands on my body. I had forgotten nothing of those forbidden sensations, and now as I tried to put them from my mind they came back more strongly. But Arthur's rough, insistent passion was something I could rely on, and eventually, eventually I began to forget, to lean into the oblivion of his touch, his rough strength. But, when it was over, and I lay awake in the darkness, Lancelot was back beside me, shimmering in my thoughts like a ghost, and I was terribly afraid that Kay was right.

We rode out in the morning, Gareth and I, before the others. Arthur wanted us to ride ahead and meet Lancelot. Gawain and the others would join us there. They wanted longer to prepare their armour and weapons. Neither Gareth nor I needed that. Before we left, I heard a little knock at my door, and I opened it to see Nimue there, and in her arms the armoured dress. We had not spoken alone before, and I was surprised to see her there, but she pressed it into my hands, telling me that it would keep me safe, she hoped. I thanked her in a daze, and was pleased for the dress. I wondered if she could hear what I thought. I did not know if the druids did that. Though I knew well enough now that they could change their shape. I was grateful for the gift, deeply. I couldn't trust her though; the blue on her face reminded me too strongly of Merlin and Morgan, and yet she had always been kind to me and gentle. I packed it with my clothes. I was dressed in the lilac silk gown Arthur had brought back from Rome. It was better that I arrived looking like a grand queen. Though I had refused to wear the heavy crown of Logrys, and though Arthur had suggested I wear the crown of snakes, I left it behind and wore my own circlet instead. I was not going to ride all day with that ill-fated lump of gold on my head.

It was about midday that we reached the town where Lancelot was waiting for us, and stopped to eat and feed the horses. We greeted each other politely, but he did not move to kiss my hand. Gareth did not notice. Lancelot seemed unwilling to meet my eye, and I was glad of it. I wished, suddenly, that I had been able to ride out alone. At least then we might have been able to speak to one another honestly, to clear the air that prickled between us.

When we mounted again to ride the rest of the way to the docks, I was glad of it. I could ride a little apart, watching the lovely green hills go by, feeling the breeze against my face, a blessing in the late autumn warmth, and be alone with my thoughts. After a while, Lancelot pulled up his horse beside mine. Gareth was ahead, excited and oblivious. I looked down, away. He had a look about him, apologetic, and I felt quickening in my heart the fear that he was going to talk, as he had in the little garden, of his loyalty to his king, of duty, that I – a woman – could never claim from him. Well, I did not mean to be denied again. It would be too much, too great to lose hope once again. Better not to hope at all.

"Guinevere –"

I shook my head.

"It is alright, sir." I looked up and met his gaze, sad and steady on me, and I was cold and stern. "We had our time, I think, and now that time has passed."

I could not read his look, whether it was sorrow, resignation, or relief. I did not know if he was hurt that I had sent him from me, or if he had wanted to come back to me. I did not know why he had not returned of his own accord, but waited for a summons. Had he stayed away from me because he thought it was what I wanted, or because he no longer wanted to be near me? I could be sure of nothing. The only thing I was sure of was that I would not hope again, only to be disappointed.

The journey over to the island of Surluse on the little ship was short and I was blessedly alone to stand at the edge and watch the waves as the horses stamped nervously in the decks below, and Lancelot and Gareth talked of jousting and fighting a little way behind me. The sunlight sparkled wonderfully on the waves, and my eyes followed it lazily, while my thoughts raced. Thoughts of Camelot, and Arthur left behind, and Lancelot unbearably close. Kay, too, back at Camelot, his thoughts on us out here. I wondered what he was saying to Arthur while we were gone. I wished the ship were not too large and grand for me to trail my hand through the water. I should have liked to feel it, cool and fresh, against my skin. I could feel instead the touch of Lancelot's voice in the distance, low and enticing, and forbidden to me.

When we arrived, the pavilions for us had been set by the servants Arthur had sent ahead. One in blue-green and white with Arthur's dragon on it for me, and one of deep purple for Lancelot and Gareth, and one of fine dark blue for Gawain, Aggravain and Gaheris. It was nightfall, and they were lit from the inside with candles and braziers, and the camp glowed in many beautiful colours of silk. I ached from the riding and was glad to slide off my horse and into the pavilion. There were some serving women there and I asked them for a bath; but they were not *my* women and I sent them away when the water was steaming in the iron tub, wanting to be alone. I regretted, then, not asking Arthur if I could have Marie, Christine or Margery with me. I missed already Christine's funny scolding manner, Marie's quick, bright little eyes, and even Margery's gentle clumsiness. My thoughts had been too full of other things to even think of asking.

I was in my underdress, about to slip it off and slide into the hot water when I heard Lancelot call my name softly from outside my pavilion. I pulled my cloak over me, holding it in my hands and crossing my arms so it covered me, and called him inside. He hovered just on the inside of the pavilion opening, as though he was afraid to step fully inside. He coughed softly, and our eyes met as I looked up to him. I felt the familiar shock go through me. No, I had not forgotten.

"My lady, is it still your wish that I should ride for you?"

I nodded.

"Of course, sir. Thank you."

It felt safer to speak to each other formally like this. He gave a little bow and left. I was shaking slightly – I was not sure if it was from fatigue or from the effort of trying to keep it all on the inside of me – as I threw off my clothes and got into the hot water. I closed my eyes in it, feeling it slough off the day, burn away my aches. But it could not burn away my thoughts. All I thought about was him.

Chapter Twenty-Five

The next morning, unfamiliar women dressed me in a samite dress of blue-green and gold, to match the pavilion, and so that those watching would know whose queen I was, I supposed. I could not avoid putting the heavy crown on my head today, though it was the one which I had worn when I married Arthur, not Cleopatra's wicked crown of snakes. The women complained in French about my curly hair escaping in little coils from the braids they tried to wind it into, thinking that I would not understand until, in my clumsy French, I sharply sent them away and they scurried out blushing. I pinned the plaits up in the gold net. I didn't look in the little mirror I had brought – I had enough gold on me to look like a queen, no matter how tidy I was.

I heard a trumpet sound outside the pavilion, announcing the arrival of the local lord, Galahalt of Surluse. I took a deep breath in and stepped outside into the bright morning. Lancelot and Gareth were already waiting outside. Lancelot, in full platemail with his helm in his hand, greeted me with a shy little nod, and Gareth in light leather armour smiled, clearly giddy with excitement. A huge palanquin embroidered in gold thread with stags came lumbering towards us, and was set down. A man emerged from it, dressed in a gold samite surcoat, gaudy and showy, embroidered with the same stags in black. He had a neat, pointy little beard that was steely-grey, short-cut grey hair and sly little eyes of grey-green that measured us up as he saw us. He stepped forward with a little bow, and then took my hand, raising it to his lips for a kiss that lasted a moment too long.

The hairs of his beard brushed it unpleasantly. I felt my body tense in response. I still had all the instincts of a warrior in me, and they bristled against him.

"Queen Guinevere, I have heard many tales of your beauty, and I see none has been exaggerated, although the tales of your husband's wisdom and prudence seem to have been if he does not accompany a lady of such beauty when he sends her into my lands."

Were his tone not one of obsequious flattery, that would have sounded like a threat. I was glad of the dagger, concealed in the sleeve of my dress. Galahalt was soft and fleshy, and looked sneaky, not strong. I could kill him, if it came to it.

"King Arthur does not send me unprotected, sir," I reminded him, coldly. He gave a deferential little nod and turned to Lancelot with a bow.

"Of course. Sir Lancelot." His lip curled in a strange, greedy little smile. His lips were too pink, too wet, seemed somehow greedy and licentious. "I am honoured that you are come to attend my tournament. The realm resounds with tales of your great deeds, sir. Your victories at the sack of Rome, and in France. They say no man can beat you in battle. My men are all eager to try their strength against yours. I do not suppose you might be persuaded to yield this lady to the victor?"

Gareth opened his mouth to protest, and seemed poised to step forward to strike the disgusting little man, but Lancelot laid a hand on his arm and he relaxed back just a little, still wary.

Lancelot gave a soft, polite laugh, but the way he stood, his hand on the hilt of his sword, was enough to show he took Galahalt's words seriously.

"My lord Galahalt, the lady is not mine to yield. My lord Arthur does not send his queen here to hazard her in battle; he sends her here as the representative of his royal person. I am sure he would be most upset if any man attempted to lay hands on her as a prize. These are not the customs of Logrys, nor of Britain, my lord." The threat was polite, but Galahalt still bridled under it.

"Of course," he replied, his tones clipped. He took my hand again. I could not hide the flinch I made against his touch, and I saw the greedy little smile curl his lip again. "My queen, I would be honoured to invite you to dine with me in my castle tonight after the jousting."

I gave a little curtsey, struggling to be polite. I pushed down the thoughts of what I would have done to this man if I did not need to be polite, what I would like to say. I supposed I had to accept; this man was vassal to Arthur, and Arthur did not have the time or energy to waste re-conquering the kingdoms of Europe just because their kings had been rude to me.

"I, and my lord King Arthur's knights, would be delighted to attend," I answered.

He blanched.

"There are more knights?"

"The sons of Lot come, at your invitation," Lancelot reminded him, firmly.

"Lot's sons are *Arthur's* knights now?" he mused aloud. He thought on it for a moment, one eyebrow raised. I was not sure why he was so surprised. "Very well. Lady," he kissed my hand again, and gave another simpering bow, "I await your company with great anticipation."

We three stood there, tense and still until the palanquin moved away. I felt my breath catch tensely in my chest. Gareth was the first to break the silence.

"What a disgusting little man. I should have hit him right in his smug face –"

Lancelot shook his head.

"That would not have done any good. He's testing Arthur's strength, testing for weakness. He seems to have been hoping that Arthur would come with us, and prove a jealous man. An angry king, a jealous king, is a weak king. After today, he will give up his little dream of taking Logrys. Gareth, ready my horse."

When Gareth had gone, Lancelot turned to me. I was still shaking with anger. He put a hand lightly on my shoulder and I turned to him. The feel of it there centred me, I felt calmer. I certainly was not alone with that disgusting little man. But, if I were still a Breton princess I would have come in my armour, and I could have fought to defend myself. Still, perhaps if he was drunk enough to forget it tonight, I would slap him across the face.

"Are you alright?" he asked me, softly, in Breton. I looked at him dumbly in surprise. I did not know that he spoke my language, though I supposed that I had never asked him. Perhaps he had not wanted to speak it in Camelot. I had, after all, only heard him speak in French there when he was reading to me.

I shook my head, but said, "I'm well enough. I wish it were *Breton* customs we lived by now, then I could have..." I didn't know what. I should have liked to have hit him, or frightened him with my dagger. I could not make a man like him respect me any other way; only with violence. I did not want to *do* anything; I just wished things were different.

"He will be sorry, my lady," Lancelot assured me.

At the jousting, I had to sit beside Galahalt, on the platform raised over the raked seating for the other noble ladies and lords that had come to watch. It was only appropriate, since I was Arthur's queen, but I was not pleased about it. The platform was covered by a canopy of pink and gold silk embroidered with little flowers in gold thread, and the chairs placed there for Galahalt, Galahalt's son's wife and myself were large and made of mahogany, with gilded scrolls at the back and arms. I wondered if the display of wealth was for my benefit, or if Galahalt was always so ostentatious. I would not have been surprised by either.

When I sat, I wished once again that I had thought to ask Arthur to send my ladies to me. I ought to have written last night. The serving ladies of Galahalt's court hung behind us, but I had already taken a dislike to them, and, besides, I wished for someone to whisper to in my own language. I wished that Kay had come with us, although he would, I supposed, have had to be fighting, too. Galahalt offered me a cup of wine. The cup was gold and studded with emeralds. This truly was a man with something to prove. I noticed that his cup was the same, and that he placed them both on the same table. To be on the safe side, I switched the cups when he was not looking. I had learned fast not to drink from a cup filled by someone I did not trust. He drank heartily and it seemed to have no ill effect on him, but I did not regret my carefulness. The wine was strong enough, and made me sleepy in the lazy heat of autumn – almost as hot here as Camelot had been in the summer – without any help.

The jousting was very dull, and almost as brutal as it was boring. Knight after knight crashed to the ground, heavy in his armour, with groans of pain that were often echoed by the audience. It was sickening, watching these brave men spar. They had fought once for the safety of their families, and they had watched their friends and brothers die in battle. Why anyone would want to play at it was beyond me. But I supposed this was the new kind of warfare. This is why Lancelot and Gawain and his brothers had had to come – to show the strength of Arthur's armies and put off another war. War was about politics and intimidation now that Arthur had conquered.

The knights in their helms all looked the same, and I only recognised a few by the colours they fought under. I saw Gawain, whose colours were the dark blue of Lothian, crash against Galahalt's son, whose lance was wrapped in black and gold to match his father's surcoat, and knock him from his horse. Galahalt seemed unworried and laughed and clapped in appreciation.

"A good bout," he said, to no one in particular.

Then I saw, at the edge of the field, the flash of cloth-of-gold – my sleeve – and I recognised Gareth, tightening the armour on Lancelot's horse. The knight riding against him was a Saracen; I could tell from the cloth that draped his horse, covered in a crescent moon and stars. He was huge and broad, his armour decorated in huge bronze lions. But it looked more decorative than Lancelot's battered iron mail that had seen many wars already.

Galahalt leaned unnecessarily close to tell me, "The Saracen riding against Lancelot is Palomides. He rides for Isolde of Cornwall. I have heard it said that they are lovers."

"That isn't true," I replied sharply, keeping my eyes on the field. Still, Palomides had a cloth of pale pink tied to his helmet. It was certainly true that he rode for Isolde.

He gave a little chuckle.

"Of course not, my lady."

He leaned away, but gestured for one of the women to fill my cup with wine again. I glanced down into the deep red pool. The sun through the silk canopy made everything appear slightly dark and pinkish anyway, and in that light, the drink in the cup looked like blood.

The crowd began to cheer as the men ran together. Lancelot knocked Palomides from his horse as if it were nothing, leaning lazily out of the way of Palomides' lance and with a swift little jab of his lance knocking the huge Saracen from his seat. I felt a peculiar sympathy for Palomides as the crowd booed him, and jeered. I wondered what they would make of me if they knew I had said my prayer this morning to the White Goddess and the Hanged God, rather than to their miserable Christ.

Then it was another of Galahalt's sons, Aggravain and Gaheris, and more of the knights from Cornwall that fell easily before Lancelot's lance, and every time he felled another the crowd cheered more wildly.

"They are pleased," Galahalt leaned over again to tell me. "He is every bit the champion we were promised he would be. Spectacular. *Spectacular.*"

Galahalt was not wrong. Lancelot rode in the lists as though it was nothing, with the easy grace of a man who knows his own strength and skill, but also with delicacy. If he could knock a man from his horse without wounding him, he would do it. I suppose his strength was so great that it was easy for him to hold back, in the confidence that an opponent he was lenient with would, if they underestimated him for it, suffer because of it.

Then came Galahalt's master-at-arms, but he was no match for Lancelot either, and Lancelot was declared victor of the day. He rode before us and took off his helm. I stood and walked forward to the edge of the platform. He bowed his head.

"You fought well," I said, more quietly than I had meant to. Softly, and close enough that if I had reached out to touch his horse, I could have done. It sounded oddly intimate, and I felt suddenly embarrassed in front of the crowd, and delicate, as though I had opened my heart to him right there. His face was dark with dirt and sweat, and he was still breathing hard from the fighting.

"Thank you, my lady."

We lingered a moment, looking at each other, as the crowd cheered again. *I should turn away; I should turn back; I should remember what I said to him.* But for a moment all I could see was him, before me, and I was not aware of the platform beneath me, just the beating of my own heart, and his eyes and mine, locked together. No. I would. I had resolved.

I turned back to Galahalt and, hiding my distaste, accepted the hand he offered to lead me to the palanquin that would take us to his castle. I climbed in first, and he after. I expected his son's wife to get in after us, but she did not come. Nor did anyone else. He called to the palanquin bearers to go.

"No, stop. I would wait for my champion."

Galahalt laughed and shook his head.

"Oh no, my lady. There is no need for that. You are quite safe with me."

The palanquin swung into motion and I checked in my sleeve for the dagger. If it came to it, I *would* be quite safe. But it seemed that what he wanted alone with me was information. He thought I was some kind of fool, obviously. Perhaps he had managed to charm everything Isolde knew out of her, but I mistrusted his reptilian charm and his sneaky little eyes.

"How fares my lord King Arthur? Does Camelot flourish?"

"Oh yes. Very well. He daily increases his retinue of knights."

If he wanted to know that Camelot was strong enough to crush him, I would tell him that. It was, after all, only the truth.

"Hmmm. They say that he brought back to you the jewels of Helen of Troy when he sacked Rome, but I do not see you wear them."

"He brought back many riches from Rome, but not the jewels of Helen of Troy. Those, I think, are at the bottom of the Mediterranean now. Besides, I think it is ill luck to wear the jewels of a fallen queen."

"Ah, my lady, beauty such as yours has no need of adornment."

I was not sure if he was suggesting that I was not dressed richly enough, but he was a fool if he judged Arthur's strength by his display of wealth. I had thought that Camelot was opulent compared to Carhais, but Surluse was something different. Closer to France in its culture, I supposed. They loved all of this in the south; the samites, the cloth-of-gold and the jewels. It was all too gaudy for my taste, as Camelot had been when I had first arrived. I settled back a little into the cushions of the palanquin, but I did not feel relaxed. I just wanted to appear so. The less I said, the better, I thought. I hoped the ride to the castle would not be too long. Through the opening of the palanquin I saw that we were already out of the camp and passing through some kind of grassy moorland. I wished I had not got in first.

"I have heard, my lady, that when Arthur marched to Rome, you fought at his side." He leaned forward, intrigued. So, I was a curiosity to him, perhaps as exotic as Palomides the Saracen, a Breton warrior-queen. A man like him could not have met a woman like me before, otherwise he would have shown me some more respect.

"That is true."

He tutted and shook his head.

"Strange customs. And yet you do not joust in the lists."

He was joking, but I looked at him narrowly.

"We Breton women never play at war."

Chapter Twenty-Six

The palanquin came to rest and he stepped out, offering me a hand to get out. The castle was small, but sturdy, built with the same heavy grey stone as Camelot, and over its towers and turrets flapped gold silk flags with the black stag on them. I turned and looked back towards the camp of knights, covering my eyes against the setting sun. I could see a band of them close behind us, and recognised the colours of Lothian. It was the first time I had been pleased to see Gawain. The gates of the castle opened as they came to us. I saw Lancelot amongst them, Gareth at his side, his head bare. He looked relieved when he saw me. I was relieved, too. I would not have wanted to go into that castle without him.

The feast was already set when we went in. Lancelot and Gareth came to my side. They had taken off their armour, but they still had their swords at their sides, wary. Gawain came in in his armour, as did Aggravain, but Gaheris and most of the other knights were unarmed and in their shirts and breeches with their surcoats thrown on top. Lancelot excused himself to wash quickly after the fighting – he had clearly ridden right after us, to keep watch – but not before he had made sure Gareth was by my side.

Galahalt had a place for me beside himself, and on the other side he had his son and the son's wife. There was a place at my side for Lancelot, but Gareth had to sit on one of the lower trestle tables with his brothers. But they were still close by. Lancelot arrived back fast, while Galahalt was introducing to me the others around the high table. Palomides was there, as a representative of King Mark, or perhaps Isolde, as was Galahalt's master-at-arms, and his two sons. The only other woman there was the wife of his eldest son, Marhalt.

The food was rich and showy. Fish and game birds stuffed with exotic spices, fruits from the south, piles of little boiled quails' eggs. I ate warily, taking nothing that Galahalt hadn't taken a bite of first. He ate heartily almost everything, and he chattered even more heartily than he ate.

"Sir Lancelot, it truly was a pleasure to see you fight today. It is rare these days to meet a man as great as his reputation. Truly, you could have gone hand to hand with Achilles."

Lancelot bowed his head modestly.

"Thank you, my lord."

"Truly, sir," Marhalt's wife piped up in a shrill little voice, "it was magnificent."

Lancelot thanked her, too.

Galahalt reached an arm around the back of my chair, leaning over towards me. I could smell the wine on his breath, and his moustache was dark red with it above his mouth, and smeared with the grease of his food. Disgusting.

"Now, we just had Queen Isolde with us, my lady, but she came with her king, Mark. I still do not quite understand why King Arthur would send his lovely wife without accompanying her. I know that King Mark would *never* have sent Isolde alone with his champion, Tristan."

I was about to answer sharply when Lancelot spoke.

"That is because Mark is a jealous coward, but also a man who would without a thought take another man's wife into his bed. Arthur is a good king who behaves with honour and trusts his people to do the same. Perhaps this is not a custom in Surluse, my lord."

Galahalt made a little noise of disdain, withdrawing his arm from around my chair, and turning to talk more of the jousting with his sons. Lancelot leaned close to me a whispered in Breton.

"Did he touch you – in the palanquin?"

I shook my head, and Lancelot nodded and sat back in his chair. He seemed angry, on edge. I think if I had said yes, he might have drawn his sword and killed Galahalt in his seat. Truly I was glad he was on edge, because I felt it, too. The man was a drunken bore, thinking himself charming, but also trying to display his superiority by mocking. But beneath this was something more threatening. If he put his hand on my knee, I was prepared to put my dagger through it. My whole body felt tensed to fight if he touched me.

I excused myself early, saying that I had to write to Arthur. I was not sure yet if I was going to or not. There was nothing definite to say, apart from that Galahalt was an idiot with too much money and bad manners, but I thought I might ask for my women. Lancelot excused himself, too, to accompany me to our camp. He went down to the stables to get his horse, and I stood out in a corridor leading to the courtyard, relishing the silence, feeling the night air cool and pleasant after the smoky closeness of the hall. I crossed my arms over my chest and leant back against the wall, feeling the cold stone through my dress, strangely comforting. I did not think I could have stood being polite to that awful man a moment longer, and I was tired from sleeping poorly in the tent and holding myself defensively all day. I just wanted to go back and sleep.

Marhalt came out of the hall, and, seeing me, came towards me. I thought for a moment that he might be coming to apologise on behalf of his churl of a father, but he clearly was not. He walked up to me, too close, and as I went to move away, planted a hand either side of me. I put my hand on my dagger. I did not want to start a war, but I was ready to do this. I was not some servant to be groped in a passageway.

"You look lonely, my lady." He slurred his words slightly, but he was not so drunk that I was sure that I would win in a fight. He was short, like his father; not quite as tall as I was, but stocky and strong, as all knights were. These were men whose purpose in life was to win in a fight.

"I'm not," I replied sharply.

"That is not what I hear." He leaned in towards me, stinking of ale, and meat, and sweat. He had not washed, then, after he had fought in the jousts. "They say that Arthur never lies with you, but prefers instead to lie with his sisters, Lot's queen and the witch Morgan. It's a waste. If I had wife as lovely as you I would not spend a night without her."

"You're drunk. You're disgracing yourself. Go back to your wife," I snapped, bracing myself to strike him if he did not.

"It's no disgrace to talk love to a beautiful lady." He leaned closer.

He did not look as if he was only interested in *talking* love. I tried to push him away, shoving both hands against his chest. For a moment, stunned, he stumbled back, but then, suddenly angry, he grasped me by the shoulders and slammed me hard against the wall. I drew the dagger. When he saw the flash of steel in the moonlight he stepped back. He was unarmed and I judged him to be too drunk to take the dagger from my hand.

"Well, it seems that Arthur has a taste for witches," he spat.

"I suppose every woman who refuses your bed is a witch," I retorted, sharp with derision. I held the dagger out in front of me. He did not come closer, but he did not look as if he was going to leave. I could see that he was angry, that he wanted to punish me for frightening him. I had counted on the dagger discouraging him enough that he would just leave, but he was angry now and had a look about him as though he would try to take it off me, as though he was thinking of forcing me in revenge for my refusal of him.

The sound of a sword being drawn turned both of our heads and in the opening of the passage onto the courtyard Lancelot stood with his sword drawn. Marhalt stepped further away. He looked warily between us, the two drawn weapons, and spat towards me.

"You can keep the witch," he snarled at Lancelot.

Lancelot slid his sword back into its sheath. He didn't speak until we were away from the castle. I sat back against his chest, in front of him on the horse. I wanted to close my eyes into it, into the feeling of resting against him, but I was afraid to. Afraid I was slipping back to where I had been, where I had hoped and suffered. There I was again, saved by him, falling into the dizziness of being close to him. I had promised myself I would not. We both held the reins and as the horse moved, our hands brushed against one another, and the thrill of his skin against mine could not be suppressed in me. But still, I felt sick from Galahalt and Marhalt.

When the pavilions came into sight, Lancelot spoke at last.

"Perhaps we should go back to Camelot."

I nodded. I did not want to stay. But I knew Gawain and his brothers would not want to go. It would look badly for us if half left the tournament early, and Lancelot as champion of the first day ought to fight in the second. Word would spread fast if he did not, and we had been meant to come here to prevent any more wars, to quash any doubts about the strength and bravery of Arthur's knights. It was more important than ever now that Lancelot and Lot's sons impressed on Galahalt the might of Camelot and Arthur.

"I wish we could," I said sadly. "I won't go to the castle again."

"I think that's wise," he agreed.

When we arrived back at the pavilions, Lancelot jumped from the horse and held out his hand to help me down. I landed face to face with him, my hand still in his, close enough that I could have leant forward and kissed him, but I did not. I felt the draw towards him, and my eyes lingered for a moment on his lips, and the sweet temptation I felt there. My pavilion was dark, and I did not want to be on my own. *Come inside.* I could not make the words; I could only think them. I felt him lean down slightly towards me, and the gravity of his presence pulled me towards him. We stood in silence, for a breath, and I felt the static strong in the air between us, and I knew that I had been foolish to think that I could decide to forget about him, to decide to stop feeling what I had been feeling.

He kissed my hand softly, shaking me from my thoughts, shattering through the tension in the space between us.

"Goodnight, my lady," he said, and walked away.

He had felt it, too. He had felt it, and that was why he had left then so fast.

In my pavilion, by the light of a little candle, I tried to write to Arthur, but the words would not come there either, and anyway I was afraid that the letter would be intercepted. If only Arthur had been able to read in Breton – though I thought it might be more trouble if I was found to be sending letters in a foreign language back to Camelot. It was probably wiser to sit it out for the rest of the tournament and resolve never to return to Surluse.

I faced the next day with trepidation, dressing in Nimue's armoured dress and hiding my dagger under its breastplate. I would go today like a Breton queen, ready for the real war that I was already beginning to feel being fought between Arthur and Galahalt. I was not even sure that Marhalt had been motivated by anything so unpolitical as desire. I thought that had been another move against

Arthur. I was right, then, not to give ground, and I went back to the chair beside Galahalt dressed like a warrior. As well as the dagger concealed in the dress, I went with a sword around my waist. It was one of Gareth's and slightly too heavy for me, but it would be well for people to see it.

When Galahalt saw me, he laughed.

"So warlike today, my queen."

I said nothing as I sat beside him, regarding him narrowly.

"My lady," he leaned over, as was his habit, "I must apologise *profusely* for the behaviour of my son. He was tired from the day's fighting and the wine was a little strong for him."

I said nothing still. I was not going to absolve Marhalt, and I was pleased when Lancelot sent him to the ground with a blow to his helm in the combat on foot.

I could barely concentrate. I felt tension all the way through me, wary of everyone around me, but it was for nothing. The day proceeded as was ordinary, and Lancelot was the victor again. We stayed with the pavilions this time. Galahalt pleaded, and sighed in disappointment, but he did not press for it.

That night, I ate in the dark blue pavilion with Gareth and his brothers and Lancelot, and Lancelot walked back with me to my pavilion afterwards. We stood at the door, under the autumn stars that winked through the clouds, and the door of the pavilion flapped lightly in the wind. He had taken a blow to the shoulder from Gawain, and, not wanting to leave him already, I asked if could look at it. I knew a little medicine from Christine. I felt light and daring, and being far from home made me more bold. He must too have been reluctant to leave, because he agreed. I could see the faint mark of dark red against the white of his shirt, so it was reasonable enough. Innocent enough.

The brazier in the centre of my pavilion was lit and I pulled up a chair for him to sit by it. I felt the tingling danger of his closeness, our aloneness. It filled me with a hazy excitement, and the air between us felt thick with potential. But I was not going back into the centre of it again. I would not be carried away with it. I only wanted the comfort of a little moment alone. He took off his shirt and sat in the chair as I kneeled before him to look at the wound. I laid my hands gently on his arm. The skin was cool and soft, but underneath hard with lean muscle. I could smell his skin, clean, and familiar to me already. It made me want to close my eyes and re-live again the moment when he had kissed me on the Round Table, the time so long ago now that we had almost come together. I was supposed to be forgetting this. I was supposed to be protecting myself from being hurt again. I was not doing very well. I was not sure anymore that such a thing could be done. I concentrated on the little patch of skin before my face, the small red scratch that was, really, nothing at all. I did not want to let my eyes wander across his body, his bare chest that I had felt against my hand, but not seen before. I could feel the heat coming off his body, his breath falling lightly on the top of my head. I tore off a strip from the linen in the little box of medicine tools Christine had given me to take, and I slowly wrapped it around the wound, tucking the end into place. My hands were light against his skin, and I felt my fingertips tingle as I touched him, and I knew he must be feeling the same.

I looked up and he was looking down at me. Our faces were close enough for me to see the thick, dark strands of his eyelashes. He put a hand on my cheek, and slowly, we leaned towards each other. My heart fluttered within me and I felt light, as though I was rushing away into something wonderful. My lips opened slightly in blissful anticipation, and I closed my eyes, but I felt him draw away.

"I should go," was all he said, leaving suddenly as he had done the night before, for me to fall into the empty space he had left. It was no good; I was how I had been again. Throwing myself into hopes that could not be. I thought of everything that he had said the night before about Arthur and I buried my face in my hands, still kneeling before the empty chair. How had he done this to me again?

The next day of the tournament was the melee, and Lancelot did not fight. It was just a wild scrabble between lesser knights, hungry for blood, or treasure and favour from their lords. Gawain and Aggravain entered nonetheless, revelling in the brutality of it, roaring like bears and cheering at everyone they knocked down. They were safe in it, all of the other men dwarfed by them, and unhardened by long wars at Arthur's side. Arthur did seem to get the best out of his men, taking boys and making them into warriors. Gawain and Aggravain might have been nothing more than provincial bully-boys without Arthur's court, riding around Lothian and Orkney burning, stealing and raping. Arthur had made them into great men, and their skill and prowess showed as they moved easily through the ranks of lesser men, impervious, it seemed, to any blows that fell on them.

Marhalt's wife, sitting the other side of Galahalt on the platform, seemed exceedingly pleased that Lancelot was sitting beside us to watch the melee. I was trying not to look at him. I felt foolish about the night before, and confused. I did not want to give anything away in front of Galahalt.

Marhalt's wife, cup of wine in hand, addressed Lancelot across me and Galahalt; hungrily her narrow little eyes fixed on him, her voice shrill with excitement. I supposed if I had a husband like Marhalt, I might look at strangers that way. I think I would be more inclined to make myself a widow, though, than look for another man who might only be just as bad.

"Sir, why do you not have a wife?"

Lancelot laughed softly, seemingly amenable enough to her question.

"If I had a wife, I do not think she would be pleased at me risking my life at battles and jousts to win my king honour. She would want me to stay with her at home."

"Well, a paramour then."

I fixed my eyes more firmly on the fighting, watching Gawain swing a huge blunted mace into some knight's chest, knocking him from his horse. The crowd cheered. They already loved Gawain.

"That can never end well, my lady," was all he said.

Was that a message to me? Or was he afraid that she was asking him to be *her* paramour? I would not blame her with that brute of a husband. I had not seen him since the first night. I hoped that he had choked on his drunken vomit in the night, but I suspected he was just cowering somewhere.

I was relieved for the day's fighting to end, as Gawain and Aggravain were the only men left standing. Tomorrow, we would ride home, and I would be free of Galahalt's slimy courtesies. As I stood to leave the platform, Galahalt announced, "I hope all those of Arthur's party will join me to feast the final night of the tournament."

I said nothing then, but I did not intend to go. I slipped away before he could try to lead me to the palanquin again. I was not going back to that castle.

When I got back to my pavilion, Lancelot was there, waiting at the doorway. He was dressed in his armour still, as he had been all day, though he had not fought. I think he was wary, not trusting in Galahalt. I could not say I was not glad of it. Even with Marhalt in the castle, I did not trust my safety with his father.

"Will you go?" he asked. I shook my head, moving to go into the pavilion. He put a hand out to catch me by the shoulder. "He has asked me to fight Marhalt for the amusement of the young boys of the castle." He looked quietly pleased at the idea of hurting Marhalt, and I could not say that I was not pleased about it, too. "I ought to go. Will you be alright?" I nodded, not trusting myself to speak, or meet his gaze fully. He looked up into the sky. "It looks like a storm is coming." I followed his gaze up and saw that the clouds that had been white and soft at the beginning of the day were dark and purpling above us.

"I'd rather take my chances with the storm than with Marhalt."
He nodded.
"You'll stay at the castle tonight?" I asked.
"If the storm breaks."
I nodded.
"Truly, you will be alright on your own?"
"I will." I tapped the sword at my side and he smiled gently.
"Alright."
There was a moment of heavy silence between us.
"Back to Camelot tomorrow," I said, softly.
"Back to Camelot," he agreed, though he did not meet my eye.
Stay with me.
I didn't say it.

I heard him leave after I went into the pavilion and lay down on my bed. Back to Camelot tomorrow, back to Arthur. Another painful almost. As I closed my eyes against the rush of memories and emotions, every other missed chance with Lancelot, I heard the rain beginning to fall.

Chapter Twenty-Seven

By the time night had truly fallen, the rain fell hard against the pavilion, and I heard thunder crack in the sky. The wooden supports creaked as the samite outer layer soaked up the rain and grew heavy, but they held. The smell of wet grass and fresh mud was gorgeous after the long dry summer and the dusty clouds that rose from the jousting fields. The knights in their metal armour, turning to rust, must have cursed it, but I was glad. It also gave me a chance to be on my own, away from Lancelot and the burning inside me that I knew I had to deny. I had stood out in the rain as it began to fall. There was no one around to see me, and I had wanted to feel the raindrops against my skin. I had hoped they would wash my thoughts away, but they had not. I lit the little iron brazier in the middle of my pavilion and sat down beside it in my light silk summer nightdress to read. I loosened my hair, damp from the rain, and felt the lovely dry heat of the brazier slowly warming it, taking away the chill, flicking lazily through the pages of the book, not really taking it in.

I heard the clank of armour, and looked up at the flap of the pavilion, reaching for the dagger beside me. A dark night like this, and a thunderstorm, I would not have been wise to be a lady, unarmed and alone. An armoured knight stepped through the opening, but as he stood to his full height the fear ebbed out of me. It was Lancelot. He had not worn his helm, and rain ran down his face in little streams, his thick hair plastered to his head. His chest rose and fell with heavy breaths. I stood at the sight of him, and the book slipped from my hands onto the rug beneath me with a dull thud. The thunder cracked into the silence, and for a moment the pavilion was lit with a cold blue flash.

"I couldn't stop thinking about you," he breathed.

I stepped forward, off the rug onto the bare grass which, under the cover of the pavilion, was still dry and slightly sharp. My feet were bare, and I relished the feeling of the ground beneath them, the blades of grass between my toes. It was as though all of my senses had suddenly become more intense. The thunder cracked again and a gust of wind, with a renewed blast of rain, shook the pavilion, but I was not afraid. I stopped a few paces before him. I had no words in me, no voice. He pulled off and threw aside his leather gauntlets and then unbuckled his breastplate and pulled it over his head. Underneath he was soaked, the white shirt plastered to his chest. I could see the shape of his muscles through it, the skin that I had been so close to the night before, but I had not touched. I longed to touch. He unbuckled his sword, and threw it to the ground. He was still breathing hard, as though he had run or ridden hard here through the rain. He must have been far away, in the castle. I reached out, slowly, and put a hand on his chest. His heart thudded against my hand, the shirt cold and wet to my touch. He leaned down towards me, only a little, but enough for me to feel the magnetism of my own desire move me towards him. He laid gently a hand, cold from the rain, over mine, and slowly, slowly, as if we were both afraid we might chase the moment away, our lips met. His were cold against mine, his face cold and damp from the rain, but I did not care. I pressed against him, and felt the wet of his clothes soak through the thin material of my nightdress to my own skin. I wound my fingers through his thick wet hair and, as we kissed, he picked me up lightly, by the thighs, holding me around him as I wrapped my legs around his waist. Against them, I could feel the damp shirt, and the cold iron of the greaves he still had on his legs. He carried me to the pile of cushions by the brazier, stepping over the fallen book, and we fell together into them. He kicked off his boots and pulled the greaves off his legs, throwing them away into the darkness. He touched my cheek lightly with his hand and I laid my own hand lightly on top of it. Through the wet fabric of our clothes, it almost felt as if we were skin-to-skin. *Almost.* It had always been almost, and now at last we were here, alone, in each other's arms. *What was he waiting for?* I was not going to wait any longer.

I pulled the shirt from him and threw it aside. I laid a hand against his bare chest, tracing the small line of soft, dark hair across it, the swell of muscle, and the scars of battle, down his stomach, hard with muscle, with a scar running down the side, white against the pale skin that glowed orange in the light from the brazier. As I followed the trace of hair down from his navel towards his breeches he took it with his own, lifting it away, twining his fingers with mine and holding it fast over my head. He kissed me slowly, deeply. I felt light rush through my body and the power and softness of his lips against mine, the bright urgency of my longing and I arched my back towards him, reaching for him with my other hand. He took this too and held them together over my head.

"Don't rush," he whispered, releasing one of his hands from mine to run it slowly down my arm, and lightly across my breast through the damp fabric of the dress, his thumb brushing my nipple, tantalising through the cloth, and slowly down to pull the dress up over my head. The feel of the night air and the warmth of the brazier on my bare skin was wonderful, intense as the feel of the grass beneath my bare feet had been. Lancelot's lips moved down my neck, and slowly, deliciously, over my whole body. I closed my eyes and stretched my arms over my head, sinking into it, intoxicated already, feeling his hands on my thighs, across my stomach, and finally, as he came to kiss me on the mouth again, winding his hands into my thick and still damp hair. I reached for his breeches again, and this time he did not stop me. I threw them aside, and as he slid his arms around me and held me close against him, at last I felt his skin close against my own, and I murmured with delight. He ran a hand over my body, down between my legs where the light flutter of his touch made me gasp and press my hips against him with desire. I felt his lips soft at my ear, my neck, and all over every inch of my skin yearned for his touch. Already my head swam with the delight of it, the feel of his bare skin against mine, his strength as he held me, the delicate power of all of his movements. At last, *at last* the moment was upon us. I laid a hand lightly on his chest and looked into his eyes. I wanted to taste it, relish it, the moment when at last the waiting came to an end. In the lovely silence, tingling with potential, another thunderclap sounded and I felt at once all the power of the wildness of nature seething around me, through me, through us. My whole body felt full of the electricity in the air all around us, full of yearning for him, reaching towards him. I felt brave, and powerful. We moved together, turning over so that I was on top of him, my hair falling thick over my shoulders. I leaned down to kiss him, and slowly drew back, sitting up, trailing my hands down his chest, feeling the breath catch in him, the beating of his heart, the powerful silent passion in the both of us. I wanted to see all of him, to run my hands all over him, I wanted to taste it all, all that I had waited so long for. I closed my eyes against the feel of his hands on my thighs, drawing us, at last, together. When I at last took him inside me, the pleasure was almost unbearable. I sighed with it, throwing my head back, feeling the heat of the brazier on my face, hearing the rain far away, and the lightning filling the tent with a cold and primal brightness, as though we two were at the centre of the world, between the storm and the fire, and apart from us and the storm and the fire there was nothingness. I felt his hand lightly on my waist and I opened my eyes, and our gazes locked together as I moved against him. I felt the heat at the core of me, the deep centre where he was, and I could see in him, too, the breath beginning to come ragged with pleasure. As I felt the heat, rising, spreading, and saw the pleasure on his face, felt him hold me tighter against him, he pulled me down into a kiss and rolled us over so that he was on me, one hand tight on my thigh holding it around him, the other tangling in my hair as we looked into each other's eyes and moved together. I felt exposed in a way I never had before, under his gaze. Arthur had always closed his eyes. I felt Lancelot at the centre of me in a new way, and I took his face in my hands, pressing my forehead into his, as I felt the rapture of his body against mine, the hot white centre of me rising, spreading through me. But then I broke through to a new place of pleasure so great it felt iridescent all around me in the night. I moaned deeply, and he followed, murmuring my name, sinking down with me as I relaxed against the cushions, feeling the glorious heat and light of it still around me – nothing to do with the brazier. My eyes fluttered closed and I sighed. His lips brushed mine, close and tender. I whispered his name.

Slowly, he moved off me to lie on his side and gather me against him, wrapping an arm softly around my waist, the other hand smoothing my loose hair back from my neck, kissing lightly behind my ear. I rested back into him, feeling the soft luxuriousness of my skin against his. The joy, the *relief* was beyond words. The rest – I would think about that tomorrow.

I woke to the sound of someone outside the pavilion calling my name and the cold, damp air of the morning clammy against my bare skin. I sat up and rubbed my eyes with a groan, feeling Lancelot's arm drop away from me. I looked down. He was still asleep. I stood stiffly, feeling the ache in my body from sleeping on the ground, looking around for my bedclothes. I picked the nightdress up from the little heap it lay in by the brazier and pulled it over my head. It was still slightly damp, and I shivered. I pulled my cloak on top. I heard my name again. I glanced back at Lancelot. I would have to go out of the pavilion if I did not want anyone else to come in. I stepped out, my feet still bare on the wet, muddy grass, into the chilly autumn morning, blinking against the light. Outside the pavilion was Gareth. He blushed to see me in my bedclothes with my hair loose.

"I'm sorry, my lady." He looked down, shuffling slightly on his feet.

"What is it, Gareth?" I asked, sterner than I had meant to, anxious to stop him coming into the pavilion.

"I can't find Lancelot anywhere. We need to leave by midday and he said he would help me get ready."

"Isn't he at the castle with Galahalt? Have you looked for him there?"

Gareth shook his head.

"Last night he said he was coming back to the pavilions. He said he was worried about the thunderstorm. I think he was worried about you."

I nodded, feeling the panic beginning to rise in me. I shouldn't have said he was at the castle, or that I hadn't seen him. I could have said that he had ridden out already for something and would be back soon.

"Gareth, let me get dressed and we can look for him."

He nodded, not looking up to meet my eye. It was childish, really, and I found myself getting annoyed. I was not in *such* a state of undress.

When I went back inside, Lancelot was standing, dressed already in his shirt and breeches, pulling on his boots. He looked up as I came in and I felt in my heart the secret flutter of joy, the fresh memory of us together last night close about me, and delicious. He pushed his hair back from his face running his hands through it, then rubbed his face. I could tell he wanted to speak, but did not dare with

Gareth outside. I ran over, light with happiness over the grass, and kissed him tenderly, then moved away to throw off the cloak and nightdress, pulling on an underdress and the armoured blue dress that Nimue had given me. I felt as if I needed it today; not as protection from the outside – I hoped that somehow the platemail bodice would help me hold in my lovely secrets, close to my chest. I turned my back to Lancelot and lifted my hair so that he could help me lace it up at the back. He pressed a kiss at the nape of my neck when he finished. I turned back, into his arms, and wrapping my arms around his neck, kissed him deeply, passionately. I felt the longing rise in me again, but I knew I had to go. I slipped away with a sigh. I plaited my hair and twisted it into a bun and set my little circlet on top. I was sure it looked wrong. I had no skill at dressing my own hair, but as I peered into the little silver mirror I thought I looked queenly enough. No different from yesterday, although I felt entirely different. I found it hard to believe that people would not be able to see it on my face, on my skin. I felt entirely changed. A woman new-made. I straightened up from the mirror and turned back to Lancelot. He stood at the back of the pavilion, waiting. He would have to wait for me to lead Gareth away before he put his mail back on, otherwise Gareth would hear the clanking.

I walked over and took his hand. I leaned up to kiss him softly on the cheek. He took my face in his hands and gave me one last, slow kiss before I had to move away, back out to Gareth, to lead him away from the tents so Lancelot could slip away.

The line was crossed and the world had changed. No more talk of *once*; no more talk of a single sacred memory, or any loyalty either of us bore to Arthur. This was something deeper, more powerful than all of that, wild with the elements, belonging to a world outside of other people, their rules, the obligations that normal men bore to one another. We *would* be together. There was no other way, now, for either of us to exist.

Chapter Twenty-Eight

The journey back to Camelot passed like a dream, in a haze. Lancelot stayed close by and it was enough, enough now that at last we knew that there was no going back and longing had been replaced with bliss. We could ride side by side, and laugh and smile together and Gareth and his brothers would think nothing of it; and I felt no knot of nerves in my stomach, only the secret pleasure of knowledge.

When we came into the great courtyard, Arthur was waiting and I slipped from my horse to run into his arms. He kissed me heartily and smiled. I took his face in my hands and kissed him back, hard. I had missed him. I was pleased to find that the secret love I carried deep inside myself did not change how I felt about Arthur. Well, they were hardly the same thing at all.

Arthur bounded past me to wrap Lancelot in an embrace, clapping him on the back.

"The news of your victories precedes you," he told him with a smile.

Lancelot laughed modestly. Kay came over to me and kissed me on the cheek.

"You look well," he said. He looked relieved. I was pleased to see him, and pleased to see that he saw nothing different in me, nothing new or unfamiliar. If anyone could have seen it, it would have been Kay. He looked well, too; tanned from the summer and relaxed. I realised that I had not seen him looking this well in a long time. He had seemed anxious, edgy, and when he was edgy he was mean. I knew him well enough to know that. So, it seemed that it was not only me that the final dissipation of tension between Lancelot and me had helped. Certainly, I did not feel nervous anymore. It was strange. Now it had begun, it was easy. I felt calm.

I went up to my rooms to bathe away the dust of the journey, and was pleased to see Marie, Christine and Margery waiting for me. I embraced each of them, and even told them I had missed them. Margery nodded dutifully and Christine nodded curtly, but Marie chirruped with joy and told me she had missed me too. Marie stayed with me to help me take off my dress as the others went to fetch water. As Marie unwound my hair and brushed it out, I closed my eyes at the pleasant feel of the rough brush against my scalp and Marie sang softly to herself in Breton. I realised that I had not been happy and at peace in a long time. Not since Lancelot had returned to Camelot from Rome, with Arthur. Now at last everything was resolved. Perhaps it was not what others would say it should be, but at last it was how I needed it to be.

When the bath came I sank into it with a sigh. Christine, Marie and Margery wanted to hear all about the tournament, so I told them. I told them how Lancelot had won every battle he had fought, how Gawain and his brothers had terrified their enemies, how Galahalt had been a simpering idiot. They gasped and laughed in all the right places. I felt I was back at home after a long *long* time, though it had only been four days. It was because I was back at home with myself.

Christine dressed me for the feast – for of course there would be one for the victorious return of Arthur's most favoured knights – in a lovely dress of dark purple velvet; new, she told me, a gift from one of Arthur's vassals in the north of France, perfect for the ripening autumn, sewn with little swirls in gold around the neck, and the ends of the sleeves, and around the waist. It felt soft and luxurious against my skin, a welcome relief from the travelling clothes that had grown scratchy and dirty with my sweat, and the sweat of the horse.

When I descended the stairs, Lancelot was waiting for me at the foot of them, and took my hand as I stepped of the final step. I smiled at him, and he pressed a soft kiss against my hand.

"You look lovely, my lady."

I did a little curtsey, proper as a queen. This was *easy*. If I had known this would be so easy, if I had known how much better this would be than longing, I would have taken the step long ago. It certainly looked the same to everyone around us. I was sure that Arthur would even be pleased to see us smile at one another, relieved that his champion was receiving the favour owed to his station.

At the feast, Lancelot sat on the other side of Arthur, out of my sight, but I could feel him there, like a fire whose heat reached me across the room. My appetite that night was hearty, and I took a bite of everything Arthur offered me. The food was delicious. I felt as though I was tasting it for the first time, the sauces sharp with citrus and thick with the lovely fats of the meat joints, the vegetables fresh and full of the life of the earth. Kay, who sat beside me, handed me a peach and I bit into it, instantly, feeling the juice trickle down my chin, and wiping it away with the back of my hand. We laughed together.

"It has been a long time since I heard you laugh," he told me, with a broad smile. He let his hand rest lightly against my knee under the table, but the touch was brisk and friendly. I kissed him on the cheek, full of a giddy joy.

"Too long, I think," I agreed.

Behind me I was conscious of Lancelot telling the others the stories of the tournament. I liked the sound of his voice close by, and the private knowledge of what it had said to me, in the secret hours of the night. It was wonderful to hear him talk freely, and I realised that this was how he had talked when he had not been around me before. Light-hearted; funny. He was a good storyteller, and his way with the other men was easy and friendly. I felt as though we had lifted a weight from both of us, and I was glad. I found myself laughing at Gawain's stories of the tournament, too, rough as they were. Everything around me seemed light, and bright, and full of hope and goodness.

Even at the end of the feast, when Arthur stood to bid his men goodnight, and took my hand in his, and we stepped from the table, leaving Lancelot and the others, I felt the thrill of the secret I shared with Lancelot glimmer between us. As Arthur walked with me from the room, his hand at the small of my back, I turned back and gazed over my shoulder at Lancelot. His gaze met mine, and a slight smile unfurled across his face, subtle and secret, but there. I would go to bed with Arthur, but we both knew that this was something else entirely. It was beyond that kind of betrayal, the love we shared. It was beyond *ought* and *must*. It was a force of nature, like the tides or the changing of the moon, and sure as I was of those, I was sure that Lancelot and I would come together again.

That night with Arthur was the first time in a long time that I did not think of Lancelot. The place he now held deep in my heart, deep at the core of me, meant that I did not feel the need to hold him in my mind lest he slip away. I was sure of him. I let Arthur take me in his arms; I let Arthur have me as a wife. I loved him as a wife, and none of that touched what I had with Lancelot, just as my love for Lancelot did not touch the love I had for Arthur. I sank into the rapture of Arthur's familiar embrace, his familiar touch, that I had longed for while we were parted, and I thought, *this is what it is like to have everything you want*.

My joy made me reckless. I held the two loves separate in my heart, and I told myself I did not care what the others thought. I sought Lancelot out often, and he sought me. We lay together reading in the walled garden, and laughing, and we sat together in the courtyard, watching the men fighting, discussing their styles, eating the last of the peaches from the summer. I spent my nights with Arthur, and sat at his side at meals and councils, but always my eyes were on Lancelot, and his on me.

The mood was festive all round the court and either everyone was full of a bright optimism, or I suddenly was. There were games, and hunts, and feasts often called. One day, in the depths of autumn, on a clear and lovely day when a few leaves still hung on the trees but were deep brown, and the air was mild and still, Lancelot and I found ourselves suddenly alone on a hunt. The faster riders – those faster than me, at any rate – had passed us by, and all at once it was just him and me, and the soft, sweet green silence of the woods. I felt my heart flutter. They would pass back this way; it would be just a moment. To my surprise, Lancelot jumped down from his horse as though he had spotted something off the path, and without a word disappeared among the trees. I slipped from my own horse to follow him into the cool heart of the wood that smelled of moss and wonderful secrets. I saw what he had seen. There was a small patch of wild strawberries at the base of one of the trees. They showed red and bright as jewels. He leaned down and picked one, and stepped forward to place it lightly against my lips. They parted under his touch, and I felt my body weaken, warm already with hunger. The berry was sweet, and pleasantly sharp in my mouth. Lancelot drew me to him gently, kissing me softly, leaning back as I moved towards him, overwhelmed already by my desire. I could hear the blood pounding with it in my ears already. I was not sure if he was teasing me, playing with my desire, or if he was afraid we would be found.

Reluctantly, I pulled away from him, and turned back to the little patch of berries, leaning down to pick one for him. As I stood, before I could turn back from him, he seized me hard, one hand burrowing into my plaited hair at the nape of my neck, the other at my hip, and kissed me, suddenly wild with it. He eased a little, pulling back, but when I kissed him harder in response he began to relent a little, sinking into it, and I felt his tongue flicker against mine, the heat of his body rising with mine. I felt my body filled with the heat of longing. I wanted his skin on mine, I wanted us to come together. I sighed his name, and he hushed me gently. He let his lips brush up my neck, and I felt myself quiver slightly under their touch, and then his hand slid from my hip to the lacing at the front of my hunting breeches, pulling it undone and sliding inside. When I felt his fingers against me, I moaned softly, and he hushed me again, turning my face to his to kiss me once more. His kiss was deep, and sensual, and his fingers moving against me brought a tight, bright point of pleasure to the soft warm cloud of heat and longing that my body had already been filled with. It was fast that it came upon me and I shivered in his hands with it, and he pressed his mouth against mine, taking my desperate sigh into him. I wanted to put my hands on his body, to feel his skin against mine, to have him inside me; it was all the more overwhelming then for everything I had already felt, but I could hear the sound of distant hooves again.

I still had the little red berry in my hand, and before we went back to our horses, I lifted it to his lips, and the rest of the day, I tasted the sweet taste of the berry on my lips and knew that Lancelot was tasting the same. I knew what we were doing was dangerous, but somehow I had never felt so safe. And I longed, longed more than anything, for us to have a night alone together once more.

I moved through my days as if I had nothing to hide, and I felt utterly ordinary and content. Slowly, the fame of the court was spreading and more and more knights came to pledge themselves to Arthur and hoped to join his band of men. There was always much for me to do at his side, and Lancelot too, but we waited and we watched for the times when we might be alone together.

It was not until the great feast at Christmas that the opportunity for us to be alone came again. Or, I suppose, that the long wait forced on our desire demanded an opportunity be made. It had been a glorious celebration, the hall decked in ivy and filled with music, more dishes than I could count of wonderful meats, fruits, nuts, and lovely soft fresh bread. Around the high table were just me and Arthur and his closest knights – Lancelot, Lamerocke, Dinadan, Perceval, Kay, and Gawain and his brothers – and all the talk was of victories past and new adventures. Lamerocke wanted to ride out towards Cornwall to find Tristan de Lyones and test his strength against him, Dinadan wanted to go out to the tournament at Lonzep; Gawain wanted to seek more adventures in France. The atmosphere was merry and I felt a happy warmth within me. Everyone was slowly getting drunk, Arthur beside me, flushed and laughing, telling again the old tale of how he had ridden into the heart of Rome with Lancelot at his side. I felt the delicious fuzziness of the wine around me, and it filled me with daring. When the eating was over, the games began, and Kay chased Gawain around the hall wearing a green monster's head he and Gareth had spent all afternoon making out of old scraps of vellum painted green, and roaring, until Gawain suddenly rounded on him and pulled the head off, and both men fell to the floor with laughter. Gareth and Gaheris were trying to teach Dinadan a dance, but the brothers were slower and clumsier than the nimble little Dinadan, and anyway they were all three too drunk to learn or teach anything. Even Perceval looked like he was having fun. When I saw Arthur take up the paper head and start chasing Kay, I caught Lancelot's eye and slipped out of the back of the hall, out into the crisp winter night in the courtyard, skipping out under the stars. A few of the lesser knights who had been gathering at court were out there, huddled around braziers with wine, and some of the women of the castle mingled among them. They nodded at me as I went by, and I waved. Lancelot caught up with me, scooping me up into his arms from behind, as I reached the shadow of the tower that held my rooms and I swallowed a laugh that might give me away, turning round in his arms to meet his kiss. There was honey, sweet on his lips, from the feast, and the same heady spiced wine that was on mine, and my head swam already with the thrill of kissing him out there in the open courtyard, but unseen, and the deep yearning woke slowly, deliciously, within me for him. As I pulled Lancelot through the doorway, over his shoulder I glimpsed little Marie jumping into the arms of Gaheris, who must have stepped out into the cool night just after me, and I was pleased that it was he, not Gawain, who she had been sneaking off to see. So, it seemed it was a night for such passions.

As soon as I slammed the door behind me, Lancelot pressed against me, thrillingly insistent, holding me against the wall, and we kissed with a blind passion, a little clumsy with the wine, but more wild with desire. It was tantalising to feel his whole body pressed against mine, and I longed to tear away the clothes that held us apart. My fingers fumbled on the buttons of his surcoat, pulling it open.

The door opened beside us and we sprang apart as Gaheris stumbled a few steps in. I heard Marie shout from outside, "Not in *there!*" and laugh. Gaheris noticed Lancelot, but not me, hidden as I was behind the open door, and gave him a big, proud smile. As soon as the door was shut again, I was in Lancelot's arms, and he drew me up the stairs as we came together in hungry, desperate kisses. I knew we would never have the time to have our passion at our leisure as we had had in Surluse, and these snatched moments had to be taken at once or lost, and this filled me with a new, wonderful fire, bold and wild. I stepped ahead of him up the stairs, eager, pulling him towards me by the front of his shirt, pulled open already by my demanding touch, and as I stepped backwards, he came with me, pulling me close, and we sank down there. I felt the cool step against my back, hard and exciting. His hands were on me, one slowly running up my leg under the skirts of my dress, the other at my breast; the press of his thumb as it brushed my nipple through the fabric made me groan softly for the feel of his skin bare against mine. I slid my hands up under his shirt, running them across his chest. His fingers found the place between my legs and I gasped at his touch. I longed to feel his tongue on me, as I had Arthur's. I felt the little gold circlet roll from my hair and fall with a delicate tinkling sound down the stairs. I did not care. I reached for Lancelot's breeches and, with a smile, he grasped me by the wrists and held my arms over my head as he had done before.

"Impatient as always, my lady," he teased as he came to kiss me, pulling at my lower lip gently, with his teeth. I sighed hard against him, wrapping my legs around him and drawing him to me. The sweet, heady warmth of the wine made each sensation feel as though it was filling my whole body, swirling in a delicious vertigo in my mind. I whispered his name, pressing against him, and with a low growl of pleasure, he too gave up his patience, releasing a wrist of mine for a moment to open his breeches, and, grasping me again, he entered me. I gasped again, and he kissed me hard. The step was rough against my back, but I did not care, nor did I care as my hair net broke and the hair tumbled around me. Lancelot held me fast, close over me. Our eyes met and I felt that, too, at the centre of me, intensifying the ecstasy growing within me. He let go of my wrists to wind his hands into the hair that fell free around my shoulders. I relished the feeling of his fingers against my scalp, the roughness of his passion, as he pulled my head back to kiss the soft skin at the side of my neck. I called out his name softly as I felt the heat inside me explode into light and he kissed me again, suddenly slow and tender, as he relaxed against me and I wrapped my arms around him with a small sigh of deep content.

He moved away slowly, but it still felt too soon, too brief. I pulled my knees up to my chest, and pushed my skirts back down over them, and rested my chin on my knees. Lancelot, who had stood to dress again, sighed sadly to see me and knelt again before me to take my face in his hands and kiss me. This was better than being without him; the pent-up passion, the desperate urgency. I wanted to take him up to my room and sleep beside him as we had done at Surluse. All of sudden it was unbearable that it could not be. He gently pulled me to my feet. I felt sober, suddenly. He wrapped his arms around me and, sliding a hand behind my head, into my hair again, pulled me into a long, deep kiss. I melted against him.

When he pulled away at last, he stroked my hair lightly, and spoke as though he was answering my thoughts.

"I am sorry, too, that this is how it must be."

He offered to walk with me to my room, but I said I would prefer to go alone. It would be too hard to say goodbye to him there. I was not sure I would be able to do it. As I walked the small flight of steps up to it, I could feel I was trembling slightly, but the comforting warmth of the wine was coming back to me. I shut the door and fell back on the bed and closed my eyes, trying to feel again what we had just had, his mouth on mine, hot with desire, the feel of his overwhelming passion, that was mine as well, both of ours at once. I wanted to hold it tight before the memory slipped away from the sensations of my body and existed only in my mind.

Then I heard the door open and sat up sharply. It was Arthur, eager with wine, and he had been looking for me. In his hand he had the circlet that had fallen from my hair, and he tossed it to the floor. He did not ask how I had lost it. I opened my mouth to make an excuse, not wanting the feel of Arthur to erase what I had just known, but he already had me in his arms, climbing on top of me on the bed, pulling his surcoat then his shirt off, ripping apart the lacing at the back of my dress and tearing it off, kissing me with a rough insistent passion. Somehow his roughness was different from Lancelot's, more animal, more muscular, more about power than desire. But despite myself, I was already losing myself in it, in his overwhelming strength. I was afraid he might smell another man on me, but he did not seem to notice anything unusual, and I was afraid that I would not desire it, but the fire that Lancelot had started within me was still there, and when Arthur tore away the underdress, ripping it apart since he was too drunk to bother with the lacing, I pushed him gently downwards. When I felt his tongue against me, I cried aloud, and grasped a handful of the silk bedcovers, lost with it. It came fast and hard, the white hot bliss, filling my body with a tingling, wonderful ecstasy, and Arthur was fast inside me, pressing his face into my neck, murmuring my name as I held him tight against me, closing my eyes, as the white hot joy turned warm and soft as honey within me.

When I fell asleep, I dreamt of both of their hands on me at once.

Chapter Twenty-Nine

The sweet memory lingered with me as long as I could have hoped, but still it was not long before once again I burned for Lancelot, and moved through my days in a kind of trance, waiting for the moment to come when we might be alone.

As the days grew longer and warmer, whenever Lancelot was about the court and not travelling across Logrys assisting Arthur, we would sit out together in the walled garden and read, but always with us were Margery, Christine and Marie, and Kay and Gareth often as well. Though, one night when the blossoms were thick on the trees, and Arthur had ridden north to King Pellinore's lands to settle some dispute there, I met Lancelot in the little garden and we were together under the clear night sky, with the winking stars, and the fresh, green spring grass tickling against my bare skin. After that, I sat with a little secret smile on my face whenever we sat there in the daytime, with the others.

It was on an early summer day that Lancelot and I found ourselves there alone. There was some kind of argument going on in the courtyard and Marie and Christine, who had been the only ones with us, rushed away to see what it was. I sighed and lay back, resting my head against his thigh as he sat beside me, cross-legged. He stroked my hair and I closed my eyes, enjoying the warmth of the sun and the pleasure of his touch. I did not know how long we would be alone, but just a moment was a beautiful thing to be savoured. I slowly pushed myself back up to sitting beside him. I wanted to lean over and kiss him, but I was afraid to start something that I might not be able to stop. He placed a gentle hand against my cheek and leaned in to kiss me softly, and just the gentle brush of his lips against mine sent sparks through my body and, grasping a handful of his shirt at the front, I pulled him closer, kissing deeper. He was slow and sensual, and it brought up memories of our first night together. I wanted his hands on me, I wanted his skin against mine, but I could hear from the courtyard that people were calling my name. *No, no, no, don't make me go.* But Lancelot had heard it too, and snatched himself away, jumping to his feet. I got to my feet slowly, feeling stunned, and followed the sound of my name out into the courtyard.

Christine was standing in the middle, her arms around Margery who was sobbing against her shoulder. She was screaming at Gawain. Christine was flushed deep with anger, and Gawain, though he was a mountain of a man, almost half her size again, stood warily back from it. Aggravain stood just behind Gawain, his arms folded and a look of disdain on his face. Gareth, Gaheris and Kay were standing with Christine and Margery. I could not see Arthur anywhere.

They all turned to look at us as we arrived, except Margery, who buried her face in the front of Christine's dress, like a child.

"What's going on?" I asked, looking between Gawain and Christine.

Gawain pointed an accusing finger at Christine.

"Your woman is diseased in the head, that's what." He turned back to Aggravain. "Get Arthur. He'll sort this out."

"He raped Margery," Christine said quietly.

I rounded on Gawain.

"Gawain, is that true?" I demanded.

He rocked back on his heels, defiant, resting his hand on his sword, but I was too angry to be afraid of him. If I had had a sword, I would have struck him. I could feel Lancelot's presence at my back, close by, and I felt safe. Invincible, even. I was sure that he was already tensed in preparation in case there was a fight.

"No. The girl's upset," he gestured vaguely, casually, in Margery's direction, "because – I don't know – she didn't like it as much as she thought she would."

"Margery, what happened?" I asked her gently, turning my back to Gawain who already I did not believe.

Arthur arrived as she began to speak, through her sobs, in a quavering voice. Christine still held her protectively against her bosom, stroking her hair with one hand.

"I went out to the woods, to swim in the little pool. When I was finished swimming, I lay down on the side to dry off in the sun, and Gawain came by, and he, he..." She began sobbing again, too hard to talk, and Christine shushed her gently.

"You see!" Gawain exclaimed, throwing his arms out in a gesture of frustration. "She was *naked*."

Aggravain and some of the other knights nodded in agreement. I glanced at Arthur. He looked impassive, and I sensed he was waiting for my judgement.

"She was a virgin, you brute. You ought to be ashamed to call yourself a knight," Christine spat at Gawain. He stepped towards her, raising a hand to strike her. At once I stepped forward to go between them, and so did Lancelot, and Aggravain moved to Gawain's side, and Margery screamed and Christine shouted obscenities at Gawain in Breton. In the background, I heard the unmistakable hiss of a sword being drawn, though I did not see by whom, and felt Lancelot's hand on my arm, ready to pull me back and step in front of me; but I was already going forward, carried by my anger, and all around everyone was shouting, until Arthur called out for silence and it suddenly fell, and stillness with it.

"*Stop*. This will be resolved, and Gawain will make reparation."

"No, my lord. I am a knight, and I will fight to prove my innocence. The girl was *naked*." He, with his hand heavy on his sword's hilt, cocked his head threateningly towards Lancelot, eyeing up the man he thought would be his opponent.

"A knight you may be, in name at least, but in this you shall have the law," I insisted fiercely.

"And what is the judgement *of the law*?" Gawain asked, derisively, leaning down close to me. He must have been angry, too, otherwise he would not have dared show me such aggression in front of Arthur.

"Exile." I crossed my arms in front of my chest, drawing myself up before Gawain. He did not intimidate me. He was a dumb animal.

He thought as a woman that I would not know the law, but I had made it my business to read the heavy, dusty books of it, and now I was glad of the long hours I had spent. I knew the law far better than he did.

There was a murmur of discontent among the knights, and Aggravain spat at his feet, but Arthur raised a hand again for silence.

"Arthur..." Gawain turned past me to him, his tone full of appeal, but to my relief Arthur was unmoved.

"Gawain, I will be sorry to see you go, but you will respect the judgement of your queen." Arthur came to stand beside me, and as he came Lancelot silently receded, as though giving his place as my protector to Arthur. Arthur turned to ask me, "What are the terms of the exile?"

I met Gawain's look of anger and resentment with an even stare. I was not afraid of a man like him, violent and hasty. He would get what he deserved.

"Two years. Or until you can bring back a woman who can attest to your virtue, kindness and gentleness. *Whichever is the longer.*"

Gawain bridled at this.

"Arthur..." he began again, but Arthur shook his head and replied in a tone that broached no argument.

"The punishment is appropriate. Don't forget, Gawain, that we all swore an oath to give our protection and kindness to the women in our care. We are not at war anymore, Gawain, this isn't the battlefield. Margery is not a woman of our enemies. You have done injury to one of our own, and you will endure the law, though you are my own dear nephew."

Gawain nodded slowly in acceptance and turned to leave, and the crowd began to disperse. It must have been strange for him to hear Arthur, who was also the friend who drank and sang lewd songs with him, pass such formal judgement upon him. But perhaps he had been foolish to forget that Arthur was his king, and just because he had his favour he was not above the law. Christine led Margery away briskly, casting a poisonous look over her shoulder at Gawain as she did. I let the breath rush out of me, suddenly conscious that I was holding it. Arthur wrapped an arm around my waist and pulled me up to him.

"What a fearsome queen I have." He kissed me briskly. A serious, concerned look passed across his face. "If I had not been there, I think you might have offered to fight Gawain yourself."

"I think Christine would have been at him first."

He nodded thoughtfully.

"But I am sorry for it, that I will lose him. He is rash. But two years is not so long, and he will learn." Arthur glanced off after where Gawain had left. "You have to forgive his rudeness to you a little. The law is different in Lothian. It's written with blood. They're feuding people, that far north, and life is rougher there than here. Well, the problem in Pellinore's kingdom – it was that Gawain had killed him, in recompense for Pellinore killing his father in battle almost ten years ago. That's the way of the kingdom he grew up in. It's blood for blood there. He would not have seen what he did to Margery as public business to be resolved by the law of the king, but something to be settled between her family and his. But the judgement is right. Whoever Gawain is, in my kingdom he will live by our law."

I let Margery leave Camelot and go back to the town that was her parents' home after that. It did not seem fair to keep her there. Aggravain seemed to blame her for Gawain's banishment and gave her cruel and threatening looks as she passed him in the courtyard. When he thought I wasn't looking he would sometimes grab at her, to frighten her. Marie said that every night she heard her crying, and so I felt I had to send her away. I missed her, her slow smile as she finally caught on to a joke, her sweet, clumsy way. Arthur considered the matter dealt with and solved, but I kept a wary eye on Aggravain, conscious now that I had made an enemy.

Chapter Thirty

The weeks and months passed, and became more than a year, and still I lived this double life, not so much half a life with Arthur and half with Lancelot, as the life of two women, and these two women became wrapped up in my one little body – one good wife, one wild and secret lover. And I could be both, and be both well. I still loved Arthur; I loved him with the deep, sweet passion that came from our happy life together, and love of our bodies that we had felt together for a long time. He had been the first man I had loved, and not even Lancelot's great passion could wash that away. I missed him when he travelled away, I longed for him. I loved him as completely as I could love *him*, because I also loved Lancelot, and that was something else entirely. It was the longing of the wolf for the moon, the sea for the shore, the quiet buds for spring. Our love was part of the world, part of existence. I knew it would always be, and I could wait, always wait, for any moment alone together. I had felt nothing more natural in my life than my love for Lancelot. And, while it was the love of our bodies that had brought me and Arthur together, from which that love had grown, with Lancelot, on those rare moments when we could come together, it all felt part of this huge, wondrous love that filled the world. I felt none of the guilt I had expected to feel, and I was sure it was because these two loves I knew, these two passions, were entirely different, and I belonged entirely to each man, and held nothing of my love back from either. They were only different kinds.

The time passed uneventfully, largely, and Camelot flourished more and more. The company of knights swelled, and more young men became knights. Gareth rode out alone on some task for Arthur and came back with a lovely young wife called Lynesse who joined my women at court, and Lancelot made him a knight. He was a man, suddenly, the shy little boy who had asked me for a kiss in the garden, and he fought more with the other men and sat less with us, reading. News came from Surluse, that the tournament would not be held because Galahalt had died. I asked about his son, and the messenger said that the son Marhalt had been dead a year. He had died on the last night of the tournament. Poisoned wine was suspected, but it seemed to have been only him. When I asked Lancelot if he knew anything later he told me that the cup had been meant for him and he had swapped his cup with Marhalt's. I was pleased that I had, also, never drunk from the cup meant for me. All the while, Lancelot and I loved secretly, and Arthur and I openly. I had been afraid at first that Lancelot would not be able to bear the thought of me with Arthur, but he seemed, too, capable of holding in himself both his love for me, and his love for his king, and he never spoke of it. When he talked about Arthur, if he talked about me as Arthur's queen, he would speak as if nothing was happening between us, as if I was just another queen he was describing.

Tristan came to court, and I found him a smug and irritating youth, but the men seemed to think he was charming. He fought well enough, reaching deadlock in a standing fight with Lancelot and earning the cheers of the people watching the games. We had more of those, too. More pageants and jousts and feasts. Things were good; all was well. There was peace, and plenty, and better still, joy. I floated around as though through a lovely dream, my happiness buoying me, a secret bliss clutched to my heart.

As two years came to an end, Gawain returned, with a sulky teenage girl who shrugged when she attested to his kindness, but Arthur was so pleased to see his beloved nephew and friend again that he declared Gawain's sentence spent before I could protest. I was not pleased to have him back when I noticed that he and Aggravain would stand together and whisper, or watch me narrowly, making me uneasy. Arthur told me I was imagining it, but whenever I was not with Arthur, I was sure I felt their eyes on me. When I told Lancelot, he said nothing. It worried him, too.

Not long after Gawain's return, I was standing in the courtyard watching Kay and Lancelot training while Lynesse and Marie watched Gareth and Gaheris do the same. It was a lovely late spring day and it was bright but still fresh and cool. The sound of horses' hooves drew all our eyes.

A knight rode in through the open gate and slid from his horse to pull off his helm. For a moment, though I knew he was there beside me, I thought I was seeing Lancelot standing before me, though his hair was the same ethereal white-blonde of Nimue's. The knight looked so much like him, had the same high cheekbones, angular handsome face, blue eyes. He, too, was tall and leanly muscled, and stood with the same leonine grace. I heard the clatter of someone dropping their sword in astonishment to look at him. I heard Kay mutter an exclamation of surprise under his breath. The knight stepped forward and sunk to one knee before me. I was frozen to the spot with surprise.

"My lady queen, I am named Galahad, and I come to ask to join your lord husband's companionship of knights, and I bring news of a great quest." He looked up at me, and the eyes I knew so well looking back caught the breath from me. I waved a hand vaguely at the building behind me.

"My lord Arthur is... within," was all I managed to say.

He moved past me into the tower where Arthur's rooms were. Open-mouthed and silent, I gazed about me at the others. No one spoke. I saw that it was Lancelot whose sword had dropped from his hands. I was not surprised that it had stunned him so. After a long, long pause where we just stared dumbly at one another, Kay turned to Lancelot and grasped him by the shoulder.

"Lancelot, that knight looked *just* like you."

"I know," Lancelot said, nodding slowly.

Kay turned to me and gestured with a little shooing motion towards where Galahad had gone.

"Go after him and find out what's going on."

I crossed my arms in front on my chest and looked at him with a sternness that was only half-playful.

"No. I'm the queen, you're my subject, *you* go after him."

Kay laughed and did a little bow.

"It ought to be you," he said in an odd tone that I couldn't place. "I'll stay out here and try to sort Lancelot out."

Lancelot was staring blankly after where Galahad had gone. When I caught his eye, he looked at me with wide-eyed panic. He had been the victim of shape-shifting before, and this strange man who bore his face seemed to threaten more of the same.

I found Galahad and Arthur in the council-room with the Round Table. Arthur smiled when he saw me and got to his feet, reaching out to take my hand and lead me towards Galahad, who stood at the window looking down at the people in the courtyard below. He turned to us both with a deferential little nod.

"Guinevere, this is Lancelot's son, Galahad. He's come to join my knights, and brings news of the Grail."

I looked at Arthur, furrowing my brow into a confused frown.

"That doesn't make any sense," I said. Galahad was young, but he was a youth, a young man, rather than a boy, and could not have been more than ten or at the very most fifteen years younger than Lancelot, which made it seem impossible or at the least very unlikely to be true. Arthur didn't look as though he followed my meaning.

Galahad spoke softly, in a neat, polite little voice. His *voice* at least was another man's voice entirely to Lancelot's; shy and light and faintly girlish.

"My lady queen, please permit me to explain. I was born in a convent on the isle of Avalon and raised by the nuns there." A *convent* on Avalon? Arthur said that Morgan had been raised in a convent, once, and a convent in a barrow-land like Avalon might raise such a strange man as this. "I did not know my mother, though she was a noble lady, the nuns assure me, but I always knew that Lancelot was my father, and heard tales of him; my mother's name was Elaine."

Morgan. This was Morgan's child. But that child couldn't be more than four, five years old. Strange, then, that I had no sense at all of the Otherworld from Galahad. Perhaps the nuns had purged it from him with their prayers. It seemed to me that Arthur's god of right and wrong could only be the enemy of the complex powers of the Otherworld.

"They always told me that a special quest would bring me to Camelot, and to my father, Sir Lancelot. Three nights ago I dreamed of the Cup of Christ and they told me it was time for me to come here, to you, my lord Arthur. It is a sign, a sign from God, that the knights of this court are ready." His eyes were aglow with religious fervour when he spoke of it, and I saw Arthur's eyebrows raise. I thought of the cursed destiny that weighed heavy on him. Did he hope for redemption? "We should gather the best, my lord, and ride out to seek the Grail."

Arthur nodded slowly in agreement, and I could see the excitement bubbling up in him. But I knew what this meant. *All the best knights of the court.* They would want Lancelot to go.

At the feast that evening, everyone stared at the strange white-haired ghost of Lancelot. I did not know how any issue of Morgan's could be so pure, but he was everything I would not have expected him to be. Arthur had called Lancelot to him when he had sent Galahad away, and had explained as best he could who Galahad was. Lancelot nodded thoughtfully. I knew he knew as I did that this was Morgan's child. When he had a few cups of wine in him, Gawain leaned across the table to bellow at Lancelot, pointing to Galahad.

"He looks just like you. *Just like you.*"

Many of the knights around the table nodded in agreement, and Arthur told them he was Lancelot's son. They seemed to accept that, unwilling to count out years on their fingers. I did not like all the talk of sons and children, did not like to hear the words. I could, besides, feel Arthur looking at me, any time those words were said, as though he were afraid I might be upset. It only made it worse. When Galahad spoke to confirm Arthur's words, and introduce himself to them, Kay caught me with his eye, and his look was unreadable. I felt as though he was taking the measure of me, somehow. I did not know what he could be looking for.

It was decided that three weeks would be given for knights to decide whether they would take up the quest for the Grail, and we would feast again in three weeks' time, and those who pledged themselves to the quest would go.

That night, as I was falling asleep, Arthur suddenly spoke.

"There are times when I wish I was not the king." I murmured in sympathy, drifting on the edge of sleep. "I can't turn away this quest, but I don't want to lose my best knights to it. They won't all come back alive, probably not even most of them. And, I will never see the Grail, won't be healed of any of my sins."

He was silent for a long time, and I wondered if he had fallen back asleep, but then he said very softly.

"I have killed so many men."

Arthur went to the chapel first thing in the morning, and I went with him. I liked the quiet, the regularity of the same little prayers over and over again. I was getting used to it; I was learning more about Arthur's god. I didn't always listen when I went with him on Sundays, but sometimes I did. I hadn't heard of the Grail, though. I didn't know if it was the same as the Cup of Christ or not, because I had always thought a Grail was a kind of long, shallow dish. I knew about the blood of Christ, about the spear of Longinus, but I couldn't piece Galahad's quest into one coherent whole in my head. I wasn't sure what exactly he wanted them to look for, or how it would help.

The smell of the chapel – old wood, leather, dust and candles – was comforting, and I was happy to kneel at Arthur's side, lost in my thoughts, while he prayed. I supposed I ought to pray, too, but I did not know what I wanted. His god did not sound as if he would be sympathetic to my wanting Lancelot to stay. I knew well enough the name his priests gave to what we did. I didn't want to pray for forgiveness, either, because I wasn't sorry. To me our love was sacred, more sacred than the chapel and the sad-faced Christ, and I would not be made to regret it.

Arthur was quiet and thoughtful, and left without a word when he had finished his prayers. I wasn't ready to leave the silence, and I was pleased to be alone for a moment. It was pleasantly cool in the big stone building and I thought I might like to read. I slipped into the little library at the back. There was a big leather-bound bible there, lettered inside with gold and drawn with lovely pictures. I had tried to read it once, but I didn't understand the Latin and I didn't want Arthur to suggest Morgan teach me again, so I had left it. Arthur didn't understand Latin either, so I didn't know why he didn't get one written in the language of Britain, but that did not seem to be the way it was done. I looked through the books but I found that I felt too restless to read. I felt as though I was waiting for something, but I didn't know what.

I wandered back out into the chapel. Galahad was there, kneeling at the altar, saying his prayers in a whisper. I sat down in one of the front pews and waited for him to be done. I felt as though I wanted to talk to him, and I was glad when he came over to me when he saw me, and sat beside me. He gazed up at the face of Christ where he hung over us. I glanced at him, thoughtfully. There was truly no way that he could be as old as he looked.

"Galahad," I asked quietly, "how old are you?"

He turned to me. His eyes were soft and kind; innocent, like the eyes of a child.

"I don't know," he admitted, quietly. "I know I grew fast into a man, because this was the destined time, the time I must come to Camelot, and to my father, with the quest."

I did not know why Morgan had given him to the nuns, nor why there was nothing *at all* about him of the Otherworld. The talk of destiny made me uncomfortable because it reminded me of Merlin. *This is Arthur's destiny.* It made me uneasy; it made me feel as if things were about to come to some kind of awful end. I was glad at least that Arthur could not go looking for the Grail.

"The Grail?" I asked.

He nodded his head.

"The vessel that bears Christ's blood. King Arthur's knights are great men of the world, but it is time they became great men of the spirit, and the sight of the Grail brings men grace. He who looks on it can die without sin."

They would want it; they would *all* want that. To live their lives as they had, as men of the world, who came and sat in chapel and nodded along to *thou shalt not kill*, but have the sight of the Grail wash that all away, and wash all their other sins. That was the problem with sin – it needed to be erased. But I thought a life without sin was different from a life filled with *goodness*. With rightness. With honesty to the self. If you killed a man because he was attacking those under your protection, I did not think that that was a sin. Sin did not make sense in this world of warriors, I did not think. Galahad would have them all thinking of sin, of the things they had done against the will of Christ and God.

I went looking for Lancelot, afraid that thoughts of sin were creeping up to him as well, but he must not have wanted to be found because he was not in any of the places we went to look for one another; in the garden, out in the courtyard, in the room with the Round Table. Gawain and Aggravain were loitering in the courtyard, and I didn't ask them if they had seen him. I still got the sense that neither of them wished to speak with me.

That night I said to Arthur, "I don't want Lancelot to go." I knew I should not have said it, I should not have voiced anything I felt about it, but I was sure that Arthur was the only one who could stop it. Arthur came over to where I stood by the window of his bedroom, gazing down at the fields below which were already filling with pavilions as the vassal knights from the outlying kingdoms of Britain came, hungry for a chance to ride out for glory, the blood of a god and the favour of their powerful king. There was not enough room in the small fortress city to hold everyone. He stood behind me, and wrapped his arms around me and kissed the side of my head.

"Neither do I," he admitted. He did not seem to see anything odd or suspicious in my desire to keep Lancelot at Camelot. I supposed he was my champion and I had a right to have him by me. "But if ever there was a man without sin who did not *have* to seek the Grail, it's Lancelot." I turned full into his arms, resting my head against his chest, strong and comfortingly familiar. He stroked my hair lightly. "Though I suppose, he too has got a bastard child. He does not seem to be taking the arrival of Galahad too well, although he seems to like the boy himself well enough."

I did not know that they had spoken. Perhaps that is why I had not been able to find Lancelot, because he had been with that strange son of his, trying to make sense of it. I could tell that Arthur was thinking of the child he had somewhere, the one his god was going to punish him for. I wondered if the child had even survived, up in the cold, hostile wastes of Lothian. It did not seem fair that the cursed child lived, and Merlin had taken mine.

I did not find the oblivion I was used to in Arthur's arms that night, and I felt quiet and half-absent, though he did not seem to notice. He was haunted by his own thoughts. I thought only of Lancelot, wondering where he was, praying that he would not go. I did not think that Arthur slept that night. I felt him get up out of the bed in the middle of the night, and when I woke he was long gone. I felt as though I was losing both of them at once.

Chapter Thirty-One

I found Lancelot at last a few days later. He was waiting for me in the walled garden. So, he had come at last, ready to talk. I had seen from the window what I thought was his pavilion, too: deep purple silk, a colour that I thought I had seen on his horse before. That meant he was preparing to leave. He had not come to me first to say that was what he planned to do.

When I walked in and saw him there, I stopped in the archway and crossed my arms, stubbornly waiting for an explanation of where he had been. He was dressed in just his shirt and breeches, but he had his sword at his side. At least he did not look as though he was riding out somewhere immediately. Around us, the garden was beginning to bloom, and I was reluctant to step fully into the space with him where I knew I would lose my resolve. He had been hiding from me, and I wanted an explanation. I was pleased that I was dressed that day in the finest of my clothes, the green and gold dress sewn with crosses, and the circlet of gold. It made me feel more like a queen, more stern and commanding. As a lover, I could only beg him to stay. As his queen I could command him not to leave me.

"Guinevere –" He reached out a hand to me, and I lingered back. I was not ready to give in until I had a promise from him that he would stay.

"I don't want you to go," I told him, firmly.

To my surprise, he nodded in agreement.

"Then I won't go." I was stunned. That was easy. Everything I had feared had not come to pass. He was not full of regret, or guilt, or longing to see the Grail. He came over to me and took me in his arms. "If you want me to stay, I won't go."

I leaned up and kissed him, wrapping my arms around his neck, pulling him fast against me. He held me close, and I felt the wonderful relief wash over me. He would stay. *He would stay.* The smell of the blossoms of the garden and his skin mingled around me, full of hope and promise. The feel of his lips against mine was like the first time, and I was losing myself in it already, the world around me receding to nothingness. With breathless delight, I murmured his name. There were words, so many words of relief and joy that he would stay, but they were all lost, lost in the blissful moment. With a sudden rush of passion he pushed me up against the wall of the garden, running his hands hungrily over my body, over the fabric of the dress. I felt the longing strong in me, and I sighed with it as he moved his lips to my neck, closing my eyes against the dizzying rapture of his touch, breathing fast with anticipation already.

"My lady queen?"

My eyes flew open, and a cold, awful panic filled me to see Aggravain standing in the archway that led into the garden. Lancelot stepped fast away, but it was already too late. He looked at us with a mean little smile, pleased with himself. I felt my face burn an awful guilty red. *It was only a kiss. That's all he saw.* But I couldn't honestly tell myself that. He had seen all the desire behind it, the rawness of our yearning for one another. It had not been the brief polite kiss of a champion for his lady. It had not been the kiss of lovers who had not yet come together in their passions. He had seen that all, I was sure, and I felt hollow with fear.

"My lord Arthur is looking for you. He said I might find you in your garden," Aggravain said, fixing me with his eyes, the smile curling further across his face.

I could not speak. I was afraid to look at Lancelot, afraid that if our eyes met everything would spill out of me, and Aggravain who had already seen too much would see into my heart as well.

"Aggravain –" Lancelot began, stepping forward, though he clearly did not know how he intended to explain himself. Aggravain shrugged.

"I saw nothing." The smile twisted away, and he bowed and disappeared from the garden. I didn't trust him, nor did I believe that he intended to keep his secret, though I thought he would as long as it suited him. He couldn't prove anything. He was just one man. A man everyone at court knew to be a gossip. Lancelot would deny it, would fight to deny it, but the perfect world I had made around myself was already fast coming apart in my hands.

I could feel myself shaking, but I held it back, forced myself to be under control. Arthur was in the courtyard, and he wanted me to meet the son of some vassal king of his who had come to join the quest. I did not remember his name, nor did I feel truly conscious of anything except Aggravain at my back, and the knowledge he carried within him.

There was a feast again that night, to welcome the men who had come. I had no appetite. Lancelot was quiet, too. He sat the other side of Arthur, and I barely heard him speak. He, like me, had his eyes on Aggravain and Gawain, who were whispering between them. Aggravain caught my eye and gave the ghost of his cruel little smile. I knew he wanted me to *think* he was talking about me, but I did not know if he was. The two of them, both huge and brutish, with the same ruddy-brown looks and huge muscular bodies like bulls, made a threatening pair. They had their mother's looks – as did Gareth, though he did not look as though he would grow to their size and his face was gentle and sweet-natured – but what was handsome and proud on a woman's face was somehow rough and threatening on theirs. Only Gaheris had what must have been the father's looks, dark and rangy, tall and wiry with a sly but benign air about him. I wondered what Lot had been like, if it was he who had taught this brutality of blood to his sons, and if they intended to teach it to me. Arthur was, after all, their kin, their uncle. Gawain had waited for ten years to take revenge against the man who had killed his father. I wondered how long I would wait before it fell on me. No, I was getting ahead of myself. Nothing had been said, no accusation had been made. But still, I could not abate the fear growing within me.

Kay beside me was laughing and joking with Dinadan. I wished, for once, that he had been watching me as he sometimes did. Somehow, that made me feel safe. I think it was the feel of the gifts of the Otherworld about him, or the fact that he seemed to see everything. I couldn't ask him, of course, if from across the table he could see the secret hiding inside Aggravain, but I was sure he would tell me if he sensed something was wrong. I did not know how much Kay knew, in truth, or how much he had guessed.

Someone was calling for dancing and there was cheering. I looked down at the food on the table. It was almost gone, but I did not think I had eaten anything. My stomach felt heavy with empty dread. The music began, and down in the main part of the hall, there was the loud screech of tables scraping against the stone floor. It was the sound of the gates of hell screeching open, I thought. I'm supposed to be afraid. *You only feel your sins when you're caught at them.* But I wasn't afraid of Arthur's hell; I was afraid of being parted forever from Lancelot.

When the space was clear and the dancing had begun, Kay took my hand beside me. He was saying something; I wasn't listening, but I followed him down to join in with the others. I saw Lancelot, Aggravain and Arthur hang back. I tried to keep my eyes on them as we swirled around, but Kay was a lithe and energetic dancer and that made it hard work. Normally I liked to dance with Kay, whose feet when he moved only seemed to brush the floor he went so lightly, but I would rather have had a more stolid partner today. Over his shoulder, just for a second, I saw Aggravain lean down by Arthur's side and whisper something in his ear. Arthur waved him away, visibly annoyed, and I felt the blood run cold in my veins. Not watching, not paying attention, I stepped the wrong way and crashed with Kay, who laughed and caught me as I stumbled back and spun me around. But I felt sick; I felt the room spin around me and I stepped away, stepped back. Disappointment and confusion flashed across Kay's face, but there was no way to explain myself. I bumped into the other people dancing as I tried to slip away through the crowd, and they apologised though it was me running into them. The music felt too loud in my ears, the room suddenly too hot, the flashing colours of the women's dresses swirling past us too bright, my limbs too slow and heavy. I looked up again towards the high table on the dais. Aggravain had moved away and was sitting with Gawain at one end of the table, and at the centre Arthur sat, deep in thought, and Lancelot stood behind him, still, but watching, one hand resting on the back of Arthur's chair. He saw me returning, but made no gesture to acknowledge it. I came back to Arthur, to stand beside his chair, and he put an arm around me, resting his hand at the small of my back.

"No taste for dancing today?" Arthur asked, kindly. I felt relieved at his kindness. He did not believe whatever Aggravain had said to him, then. I shook my head.

"No."

He nodded. Behind him Lancelot moved forward to stand before him.

"My lord Arthur, I am going to take my leave of you now," he said softly.

"Oh, Lancelot," Arthur complained, "it's early."

Lancelot gave a little bow of his head, but did not relent. Arthur stood, and the men kissed each other on both cheeks and Arthur gave Lancelot a hearty slap on the back. Then Lancelot stepped over to me and took up my hand. I knew Aggravain and Gawain were looking. The skin of his hand against mine filled me with a sudden heat, but I held it back.

"Goodnight, my lady," he said, loudly enough for those close by to hear, and then he leant in fast and planted a brisk, courteous kiss against my lips, right in front of Arthur. My stomach jumped within me in surprise and pleasure, but also fear. But I knew what he was doing. He gave a little bow again and went from the room. I glanced back in time to see Arthur give Aggravain a sharp look of disapproval. It gave me a sweet secret thrill that Lancelot had thought of it. It was enough to protect us for now, I was sure.

As quickly as I had felt the danger close, I felt it pass. Arthur didn't speak of it, and I didn't ask. I thought it was better if I did not seem to have noticed anything unusual at all. Things were as they had been between us, and it seemed that he blamed Aggravain entirely for spreading idle gossip.

The next few days passed without event, though more and more knights gathered for the Grail quest, and it was all anyone talked about. All of the young men were excited at the prospect of winning adoration and fame, and a chance to sit around Arthur's Round Table. *My* Round Table. I didn't correct them. I stayed away from Aggravain, but apart from that, it was as though our secret had never been discovered. We were wary, though, Lancelot and I, and we held back from trying to see each other alone. Without discussing it we had both decided that it was best to avoid danger for the time being. He hung close by me, and I by him, but we did not try to meet alone.

Still, it gave me comfort to have him close to me in the crowd of people, to know he was there.

So, I was surprised when, one night when I was alone, Lancelot came to my room. He stepped swiftly inside and bolted the door. I was sat by the window, looking out onto the moonlit garden, and when I heard him, I jumped to my feet.

"Lancelot..." I murmured in surprise. My heart was fluttering within me already. He looked a little wild about the eyes. He strode across the room and took me in his arms. I pressed my hands against his arms, feeling the muscles hard underneath, and gently pushed him back. "Arthur might come."

"He won't," Lancelot whispered, kissing softly beneath my ear. I felt my body relax in his hands, but I was still worried.

"How do you know?" I asked softly.

"Nimue has just arrived," he whispered, his lips against my ear weakening me at the knees. So Arthur would be taking her counsel. Whenever she came they would sit in the room with the Round Table all night and he would listen to everything she had to say from Avalon. I never asked if they did anything else, and I did not want to know, though I had heard people say that she had killed Merlin not for Arthur's sake or mine, but because he had tried to take her maidenhead, which was dearer to her than anything else, so I did not think I had any reason to be jealous.

He kissed me, and I sank into the feeling of his lips against mine, the soft sensual touch of his tongue against mine, but I fought through the mist of desire rising around me, and pushed him gently away again.

"I don't think it's safe with so many people around. We shouldn't."

He pressed his forehead against mine, and I felt his quick desirous breaths against my lips.

"We're alone now." He held me close, up against the window frame. I felt the cool air at my back, the heat of his body close by me, and I leant towards him. He brushed his thumb across my lips, and they parted at his touch. I was flushed already, dizzy. I fought through it. I wanted him, but I was still afraid.

"Someone might come looking for me."

"Let them." He kissed me, sliding his hand into my hair at the nape of my neck, his fingers firm against my scalp, pulling my hair loose. "It won't be Arthur, and this is no one else's concern."

"No," I whispered, but I was saying it to myself, not him, and certainly, as I felt his hand against the bare skin of my back, the lacing of my dress already falling open under his quick hands, it sounded in the air between us a lot like *yes*. He slid the dress off one of my shoulders and the gentle touch of his lips there, across my collarbone, sent a wonderful weakness all through my body. I was lost already. I could not have turned back. I leaned my head back against the window frame, breathing the cool night air in in fast, eager breaths, as I felt his lips against the bare skin of my breast. I wrapped my legs around him and pulled him tight against me. His hands ran up my legs, holding me against him. I loved the touch of his hands on my bare thighs. I kissed him, hard and urgent, filled with the heat of yearning, and pulled his shirt over his head, throwing it down beside us. The moonlight picked out the powerful shape of his body, the lithe, muscular frame, and across his fair skin, the scars of old wounds on his chest and arms, the marks of a man who had already fought long wars. I trailed my fingers lightly across them, familiar already, and, fading already on his arm, the red mark turning to purple of the wound he had taken at Surluse. It had been nothing, of course. He lifted me lightly, as though I were nothing at all, and carried me gently to the bed, where he lay down on top of me. I remembered that we had not been together in a bed, and it gave me a dangerous, forbidden thrill. The thought of us in the bed where I had lain many times with Arthur, and us safely hidden away, while around us in the castle everyone carried on, knowing nothing. Lancelot kicked off his boots and I hooked a finger into the front of his breeches pulling him down towards me into a slow, passionate kiss. I pressed my body against his hands as they ran across it, across my breasts, pulling the dress down to my waist as I slipped out of it. The bare skin of his chest against my own was delicious, blissful, and my head was full of him, swimming with pleasure already. Lancelot grasped the dress and finally pulled it away and I felt the wonderful freedom of my nakedness against him, as he ran his hands slowly all over me, and I sank into it, into the wonderful taste of his touch, and then his lips moving all over me and finally, as I had longed for, down, down towards the place that made me cry out with bliss, and I felt the spark of light at the centre of me grow fast, fast under the touch of his tongue, and I was gasping for my breath already. I pulled him up, suddenly hot with a yearning to have him inside me, pushing him over on the bed, pulling away the breeches, moving on to him. He took me by the hips as I sat over him and for a moment we paused, looking at one another. His chest rose and fell softly against the hand I rested on it, and I felt the electric desire in the air, the desire for us to come together, almost unbearable, but also ecstatic in that single moment of deferral, that second's wait for it. Then, I took him inside me and he groaned deeply. I saw the pleasure on his face and it rose fast in me as we moved together. His hands ran up over my body, gently brushing against my nipples and I sighed for him, for his touch, and threw my head back as I felt the rising white-hot bliss; but then he held me fast by the hips and moved me slowly against him and I felt it gloriously slow inside me, around me, all the air full of heat and light as at last it washed over me in a wave of ecstasy and I cried out for him, and felt him shudder against me. I sank down slowly against him and he rolled me over to hold me in his arms, kissing me with the soft, slow kisses of satisfaction. I stroked his hair lightly, closing my eyes and draping an arm across him, and a leg around him, kissing softly against his shoulder. I knew he would go, I knew he would have to leave before the morning, but in that moment I did not have to let go. I could forget the danger and the rest of the world around us. It was only after I fell asleep that I felt him move away and, half-waking, turned over to find that I was alone in the bed. It was only then that the fear struck me, cold at the centre, full of irrational panic, that that might be the last time.

Chapter Thirty-Two

I woke the next day when Marie and Christine came to dress me. I had not missed Margery often before she was gone, but now the thought that it would never be her who came through that door in the morning made me feel a little sad. They had prepared a bath and I was grateful. It had been a strange night's sleep, hot and close, full of fearful dreams.

Marie gossiped fast in Breton as she brushed my hair, and I enjoyed the idle chatter of her sweet little voice and the deliciousness of my secret.

"Gaheris said that Lancelot wasn't in his pavilion last night *all night*. They all say he has some lady in the castle."

Christine clicked her tongue, casting me a wary look. So, she didn't know, and she was afraid I was jealous, or upset. I shrugged and the bathwater splashed gently around me.

"Perhaps it is Christine," I teased. She put her hand into the water and splashed some at my face, but she smiled, pleased, I think, that I was not upset. Marie laughed.

"He says Aggravain knows who it is and won't tell anyone, but I think if Aggravain won't tell, he doesn't *really* know."

The water suddenly felt cold around me. I pulled my knees up to my chest and wrapped my arms around them. We had been so foolish. Reckless. *I* had been foolish to think that it was over already, that anything Arthur said would stop Aggravain from talking. I had *told* Lancelot that he should not have been there last night. I hadn't been thinking. How could I have thought I was safe? How had I been so stupid?

I winced in pain as Marie's brush caught a knot of hair.

"You must have been thrashing around in your sleep," she complained. I wondered how much she told Gaheris.

"It was hot."

Christine nodded in agreement.

"It's going to be an uncomfortable summer, I think," she agreed. "It's hot already this early in the year. I don't envy those knights riding out in that heavy armour. I don't know what they want with the Grail."

"The Grail is the cup of Christ's blood," Marie told her, authoritatively, "and its achievement is the greatest spiritual victory an earthly man can have."

Obviously Gaheris had been talking to her about the Grail.

"I'm sure it is," Christine replied curtly. "But I think the greatest deed an earthly man can do is stay at home and protect his wife and children."

Christine's husband and had sons had ridden out with my mother and brothers to fight alongside King Lot. None of them had returned. I thought suddenly of Arthur's half-confession in the darkness, *I have killed so many men.* No one had come back from that war alive to Carhais. There must have been total slaughter. Once people had said she was lucky to have had so many sons, but I knew when it was time to go to war, she had wished painfully that she had had a single daughter. All she had now was me, not quite her own child.

I was surprised, because Christine was named for Christ, and her father had been a Roman man come to Carhais to trade in spices and silks who had loved Christ and God, though I did not know exactly who Christine herself prayed to. Of she and Marie, it was Christine who I might have suspected of being in agreement with Arthur's quest for the Grail.

"Will Gaheris go?" I asked Marie.

"Oh no. He doesn't care about the Grail. He wants to stay with Gareth, I think. Lynesse is going to have a child, and he wants to see his little nephew or –"

Christine shushed her sharply, and I felt myself blush. I would not have minded if Christine had not drawn attention to it. So that was how it was going to be. Because I was barren, women were not going to talk about children in front of me. Lynesse had, after all, said nothing about it to me. She was probably afraid of upsetting me, too.

"It's fine, Christine." I stood up suddenly, the water sloshing from the bath, and stepped out. Christine handed me a silk sheet to dry myself. I wish they had not reminded me about it. Unconsciously, I pressed my hand against my stomach. Now, I too bore the curse of Arthur's destiny. I felt a sudden need to see Arthur, to feel his arms around me. I wanted to put my head against his chest and share that one little loss again with him in whispers. No one else understood it quite the same. Thoughts of it had chased from my mind all my fears about Aggravain.

I turned to Marie.

"Will you go to Arthur and tell him I want to see him?"

Marie nodded. She was flushed, too, embarrassed. She had meant no harm, but the words had been spoken and the memory of it was, even after all these years, fresh and raw, as was the knowledge that I would never have a child. I would have loved to have a child.

Christine stayed with me and dressed me in silence in the lovely light dress of lilac silk brought from Rome. When she put the little gold circlet on my head she pressed a motherly kiss against my forehead. I closed my eyes and leant against her for a moment. She, too, was a woman without children, and I had not suffered the pain of losing sons I had known. And we had one another.

Marie had not come back and I was restless, so I went to look for Arthur myself. I brushed past people as I went, wrapped up in my thoughts and clumsy with it. Lost somewhere in the awful swirl of those thoughts was the wild little girl I had imagined for myself once, with my red hair and Arthur's fierce grey eyes, savage and wonderful with the blood of witches and conquerors. I did not notice who I was passing until I felt a hand on my shoulder and looked up, jarred from my thoughts of loss and children that could have been, and saw Gawain.

"Gawain," I half-asked, puzzled and disorientated, shaken from my painful daydream. I had not even realised where I was in the castle.

He slammed me against the wall, catching me off-guard and pinning me there. The shock of it knocked the breath from me and I winced in pain. My mind could not catch up with what was happening to me. He leaned his grizzled face in close to mine with a cruel leer. I saw the scar across his cheek standing out white against the dense-freckled skin of his face. I could smell meat on his breath, and the leather and stale sweat of his armour, acrid.

"Where do you think you're going, you little Breton whore? You've been letting Lancelot fuck you, haven't you?" He pushed one of his legs between mine, pinning me against the wall. I slapped him across the face, and he grabbed my wrist, pressing the length of his other arm across my chest, holding me down so I couldn't move. "You foreign sluts, you're all the same. Is this what they all do, where you're from?" He let go of my wrist to grab the skirts of my dress, pulling them up, pressing himself harder against me, squashing the breath from me so I couldn't scream. He didn't even seem to feel my free hand beating against him, trying to push him off. "Well, if you're letting Lancelot fuck you, I think it's only fair if everyone else gets a turn."

He shoved his hand up between my legs and I kicked against him.

"Gawain." A cold, threatening voice called from the end of the corridor. Gawain stepped away from me, letting my skirts fall back down to the ground. I was struggling for breath, collapsing back against the wall, my mind scrabbling to get hold of what was happening to me all of a sudden. I looked up. Standing at the end of the passageway was Kay. At his side a naked two inches of steel shone hard and cold in the light that came in through the narrow windows where he held his sword, loose in its scabbard and ready to be drawn. Gawain could have killed Kay easily in a fight, but then he would have to explain to Arthur why he had killed his Seneschal and foster brother. A wave of relief ran over me. *Kay.* Kay.

Kay strode down the corridor and grabbed me roughly by the arm and pulled me away with him, fast. Gawain skulked back into the shadows. I felt sick and I was beginning to tremble, and to ache, and I felt, close by, barely suppressed sobs creeping towards the surface. For now, the shock of it was holding them back.

I could barely keep up with Kay's strides, he was marching so fast. A sudden fear quickened in my chest.

"Are you taking me to Arthur?" I asked breathlessly.

"No," Kay said, flat and cold.

He marched me out of a back door to Camelot keep, one that was invisible to the eye when shut. Kay knew all the secret places in the castle, so I was not surprised that it was not a way I knew, nor one I had seen before. Kay led me across the wide green field that lay behind the keep to a silk pavilion that I knew as Lancelot's from its deep purple colour.

I had hoped beyond reason that when we arrived Kay would comfort me and be forgiving, but when he burst through the silk door flaps of the pavilion and saw Lancelot was alone, he threw me into him. Lancelot caught me, and I let myself crumple into him, the tears I had held back rolling down my cheeks, silent. He picked me up gently and wrapped an arm around me, looking in bewilderment between me and Kay. Kay's chest was heaving with anger and his face was flushed. I could see the fury in his dark eyes.

"I just pulled Gawain off her," he shouted. He was so loud that anyone outside must have been able to hear through the thin walls of the tent, "*You.*" He pointed his finger accusingly at Lancelot. "You need to be more careful about what you're doing. I don't know *what* you were thinking." He drew his breath in heavily, still incandescent with rage. "End this. Now. You have an hour, then I'm coming back to get her. To take her to her husband. *Your king.*"

And then he left.

Lancelot looked down at me, gentle and sad. He brushed the tears from my cheek with his thumb.

"What does he mean, 'I just pulled Gawain off her?' What happened?" he asked.

I shook my head. The tears filled my throat and I couldn't speak.

Bruises were already darkening across my chest. Lancelot trailed his fingers lightly across them and sighed deeply.

"If I could, I would kill him, for that." He kissed my forehead, lightly. "How does Kay know? Did you tell him?" I could hear the panic creep into his voice. "Did you tell Arthur?"

I shook my head, gasping for little breaths of air.

"I didn't think he knew," I managed to gasp out. I had thought he suspected, but it seemed as if Kay already knew *everything*. Lancelot nodded and held me tight against his chest, smoothing my hair. The skin of my damp cheek pressed against the bare skin of his chest where his shirt was open and I could smell his smell, of grass and horses, of deep, dark forests.

We stood in silence for a long time, until I felt my breath slow down and grow steady, and I began to feel calm enough to talk. I wrapped my arms around his neck and pulled myself up to stand facing him and rested my head on his shoulder. He put a hand on my cheek and kissed me gently. Then he said, softly.

"I think I should go."

I closed my eyes against the tears rising again.

"I'm sorry," he said. I sank away, moving from him to sit in one of the wooden chairs nearby. His pavilion was richly furnished inside with heavy wood chairs, silk cushions, a large bed with silk coverlets. It struck me distantly that he must have been lord of very rich lands that he had left behind to come here. I rubbed the tears from my face and drew in a deep breath, gathering the little strength I had left. I pushed the hair that was already falling loose back from my face, tucked the strands back into place, automatic.

He was right, of course. But I did not want him to go.

He stood where I had left him, uneasy on his feet, looking to me for what I would say. I looked at him sadly. I could not find any words within me.

"Kay is right, we have been reckless. *I* have been reckless, with your safety. It's unforgivable." He shook his head, and rubbed his face with one hand. "I was supposed to protect you, and I have brought us to this."

I stood up and went back over to him, taking his hands in mine. I could feel the tears falling on my cheeks, still, but the horrible sad calm of resignation settled over me.

"Promise me you'll come back."

He nodded, and leaned down to kiss me. I tasted salt, and loss. I felt his lips against mine after we moved apart, and I wanted to hold onto the sensation there, but I knew it would fade soon, and he would be gone. I could feel nothing but despair now, but perhaps later the delicious familiar memories of our love would creep back to me, and give a little comfort.

I rested my head against his chest again, and he wrapped his arms around me and kissed the top of my head. We stood like that in silence for a long time. There was nothing left to say.

Kay seemed to return too soon. He stood with his arms crossed in the entrance to the pavilion.

Lancelot took my face in his hands.

"I will always love you," he said, and in front of Kay he kissed me, deep and passionate, and I melted against it, leaning into his body for what might have been the last time, winding my hands in his thick hair. And then too soon it was over, and I felt Kay's hand rude and rough grasp me by my arm and lead me away as I stepped back from Lancelot, leaving my hand to trail out of his until the last moment. I turned back to look over my shoulder as Kay pulled us out into the fresh air, but he had already turned away and sunk back into the depths of his pavilion.

Kay led me to somewhere I had never been, which must have been his rooms. In one was a bed and a small steaming bath. Everything was clean, simple and functional. No silk, no gold. Kay did not seem to have seen the attraction in Camelot's new-found luxuries. He locked the door behind us and gestured to the bath.

"Get in," he said brusquely. "You'll feel better for it."

I stood my ground, resistant. Still upset, angry and resentful. He had *pulled me* from Lancelot's arms.

"Can one of the women not help me with this?" I crossed my arms stubbornly.

"Do you want *more* people to know?"

He turned me around impatiently, and loosened the lacing of my dress as if he was helping a child. He turned away for me to slip out of it and I stepped into the bath. The hot water, almost painful against my skin, did make me feel calmer. I noticed I was still trembling slightly, but I was beginning to feel more steady. And I was glad of the hot water. I pulled my hair loose, though it was almost loose already, and it fell around my shoulders, the ends trailing wet and dark in the bath. I pulled my knees up to my chest and rested my chin on them. Kay turned back and sat down cross-legged on the floor beside me. He sighed to look at me.

"It will be well," he said, the anger all gone from his voice. I glared at him from under the locks of hair falling before my face. "Oh, I'm sure now it seems like the end of the world. But it's better this way, Guinevere. Arthur doesn't know, and the gossip will die down." He paused for a moment, glancing down at the floor thoughtfully. "Arthur loves you, you know."

I put my head down on my arms, folded around my knees, to hide the tears of guilt pricking there. I knew that I was lucky, I knew I had something good, but I had wanted to *choose*. It all seemed so unfair. I hadn't asked for any of it. I hadn't asked for Lancelot to come into my life and change everything; nor had I asked Arthur to take me from across the sea to be his wife. I didn't see why I shouldn't love as freely as everyone else seemed to just because I was someone's queen. I hadn't had *any* control and now I was being punished. I was suffering because I had wanted to be happy, and make my own choices like a man. I didn't think Arthur owned me, but everyone else seemed to think that he did. Tears choked my throat, but didn't fall. This was the way it was, it had always been. I had longed for something more, but the world had closed in around me, and reminded me that I was not somehow above it.

"Arthur has had other women," I replied sulkily, flicking at the bathwater with my fingers.

"Guinevere, this is just the way of it." Kay put a comforting hand on the back of my head, and rubbed lightly. I looked back up at him, and for once his deep brown eyes looked serious, and sad. "We can't always have the life we want. We have to learn to be happy with the life we have."

He kissed me softly, just for a moment, on the lips. I tasted the salt of my own tears in the kiss.

"Kay..." I began, searching for the words, though I knew there were none.

He shook his head, moving away.

"I know, I know." He stood up again, and I heard him pace away. He came back with a sheet and held it out to me. "Come on."

I didn't move.

"Look away," I insisted. He laughed softly and turned his head away. I stepped out into the sheet, wrapping it around me. I felt small and frail. I wanted to be alone; I didn't want to be taken back to Arthur like a *thing*, like an object he had lost or that Lancelot had borrowed. I wanted to go and lie on the table.

Kay stood with his back to me while I pulled on my underdress, but I had to ask him to tie the laces at the back, and the laces of the lilac silk dress that I slipped over the top. I could feel his breath on the back of my neck. He was quick and business-like with it, but I felt suddenly strange with him so close. I wondered if this was what they all thought of me now, him and Gawain and the others who knew. I felt simultaneously sick and as though I wanted to cry, but I was not going to cry again. I bit it back.

I moved away from him fast once I was dressed and plaited my hair. I couldn't tie it up myself like Marie did, but it would be good enough, and I set the little circlet on it. Kay watched me from the side of the room. When I was dressed he came over and laid the fingertips of one hand on my collarbone. I glanced down. Under his fingers were the ugly purple marks of a bruise already. He traced along the line of them and sighed.

"Not much we can do about *that*." He put his fingertips against my cheek. "Don't tell Arthur about Gawain." I opened my mouth to protest, but he carried on. "If you do, it will force Gawain to make a public accusation. You don't want that."

I wanted to make Gawain pay, but perhaps Kay was right. Perhaps it was better to forget and survive. I wished I was strong enough to hurt Gawain, to fight him, feel the satisfaction of knowing

I had made him feel his own weakness, but I had no way to do it. I didn't want to ever feel how weak my body was under his hands again. I pushed away thoughts of Margery as quickly as they came.

I nodded. I would find a way to punish him in my own time. Kay gave a small sad smile. He lingered near me, and for a moment I thought he was going to try to kiss me again. *Kay, don't.* But he did not, and slowly he moved away. He turned aside to a little table in the corner where there was a plain cup of something that looked like wine that he handed to me.

"Drink that. You'll feel better." It looked like wine, but it was something stronger, something fortified. It felt hot in my stomach, but good.

"Are you ready?" he asked.

I nodded again, but I was not. How could I ever be ready for this?

Chapter Thirty-Three

Kay led me up to Arthur's council room, and when Arthur saw me he leapt from his chair and came around the Round Table to pull me into his arms for a swift kiss. Gawain and Aggravain were there, too, but comfortingly at the back of the room stood Nimue. I wished I had worn her armoured dress today. But I was glad she was there. Despite her woaded face, I was coming to trust her. She was always gentle and quiet. Besides, she was smaller than me and it made me feel better to be in a room with at least one person who I did not think could have killed me with their bare hands, if they had wanted to.

"I have been looking for you," he said gently, smiling. I didn't trust myself to speak and I laid my head on his shoulder in response. He stroked my hair. "Oh, you're upset." He sounded sad but not surprised. I supposed he had heard about Lynesse as well, but that seemed like a distant sorrow already to me, the morning an age ago. He kissed the top of my head. "It's alright, I know." I heard the loss in his voice as well. If only that was what could have happened, that I could have found my way to him and we could have comforted one another. "Go and lie down. We will be finished soon."

I nodded and left, closing the door behind me and leaning back against it, pressing my head hard into the wood, trying to clasp all of the disintegrating pieces of myself into a whole. Then, through the thick door, I heard voices. I pressed my ear against it. It was Aggravain.

"I know what I saw." I heard the crash of a fist on the table. So it was already heated, and I knew it was about me.

"You were mistaken," I heard Kay say, evenly.

"You were," Arthur agreed. "I saw this 'kiss' that was bothering you, at the feast. That's just Lancelot's way, the way of the French. It's very common for a queen and her champion to show favour to each other in public. It's not the way of Lothian, I know, but it is not necessary to make conflict over this."

"I kissed her just now," Kay said, unhelpfully.

"Don't bait him, Kay," Arthur scolded, stern. He thought Kay was joking.

There was silence for a moment, that must have been Aggravain saying something quiet, because the next thing I heard was Arthur's voice, raised in an anger that I had not heard for a long time.

"You be careful what you say about her, Aggravain; she is my queen. Come to me again when my queen births a black-haired child and I'll take your quarrel to Lancelot. I *won't* have my knights starting fights among themselves about nothing, about idle gossip. Do you think I haven't heard it before?" That struck me hard. *Who had he heard it from?* "We have a *hard-won peace*. Don't waste it by fighting over nothing, and if you're going to make accusations against my wife again, be prepared to make them good *on your own bodies*, against Lancelot. Don't think I don't know what this is *really* about. If you can't beat a man in the lists then it's low revenge to spread gossip about him."

I moved away, slowly, up the stairs. I could hear the shouting getting fainter and fainter behind me. Arthur, at least, did not think it was true. I felt innocent in that, although I knew his belief it was not true did not make me innocent; but somehow I felt innocent, because that meant it did not touch him. It did not hurt him, and the two loves could sit separately still inside me.

It felt hard, the few steps suddenly steep, as I climbed them to Arthur's room, and when I got there I fell back on the bed, wrapped my arms around my face, and let the tears come, finally, blissfully alone. Whatever Kay had given me to drink was beginning to fill me with a sleepy languorousness and my limbs felt pleasantly heavy. I let my arms slip away from my face and felt the tears dry against my cheeks, my eyelids too heavy to lift, but my eyelashes fluttering, still damp. After a while, I heard Arthur come in, and sigh sadly at the sight of me. I was too heavy with the sudden sleepiness to rise or open my eyes. It was merciful, really; the hazy drowsiness pushed everything that had happened that day to the edges of my mind. I felt

Arthur sit on the bed beside me, and with all the lazy strength I had, I slowly reached a hand out towards him. He took it gently for a moment, turning it over and pressing a kiss against the palm. It felt wonderfully intimate and tender, somehow, that little gesture. I felt it strike at the centre of me, and somewhere beyond the haze of Kay's drink, I felt love, and guilt, and loss. Then he put it down and I felt him lift the little circlet from my hair, then unlace and pull away the silk dress. I murmured to him through the haze of sleepiness, but I was not sure what I was trying to say. He shushed me gently and lay beside me on his side, pulling me against him and wrapping his arms around me. I felt a kiss against the top of my head and sank back against his warm, familiar body, letting the lovely forgetful sleep pull me down with it.

Whatever Kay had given me was strong enough that I only woke the next day when the sun was high in the sky and streaming through the window. I was still in my underdress in Arthur's arms. When I sat up and looked at him, he was still dressed in the clothes he had been wearing the day before, or the shirt and breeches at least. The red and gold surcoat lay draped across the chair by the window. He still had his boots on, hanging over the edge of the bed, and he was still asleep. I turned around and kissed him gently, and he smiled in his sleep. He must have been exhausted, too, to sleep for so long without any of Kay's drink. Though it was not strong enough to keep the thoughts from my mind now that I had woken. Tonight the knights who would ride for the Grail would declare their intention, and I would say goodbye to Lancelot, maybe for the last time. He had promised to come back, but a man cannot promise to live.

I went down to the courtyard while Arthur was still sleeping. On my way down, I glimpsed Nimue in the room with the Round Table, sat cross-legged on top of it in another armoured dress like the one she had given me, reading in Latin from a huge book laid open before her. The words sounded alien and occultish as they drifted past me. I wondered why the Grail had brought her, too, to Camelot. It could not have been the blood of *her* gods.

Out in the courtyard, Gawain and Gareth were practising together, casual and lazy, and Gaheris stood at the edge with Lynesse and Marie, chattering. It was easy for him; he had decided not to leave in search of the Grail. Aggravain stood at the edge, too, alone, and I felt his eyes on me as I walked down, going over to Christine, who stood with Kay. She was shaking her head about something and clicking her tongue in disapproval.

"Half of these men are boys, really, and most of them want favour from Arthur rather than the Grail," she was complaining.

Kay gave a non-committal shrug of agreement, already no longer listening to her, watching me come over. I didn't want him to look so concerned. I wanted him to pretend that nothing had happened, that he knew nothing. Though it was too hot for it, really, I had pinned a wool cloak around me, to hide the marks of Gawain's hands. I stopped beside them, and Kay opened his mouth to say something when a murmur of excitement went around the gathered crowd of women and young men who had come to watch the knights train before they declared themselves for the Grail. I looked around, and saw that the murmur of excitement was because Lancelot had stepped from the crowd of knights into the open circle of flat ground where the fighting was taking place. Gawain had already slipped away, back into the crowd, by the time that Lancelot had come forward, but Lancelot had him in his sights. I felt my heart beat faster within me. Just the sight of him was enough, and close, too, paces away from us, but unbearably far.

He looked purposeful, as though there was something other than the casual pastime of swordplay that he had come for, and I was afraid I knew what it was.

Lancelot stood in the centre of the courtyard, the tip of his sword resting on the end of his boot. It was blunted for practice, but threatening enough the way he held it, and real steel, not the wood the squires used. I could see the tension in his muscles already, preparing to strike, the readiness all over him for a fight. He lifted it, only slightly, and pointed it towards Gawain.

"Gawain," he said, in challenge.

Gawain leaned back against the wall of the courtyard casually, one foot against the brick of the wall. For all that he was, he was clever enough not to take the challenge. He saw the desire for blood in revenge in Lancelot's eyes. I felt the fear quiver within me. I was not sure what I was afraid of. Christine beside me seemed tense, too. The air felt full of it, like the sense of a coming storm.

"I have no taste for it today, Lancelot," Gawain answered, nonchalantly. Lancelot was about to question this when Aggravain stepped forward from beside Gawain, taking Gawain's practice sword from his hand.

"I'll take the challenge," he said with a grin, already relishing the thought of a good fight. He had revenge *he* wanted to get, too. I was sure he was angry that Arthur had not believed him. He stepped towards Lancelot and both men braced for it to begin, raising their swords, Aggravain shifting Gawain's sword in his hand, taking the balance of it. Gawain was just a brute, but Aggravain had something crueller and more calculating about him that made him seem the more dangerous of the two to me. "You know, Lancelot, I have heard it said that Isolde of Cornwall is the mother of Galahad, and that that is where he gets those fair looks. That you keep her for your pleasure in your castle Joyous Guard, and search for more lovers of the same kind, because you have above all things a special desire for *a queen's* cu—"

Lancelot was on him already, but not before Christine beside me gasped in disapproval. The women around me were tutting among themselves, clucking like hens at the gossip, and the promise of more crude words and fighting, but I felt cold and still and empty. Their swords clashed together loud, louder than the noise that ten or more men fighting usually made in the courtyard. For once both of the men were fighting with all their strength, aiming to injure one another. Lancelot had easily the upper hand – not only faster and more lithe, the strokes he struck with the sword were more powerful. Aggravain was the larger man, but he moved like a bull, and seemed to handle the unfamiliar sword like an axe, swinging it heavily down with each blow. Lancelot was driving him into the corner with little effort, it seemed, though I did not think I had seen him angry like that before, not in a fight, and I was afraid for him that he might lose his focus, and the lesser man would win. Then, with a screech, Lancelot caught Aggravain's sword under his own and forced it down, slamming a foot onto the blade, which skittered down from Aggravain's hands. Lancelot kicked it away. They stood for a moment facing one another, Lancelot with his sword held out in one powerfully quivering hand towards Aggravain's throat, Aggravain breathing hard from the exertion, backed against the wall. For a moment, we all thought the fight was over, but Lancelot was not finished. He threw his own sword away and they rushed together again, Lancelot going down under Aggravain's bulk as the bigger man threw all his strength at him. For a moment I panicked, but Lancelot slid out from under him with that panther-like grace and seized him by the arms. Lancelot was shouting in French, too fast and violent for me to understand, and Aggravain was shouting too, in his anger his accent thickening, blurring out the words; but I knew what they were shouting about. They grappled together for a moment, before Aggravain freed an arm long enough to strike a blow across Lancelot's jaw. Lancelot stumbled back. The silence in the courtyard had changed from one of excited interest to one of danger, and everyone was watching, stock still. This was not how knights fought, nor men who were supposed to be companions in Arthur's band. I wanted to look away, but I couldn't. I wanted to shout *stop*, but the breath was still in my chest. *Lancelot should not have thrown away his sword. He had won.* No, but he wanted the satisfaction of tearing into Aggravain with his bare hands, of punishing him. I could see that in him, in the way he squared up to Aggravain again, and struck his own blow, ducking under Aggravain swinging at him again to catch him under the ribs, and Aggravain went down. Lancelot jumped on him, grabbing him at the neck of his shirt and striking a blow that might have cracked the bridge of his nose. One of the women behind me made a sympathetic little groan of pain as she saw it. Lancelot raised his arm to strike again when finally *finally* someone shouted for them to stop. Everyone looked around. It was Gareth.

Lancelot dropped Aggravain with one last shove of anger against the ground, and stepped off him, moving away, gazing around at the crowd gathered watching, stunned for a moment until he saw Galahad. He gathered in a breath, enough to shout, pointing at the youth.

"Isolde of Cornwall was *not* your mother." Then he turned to the others, the knights gathered around, picking up his sword from the ground. It slid from the packed earth floor with a threatening hiss of steel. "And any man who speaks dishonour about *any* of the ladies under Arthur's protection should from now on come to me with his sword drawn, and prepare to make that accusation good *with his body.*"

He pushed through the crowd, out through the gates, out towards his pavilion, wiping the sweat from his brow with the back of his arm. In his anger, he had not even seen me, or perhaps he had not wanted to look, not wanted to draw people's attention to me, when the accusation had, to anyone who knew or suspected the truth, patently not really been meant against Isolde. The silence of so many people was deafening, but thankfully it quickly descended into excited, scandalised whispers. I watched Gawain help Aggravain, who was pouring blood from his nose, to his feet. Gareth stood beside his wife, staring at the space where it had happened, where the man who had made him a knight, and who had trained him to be what he was, and his brother had thrown their swords away and come to blows. He was not so innocent anymore that he was not realising that the time would come when he might have to choose a side, to choose if the blood laws of Lothian would be his as they were his brothers. Where Aggravain had lain, on the earth, were little red spots of blood. *Blood is paid with blood.* And these men would go out looking for a cup of blood. I hoped it would be enough to satisfy them all.

I heard Tristan say, not far from me, indignantly, "That was my quarrel, really." Funny, really, that the slight, proud youth had not stepped forward to offer his own challenge to Aggravain.

Chapter Thirty-Four

There was a feast again that night, but the atmosphere was tense and subdued. Arthur was unhappy. He didn't want to lose his knights, his friends, to the quest for the Grail, and at the same time he was jealous that as king he could not go himself. Nimue sat in Lancelot's place by his side, and Lancelot beside her, further from me than usual, and I sat as I always did between Arthur and Kay. With Kay's eyes on me beside me, I dared not try to catch Lancelot's eye, to take the last opportunity to beg him not to go. Opposite me, Galahad waited with eyes wide with religious rapture, slightly damp with anticipation, a look of blissful innocence and total belief written on his face. How could Morgan have birthed such a child? Was Arthur's god truly powerful enough to make something of hers into something like Galahad?

I didn't eat much, and neither did Arthur. I could feel his disquiet as he sat beside me, and it heightened my own, the dread I felt gathering about me and what I knew had to, and what I longed not to, happen.

Arthur was tense and quiet until the fruit and cakes were brought and it was at last time for him to stand and call the knights to his council chamber. I went too, and so did Nimue. Behind me, Kay reached out and took my hand, and I was surprised to find I was glad of it. Glad that there was someone who knew, who could guess at, the emotions raging inside me. I felt, too, the Otherworld strength of him, and that reminded me of my own strength. I would be strong in this.

The table was not really big enough to hold all of the knights who had come to court, and once those who habitually gathered around it and their kinsmen had sat, the other knights had to stand around it without chairs. I sat beside Arthur, the heavy crown of Logrys already making my neck ache, and my skin cold and clammy under the rich samite dress of red and gold. The knights had come dressed in fine surcoats and doublets and the room was filled with a brightness that I found unbearable to look at, though I could not explain why. Lancelot wore a surcoat of deep purple silk sewn in silver at the neck and sleeves. I had not seen him dressed so finely before. Somehow it was painfully impersonal, the sight of him dressed in the colours of his house, when I had known his skin against my own. It was as though he was holding it out as protection against me, though I supposed the crown must have looked the same to him, although I had worn that for Arthur's sake. Kay alone was dressed in shirt and breeches, all in black, lounging in his chair with one leg hooked over the arm of it, quick dark eyes taking in everyone in the room. Kay, clearly, had no intention of going in search of the Grail.

Arthur, beside me, took my hand, entwining his fingers with mine. I turned to him with a comforting little smile, the best I could muster. He was dreading this as much as I was, though I was sure it was for different reasons. He took a deep breath and nodded to Galahad. Galahad cleared his throat and glanced around at the knights close by him. He was dressed in a blue and silver surcoat, the insignia on it a sign I did not recognise, a four-pointed star, long and thin.

"My friends, fellow knights of the Round Table." So, Arthur had welcomed Lancelot's son to the Round Table. I supposed it was natural enough. "The time has come to declare yourselves, whether you will take the quest, and join me in search for the Grail."

His quavering treble cut through the silent air of the room. There was a heavy silence. I squeezed Arthur's hand. Lancelot's face was turned away from us, and the candlelight lit his thoughtful profile, the high cheekbones, the dark waves of hair. He might change his mind. He might decide to stay. He had made his stand against Aggravain, after all. I hoped beyond reason that he had changed his mind.

"I will take it." To my surprise, Gawain was the first to stand and, pressing his hand to the table, pledge himself to the quest. Arthur was surprised too, though he was not so pleased as I was.

"Gawain, *no*," Arthur protested, but Gawain had already sworn. Perhaps Gawain thought it was wise for him to leave court for a bit since he had had a taste of Lancelot's anger. Perhaps this meant Lancelot would stay.

"I will go, too," Perceval declared seriously, standing to plant his hand beside Gawain's.

"And I." Tristan was next. Leaving Isolde, I noted, to wait for him alone at Joyous Guard while he sought glory among men.

"And I." Bors followed him, one of Lancelot's kin. I glanced to Lancelot. His eyes were on the men around the table, watching who would be next. One after the other the knights pledged themselves until the only ones left to pledge were Kay, Gareth, Gaheris and Lancelot. Arthur was pale at my side. He drew in a deep breath. I could not breathe. *Lancelot had not pledged to go.* As each man pledged my heart jumped, fearing that he would be the next. The tabletop was covered with hands pressed flat to swear their intentions to the Grail. If everyone else left, then perhaps he would stay. We would have to be more secret, more careful, but I could keep him near me. Arthur pressed his hands into the table, leaning heavily down against it, and was halfway to pushing himself to standing when the voice I dreaded came.

"Wait." All eyes turned to Lancelot, who had stood, but his hand still hovered just above the surface of the table. Arthur froze where he was and half turned his head as though he was about to shake it. *No. NO.* I screamed inside myself with him. Our eyes met and I felt my insides twist with an unendurable pain. My knees felt weak, and I felt powerlessly frozen to the spot. There was apology there, in his look, but also resignation, an unbearable resignation that meant I had lost him. And he thought he was doing this for me, to protect me. I drew in all the little breath I could through the tightness in my chest. He was going to do it. "I pledge myself to the quest, also."

Arthur groaned and pinched the bridge of his nose, screwing his eyes shut. I felt the ground shift under me and leaned my head against the back of my chair, steadying myself as much as I could.

"Very well," Arthur declared, getting slowly to his feet, leaning down on the table, as though he needed it to steady him. "I am lucky to have so many brave knights at Camelot." He looked slowly around the room, full of a heavy sadness that I had not anticipated in him. "Though truly, I am sorry that so many of you have pledged to go. The quest for the Grail is known as a perilous one. Most of you will not return alive."

I felt a wave of nausea pass over me. The knights were variously clapping each other on the back and congratulating each other on their bravery, or already discussing plans to depart together in the same direction. All I could think is *what will we do if there is war?* There is no way Arthur could call back enough knights to defend Camelot. These were not the only fighting men; their younger brothers, squires and the lower men, the men of the fields and the markets, would stay, but they were not the men for defending a kingdom. However, I noticed that many of the knights here were from Lothian, or Cornwall, or other border countries, those most likely to rise up against Arthur. Perhaps emptying the land of fighting men was another way of achieving peace. Arthur, though sorry to lose them, began moving among them, giving the young men words of encouragement. He was good with his men, I could see that. A natural leader. I remembered that that was when I had first begun to doubt my ability to hate him, the day we were married, when I had seen how his people already loved him. He did not begrudge them their quest, though he was sad to see them go. And he longed for it, too. Were he not king, he would have been among the first to pledge, and I would have lost him, too.

I caught Galahad's eye. Under the pale hair, his light blue eyes and his pale face made him look like a creature from the barrow-lands, and suddenly he did not look so much like Lancelot to me at all. He was a shell of a man, moulded for one thing, to bring this cursed Grail to Camelot and tear it apart. I looked for Lancelot, but he was swallowed by the crowd, talking to Gareth, who was wide-eyed with excitement on his behalf, perhaps half-reluctant to hang back with a pregnant wife while his friends went off to find adventures. I felt the wave of nausea again and pushed myself up from my seat. I heard Kay say something to me, but I didn't take in what it was.

I was glad to be out of the room, hot already from all of the bodies crammed into it, and full of sickening pride. Arthur was right. Most of them would not return alive.

When I got back to my room, I threw the window open and stuck my head out into the night air. The smell of the flowers in the garden beneath was suddenly sickeningly sweet and I stumbled back into the room, retching. I took the heavy crown off my head and set it down on the table beside the window. I sat in the chair beside it and rubbed my face, drawing in deep breaths.

The door opened, and I expected it to be Arthur, but it was not. It was Lancelot. I got to my feet unconsciously. I could feel the tears gathering in my eyes already. He shut the door softly behind him.

"I saw you leave," he said, leaning back against the door. He looked sad, but wary. In the faint candlelight, the silver thread in his surcoat glinted, coldly. The little space there was of the room between us seemed impossibly large.

"Truly," I whispered, "truly you're leaving us?"

It was all I could manage before the silent tears began to roll down my cheeks. I did not want to cry. He strode towards me and took my face in his hands, wiping them away. I didn't want him to touch me if he was going to go, but I did not ask him to stop.

"I don't have a choice," he whispered. His lips brushed mine softly, and I leaned up into him, and he took me into a kiss that felt unbearably like the last kiss. Slow and deep, we savoured it both. It might have to last me forever. He moved away slowly. "And I *will* return."

The door opened again and it was Arthur. He clapped Lancelot on the back and half-reprimanded him for leaving Camelot against our wishes, but as they spoke their words were lost to me against a rushing noise that filled my ears, and the room shifted away from me. *That might have been the last time we were alone.* And I looked down into the deep, deep void of the rest of my life without Lancelot, and I closed my eyes against its chill.

The next day Arthur and I stood out in the early spring morning, bright but still cool, to watch the knights ride out. Two columns gathered to go, headed by Lancelot and Galahad as champion and the knight who had called the quest. In the light breeze, their banners fluttered, thick in the air of the courtyard. Horses shifted their feet, armour plates scraped against each other. Arthur and I were dressed in all the finery of king and queen, he in his crown with the red and gold surcoat patterned with his father's dragon, I in the green and gold dress sewn with golden crosses, the gold and emerald necklace at my neck and my wild hair wrapped in a neat, white silk scarf with the crown of Logrys heavy on top. Today it all felt like armour, and I stood there as a queen rather than as myself. Lancelot before us was dressed in his armour, his sword at his side, but his head free and his hair lifting slightly in the breeze. It hurt to look on him, so close, and now forever utterly out of my reach. *I will return.* So many had once said the same.

As Lancelot began to speak, taking his leave of us on behalf of them all, I closed my eyes as the tears began to fall again, and my memories of him from the first time rushed close around me: stepping into my pavilion at Surluse, his hair wet from the storm, that moment there before we came together when we looked into each other's eyes in the light of the brazier, the skin of his chest cool from the rain and delicious under my touch, his hands in my hair, his lips on mine and the slow longed-for love we had shared there, at the beginning, when we had all the daring hopes of it before us. Would I have begun if I had guessed the pain of the end?

I did not open my eyes until I heard the hooves of the horses again. I was sure I could not bear to watch him turn away.

That night I came to Arthur, ready to forget. I wanted his rough hands on my body; I wanted his powerful, hot desire to burn through me and leave me clean. The warmth and haze of wine flushed me, dulled down the ache within me, and I knew that oblivion in Arthur's arms would give me what I needed.

    He usually came to me, and was not expecting it, but I could see in his eyes that he wanted it. When I stepped into the room in my nightdress, throwing my cloak from my shoulders, and shut the door behind me, he looked up from his chair, where he had been sitting by the window with his head in his hands, and the sight of my hair loose, and the shape of my body through the thin fabric brought him to his feet. I pulled loose the three small ties that held the little dress together and let it fall to the ground. Arthur stopped where he stood and looked at me, as he had done long ago on our first night together, and I relished the hungry touch of his eyes against my skin. He pulled his shirt over his head and threw it aside, and kicked off his boots, stepping towards me and seizing me, throwing me up against the door. The hard wood was cool and rough against my back, the iron brace along it cold in the small of my back, and hard. But I wanted it; I wanted his roughness and urgency. I tasted wine on his lips, too, and felt him respond powerfully to my need for his body. He gripped me hard by the thighs, lifting me up against the door, pressing against me, his kisses rough and wonderfully intoxicating. I reached down to his breeches to find him hard already, and as I felt his lips, and the light flutter of his tongue, against my nipple and moaned for him, I pulled them open and slid my hand inside. He moaned too, deep and thick with desire. His hands were hard and rough against my breasts; it hurt me slightly, but I wanted it. I wanted to feel the power and strength of his body, to feel overcome. He kicked his breeches away and thrust hard inside me. I cried out his name and he buried his face in the hair at my neck, his breath close at my ear, his low groans of pleasure, as he held me fast against the door by the hips and moved hard against me, rough and urgent until at last I cried out again; and he sighed against me just after, and slowly moving from me, released his grip and let me slide to the floor. He gathered me up in his arms and carried me to the bed where I lay with my head on his shoulder, resting my hand on his chest, still rising and falling hard. No, I had not forgotten, but I had Arthur's familiar body beside mine, and his absorbing love that seemed that it would always be the urgent passion of a young man, and I was happy, or half of me was. Half of me lay side by side with Arthur in perfect bliss, and I had to let the other side slip away and become nothingness, if I was ever to survive this.

Chapter Thirty-Five

I did not forget, nor did the memory of Lancelot fade, but as the days went by, it became easier. Arthur and I did not talk about the empty seats around the Round Table, nor the friends we missed, nor did we talk very much at all, but whenever we were alone we came together as though we were trying to destroy each other, or to obliterate ourselves; rough, urgent and deliciously anaesthetic. I thought I would see him less as he worried about his absent friends, but it seemed that he longed for the forgetting touch of my hands as much as I longed for his on me. Only in those moments when we came together did I feel my whole self. The rest of the time I moved through Camelot like a ghost, half Arthur's queen, half the woman I might have been with Lancelot, lost in memories and longing. Stuck between the two, unless I was in Arthur's arms. I did not know what it was for him, if it was only that I was the only creature he could hold to him, possess – he thought – all his own. Kay was always too much of an enigma to be *possessed*, though the brothers were close, and Gareth and Gaheris belonged to each other, and to the little fair-haired girl Lynesse produced, screaming like a wounded boar, in the depths of winter. I did not think I would have screamed like *that* if I had brought my child to birth. I liked Lynesse, but I thought she was weak, a little simpering. There was something about her that reminded me of Isolde, a certain brainless sweetness. But she made Gareth happy. My days were spent with Marie and Christine – sometimes Kay, Gaheris and Gareth as well, although the brothers now spent most of their time with Lynesse and the baby girl, reading or listening to Marie sing. I wrote letters to Isolde, who, waiting at Joyous Guard, was constantly anxious about Tristan, or worse, about Mark finding her and putting her to the fire. I was surprised at how well she wrote, and the neatness and attractiveness of her hand, which was far finer than my own. Sometimes, too, I sat with Kay while he sang and played the lute, which he was good at; but I did not often like to be alone with him, because he knew it all, and I was afraid he would ask me about it. I did not want to speak the words of it in front of another, in case I suffered the loss again. I dreamed of Lancelot often, but the dreams were often painful and confused: I would search for him through the castle, but find him nowhere, only to feel him catch me in his arms from behind and turn around to find it was not him at all but Arthur, or Kay. And when I dreamed of us together, the sensations of the dream felt almost real, brought me to the edge, but were never enough and I would wake suddenly, mad with longing and alone. Or with Arthur beside me. Sometimes he would wake as I did, as though he sensed the desire lingering about me, pull me into his arms and roll on to me, and with the dream still lingering around me it felt as though I was with both of them at once. But that was not often, and never quite enough for me to stop feeling the loss of Lancelot when I woke again in the morning. In the daytime when I could be alone, if it was warm enough, I lay in the garden with my eyes closed and let all the small sweet memories of Lancelot I had stored inside me wash over me, and held them, warm and close, to my heart. It was not much of a comfort, but it was all I had.

Gawain was the first to return from the quest for the Grail, almost a year and a half after they had set out. He did not seem to have tried very hard, saying he had returned because a hermit had demanded he do penance, which he deemed 'not needful for a knight who has taken many wounds in battle', but Arthur was pleased to see him.

Aggravain came soon after, near Christmastime, with quite a company of knights, who had ridden around and found nothing. Arthur commiserated with them and commended their valour, but from what I understood from what Galahad had said, success on the Grail quest was an index of the knight's virtue. I was not surprised that Aggravain had seen nothing, but I was surprised to see Lamerocke, whom I had always liked, return with his band; but then it was said that he was a lecher and had had too many women to count, so perhaps that had held him back from any sight of the Grail.

It was good to have Camelot more full again, although it meant I saw less of Arthur, and when I did his passion had lost some of its desperate ferocity. He no longer needed it, as I did. He was so happy to see his nephews Gawain and Aggravain again that he did not notice anymore that I was still lonely and sad, and he often rode out hunting with them or asked them to recount stories from their travels again and again. I was sure, also, as I left the room once I heard Gawain begin some awful tale from when he was exiled for rape. Still, he was not foolish enough to do this in front of me, nor did he or Aggravain make any more accusations. Kay was often by my side, or Arthur, and that was enough to make them wary.

I found myself spending more and more time with Kay. He often sat with me, Christine and Marie, and he was beginning to pick up enough Breton to enjoy Marie reading from her book of *lai*. His mind was quick and sharp, and often he made even Christine laugh. As the time passed, and the rawness of his part in my separation from

Lancelot began to fade, I enjoyed having him around more and more. It made me feel less lonely.

Still, every day, I had one eye on the gate, waiting for Lancelot to ride through. As spring came and turned to summer Dinadan returned with a small group of knights who all said they had been trapped a year in a castle full of maidens and seen an altar covered in a sheet, but not the Grail itself. Dinadan said that twice the number that returned with him had ridden out together.

I began to go to with Arthur to chapel more often. He went every day. I did not go with him that often, but I felt that the Grail belonged to Arthur's god, so if I wanted Lancelot returned to me then it was to the god of the Grail that I would have to pray. By the time two and a half years had passed and Ector returned alone, saying he had heard Lancelot had been with a hermit in the woods but had seen nothing of him, I was beginning to lose hope that Lancelot was alive.

Tristan did not return to Camelot, but I heard in a letter from Isolde that he had joined her at Joyous Guard, though they had quarrelled there about some other knight, and he had left. Without Tristan to protect her, I was worried that she would return to Mark, and I wrote to her to tell her not to go. I did not envy her, alone in that siege fortress. She must have been bored. I was lonely, certainly, but lonely in the deep place within myself that could only be comforted by Lancelot. If he was gone for ever, I would never be whole.

It was when high summer had given way to autumn, almost three and a half years since they had left, when more news came. But it was not news of the Grail. I sat with Arthur and Nimue in his council chamber, maps spread out before us. Arthur had it in his mind that he would ride out and look for Lancelot, Bors, Perceval and Galahad – of whom we had had no word – himself. It was Lancelot particularly whom he was eager to find, missing the friend who had been like a brother to him. It was deadly sweetness to me, his desire to find Lancelot, because it was my desire as well, but I felt the wickedness within me that did not want him to be reunited with his friend, but wanted my lover returned to me.

I had asked Nimue to have another armoured dress made for me, and as well as the light blue one I had had as a gift from her, I had a dark green one all of my own, with gold-plated greaves up to the elbow and a gold-plated platemail bodice embossed with Arthur's dragon. Arthur thought this much more fitting for a queen. I liked it;

it made me feel more like the warlike queens of my ancestors, less like a woman forced to wait in a castle for news from far away. I was pleased, too, to have Nimue at court again. She rode out hunting with me sometimes, and Kay would come with us, although he was quicker than us both and that left us with less sport.

As we sat there, tracing paths through the woods for Arthur with our fingers, discussing the merits of each, a soft cough came from the doorway. I looked up and saw Ector standing there, lingering on the threshold. The kind old man – for old he was now, his beard steely grey and half the black gone from his hair – was usually forthright and open. Something was making him nervous.

"Morgawse of Lothian is coming to Camelot. With her son." Ector's gaze on Arthur was wary, his voice uncertain. Arthur leaned forward and put his head in his hands. Ector looked to me, and I gave a hopeless little shrug.

"What does she want?" Arthur asked thickly, without looking up.

"I think she wants the boy fostered at court."

Arthur looked up in panic and disbelief.

"Ector, she can't..."

So, this was not just another one of Gawain's brothers. This was Arthur's child. Arthur's only child, since I had not – and would not ever – give him one. Once again, I was reminded of that loss, that emptiness inside me.

The trumpets in the courtyard were already sounding an arrival, and Arthur's surprise turned to anger. He jumped from his chair and shouted, *"You did not tell me they were here now!"*

Ector's kind eyes crinkled in sadness in his weatherbeaten face.

"I only came to warn you before they arrived. She did not send word that she was coming. I think she suspected that you might command her to keep the boy in Lothian."

Arthur sighed and bowed his head in defeat and Ector led the way down to the courtyard.

Through the great gates they came riding, Morgawse first, on a handsome chestnut horse, the spiked crown of Lothian on her head, wrought in dark gold, studded with rubies like blood. It was certainly the crown of a warrior people. She had a grandness about her, and she did look beautiful, dressed in white furs over a dark red robe of samite, edged with the same white fur. It must have been cold as midwinter already in those northern wastelands. Her broad, proud face was unmistakably one of a woman who had been a great beauty in her youth, and her eyes were full of an intelligent kindness. Behind her rode a stern-faced youth on a huge grey warhorse. I would not have called him a *boy*. He was young, certainly, but he was tall and broad already, and when he jumped down from his horse it was clear that he was easily as tall as Arthur and, without a doubt, Arthur's son. He had the same fair looks, the golden hair, the easy handsomeness, the strong frame, but his eyes were dark, serious and intense, and he did not have the look about him of one quick to smile or laugh.

He offered his mother his hand and she took it to slip from her horse with an easy grace. She curtseyed before me and Arthur, and the youth bowed. As he looked up, his eyes met mine and I felt a stab of panic in my heart. I did not know why, but the look of him unsettled me right to the core. Perhaps it was how much he looked like Arthur, and yet entirely unlike him. It was like staring into the eyes of the Arthur I met at Dover and seeing an entirely different man, and an entirely different future. It was not one I would have liked, I thought instinctively. I hugged my cloak around me more tightly, suddenly feeling the cold.

"Why did you bring him here?" Arthur demanded, without greeting. I could see he was flustered, embarrassed, angry. Morgawse did not look worried or ashamed, but she was older and had buried a husband and a king, had ruled her wilderness in the North alone and raised a child born from incest. Her husband had died for her sins, but Arthur was still to pay for his.

"It is fitting that he comes to fight for his king, Arthur. Lothian is still a vassal kingdom of Logrys, so it is only right that you accept my sons – *all* my sons – as your knights. You can't just take the ones that please you. Besides, Mordred will please you." *Mordred*. An ill-sounding name. I wondered who had named him. "He is strong already, and it is his wish to become one of your knights."

Mordred said nothing, eyeing me and Arthur with cold, steady eyes.

That night I went to see Arthur; I wanted to try to offer him what comfort I could, but as I reached his room I could hear shouting within. I pressed my ear against the door. I recognised a woman's voice; it was Morgawse.

"He hasn't done you any wrong, Arthur."

"I don't want him here. I don't want to *see* him, I don't want him near me. Why can't you understand that? And I don't want *you* here, either."

"Oh come on, Arthur, don't be a child. It's time you took responsibility for him. If you want to stop feeling ashamed about it, then act honourably by your son and take him as your knight."

"You *aren't* ashamed?" He sounded furious still, but also as though he was tiring, weary and defeated.

"Why should I be? We didn't know."

There was a long silence, and I pressed my ear closer to the door.

"Very well, he can stay. But you should go."

The voices fell quiet and I tried to slip away, wanting to be gone before they noticed I had been there. When I was halfway down the stairs, I heard the door open behind me and turned. It was Morgawse. She sighed when she saw me, and ran down the stairs to catch me as I tried to scurry away, pulling me into the room with the Round Table.

"Guinevere, I don't know what you know –"

"I know. Even if I didn't, it's quite plain to see, isn't it?"

She nodded slowly, and rubbed her forehead with the heel of her hand.

"I suppose you aren't pleased either." I didn't say anything. I did not really know what I thought. "I knew Arthur wouldn't be. He doesn't like the sight of me, because it reminds him, and having Mordred here, well... I don't know why it makes him so ashamed. It was a mistake, and I have had to move on, live with the consequences. I was young, and foolish I suppose. I was sick of Lot, who had me pregnant all of the time, making him more and more sons, and when he asked me to come and spy for him at Arthur's court I was relieved to go. Arthur was young and kind, and Lot had been old and cruel, and it seemed natural enough to me at the time. Arthur was very charming, not that he needed to be in comparison with the disgusting old brute I was married to. I was given to Lot by my stepfather when I was eleven, maybe twelve, and by the time Arthur was born I had had Aggravain and Gawain already. I didn't know who he was. People said he was Uther's son, but others said that he was some little changeling fostered by the witch Merlin, and our mother was hiding from Uther's enemies in Cornwall. Uther had not been *my* father. I find it hard to think of Arthur as my brother even now. We didn't grow up together; I know we shared a mother but honestly I don't see much of her in him, even now I know who he is. I'm sorry it haunts him, I am, but it is long done. I am sorry that he will suffer to have his son here. But, Guinevere." She put her hand on my arm and I met her look. She looked sad, and sincere, and I felt an overwhelming rush of pity for her. "I had no choice. I can't keep Mordred in Lothian. He was starting to talk to the knights of riding out against Arthur, and he's getting older, stronger. They're listening to him instead of me. They've stopped thinking of him as a bastard child and they've started seeing a king, which he can't start thinking he is. He has to be here; he has to pledge his faith to Arthur if there is not going to be another war in Britain."

I nodded, and took her hand, giving it a gentle squeeze. Hers must have been a hard life, alone far up in the north, losing her husband who, though she had hated him, had kept her place in the realm safe, and then, slowly, her sons.

I was sorry to see her go, just as soon as she had come, but there was open relief on Arthur's face as we watched her ride away. Aggravain, Gawain and Gaheris were pleased to have their brother there, and set to be made a knight alongside them, but I was sure I saw Gareth regard him with a wary, uncomfortable fear.

That night in the darkness, Arthur said, "It is true what they say, that our sins come back to haunt us."

Chapter Thirty-Six

So in the days that followed, Mordred was made a knight and took his place at the table beside his brothers. They called for a feast to celebrate them all being there together, and out of affection for Gawain, Arthur relented. I noticed that he only ever called Mordred his nephew, though everyone could see the boy was clearly his son. Mordred himself was quiet and watchful, and I did not like the way he was always close to Aggravain.

Beside me, as the food was brought out before us, Kay leaned close beside me.

"So, that is the boy," he said, thoughtfully. He was looking at Mordred. I could see that he did not like the look of him any more than I did. I wondered what he thought of all the talk of sin and curses, of Arthur's bad destiny.

"Hardly a boy anymore, really," I answered.

"Hmmm." Kay's tone was unsettling, as though he was, for once, unsure what to make of it. Arthur beside me was tense. I could feel it. He wasn't eating; nor did he seem to be enjoying Gawain's storytelling, which he usually loved. I felt strangely about Mordred, but from what Morgawse had told me, I felt it was my duty to encourage Arthur to look kindly on his son. Mordred turned towards us and I looked away, not wanting him to think that Kay and I had been talking about him. It must be hard, to carry such a dark history inside oneself. To know that people are talking about you wherever you go. The conversation was loud and hearty, but it was Gawain, Lamerocke and Gaheris who carried it. Arthur, Mordred, Kay and I were silent, each watching the others, trying not to show it. I wished that Lancelot had been there. I would have felt comforted by his presence, and he would have been someone else close to Arthur that was not Mordred's brother. Arthur could hardly confide in Lot's sons about it. Everyone knew the truth of it, but no one dared speak it.

At last, the food was taken away and the music for dancing began. I was relieved, and hoped that this meant that I could slip away, but to my surprise, Mordred stood and came over to me, offering me his hand to dance. I glanced uneasily to Kay, but all he gave me was a blank look of confusion in return. I did not much feel like it, but I thought if I made an effort at kindness it might encourage Arthur. I stood slowly and gave him my hand, and we stepped forward to join the dancing. Something about the touch of his hand repulsed me, and I could not say why. I pushed the feeling away; I was being silly because of Arthur's superstitious belief in a curse. I could feel Arthur watching, and Kay, but far out in the crowd I felt suddenly alone and without their protection. I did not know what it was about Mordred that made me feel so fragile. Close and alone in the crowd now, I felt it more intensely, and I felt myself shrink back from him instinctively, as far as I reasonably could. As we danced he spoke softly, so only I could hear him, his voice lost in the music to anyone further away.

"I would like such a lovely queen as you for myself." His look was uncomfortably intense, serious and steady.

I laughed, attempting to shrug it away. "Would you not prefer a girl your own age?" Perhaps he was trying his hand at knightly courtesies. He could not have had much practice at them in Lothian.

He pulled me slightly closer, sliding an arm around my waist. I was wary but unwilling to push him away in public, still eager to mediate between him and Arthur. Maybe the boy thought he was being charming. He had listened to too many tales of knights praising and wooing the wives of their kings. I turned my head slightly away, looking down. The way he was looking at me made me feel uneasy, exposed. But still I felt his breath against my neck, and in the hand at my back the threat of strength, and the smallness and vulnerability of my own body in comparison. The music and the other dancers seemed impossibly far away, and I wished that I had thought to wear Nimue's armoured dress.

"I don't think that I would," he whispered, right by my ear. I could not suppress a shiver. I looked up at him, but he was looking away. Over my shoulder, he was looking at someone. Perhaps Arthur was watching him, wary too. I felt my body tense in anticipation of a struggle, but none came. He did not speak again, nor did he try to hold me closer against him, and when the music ended he bowed and moved away. It had not been so unusual, nor had anything *actually* been said, but somehow it had felt like a threat. I wished that Morgawse had not gone. She would have known.

When I sat back beside Arthur, he leaned over to me and asked in a hissing whisper.

"What did he say to you?"

I shook my head. "Nothing much."

I would bide my time, and keep my watch. It was not worth worrying Arthur over, and there was no good beginning a conflict over nothing, but I could feel still the press of his hand against my back, as though he was reminding me that he was stronger that I was, that he had come with something to prove. Maybe he was just one of those young fools that liked to talk empty little compliments to every woman they met, but it felt darker somehow and more violent than that. I could not put my finger on why, but deep in my stomach there was a flicker of fear, and more than anything, I wished again that Lancelot was here.

Days passed without event, and Mordred joined the other knights in their routine of training and riding out hunting. I would have liked to go out hunting more, but few opportunities came. Winter gathered fast around us, and I missed lying in the garden, half-dreaming, half-remembering Lancelot. Arthur grew less quiet and withdrawn around Mordred, though he never openly called him his son. He did not see much of him; Mordred spent most of his time with Aggravain and Gawain. I did not like the feel of their eyes on me as I passed them in the courtyard, or in the halls, but I said nothing. It was half for Arthur's sake, half for my own; I did not want to push Aggravain into making accusations again, nor bring such accusations to Mordred's ears.

I felt lonely and restless. The festivities of Christmas felt empty and false, as though all of us were going through the motions of it. I was pleased, at least, that Mordred did not ask to dance with me again, but he did seem often close by. The smell of the fires, their smoke, was thick and heavy in the air, the wine made me sleepy, and it made me think of Lancelot, and the night so impossibly long ago that I had shared first with him and then Arthur. If I closed my eyes I could almost feel Lancelot's hands on my thighs, pushing me against the stairs. I dared not slip in to it. Not in front of everyone. Arthur tonight was singing with Gawain, some song I think Gawain had invented about the Grail, though he had hardly participated in the quest at all. The sight of the others all around me drinking and celebrating made me feel hollow, and even more lonely. And I could feel Mordred's eyes on me.

I stood to go, and as I did, Kay stood with me. He, too, did not look as though he relished the thought of the festivities he usually loved.

"Are you leaving?" he asked. I nodded. "I'll go with you."

As we walked out into the courtyard, it began to snow. I turned my face up against it and felt the little chilly kisses of the snowflakes against my hot face. It had been too hot in there, and too loud. Kay sighed into the night air, stretching his arms out and up. He was clearly grateful, too, for the air. I turned to him.

"Arthur will be sorry you're gone," I told him, playfully. Arthur liked nothing better than Kay's Christmas games.

Kay relaxed his arms by his side, suddenly serious.

"Well, I didn't want you walking out here by yourself."

"What do you mean?" I asked, noticing at once that he had his sword at his side, that he had had it there for the whole meal – he must have done. I felt afraid suddenly that Kay would think I was in danger. It must, then, not just have been in my imagination.

"Oh, well." He shrugged back, not willing to commit to anything definite in his warnings. "It's just... Mordred. He's... strange. He watches you a lot, and I thought if I followed you, he wouldn't."

I supposed he was right. Though I thought Mordred was more odd than dangerous, more the awkward boy who did not know how to behave. Besides, I was thinking about Lancelot, letting the feeling of the wine swirl through me, the memories hang close around me. The worry had passed in a second, and I had a thought I might be alone soon, and I could relive the memory of that night from the comfort of my bed. I turned my face up to the sky again and stuck out my tongue to taste a little point of snow. Delicious. But I was beginning to feel the chill in the air, and the longing to be alone with my memories, so I walked towards my rooms, and Kay came with me. I was not surprised, because Christine had not gone to the feast, feeling tired and having a chill on her, and Kay had been going to read to her in the evenings. But, when we passed the door to Marie and Christine's rooms, Kay did not go in, but came up the last flight of steps to my door. I stood with my back against it, unwilling to open it with him there. I could not put my finger on why, not through the haze of wine and half-remembering. Perhaps that was it. Kay stood before me, and in the dark half-light of the torch in its sconce on the wall I could see the vague resemblance he bore to Lancelot, though it might have been the wine. The same dark looks, though Kay's hair was short and straight and fine, and the same tall, lithe frame. I knew I should not be looking at Kay like this, though I could not deny that I had wished for him, not Arthur, when they had come for me at Dover. He was kind, and I was lonely. I did not know if Kay was thinking the same thing, but he did not speak and only took a step closer. I began to doubt that he had followed me out of concern. He leaned against the door with one hand, close enough by my head for me to feel about him the savour of the Otherworld, the dark strength as he moved a little more towards me. He hesitated there, and I too. I felt the flutter of anticipation within me, *was this going to happen?* He leaned in slightly, slowly, just until I felt his nose brush against mine and my heart begin to race, and the wine hot in my blood, and the longing telling me *yes*. But, just as I closed my eyes and tilted up my face to meet his lips with mine, I thought, *It wouldn't be Lancelot*. It was not Kay that I was yearning for, nor the body of any man apart from Lancelot. I turned my face away, blushing hard with guilt and shame. I was angry with myself for coming so close. Worse, for thinking that any man could stand as substitute for Lancelot if Arthur could not. Kay stepped back, mumbling an apology, or an excuse – I could not tell. I closed my eyes and leaned my head back hard against the closed door, catching my breath, trying to still the swirling in my head from the wine, the desire, the memories of Lancelot.

Arthur came to me late, and woke me gently from a dream where I was with a dark-haired man whose face I could not see, who sometimes was Lancelot and sometimes Kay, and sometimes, confusingly, both at once. I was pleased to be woken, and to see the golden hair that could only be his, and to have him on top of me, hot and hard and real, chasing the dream away.

The next morning, Kay came in after Arthur had left, while Marie was braiding my hair into little plaits and weaving them into a little bun. When Christine, who was fixing some stitching on one of my dresses, torn (I had not told her) by Arthur's eager hands, saw him come in, she put down the dress hastily and, flustered and blushing, made an excuse to leave. She still had the chill on her slightly, and in her hurry to leave the room, she set herself coughing hard.

"Good morning, Christine," Kay called after her, as she hurried down the stairs.

Behind me, Marie giggled.

I turned to Kay.

"Have you upset her?" I asked, haughtily. Kay, seemingly unchastened by our encounter the night before, gave a slight and knowing smile.

"I think she's just a little embarrassed."

Marie giggled again. She tried to swallow them down, but they burst out of her nonetheless.

So, Kay had not gone all the way downstairs when he had left me, nor had he returned to the feast. I was surprised – Christine was half Kay's age again, or more – but not unduly. Christine was still beautiful in a neat, dignified kind of way, and they had grown close, but I felt a hard knot of guilt in my stomach that Kay might have gone to her as I would have taken him to me; thinking of someone else.

"And are you here just to embarrass Christine?" I asked, my tone imperious.

"Well, would you rather I was here to embarrass *you*?"

I felt the heat light up my cheeks; both anger – *I could not believe he said that in front of Marie* – and shame.

"I don't know what you're suggesting," I told him coolly. Marie's hands were still in my hair, but unmoving. I could not see her, but I could imagine her eyes wide with anticipation of some kind of dramatic argument. Marie loved gossip, especially if it wasn't about her.

"Actually, I just came to tell you there's news from the Grail quest. Arthur wants to see you. He's in his chamber, I think."

I got to my feet fast, Marie scrabbling away in surprise. My heart was beating fast within me. I knew Kay saw in me what I was thinking, but I didn't care.

Chapter Thirty-Seven

When I got to Arthur's chamber, he wasn't there; nor was he in the room with the Round Table below. I did not want to search for him through the whole castle and risk missing the news. *News from the Grail quest.* I decided to wait for Arthur in his chamber, but I could not sit still, could not still my restless heart, and instead waited for him pacing slowly up and down. *News from the Grail quest.* I was suddenly filled with a desperate hope that it was *not* news of Lancelot. Whatever it was, I would not want to hear. I did not want to be reminded, did not want to think about him. I had to learn to be content with a life without him. I had been happy before. I *could* again. No, no it was not true. I had spent what was almost four years now watching the gate, listening to every conversation for the sound of his name, dreaming of him, still as often and as vivid as the months after he had left. I had almost taken Kay into my bed just to feel a tiny bit closer to Lancelot. But the thought of having him at Camelot again was overwhelming, unbearable in its joyfulness, and I was not sure I could bear to hear it in front of Arthur. If he was to return, I did not want to be warned. Otherwise, I did not know how I could stand the last few days of waiting for him.

The door opened and I turned to look. For a moment I thought it was Arthur, but then I saw it was the boy Mordred, which I could not help thinking of him as, though clearly he was no longer a boy. I supposed he must have been as old as Arthur was when we married. There in him were Arthur's looks – the golden hair, the big, muscular frame – but where Arthur's eyes were kind his were dark and sly; cruel, I thought, though I did not dare to say so to Arthur when he was just beginning to warm to his son. He had little of his mother about him, who was kindly of look, too, and I wondered if his ill-fated birth was what had made him appear so cruel. It could not have been an easy life for him, a bastard's life, and worse, a child of incest.

"Arthur isn't here," I told him, gently. I expected him to leave, but he shut the door behind himself and drew the bolt. The sound of it shook me to the core; I began to feel nervous and I moved towards the bed where I knew Excalibur was hidden. That was strange, truly, to draw the bolt, though I had learned too well on my first night with Arthur that any of these men could wrench the doors from their hinges. Still, I wished that Arthur would come soon rather than later.

"That is well enough. I hoped to find you alone." His tone was direct, casual. Perhaps he only wanted to speak about something. His voice, too, was like Arthur's, low and pleasantly rough. Only the tone was different, sharper somehow.

"Are you well?" I asked, searching for some easy topic of conversation.

He laughed, and it was an odd, harsh laugh.

He stepped towards me, and for the moment I held my ground, but I was tensed and ready to run, or attack. I was glad that I had worn the green armoured dress, though if I could have had my choice, I would have been armoured head to toe alone with a man his size and strength that I did not trust. And I would have been armed.

"Am I well? Quite well. But I am concerned, my lady. And often, *often* I ask myself, *where is my lord father the weakest?*" Before I could react, he lashed out fast and caught me by the hair, pulling my head back, and pulled me fast against him. *What was he talking about?* He hissed close to my face, "I think I have found it." I pushed him back, but he did not move, nor loosen his grip. He had all of his father's strength, but none of his mercy. I reached up to try to pull his hands from my hair, but his grip was hard as iron and would not be moved. "I hear it said openly in the court that you and Lancelot are lovers."

"You don't know what you're talking about. People in the court also say Arthur isn't your father, but that you are the witch Merlin's little changeling made in Arthur's image." They said worse things as well, but I valued – and feared for – my life more greatly than that. He put a hand against my throat, pushing us back against the little table by the fireplace. I felt it dig painfully into the small of my back. I tried to catch my breath to speak again, I wanted to muster a little power, but the words came from me in a tight gasp. "Arthur defends you and protects you, gives you a place here. Why would you try to hurt him?"

He laughed again. My scalp ached under his violent grip. I wished I had moved faster towards the bed, I wished I had not hesitated, still giving him the benefit of the doubt; I wished I had had time to get Excalibur in my hand. Now we were this close, I could feel, beneath the brute force, the strength of the Otherworld. How he could have it, I did not know, but it was there. His face was close enough to mine that I could feel his breath, and see the dark manic flash in his eyes.

"Arthur tried to have me killed when I was nothing more than a babe in arms. Because of him, and his unnatural lusts, I live a cursed life. I have had one father who hated me because I was not his child, and another father who hates me because I am. People cross themselves when they pass me in the streets. I will have *nothing* from my father when he dies, though he is without an heir, because he killed my mother's husband, and though he can bear to have me at court, he will not openly call me his son. Every day he bends his head in chapel to repent my existence. I am a worthy son of his. I am strong and brave. But all my virtues count for nothing in his eyes, though he made me as I am. I have the same valour in me as he has in him, and I deserve everything he has." He let go of my throat to put his arm around my waist and pull me against him. To my disgust, I felt that he was hard. I pushed him away, but my strength was nothing against his, and he kissed me violently, twisting my hair harder as I tried to pull away from him. I scrabbled on the table with my hand to find any kind of weapon and my hand closed around the cold metal of a candlestick. I brought it hard against the side of his head and he stumbled back. He raised a hand to his bleeding nose, where the candlestick had caught him hard, and felt the blood there. He looked from the blood on his hand to me with a cold cruelty.

"I will punish you for this," he said, his chest heaving, his eyes dark with anger.

He moved back towards me, but I was quick this time, darting out to where I knew Excalibur was hidden and drawing it from its sheath. He backed off more when he saw the point of the Otherworld sword. I felt it trembling in my hands, against the strength coming off him even stronger now. Either he had been born in the barrow-lands or he had sold his soul to some demon for that strength. It was more than anything I had ever felt, and hidden most of the time, for I only felt it fully at last now I held Excalibur to him.

"Perhaps you will," I replied evenly, "but it will not be today. It will not be while Arthur lives."

He laughed again, and gave a cruel smile.

"Oh, you will not tell him."

"Will I not?"

"A word of this, and I will tell him everything I know about you and Lancelot."

I felt less safe, but I did not back down.

"There is no truth in it, and he will not believe you."

Mordred gave an insincere little bow. "My lady," he said, as he turned and slipped out of the door. I let Excalibur fall from my hands with a clatter and sat down hard on the edge of the bed, catching my breath. I hoped that when the news came it would be news of Lancelot.

Eventually, when I had gathered myself, I went looking for Arthur. I did not want to be trapped in a little room with a bolted door again. He was down in the courtyard, watching Gareth and Gaheris fight, though they were only throwing soft and playful blows at one another with wooden swords for the benefit of Lynesse who was watching, the little fair-haired girl in her arms. I saw what the news was before I heard it. Ector's brother Bors had returned from the quest for the Grail. He was clearly new-returned, his face still dark with the sweat and the dirt from the journey. He stood awkwardly, one arm curled around his stomach as though it was injured, and his platemail was dented and, over the right hip, cracked. As I approached, he was telling Arthur what he had seen. I scanned the courtyard for Mordred, and saw him at the edge, the blood from his nose staunched, but nothing changed from the vengeful anger in his eyes.

Bors was shaking his head. "Lionel, my brother, is dead. We were set upon by enemy knights, I did not know whose, and I was separated from him, and when I looked back for him, he was already dead. I saw it, though, the Grail. A glimpse from far off, beneath a veil, but it was as though the light of God filled me from head to foot at the sight of it." The words were slow coming to him, as though he had not spoken for a long time. His breath wheezed from him slightly, as though he were injured in the ribs, too. "I saw Perceval. We travelled on a ship; I don't know where. That was where I saw the Grail, the little glimpse of it I had. But we lost each other in the forest coming off that ship, and I do not honestly know how I made my way back here. I don't know what land we were in. But I saw it. I saw it."

Arthur put a hand on his shoulder and kissed him heartily on the cheek, the black of dirt smearing on Arthur's own clean face. I did not expect Arthur cared. He would have loved some of the dirt of adventure about him, I was sure.

"You have done well, Bors. The best of any who have returned to us. But, did you see Lancelot and Galahad?"

Bors shook his head sadly again, and I felt my heart within me sink. Four years, almost. How much longer would it be before news came?

"I have not seen them alive or dead in more than a year. Last I saw Lancelot, he had seen the Grail pass him in a dream and been unable to wake from it until the Grail had passed, and when he woke it was not where he had dreamed it to be. Galahad... Perceval had seen him, but a long time ago. A long time. I'm afraid, my lord Arthur." Bors glanced warily at me, and at Lynesse standing close by, and I knew what was coming. "I have heard it said that they are dead, all three."

Arthur pinched the bridge of his nose, shutting his eyes tight and looking down, deep in thought for a moment. I could not feel the ground beneath me, nor the air around me. It might not be true, but it did not seem likely that Lancelot was coming back; dead or lost, it was all the same, and for the rest of my life I would be locked in this half-life of ceaseless longing.

"Yet I hope it is not so," Arthur replied slowly, glancing up at Bors. "You should rest, Bors." He turned to me. "Is Christine well enough to see to his injuries?"

"I'm not sure," I admitted. I did not think that she had looked fully well in a long time, and I was loath to do anything that might risk losing her.

Arthur nodded, and called for Ector, who came across the courtyard to lead his brother away. Across the yard, Mordred and Kay were fighting. Mordred was so clearly stronger that although Kay was quicker and more skilled, every time the younger man's practice sword struck against the light leather armour they wore to train, Kay stumbled back. Mordred's style was ruthless and he moved with a reckless carelessness, throwing himself into each blow. But it was working. Kay, who had come so close at the first tournament I had seen to besting Lancelot, was being slowly driven back, losing ground. I felt as I watched that I, too, was losing ground. The hope of Lancelot returning was slipping away from me, and Mordred was advancing on Arthur, though Arthur did not know it, and had made it clear that I was the first piece of territory he intended to take.

But after that the days passed without event. I felt listless and miserable, but Arthur was listless and miserable too and did not notice. He said often that he believed Lancelot would return, aloud to no one in particular. I felt that like a knife into the centre of me. I did not want to be tortured with a hope that was never to be.

By the time summer and the warmer weather came, mercifully Christine grew well again, though she was weaker than she had been before, and liked it less when Kay sat with us to read, casting a narrow eye on him and curtly correcting his Breton when before he was one of the few people along with myself that she favoured with her smiles. Kay seemed unrepentant, though I noticed he had not offered to read to her at night anymore after Christmas. Marie told me once, quietly, while Christine had gone to fetch something, that Christine was angry that he had come only the once, and drunk, and never said a word of it to her afterwards. This distance seemed strange now since I had thought they had been so close before, and Marie told me that long ago she had seen Kay kiss Christine once, in the garden, when he thought they were alone, though I was not sure I believed her. I felt I ought to chastise him about that rudeness in some way, but I did not know what to say, and anyway I did not feel the relevance of it as I once might have done. It all seemed far away and faded, the life I moved through.

Mordred did not make another move against me. He seemed to be biding his time, though I knew he and Aggravain always watched me. I did not think they could do anything to me, anyway, since Lancelot was gone and I had no hope left that I would see him again, only the constant ghost of his memory that I carried close to my heart, and against my skin.

Chapter Thirty-Eight

It was a year since Bors had returned, and early spring, when I found myself alone and decided I would go to the chapel and pray to the god of the Grail once more, and beg him to return Lancelot, or bring news of his death. I just did not want to carry on not knowing, staring out across the fields every day, waiting for news. I went often those days, whenever I was alone and at a loss for what else to do, and could not face the tedium and the thoughts of Lancelot that came with it, if I stayed in my room. It seemed more appropriate to apply, with those thoughts of Lancelot, to his and Arthur's god, and wish for his return.

I came to kneel before the altar and a small cloud of dust rose from the old cushion as I sank on to it. Though Arthur's kingdom was new, everything in this chapel was old, and carried with it the smell and feel of age. I liked it. It made me wonder if Arthur's god might not really be as old and powerful as my gods after all. Though Arthur's chapel was younger than the hills, and the trees, and the moon, still. I pressed my hands together, twining my fingers, whispering the words I had learned by heart, but that still sounded unfamiliar and alien to my ears, the Latin as incomprehensible as a spell. *Bring him back, bring him back*, I thought, my wishing mind disconnected from the automatic words of my mouth. I did not know what I could offer in return. Christ was not like my old gods, and I had brought no offering for him. He did not like such things, I had learned from the times the sermons in chapel had reached me through my daydreaming.

Bring him back.

"Guinevere?" I heard my name and froze. The voice was unmistakable, but I did not believe it. I stood, slowly. I felt my whole body trembling, my heart racing, my palms suddenly sweating hard. I dared not turn around, not right away. I could have imagined that voice, that single soft word. I drew in a deep shaking breath and closed my eyes. I was sure I was not dreaming from the pain deep inside me, which would have woken me from my sleep, that shot through me at the sound of his voice, so familiar, and lost so long. I pressed my hand against my ribs, below my breasts, trying to steady my breath, to hold myself together. Slowly, slowly, I turned, as though I were afraid if I turned too fast I would shatter the dream I had dreamed for so long and prevent it from becoming reality.

But there he was, standing in the aisle, dressed still in his platemail, his helm in his hand hanging by his side. I felt a wave of rapturous dizziness pass over me at the joy of seeing him. The years had been kind to him, and if anything he had grown ever more handsome. He was dirty from the road and a dark stubble shaded his chin, but it suited him well. He looked strong and valiant. I was aware suddenly that five years, *five years*, had passed since we had looked on each other, and I was no longer young. The plumpness of youth had left my face and I looked proud and angular now; more like a queen, less like a desirable young maid. I had grown out of youth into womanhood without really noticing it at all. I stood still and took it all in; the mouth I had felt against mine, the hair I had wound my hands in, the strong, true body I had held against my own. All returned to me. The helm fell with a clatter from his hands as he stepped forward towards me, and I towards him. An impossible stretch of space stood between us, half the aisle of the chapel, but I could only move my stunned limbs slowly, towards him. It felt like an age until we stood before each other, close enough that I could reach out and lightly touch his cheek with my fingertips. Skin, desperately, dizzyingly familiar, met my touch and I gave a gasping laugh of relief when I could at last be sure it was not an illusion.

"You're *alive*," I whispered.

He took my face in his hands, and I felt the rough leather of the gauntlets and longed instead for the touch of his hands, his skin bare against me, as he pressed his forehead against mine and whispered in return.

"I returned to you, as I promised I would."

I leaned up to kiss him, to taste again the lips I had remembered on mine for five years without their touch, when I heard Arthur call from the door of the chapel.

"Lancelot!"

The tears came hard, shaking me all the way through my body; tears of relief and tears already of new loss as Arthur had come crashing in on our reunion. I had not got even a kiss. He was close enough to touch, but impossibly far with Arthur there. Lancelot turned to Arthur and the men embraced, each clapping the other on the back as I leaned back, steadying myself against the pews, as the sobs of joy, of relief, of the infinite closeness and distance of Lancelot racked me to the core. *But he is alive, and he has returned to me, as he promised he would.*

Arthur looked to me and laughed gently and pulled me into his arms. I went like a child, stunned, weak and obedient. I let him hold me to him, glad of the comfort, though it was Lancelot I longed to hold. He hushed me gently and stroked my hair, and I sank against him, my tears darkening the red fabric of his surcoat. "My love, he is well. Look." I knew that he was well, I could see that, but I could not voice – especially not to Arthur – what I felt. "We have thought of you often, Lancelot. In truth, we heard you were dead," Arthur added, as though apologising for me. I supposed to him I seemed to be being hysterical. Lancelot nodded sadly, looking at me. I leant my head back against Arthur's chest and looked back, hoping that he could see it all there in me: the relief, the longing, all of it.

"I did not come back easily with my life," Lancelot admitted. Then, after a pause, and a sigh, he added, "Galahad and Perceval are dead."

"The Grail?" Arthur asked eagerly. "Did you see the Grail?"

It was as though in his eagerness for stories he had not taken in the loss of his friends.

Lancelot shook his head again.

"I saw it far off, or in dreams, but no, not truly. But Perceval and Galahad did."

Arthur nodded beside me. His voice had the surety of total belief, total trust in his god. His god ought to have loved him for that. "Then they died without sin, and they are in heaven." Arthur seemed pleased at this, seemed not to see the wary sorrow that hung around Lancelot. Arthur was too excited to have Lancelot returned, too excited at the thought of knights of his having seen the Grail to notice that something was not right.

"Well, Lancelot, we will have a great feast tonight and you must tell us all about it. *Five years* of adventures." Arthur grinned broadly and slapped him on the back again.

"My brother Bors. Did he return?" Lancelot asked quietly.

"Yes, yes. He has seen the Grail, too, though covered. I'm very glad it's over, and so many of you have returned to us whole and sound."

Arthur was talking and talking, excited and eager, while Lancelot and I stood quiet and weary – he from his travels, and I from the sight of him once more after so long. Eventually Arthur noticed Lancelot's quietness, and bid him go and rest. Lancelot left us with a little bow and once again was gone. I was frightened to see him walk from the chapel door, as though I might have imagined it, and he might be gone again. I told Arthur that I wanted to get ready for the feasting, and he kissed me lightly on the forehead and let me go.

I was relieved when I came at last up to my chamber and could be alone. I called to Christine for a bath and paced the room until it came. I felt full of an awful anxious energy, desperate to see Lancelot again, but not knowing how long I would have to wait until we could be alone. He had been long missed at Camelot by all the other knights, and I still had Mordred and Aggravain and Gawain's watchful gaze to hide from. I did not think I could bear their looks on me tonight. I was afraid that my heart and my thoughts were painfully close to the surface of my skin, and would show through me. When the bath came at last and I could sink gratefully into it, I closed my eyes and leaned back into it, feeling the hot water soak through the thick curls of my hair. The heat felt cleansing, and strengthening, burning away the years of waiting. Whatever it would be, surely it could not be long now. Christine pulled the chair around behind me, and began combing my hair as I sat back up, curling my arms around my knees. Periodically she coughed into the back of her hand. I feared that the cough would never leave her. It had been a cold winter, and Christine had not been young for a long time.

"So," she began quietly, in Breton, "Lancelot is returned at last."

I didn't say anything. I did not know what I could say to her that wouldn't spill everything out of me. I was sure she already knew, anyway. She clicked her tongue softly as she pulled away the knots with the comb, the hair jerking sharply against my scalp. I was glad of it. It meant that I could be sure I was awake.

"Would you like me to ask him to come to you before the feast?" she asked, after a long pause. I was not sure I had heard her right, and I sat up sharply, the water sloshing around me in the iron tub. "So you have not gone deaf after all, my lady." I could not see it, but I could hear her smile. But then, her voice turned serious again. "Just do not be surprised if he is much changed. Five years is a long time."

I didn't know what Christine knew, or what she thought. I supposed she just thought he had been a dear friend to me. I wished I could have told her, could have asked her. I would have liked to have had a woman to whom I could talk about it, but I dared not bring her or Marie into danger with the truth.

Marie came to help me get ready, as Christine went to pass the message. My heart was thudding within me already. I did not know how my body could sustain it, if I had to wait for long. Marie tied up my hair, braided through with a gold ribbon, into a bun. She had brought a dress of pale green silk, thin and light for summer, that flowed around me in the breeze from the open window. She brought the necklace hung with little emeralds, and had also brought the heavy crown I hated to wear. I supposed that Arthur was keen to celebrate in the most ceremony possible. I did not want to put it on until I had to leave. I let her go to make herself ready and sat by the window to wait, looking down at the garden below in the late evening light, not yet orange at the edges, but the brightness of the sun fading, and the shadows long and dark.

I did not have to wait long. Lancelot came through the door quietly, and closed it gently behind him, but I had been tense and listening for so long that I could not miss it. He, too, had bathed, and his hair was still damp. My fingers remembered the touch of it, and the memories of Surluse hovered close about me. I wondered if he was thinking about it, too. He had shaved away the rough beard that travel had grown on him, and he looked just as young as he had when we had five years ago said our goodbyes. It was, blissfully, as though no time at all had passed. I wondered if he looked at me now and saw a different woman, or if for him, too, it was just the same. He was dressed just in his shirt and breeches, either not yet in finery for the feast or not intending to be. I stood slowly, my body moving sluggishly behind my racing heart as though my heart had taken all its strength.

"My lady?" he said, quiet and hesitant, awkward and painfully formal, hovering by the door. At once I rushed into his arms, the longing overtaking me in a wild whirl of joy, to hold him, to be close to him. But, as I came to him he caught me lightly by the arms and gently, but definitely, held me away.

"What's wrong?" I asked, my voice small and fearful.

Lancelot sighed.

"Sit down."

I did not move, resistant. He released his grip on me and moved away, going to sit at the window. He rested his arm along the ledge and looked out, the late sun lighting his profile. I did not move or speak, crossing my arms in front of me and standing by the door, still, as though I was guarding the way out. After a moment, he began to speak.

"Guinevere, it was awful. *Awful.* Most of the knights who rode out with us were nothing more than boys in borrowed armour, sticking close to me because they thought I could protect them." He shook his head sadly, still staring out across the garden. "I did what I could but... and Galahad, he didn't know how to fight, he looked as though he had never held a sword. He was *my son*, so I stayed with him and Perceval went with the others. Half of them were princes, not fighting men, their horses covered in gold and jewels. Arthur's peace is a long-needed mercy, but it has not bred warriors, and there were men in the woods – bandits, outlaws, I don't know what – and they fell on them and they tore them apart. I did what I could, but there were so many. And Galahad, Galahad was always riding ahead, the Grail in his eyes, following the sense he was so sure he had of it. I didn't want to lose him, because I knew he couldn't fight, but we got separated. I didn't know where I was. I wandered for months. I didn't know if I was still in Britain. Sometimes I dreamed the Grail was before me, and I could not open my eyes to see it. I lodged with a hermit, and when I confessed my sins to him, he told me they were too heavy for me to ever see the Grail." Lancelot turned his head to look at me, and I shrank back against the door. *My sins.* Oh, I knew I was one of those. He hesitated for a moment, and I could see the sorrow all about him. "Then, I found Perceval. I came to a ship docked by a river, but it seemed to be empty. When I climbed aboard I saw it was not. It was a plague ship, full of the dead. It stank of death. I could smell the dead below decks, and there were a few bodies strewn on the deck up top. I recognised Perceval. He lay at the bow, half-propped against the edge. His skin was grey, his eyes red. He had this huge wound, at," Lancelot baulked for a moment, as though it was hard to speak of, and I knew he was seeing it again before his eyes, "at his thigh. When I came to him, he recognised me, but he was babbling on and on about a wounded king, and the Grail, saying he had seen the Grail in the castle of a wounded king. He was feverish, and his wound smelled of the death that was coming for him. I –" Lancelot stopped again and rubbed his forehead hard with the heel of his hand. "I could not bear to see him suffer a slow death." In the silence, I understood what Lancelot had meant. I should have said something, should have told him that it was the kindest thing to do, but I could not. "It was months after that that I found Galahad at last. I came upon a ruined chapel deep in the woods. All the windows and doors were broken in, and part of the roof had fallen. I only saw him because the sunlight caught his pale white hair. He was lying by the altar. He was thin, his lips were white and his skin was pale and cracked. There was no mark of a wound on him, but when I saw him there and I took him in my arms, he died. He died muttering about the Grail. He said that he had seen the Grail, and that he was with God." Lancelot looked up and fixed me with his eyes. I felt them go right through me, hold me to the spot. "I don't know if there ever was a Grail, but I *do* know that Galahad died for my sins. He would not have been born but for them, and he suffered and died for my sins."

"If you had truly been with me, that night, then Galahad would not have been born at all," I replied, my voice quavering. Lancelot sighed, rubbing his face in his hands. After a moment, he got to his feet. I could see him bristling with frustration as he paced before me, desperate for a way to make me understand, I think, what he had understood. But either I could not, or I did not want to, but I knew either way I would not.

"Don't you believe in sin?"

"I do. And yet Gawain has returned alive." I could hear the stubbornness in my own voice. I did not want to give it up. I had a right to it. I had waited. I had not changed.

"Guinevere, *please* –"

"What about love?" I stepped forward towards him, and I felt the anger light within me, the spark of it spreading through me. "Love is sacred. And truth."

"Guinevere, *marriage* is sacred."

That took the strength out of me as fast as it had come and I felt myself reel back from it, as if it had been a blow. So that was the way he saw it. Lancelot groaned in despair, turning away from me again, running his hands through his hair.

"Don't you... want me... anymore?" I asked, the words only just managing to escape me. I felt as though I was shrinking away, growing weaker. All of this waiting, for nothing. He turned back to me then, and it was as though all the air and anger rushed from him and he sighed away. I saw the sadness there, and longing, but I was still sure it was nothing to my own.

"From the moment I saw you," he said gently, as though he was answering a different question entirely. "I saw you first on the battlefield. You were so brave, and fierce, and beautiful. I thought I was looking into the past, at one of the celtic warrior queens from long ago. I was young, and still hopeful for a wife to take to my own lands. But, when I asked who you were, they told me you were Arthur's queen. *Arthur's*. Arthur is like blood to me, like my own brother. I should have forgotten you then, but I could not. And then you fell, and I had you in my arms, and –" he sighed heavily again, taking his gaze from mine to pace again, "I thought it would be enough to be close to you, so I accepted Arthur's invitation to court. And –"

"And now here we are," I finished, coldly. I did not want to hear him recount his love for me with regret. I did not want to hear his talk of sin. He would not stand there and unwind the whole brave thread of our love until it came to pieces. It was not a tale, not something that had been. It was real and raw and all around us, and I would not let him give it up.

"Guinevere, please. I love you. We should not be as we were. We should not –" He searched for a word, but found none that he was brave enough to say aloud. "But let me stay close to you."

I did not want him to go. But I did not want him to look at me as though I was some vessel of sin. He came towards me as I looked down and away from him, and felt the tears beginning to roll down my cheeks. I had not realised that I was crying. Lancelot took my face in his hands and wiped them away with his thumbs, softly. The touch of his skin on mine for so long made me shudder with yearning for him, but I dared not lean towards him, because I knew he would lean away. Perhaps this was as close as I would ever get. I closed my eyes and put my hands over his, holding his to me. I nodded, accepting what little closeness he might offer me, and he kissed me on the forehead, and left.

I waited until I was calm before I went to find the celebrations. They were not in the great hall, but in Arthur's council chamber, around the Round Table. When I entered the room, it struck me that the knights were now so much fewer than when they had left for the Grail quest that all could easily fit around the table. I found to my surprise that I suddenly missed the stern, unsmiling face of Perceval. At least he had always been constant. When I stepped into the room, the first eyes that met mine were Mordred's, and a chill went down my spine. He was sat with his half-brothers opposite my place beside Arthur. Lancelot was already sat at Arthur's side and he tried to give me a small smile as I came in, but I was not yet ready for the half-love that was all he was offering me. I would take it for now, but I was not sure that I did not deserve more from him, after everything. He was wearing the purple surcoat, and beside Arthur in red and gold they made a dazzling pair. One fair, one dark, both men tall and strong, moving with the easy grace that comes from a powerful warrior's body, Arthur broad and Lancelot lean and feline. As I sat beside Kay and Lancelot shifted out of my view behind Arthur beside me, Kay patted my shoulder in what I supposed was meant to be a comforting manner. He was strange, Kay, and I never knew how kind he would be. But I was glad of this kindness.

The story Lancelot told to the knights around the table of his quest for the Grail was wildly different to the tale he had told me. In this tale, he had watched as a shaft of light lifted Galahad to heaven as he stood before the Grail, and he himself had been shown the Grail behind a veil by a beautiful maiden who trapped him in her castle for a year, testing – he said – his virtuous suitability for the Grail. Gawain had liked that part, though had suggested that Lancelot might have enjoyed his quest more had he failed her test. Perceval had slain a dragon, and died in rapture at the sight of the Grail which came to him when the deed was done. The others laughed and cheered – Gaheris especially when Lancelot mentioned the dragon. I remembered hearing some story once about Gaheris fighting a dragon, but if Gawain had told it – as I suspected he had – I thought it more likely that the truth was that Gaheris once trod on a frog. He and Gareth seemed to be drunk already, celebrating hard. Aggravain and Gawain probably were as well, but the older brothers being larger wore it better. Mordred, his wine untouched, kept cold, watchful eyes on everyone around the table. I drank heartily from my cup, eager to feel less, to feel soft and fading around the edges and a little numb. I wanted to feel the wine in my blood and have Arthur take me in his arms and drive all the thoughts of Lancelot from my mind. I wanted his rough, demanding touch on my body, his insistent need for me. Now Lancelot was there before me, the memories came back, thick and fast and unbidden, of the sensation of his hands on me, his lips, his skin against mine, and I drank hard, trying to drive the thoughts away. When they were taking away the meat and fish and bringing the little honeyed cakes, Kay put his hand over my cup.

"Steady," he said. I pushed his hand away, and drank again. Enough wine, and enough heady memory, and it would be as though they were both there tonight.

When the food was finished and the knights sat back in their chairs, groaningly full and flushed and grinning with wine, and we all sat in a warm, satisfied stupor, the knights began to get up and mill around to talk with one another. Arthur went to Gawain, asking to hear of Gawain's quest for the Grail again, I suspected, and Kay went to Lancelot, who I supposed he too had missed. I sat back in my chair, feeling the pleasant swirling of the wine inside me, letting my eyes lie heavily half-shut. It was pleasant to look at the room that way; the men in their bright surcoats blurring in to one another in the candlelight. Because of this, it took me a moment to realise that Mordred had slipped into the chair Kay had left empty beside me. He put an arm lazily around the back of my chair and leaned slowly down by my side. Lancelot, two seats away, seemed to notice, though he gave nothing away, neither stopping his conversation with Kay nor making any move towards us. Kay, sat on the table, his back to us and facing Lancelot, half-blocked his view, but I felt his eyes on me and felt a little safer. But Mordred had not come so close to speak to me.

"Sir Lancelot," Mordred called out loudly, "I have heard many tales of your prowess in battle. They say no man can defeat you."

As Mordred spoke, I felt the fingers of the hand he had reached around the chair brush my throat. It was soft as a whisper, but it was a threat. But it wasn't aimed at me; Mordred had sensed a rival, a man strong enough to stop whatever it was he was plotting, arrived at court. The way that Kay was sitting blocked Arthur's view of us, and I did not want to call out, did not want to encourage Mordred or Aggravain to make any public accusations. Lancelot was just returned and I would not risk chasing him away. I stiffened in my chair, holding my breath. I wished I was wearing my armoured dress. I wished I had brought my knife. I had been thoughtless. Lancelot's eyes fixed on Mordred behind me, full of danger. He did not respond.

"I should like to feel your strength in battle," Mordred continued, trailing the fingers down my neck, down towards the neckline of the dress. I reached forward slowly, only moving my arm, and wrapped my hand around the stem of my metal cup. It would be as well to have a weapon of some kind in my hand. Kay had turned now, and I saw that his hand rest against the hilt of his sword. So, Kay had come to the feast armed. Lancelot, I noticed, had not. "My brother Gareth tells me it does a man good to feel your might against him." He pulled his hand back up, dragging his fingernails across my skin. I suppressed a shudder. "I think you would find me a worthy opponent."

Then he moved away, as suddenly as he had come. Lancelot and Kay looked at one another, and then at me. I let the breath rush out of me. I did not realise how hard I had been holding it. Arthur, on the other side of the room laughing with Gawain, had not noticed. I felt suddenly cold, and sober, and Lancelot's eyes lit upon mine, heavy with dread.

Chapter Thirty-Nine

Lancelot was often near me after that. I think he was afraid to leave me alone with Mordred. I was pleased, anyway, to have him nearby, though we were never alone. Marie and Christine were always near me, and sometimes Lynesse with the little girl, whom Lancelot was always pleased to see. To watch him pick up the little girl and throw her lightly in the air to make her giggle made me wonder painfully if he would not have liked to have had a child and a wife of his own. Perhaps it would have been for his own good, a kindness to him, if I had sent him away for good. But he must have felt as I did, that he would never be whole if we were apart. He had had, after all, opportunities before to leave me and find someone who could give him a child.

And then, suddenly, one late spring day, we were alone. We had been sitting with Christine and Marie in my audience room, the bright light of late afternoon streaming through the windows leaving lovely diamond patterns of light and shade on the wooden floor, and making the specks of dust that flew lazily through the beams of light glow, when Marie was called away to help Lynesse with something or other – I did not pay attention – and Christine fell to coughing too hard to breathe and had to go to lie down. I offered to go with her, but she insisted she needed no help. And suddenly, for the first time since I had turned around to see him in the chapel, we were alone. This time, there was no likelihood of someone wandering in. I wanted to ask him if he had changed his mind about sin, and the love that I still felt strong and hot between us whenever he looked at me. *Surely* he could not be so sure after we had spent so many days just across the room from one another, in each other's company, but tantalisingly apart. I felt him look at me; I did not imagine that. I pulled the big book that Christine had dropped to the floor onto my lap. It was heavy and huge, covering most of my thighs as I drew them up towards me to lean over the book. Lancelot moved closer beside me. I felt the magnetic presence of his body, smelled the longed-for smell of his skin. But I did not move towards him, or speak, afraid to break the spell and scare him away. He rested one hand against the floor behind me to lean forward and look at the book. It was a silly old story about a man and a fairy in Breton. Lancelot tried to read it, but he mispronounced the words, the written Breton unfamiliar to him, though he spoke it well. The words sounded funny in his southern accent, so familiar to me in my own, and I felt the laughter bubble out of me, as it had not in such a long time, and he was laughing too. I did not want him to stop reading, because I loved the sound of his voice so close to my ear, deliciously intimate, but I could not help it. His hair brushed my cheek as he leant forward to peer more closely at the letters on the page and I closed my eyes, letting the delight of it rush over me for a second. I could reach out and touch it. I could smell it, clean and close. I felt that if I held him now, he might relent. He tried the word again, and laid his hand lightly on the book where it was, and I laughed again, reaching out to point to it, too. Our hands brushed, lightly, and I felt it go right through me. He didn't move his hand away, and we had stopped laughing. I felt the tension gathering between us, neither of us sure if we were about to begin it all again. He turned to me with a gentle smile, still lingering from his laughter, and as our eyes met, I felt the shock go through me, the old familiar shock, and neither of us were smiling anymore. He was close, so unbearably close. I leant towards him slightly, closing my eyes as our noses brushed together, and I felt the velvet brush of his hair against my forehead. My breath caught in me, and I felt the heat rise in my cheeks. I could hear his breath fast and nervous, too. Then, glorious and longed-for as the earth longs for sunrise, I felt the brush of his lips against mine, and felt my lips part in automatic, yearning anticipation. But he moved away. I gasped for my breath, blushing harder now, hearing my heart beat in my ears, frustrated, angry and burningly rejected. I stood fast, letting the book fall to the floor, walking fast to the window and crossing my arms protectively around myself, turning away from him and looking out.

The door opened and Kay came in, looking for Lancelot to train with him, but I had no way of knowing if Lancelot had heard him on the stairs or simply been repulsed by the thought of the sin that waited for him in my body. I felt Kay's questioning eyes on me as he stood in the door, but I did not turn to him. I didn't answer Lancelot as he took his leave of me or turn to look at him. He would get nothing from me.

That night when Arthur came to me, I was fired with a desire born from anger, and a need for revenge. If Lancelot would not have me, then I would give myself to Arthur with the ardour I had saved for him.

"I have been waiting for you," I told Arthur, as he came through the door, and he gave me a knowing, desirous little smile. He pulled me hard into his arms and he kissed me eagerly, excited already by my desire. I was cruel, and angry, and I wanted control. I knew Arthur, I knew he would never change, he would always want me, and I needed it then. I needed to be able to rely on his ceaseless desire. I drew back from him, teasing, testing, making him press towards me, pretending I might slip away from him until, as I longed for, as I needed, with a groan of frustrated hunger he grasped me hard against him, insistent, demanding. I closed my eyes and sank into it, the wonderful oblivion of being wanted. He tore away my dress, and ran his hands through my hair, letting the pins fall to the floor. I heard him say my name and I knew he was lost, too, and utterly mine. I led him to the bed and pushed him down. My touch would have been nothing but a feather's to him, but he lay obediently down, pulling off his breeches and kicking them away. I pulled my underdress over my head and felt the appreciative touch of his gaze on me as I climbed onto him, feeling him slide his hands up my bare back and into my hair. I could see in his eyes that all his thoughts that moment were of me. I knew him. I knew how he would have me now, that there was no other way for him. There was a man, still, who would not deny me. Not refuse me. I had some power still. I leaned down and kissed him. I was slow and sensual, but he was hot with urgency already and he drew me into a rough, passionate kiss. I felt his hands, firm and hungry, against my breasts, and pressed myself back into them, lost in the pleasure of his touch. He was keen and excited, and fast he pulled me onto him, and I took him inside me with a little cry of joy, and I sat up, leaning back into it, throwing my hair back and feeling his strong hands against my hips, moving me with him as he groaned with pleasure beneath me and I felt the heat of pleasure rise within me. Thoughts came unbidden to me of Lancelot beneath me, the sensuality of his touch, the feel of his lips soft and light against my breasts, the last night we had spent together, and I flushed hotter with pleasure and heard a little cry of it escape me. I closed my eyes as I felt the wave of bliss move through me and Arthur groan and sigh beneath me. I fell forward onto him and he wrapped his arms around me and rolled over on to me, his kisses gentle and satisfied. I sighed against him, nestling my head into the crook of his arm. He stroked my cheek gently and smiled.

"You are still full of surprises, my love."

I felt suddenly cold. *I had only been so before with Lancelot.* I had been thinking of him, thinking of trying to forget him, when Arthur had come to me, and I had forgotten that Arthur and I had never loved thus together. He did not seem to think it too remarkable, though, and was soon asleep beside me while I, with thoughts of Lancelot pressed close against my bare skin, and the man himself unbearably far away, lay awake staring up into the empty darkness long after the last candle had guttered out, wondering if I would ever learn to live without his touch.

Arthur called a tournament to celebrate the final return from the Grail quest. I was not that interested, and had never enjoyed the sight of grown men playfighting, but I thought it might do me good to see Lancelot fight with my sleeve on him. It might remind me of Surluse, and give me some comfort. Besides, as Arthur's queen I ought to make an appearance, and clap and cheer in the right places. But I wore the green armoured dress and the crown of Cleopatra. I had not worn it in a long time, feeling that it was an ill omen from Morgan, but I thought its fearsome cobras were a fitting match for the armoured dress, and I wanted to feel strong and queenlike. I wanted Lancelot to look at me and see the woman he had dreamed I was when he had seen me on the battlefield. I also wanted to feel prepared if he tried to reject me again. I would fight for what I had deserved, what I had earned through my long waiting.

Arthur was pleased when he saw me, and kissed me tenderly when I joined him on the raised platform.

"I am glad to see you wear that again."

I kissed him in return, holding his face in my hands, pressing my body against him. I was suddenly filled with the strength of my love for Arthur. Arthur, who was always there, always simple. Always kind, always desiring. I loved him. I loved him with all my heart. But I knew, I knew deep inside me still that I was a woman born with two hearts within me, and though one was full of love for Arthur, that was not enough.

I looked for Lancelot in the lists, but I couldn't see him there. Knight after knight clashed together and nowhere did I see my gold sleeve or a man dressed in Lancelot's armour.

"Where is Lancelot?" I asked Arthur. Arthur shrugged beside me, not taking his eyes from the jousting.

"I don't think he is riding today. Men don't want to ride against him anymore because he always wins."

I could understand that, but I was disappointed. I sat back into my seat, less interested in what was happening before me. Mordred was doing well. He knocked Kay, who usually did well, easily from his horse in the first round. When he came up against his brother Aggravain, it was a harder-won match, but he knocked Aggravain down in the end. He beat Lamerocke and Dinadan easily, and at last the only knight left to face him was one I did not recognise, who bore a sleeve of red and white.

"Whose sleeve is that?" I asked Arthur, pointing to the knight who was gathering himself to ride against Mordred, who rode without a woman's favour, at the other end.

"That's the sleeve of the girl they call the Fair Maid of Astolat." Arthur sounded surprised.

I had heard of her. Some nymphish fourteen-year-old from a nearby castle town. People said that she was just as fair as Isolde, and besides, she was young and unwedded with a rich castle. I supposed a lowly but strong knight would be well-advised to ride for her sake.

Though I did not rate his chances against Mordred's brute aggression. I gazed around for her in the crowd, but I did not see anyone that could be her.

When they came together, a huge cry went up from the audience as both spears shattered, and neither knight fell. So, he would not be easily defeated. They came together again and again, each time with fresh spears, until at last the knight that rode for the Fair Maid of Astolat caught Mordred in the ribs with his spear and Mordred crashed to the ground. I was on my feet cheering with the rest. I was pleased to see Mordred knocked to the ground. If I could not see Lancelot fight for me, at least I would enjoy the memory of Mordred being unhorsed. Arthur jumped to his feet beside me, clapping and cheering with everyone else. The knight rode around the jousting field once, and came to stop in front of us. I stopped cheering and clapping as the knight pulled his helm from his head. It was Lancelot. The blood rushed in my ears and I felt the shock of it move me from my body. My arms fell limp by my side as I felt the numb, cold shock spread through me. As though from underwater, I heard Gawain remark to Arthur with cruel pleasure.

"It is a marvel, they say, what great love Lancelot has for the Maid of Astolat."

As soon as I could I rushed back up to my room. I was trembling, hot all over my skin, and cold with dread within. *Betrayed*. I poured water from the brass jug into the basin by my window and splashed it on my face, but I didn't feel any better. I forced air slow and deep into my lungs, trying to make myself feel calm.

The door burst open without a knock and I turned to see Lancelot, dressed in the clothes he must have worn beneath his armour for the jousting; shirt and breeches with a small leather jerkin, all marked and scuffed from the fighting. I took a step towards him, feeling my fists clench automatically, the power of my anger gathering in me.

"How *dare* you come to me now?" My voice was low and threatening. I could feel myself quivering with rage within, but I held it down. He opened his mouth to speak, but I spoke again. "After you let me stand there and cheer for you fighting for another woman, listen to people talk about the *marvellous love* between you and this Maid of Astolat. How dare you show your face before me?"

He moved another step into the room. Why did he not leave? I did not want to see him.

"Please, Guinevere, let me explain." He came closer and I turned away from him, pacing back towards the window. I did not need him here now, I needed the space alone with my thoughts. As I was now, I wanted to tear into his flesh with my nails. If I had had a weapon in my hands I was sure I would have tried to kill him.

"I don't want to hear it."

I could feel myself shaking with rage, I could feel that I was out of control. I hadn't wanted to see him, I hadn't wanted to until I felt calmer, but he was *pushing* me, pushing me into this angry little corner. I pressed a hand against my forehead, trying to still the racing thoughts, cool the rage within me, but I heard him step towards me again, and I rounded on him.

"Lancelot, *I don't want to see you*." I was struggling to keep from shouting, and this gave my voice an unsettling quavering calm. I crossed my arms in front of me, a vain attempt to hold the wildness of my rage tight against my chest. "You show me disrespect in public and disdain in private. You shy away from me and the love I have had for you *for years* as though it disgusts you and you *wear another woman's colours* into the field. *Another woman.* A young girl, a woman half my age, I hear, as well. *Less.* I see now what your rejection of me is really about. After all, you're nothing more than a common lecher. All of your talk of piety and God was just a lie. You're a man of no faith."

He paced before me for a moment, clenching and releasing his fists in frustration, searching for the words. I could see that he was angry, too. I was glad he was angry. That was better than all the praying and silence. He ought to feel angry. He ought to come here to fight to the death for me, to fight until I believed he still loved me if he truly did as he had pretended he did when he had returned. If he was angry then there were still feelings in there, still a human heart; he still had a man's blood rather than a saint's, or a coward's.

"Guinevere." He spoke slowly, his voice soft and controlled, but powerful. I did not like his tone, though. He was slow, as though he was explaining to a child, and it only made me angrier. "People are talking. About us. Mordred watches us all the time. I took the girl's sleeve for *your safety*. We are in danger here, even now. Our boldness has put us both in danger before. We have to be prudent." He gave a frustrated sigh and looked up at me, but I was cold to the appeal in his eyes and in the face of his cold rationality I had already lost control.

"It's clear to me now that you're nothing more than a *coward*." I stepped towards him in anger, and he did not back down. I was shouting now, the words tearing out of me like a storm. "What is a coward knight worth? Oh, you're brave enough in battle, but that's only because you're sure of your strength. It seems to me that my woman's heart is braver than your man's one. You take another woman – hah! – a *girl*, because she's *safer*, because – don't pretend this is about *me* or what *I want* – safer for your precious reputation. I didn't care about *anything* apart from being with you." The strength drained out of me suddenly as I said that, and I gathered myself back. I had been given from too deep in the centre of myself, and torn its core out with it. It had all the painful effectiveness of the utter truth. I was angry, because I loved him more than he loved me. I felt hot, frustrated tears prick at the back of my eyes, and though I struggled I could not hold them back. Lancelot watched me with sad eyes, his chest rising and falling with heavy breaths as he held his own anger back, but he moved closer and I did not move away. I drew in my breath and began again, the words now almost a whisper in the intensity of my anger, shaking through the burning tears of rage. "You let me wait. You let me wait for you for *five years*. I didn't know if you were alive or dead. Then you came back like it was nothing at all, and you wanted to walk with me and sit with me and talk with me, but you wouldn't let me *touch* you because my woman's touch carries the poison of sin. *You* changed when you went looking for the Grail – *you* did. I didn't change. I stayed here, and I waited, and every day I loved you just the same. I *dreamed* of you. I waited for you, while you were forgetting me. While you were thinking I was nothing but a sin. But this isn't even about sin!" The rage fired in me again, and I leaned into it, relished it, felt delight as it lifted through me. It was making me strong again. "No, this is about your coward's heart." Lancelot reached out to take me into his arms but I pushed him away. He seized my arms as I pushed him and pulled me hard against him, holding my wrists in front of his chest, for a moment, holding me fast against him. I felt his chest against mine, the closeness and heat of his body. We had not been this close, I had not felt his body against mine, in more than five years. I could have lost myself in it, then. I pushed back the memories that were rushing to me, the longing to cast away my clothes and feel his skin on mine, and held on to my anger. I leaned up towards him, and hissed, "*Go then*. Go and find a safer woman. I don't want to see you again."

He did not speak. Our eyes were locked together. I could smell the musky sweat of his body; I could feel the dangerous gravity of my desire pulling me towards him. My body in its yearning leaned into his, and I could feel his intoxicating closeness beginning to cloud my mind. He leaned down towards me. I felt my mouth move instinctively towards him. I wanted him, I knew it, and his lips were seconds from mine. I remembered it all, all the times he had pulled me close and kissed me, and I had melted into his arms, all the times I had felt his skin on mine, his lips on mine, everything we had whispered to one another. But I could not forgive him, I could not *trust him* now. But it would be so delicious to give in. *No.* Just as our lips were about to meet and I could feel his breath soft on my face, I wrenched my hands free from his unsuspecting grip and pushed him hard away. He had betrayed me. There would be no going back. He could not have me *and* someone else. "Lancelot." My voice shook with anger, and I could feel the tears of rage prick again at my eyes. He looked back at me, lost, helpless in the face of my rage, the power of it. "*Go.*"

The next morning, when Arthur found that Lancelot had gone, he turned to me and grumbled,

"I don't know what the matter is with you that you can't keep Lancelot here at court."

He then turned to Gawain and asked if he knew where Lancelot had gone, and Gawain replied.

"To Astolat, I expect."

And I felt Mordred watching me, to see if I would give myself away.

Chapter Forty

The anger I nursed within me made the loneliness more bearable; the longing I felt for him was worse than ever now I knew he was close, and alive. His love had not been a strong as mine, had not been as bold or daring. But, as the days passed and news came back of his victories abroad, in tournaments, in battles defending Arthur's borders, always wearing the golden token I had given him, I began to wonder if I had not been rash. But I could not send for him now. Besides, if I did and then he came he might talk, as he had before, of sin and regret. It had only been in the heat of his anger when he left that he had held me to him. I did not think I could survive another lecture on *sin*. Still, I hoped that I would see him again.

News came to court in the winter that Tristan had died in France of wounds sustained in battle, crying out for Isolde of Cornwall. He had, confusingly, she said in her letter to me, married another woman whose name was also Isolde while he was travelling in France. Perhaps one was just as stupid as the other, but still I was sorry for her. She would, she said, at last go back to Mark, and beg him not to try her for treason and have her burned. I wrote back something vague and comforting, wishing I could have done more. Lancelot must have been far from his castle Joyous Guard, because if he were there, I was sure he would have stopped her from leaving its safety.

That winter, too, saw the end of Christine. She was weak from the last winter's cold, and when she caught another chill, Kay, Marie and I sat with her around her bed until she went, sometimes reading to her in Breton, sometimes talking quietly. Kay was silent, mostly, but I think he wanted to be there. It was slow, but it came for her at last. I knelt down beside her to kiss her on the cheek and whisper goodbye to the woman who had been like a mother to me since I was a girl. She laid her hand on my head, like a blessing, but she could not speak. I cried for her, we all did, until they laid her to rest, and I knew I had to say goodbye in my heart as well. The prayers they said for her were Christian prayers, so Kay and I sat up one night alone and prayed to our ancient and forbidden gods, in case either god could hear, and would give Christine comfort after death. I felt more and more alone. I could not bear to find someone else, so I had only Marie to help me. I thought of sending back to Brittany, to Carhais, for someone, but I did not. I would not have known them, and it would remind me of how far from my old home I had come. It was quieter without Christine, although she had never talked much, and sadder, and I wished all the way to the core of me that I had not sent Lancelot away.

Arthur was cheery enough, though he often talked of calling Lancelot back. He sent messengers to Joyous Guard a few times, but every time Lancelot was away. I held tight to Arthur, the warm, solid centre of my world. I understood him, and he never changed, and we could share, in half-honesty at least, our longing for Lancelot to return.

The spring came again, and I realised how much time I had let slip by. I had not thought of Lancelot less each day, and though I thought the white-hot anger would scorch me clean of love for him, it had only faded away, leaving the love untouched and a bitter black coal of regret heavy at my heart. I should not have sent him away. I should have been satisfied with having him close by me, his love without his touch. He had not, after all, gone to Astolat, and the frail little Maid had died. I had heard that she was a hysteric, and when Lancelot had not returned had starved herself to death because of some imagined hope that he had intended to take her as his wife. He had been thinking of me, thinking of keeping me safe. I thought of sending him some gift, some token that would require no words to send to him, to call him back to me, but I had nothing that seemed suitable that Arthur would not miss. I did not think I could send a ring, too obviously a lover's gift, and I did not want to part with any more of my precious books, having lost my little book of Ovid into the hands of Morgan, so I sent nothing.

There was talk all about Camelot of a Mayday hunt, and I was eager to go, eager for the distraction. Afterwards there would be a great feast, and games and celebrating, and that would keep my mind busy for a little while. I hoped that Lancelot might come back for it, for Arthur sent for him again, but he did not.

When I woke on Mayday morning, it was already bright and light and I could feel against my skin that it would be an unusually warm day, lovely for riding. The night before, Arthur, thrilled with excitement at the great hunt, had rushed me up to his room as soon as the sun was beginning to set in the sky, and had me with all the rough eagerness I needed to forget, for a moment, about Lancelot. I woke with the half-dreams, half-memories of Arthur's touch around me, his mouth against mine, our bodies pressed close together, and for a moment I was immersed in that happiness, forgetting what I was missing. *If only*, I thought, *If only there could be more times like this*. But I was not by nature a woman of forgetting.

I sat up in bed to see that Arthur had already gone, and I was annoyed. He knew I had wanted to ride out with them, although I supposed he had thought it rude to wake me, and had been keen as a boy to get out on his horse. There was once a time when he would not have forgotten to wake me. He was his men's man as much as he was mine now. Or perhaps he had just been too excited to wait, thinking I would catch up. The sun was not so high in the sky. I thought I could.

My hunting leathers were in my own chambers, across the courtyard, and I did not fancy the thought of walking across to get them in my underdress, so I called down for Marie. I did not like it so much to sleep in Arthur's room as my own, because it meant I was far from my own clothes and had to wait in bed for someone to fetch them for me. But it was not Marie who came, it was Kay. I was surprised; I had expected him to ride out with the hunt. He came dressed in light leather armour for hunting, but in his hand for me was not my hunting clothes, but a green dress of light silk sewn all over with little ribbons. A maying dress. I drew my knees up and gathered the sheet around me as Kay bounded in, unabashed as always.

"Have they gone already?" I asked him, disappointed. He nodded.

"It wouldn't have been any fun anyway. Arthur and Gawain would have killed everything good before we got there, and I would have been stuck at the back with *you* because you ride like a woman."

I threw one of the pillows at him, and he caught it, laughing.

"I'm better than you," I told him. Then I eyed the dress he had lain on the bed. "I suppose that's for me, rather than you."

"Oh, come on," Kay grinned. "It will be fun. Let's not go and find them hunting. It's a warm day; we can just ride about and please ourselves and go and watch the people in the village dancing."

"Very well." I sounded more reluctant than I felt. It sounded like a pleasant way to spend a day like today. So I shooed Kay away, and dressed myself, pulling the dress on over my underclothes. It was more a costume than a dress, so it was simple to put on, and I did not have to call for Marie again. I was sure Kay had sent her away anyway, wanting to have some fun surprising me himself. Well, I was not surprised by Kay. Not any more. I plaited up my hair, all I could do on my own, and I considered not putting on my circlet, thinking it might be fun to go into the village without giving away my status; but then I thought it safer if people knew. I had been to the village nearby to watch the maying before, and it was sweet and vibrant enough as a country ritual, but if you stayed too long the men were all drunk and the women all complaining about childbirth. I would, I thought, prefer to watch the dancing from a distance.

Kay laughed when he saw me walk out into the courtyard in the maying dress. I don't know where he had got it from, but I did not think it looked so very bad; it fitted well enough, and the green suited me. He held both our horses by the bridles, eager to go. I swung easily up into my saddle, breathing deep of the fresh spring air. I had not felt so full of hope and joy in a long time, as I did then at the prospect of riding out on my own little adventure.

When we were mounted side by side, Kay leaned over and playfully tried to grab the little circlet of gold ivy-leaves from my head. I batted his hand away.

"You should have a wreath of real flowers on a day like today," he told me, laughing and kicking his heels lightly into his horse, trotting away. I followed close behind. It had been too long since I had ridden through the fields around Camelot and properly looked at them. There were wildflowers springing up around the edge of the wood; I could see the little white elderflowers, pink crocuses, and deeper in the woods, bluebells. The air smelled of spring, and under the bright sun the grass looked lush and inviting, a bright green. Kay was in spirits as good as mine and we laughed and joked as we rode along. Kay did a rather good impression of Gawain's storytelling, all waving arms and wide eyes, but better still was his imitation of Lamerocke, smoothing down his hair. I wondered obliquely what Kay did when he was imitating me to someone. Probably crossed his arms before his chest and frowned.

It was when we came over a little hill and the castle passed out of sight behind us, that we came upon a small band of knights who seemed to have got separated from the hunt. At their head was a slight man with a tawny beard cropped close to his face. I recognised him as one of Arthur's knights, though I did not know his name, and smiled to see him, raising a hand in greeting. Then I realised these knights could not be out for the hunt, because they were all dressed in platemail. There were perhaps as many as eight of them. I wondered what they were out doing. The man at their head gave me a nod of greeting as he rode up to us, his knights close behind. I noticed Kay shift closer to me and rest his hand on the hilt of the sword. I was glad to see it, for having nowhere on my person to hold a weapon I had ridden out without one, but it now seemed impossibly inadequate faced with this band of knights. But there was no reason for us to be wary of them. That was, at least, what I told myself.

"My lady queen." He bowed in his saddle. "I am pleased to come upon you thus." I did not know quite what he meant. Kay did not release his grip on his sword.

"I am glad to see a knight who has been loyal unto my lord, King Arthur," I replied, the formality the only defence I had, drawing myself up in my saddle. I wanted him to be sure who I was, what the consequence would be to him if he did me or Kay any harm. The man smiled, and the smile was crooked and insincere.

"I must confess that I have loved you many long years – why since I set eyes on you – and never did I dream the day would come when I might get you at such an advantage." I felt my heart begin to race within me, and through the sun on my skin I felt a chill. "Yet, I intend to take you as I find you."

"You know, sir, how Sir Lancelot deals with traitor knights like yourself," I warned him. I could feel my heart racing already, my blood pumping, and I gathered the reins of my horse tighter, prepared to turn and run. But I could not really. There were eight of them, and two of us. I could hardly run from this, if it was as I feared. His disgusting smile spread deeper across his face.

"And yet, I hear Sir Lancelot is gone from here, and no one knows where he is, so I think I may do as I please."

Beside me, Kay hissed grimly, "That was a clever idea of yours, to send Lancelot away."

"My lord Arthur will find you."

The knight shrugged, "Perhaps he will, but he is hunting now, and may not be back until gone dusk. By then we shall be far away."

Kay drew his sword, moving forward slightly, and the knight laughed.

"Sir Kay, I am pleased to find *you*, also, as I have heard them say, brave, but foolish."

"If you intend to take her, *sir*, come forward and draw your own sword."

Kay, sword raised in front of him, stood between us, but the knight clearly did not intend to fight. He was not armoured like the others, but in a rich silk doublet embroidered in gold.

As I shouted "Kay, no!" Kay spurred his horse forward and four of the eight knights sprang forward at him. His horse went down beneath him first, its neck sliced open by the first knight that reached him, and the other three fell on him.

I screamed, "Stop, *stop!*" until the leader of the knights raised his hand, and they stepped away from Kay, climbing back onto their horses. My own horse stamped its feet and edged away from Kay's dead horse, smelling the blood of its own kind, which made it anxious. I knew how it felt. Kay pushed himself heavily up from the ground. I could see he was bleeding at the shoulder, and at the side. One of the knights who had jumped on him was slumped forward on his horse, but the others were unharmed, and they had taken Kay's sword. I felt sick in the pit of my stomach with dread. I gathered myself, forcing myself to be calm. "I will go with you, then. Without complaint. Provided," I fixed him with the most authoritative look I could muster – he might have me at the advantage, but I was still his queen, and I would not let him forget that – "that no one harms Sir Kay, and I may bring him with me."

The leader knight considered it for a moment, then nodded curtly, bringing his horse forward slowly, past Kay, to seize the reins from me and lead my horse towards his.

"Very well, my lady. But, if I hear the slightest whisper that you have sent for Sir Lancelot then this man's life," he pointed down at Kay, "will be forfeit."

"So will yours, sir, when Arthur hears of this," I told him, but he simply shrugged, as though he thought he was safe and Arthur was nothing but a lord in a castle, not the warrior emperor who had conquered Rome. He was a fool, and I would make him pay.

As he led me past Kay, who had stumbled heavily to his feet, I reached down and helped Kay into the saddle behind me. He slumped against my back, and I wrapped his arms around me. *Don't die, Kay*, I thought, screwing my eyes shut, pushing away the tears. This man would not beat me. I felt Kay free a hand and pick at something in my hair.

"Shhhh," he whispered at my ear as I opened my mouth to speak, and I turned behind me to see glinting against the grass the gold of the circlet he had just pulled from my hair. He rested his head against my shoulder, and I felt his weight press heavy against me. He did not have the strength to hold himself up. But, following his example, as we went I pulled the ribbons from my dress whenever the man leading me was looking away, and dropped them on the ground. If someone found the circlet, they would know it was me, and they would follow the trail. I prayed to every god I knew that someone would come in time.

The castle our captor led us to was not far, and the sun was only just beginning to sink in the sky as we arrived. It was oddly empty, I noticed, as we came in through the main gates, under the threatening teeth of a rusting portcullis. It could not have been anyone's home, that castle. There were no servants, no men for the horses. This was not a place anyone would think to look. I hoped that birds had not carried my ribbons away, nor had someone hungry for gold who did not recognise it picked up my circlet.

I slid down from my horse, turning to catch Kay as he slipped into my arms, heavy and sudden, leaning against me to stand.

"Kay," I whispered, sad and close.

"Don't worry about me," he replied, grimly.

"Come, my lady," the bearded man declared, offering his hand towards me as though I were a guest, as though he was the very pinnacle of courtesy. I stood back, not letting go of Kay's arms as I held them around my shoulders. "I will show you and your," he paused for a chuckle, "*brave knight* to your chambers."

I could not work out yet exactly what he wanted with us. It was clear whatever it was did not involve either of us being able to leave the castle. Perhaps he wanted money from Arthur. But his ridiculous talk of *love* unsettled me, and I regretted heartily not thinking to carry even a little dagger about me.

After he led us to the rooms, he left, leaving half of the knights he had brought with him on the corridor that led to the stairs to guard us, saying he was going to take his evening meal, and food would be brought to us in turn. At least that gave me a little time.

I led Kay over to a bed in one of the rooms, and laid him down. He groaned in pain. I put my hand against his brow. It was cold and clammy. At least not feverish. I pulled the boots from his feet and climbed onto the bed with him, leaning over him to unbuckle the leather armour and lift it away. I could see against the shirt underneath deep red stains of blood, one beneath his ribs, and the other at his shoulder. I peeled back the shirt at his shoulder and Kay hissed through his teeth at the pain. The wound was not deep, at least. I reached underneath the end of my skirts and tore a strip of cotton from the underdress, rolling it up and pressing it against the cut. Kay winced, but he was quiet. I moved half over him, sitting over his legs to look at the wound at his ribs the other side. When I lifted up the shirt, I saw it gape deep with his breath, and I heard the air wheeze slightly in and out of him. I had an awful sinking sensation, and I was sure I could not hide my dread and that Kay saw it on my face. I tore another strip from the underdress and held it against the deep cut. I felt Kay's hands slide up my back.

"Oh, sweet lady," he sighed, "this is how I always dreamed I would die; in bed with you on top of me, ripping off your clothes."

Even now Kay was full of jokes. Wonderful, sweet Kay. I laughed, but the tears pricked at my eyes and I leaned forward to kiss his cheek.

"Kay, you won't die. Knowing you, you will live forever." The words sounded hollow even as they came from my own mouth and as I leaned back to press the wad of cotton against the wound beneath his ribs, our eyes met and Kay held me with a look of wry resignation.

"We are far away from your witch's table now."

"Kay..." I whispered, as the tears welled up in my eyes, and I could not keep them away. I could not lose Kay, who had always been my friend. I had no words for him, no words of comfort. I instead lay down beside him, my head against his chest. Against my ear I heard the awful wheeze of his breath, in and out. He put a hand against my hair in comfort, but it was I who should have comforted him. I closed my eyes and pressed my face against his chest, letting his shirt soak up the tears.

Then, all of a sudden, I felt arms grab me and lift me from the bed, dragging me away from Kay. I shouted and kicked, but there was more than one pair of hands holding me, and one of them was tight in my hair. The man who had led us here was standing in the doorway, his arms folded over his rich coat. The knights holding me pinned my arms behind my back and twisted my hair tight so that I could not look away from him. He shook his head.

"My lady, to be caught in *shame* with your king and husband's own dear foster brother," he tutted, stepping forward to tug at the patches of my dress that were stained already with Kay's blood, as though they were evidence.

"I was seeing to his wounds," I spat, furious, pulling against the arms that held me. "You should have brought us to somewhere where someone knew medicine. Leaving him here without any help is tantamount to murdering him. Arthur will have you killed. He will –"

Fast as an adder he sprang forward and struck me across the face, making me gasp in pain and shock. He put his fingers under my chin, turning my face up towards his, so that I had to look him in the eye.

"Hush, my lady. It is not seemly for a queen to speak so, even a queen caught in shame. But I shall forgive you, and later I shall come for you. And when Arthur hears of this," he gestured lazily towards Kay on the bed, "I shall protect you from him. So I urge you," he leaned in closer and I felt his spittle fall on my face, "to *show me some appropriate kindness.*"

He made some gesture of command to the knights holding me and they dragged me from the room as I shouted, for Kay, for Arthur, to be released. I dared not shout for Lancelot, after what the man had said. I doubted, anyway, that anyone could hear me. As they dragged me through the door I glanced back over my shoulder to see four of the knights holding Kay down as he struggled against them, and his wounds, to rise. I prayed deep in my heart that he would survive this.

They threw me into the next-door room and slammed the door, bolting it behind. I heard the scrape of the iron, shutting me in, and the cold dread filled me to the core. The room was dark, and in the fading light I could see the window was barred with iron. When I went closer, I saw the iron was old and rusting, but hard as I pushed it, I could not break the bars, and besides, it was a sheer drop, many feet to the ground. There was no way for me to escape.

As my eyes adjusted to the darkness, I saw the room was small and bare, the walls rough grey stone, with only a bed up against the same wall as the window. The bed was strangely grand for the cell-like room, draped in red silks and hung with curtains, and it gave me the uneasy feeling that the man who had brought me here had been planning this for quite some time. I crawled onto the bed and over to the window to look out again. The light on the horizon was fading ominously red, and all I could see between here and there was empty fields and dense patches of trees. I wrapped my hands around the bars again and tugged as hard as I could, but though they were crusted with orange-brown rust and slightly bowed, I could not move them even the slightest bit. I could reach my arm out, but there was no way I could fit my head between them. If only I could have moved them enough to slip out, I could have made a rope with the bedcovers, I thought. But then I would have had to leave Kay behind, and it was for my sake that he was here, and injured.

    I crawled back on to the bed, and sat against the wall, beside the window, gazing into the murky darkness of the room. I didn't want to look out of the window, to watch the sun set on a blank horizon. I could not even see Camelot from where we were. Back, far far away at my home, Arthur would be riding in from the hunt, and jumping from his horse. He would look around for me in the courtyard, and I would not be there. He would go up to my room, and then his room, and he would not find me. Perhaps he would call for his knights, and they would ride out into the night to look for me. Or perhaps Arthur would ride back from the hunt, and I would not be there in the courtyard, and he would shrug and take some other woman up to his chamber, and lie her down in his bed. He might not know I was missing until late tomorrow. I wrapped my arms around my knees, and rested my forehead against them. Arthur was Arthur, and he would come, or he would not come. I could not have changed that. I did not mind so much the thought that Arthur would not come in time to save me as the thought that I had sent Lancelot away. If Lancelot had been at court, even with his half-love, his God, his talk of sin and shame, I could have been sure beyond doubt that he would miss me before the sun had set, and that he would come for me. But I had sent him from me because I was rash, and selfish and cruel. I had not wanted to compromise on our bright, bold love, and accept something muted and safe. And I had sent him away. I did not even know if he was still in Britain, or if he had gone to his father's old castle in France. Still bright in my heart I had the hope that somehow he would come. That he would sense my danger, and he would come for me, though I knew this was a foolish hope. I supposed I had nothing else. I knew well enough now what this man intended with me, and I did not think he would afterwards let me go home safe to Camelot, to bring Arthur's revenge on him. He would kill me afterwards. And Kay. *Kay.* Kay dying in the room beside me. Kay, who I had brought to this, Kay who would not be saved by Lancelot either, because I had sent him away.

I turned and looked out of the window again. I could not hide from it. I was beginning to feel strangely calm. *So*, I thought, *this is the end*, as I watched the sun dip further and the light fade from pale orange to a furnace-red. I thought of Kay, and the joy of our friendship, and I thought of Arthur, and the constancy of our love, but those were passing thoughts, like dreams. As I waited for the man to return, what I thought of most of all was Lancelot, and I wished a painful, regretful wish that I had not sent him away. I wished that I could have been different. More forgiving. I wished that as he held me to him, I could have forgotten my anger, and kissed him. I played the moment over in my head once more. Me shouting, him gathering me to him, holding me tight against him. This time when he leaned down, I leaned in, and our mouths met in a wild, passionate kiss. I wound my hands into his hair, and he wrapped his arms around my waist and held me close. I could almost feel it, almost feel the softness of his lips, the power of his love, the overwhelming rush of our passion together. I would have given anything to feel that, once more, for real. I almost could. Almost.

But the dream passed away, for what it was, and I was alone in the dark, painfully aware that no one had come for me, and in sending Lancelot away, I had sealed my fate.

Part III
The Day of Destiny

Chapter Forty-One

The sunset deepened to an ugly blood-red, and the grim shadows of the bars of the window grew black against it, like the teeth of a skull. I sat on the bed with my back against the wall, staring into the darkness, waiting for the sound of the feet down the hall of the man who had taken me prisoner. Waiting for the sound of the bolt drawing back. I would be ready for him when he stepped through the door. As ready as I could be.

I was alone. No one knew I was here except Kay, lying wounded in the room beside me, breathing awful, wheezing breaths. I was not sure I had not heard his death upon him when I had laid my head against his chest. He would not come for me. Then there was Arthur. Arthur might not even have returned from his day's hunting, might not yet know I was gone. Lancelot was far away, in the exile I had sent him to in a wild anger I no longer remembered the reason for. Not now. Not in this awful moment.

It was hopeless, truly. I had no weapon. No rescuer. I was a woman alone, trapped in this madman's castle. Yet if he thought I would go willingly, then he was wrong. I had not gone even to the marriage-bed of a great conqueror without protest. I was not going to lie down for this coward. I would rather he killed me.

It was not long before he returned. I had hoped for moments more. More time to gather myself. More time to run through my mind for the last time my memories of Lancelot, and Arthur. The love I had had from both of them. The happiness. I wanted to be holding those tight to my heart when the moment came.

But he came back fast, and as he stepped inside the room I heard someone on the outside slide the bolt shut behind him. So, he had one of his knights waiting out there. Or more. I stood on the bed where I had sat, backed against the wall. He had a repulsive leer on his face, and he seemed relaxed, as though he was enjoying himself already. He shrugged off his faded red and gold surcoat and folded it carefully before placing it at the foot of the bed. Underneath I could see that he was small and slight for a knight, though slightly paunchy. If I had had even the smallest weapon, I would not have been afraid of him.

"My lady." He held out his hand towards me as though in invitation, but I did not move. He sighed sadly, shaking his head. "Very well."

He darted forward and, grabbing me by both ankles, pulled me off my feet so I fell back on the bed. I kicked and shouted for Kay – I knew he could not help me, but I had no one else to cry out for – but he was already on top of me, his weight pinning me down as I struggled against him. He was not nearly as strong as Lancelot or Arthur, but his weak coward's strength was still that of a full-grown man, and more than I had in me. And besides, he did not care if he hurt me.

As I screamed and kicked at him, beating my hands against him, trying to push him off me, he clamped a hand over my mouth, half-covering my nose as well so that I could hardly breathe and the strength went out of me fast. His hand smelled of meat grease and oil. I felt him tearing at the fabric of my dress as I still kicked at him, all the time muttering, to me or to himself, his disgusting face right over mine, until the thin silk of the overdress ripped right up to the waist. He gave a satisfied little laugh that made my skin crawl, and grabbed at the underdress beneath. That was when my hand, still trying to push him back, hit against something I recognised, with a little leap of joy, against his hip. The hilt of a hunting-knife. He had, like a fool, come armed and forgotten it. I supposed that he had thought he had already won. I grabbed it from its sheath and stabbed up, fast, underneath his rib cage at the centre. His eyes above me widened in sudden surprise, and he made a coughing noise, spattering blood across my face. I shoved the knife in harder, and pushed him off me. He rolled limply off the bed and on to the floor, leaving the knife shining dark red in my hands. I leaned over the edge of the bed and peered down. He was twitching, slightly, and making a dreadful gurgling noise. He was not going to rise again. Just to be sure, I sliced the knife across his throat, and his eyes fell shut, and he was still. My hands were plastered in blood up to the wrist, and my torn dress stained with red. I sat back against the wall again, catching my breath. I could feel the air burn in my throat, and my heart pounding in my ears. I felt shaken through with relief, though I knew it was only for the moment. I was still trapped. I wished I could have rubbed the blood from my face, but my hands were too smeared with it for me to bother trying. The aches were coming to me now. I could feel them where his hands had grasped me roughly, against my thighs, my wrists, my ankles. I did not know what to do now. I had a weapon, so

I was gaining ground, but the little knife was nothing against the swords of the knights, and I had no way to leave the room.

I heard suddenly then the scraping of iron against stone beside me, and jumped back, seeing a pale hand wrapped around the iron bars of the window. Slowly, slowly, the hand pulled back an iron bar until it bowed and snapped, and threw it away. I backed against the wall, holding out the knife in front of me. I was not sure if I had the strength in me to fight another man, one stronger and better prepared than the madman I had killed. Not a man who had the strength in his hands to tear the iron bars from the window.

But, when the bars had been torn away and I saw the top of a head emerge I felt the wave of sweet relief wash over me, and I dropped the knife. *Lancelot*. I rushed to the window and grabbed hold of him, pulling him in. We knelt face to face on the bed before the window, me soaked in blood, trembling, he breathing hard from the climb, his face darkened with dirt from travel. It was but a second as we knelt there, looking at one another, before he took my face in his hands and kissed me hard, whispering, "You're alive; you're alive."

I pressed into his arms as he put them around me and, forgetting the blood on my hands, I buried them in his hair, pulling his mouth closer against mine, responding with desperate relief. I tasted the iron of blood on my lips, but I didn't care. A moment ago, I had been prepared for death. A moment ago I had not known if Lancelot was even in Britain, if he would ever have forgiven me for sending him away. Or if he would ever have held me to him like this again, for all his fear of God. Suddenly, all that was washed away, and all I was aware of in the whole world were his lips against mine, the desperate, rushing relief that ran through my whole body, not just to be alive, but to be alive and to have him in my arms, at last. Our kiss was long and passionate, wild with our relief, and it was as though there had been no Grail, for all the raw desire with which we met in it. I felt the potency of our love all around me. I felt small in his hands as he held me close about the waist, but wonderfully so; small and safe. He had come for me as I had not dared to hope that he would.

We sank apart at last, our foreheads still pressed together, and through my shaking breaths I said, "You found me." I wanted to say so much more, but this was all I could manage.

He nodded, brushing his fingertips across my cheek. I felt my skin glow under his touch. I noticed then that his hand, where he had torn away the iron bars, was bleeding. He did not seem to notice.

"I came for the Mayday hunt, hoping I would see you. But I came late, and everyone was gone. I... I thought it was best for me to just return to my home, but then as I rode back, I saw your circlet lying in the grass."

He seemed to notice only then that I was covered in blood. He took my hands in his, turning them over.

"Are you hurt?" he asked. His eyes caught the tear in the dress, my hair torn free and tangled, and matted with blood. I shook my head. "I heard you shouting out for Kay, as if someone was... hurting you."

I led him over to the edge of the bed and he looked down.

"I know that man," he said, softly, but he did not explain.

He got off the bed, stepping over the body, and tried the door. When it wouldn't open, he threw his shoulder hard against it, and I heard the hinges crack. On the second time, the door crashed open. The knight on the other side turned, ready to draw his sword, but when he saw it was Lancelot, though Lancelot was without armour, the knight turned and ran. Lancelot drew his sword and I ran out into the corridor to join him. I wished he had not destroyed the door. I would have liked better to shut away the body of that man in the room full of blood.

He strode ahead of me, until I called out.

"Wait. Kay."

He turned back.

"Kay is... *here?*"

I nodded. If there had been knights guarding the door to the room Kay was in, they had run already because no one was there. I slid the bolt back and pushed the door open.

Kay lay with his eyes closed, his chest rising and falling gently in sleep, but as I moved closer I could hear the awful wheeze underneath his breath. Lancelot walked over and leaned down to look at Kay, touched his hand against Kay's brow. He came back to me and said, quietly.

"I think he will be well enough, though we cannot move him tonight."

I nodded. I did not want to stay in this castle overnight, but I knew we could not ride safely back to Camelot in the middle of the night, not with Kay like that. I hoped that Lancelot was right, and that Kay would be whole again.

Lancelot looked at me and brushed the tangled hair back from my brow, thoughtfully. I wanted to lean into his touch, but I held myself back, for the moment.

"We should find somewhere for you to wash this blood off you."

I followed him out of Kay's room, gently shutting the door behind me, glancing back at the last moment. He was still breathing. *Let him live*, I thought, picturing the Round Table in my mind.

Lancelot tried a few doors until we came to a room with a fire burning in it. It must have been the room of the man who owned the castle, because there was a rich bed covered with fine silks and a wooden table with a pitcher of wine on it, and a bowl of fruits. It seemed as though the knight who had fled had spread the word of Lancelot's arrival to the rest, because the castle appeared to be totally deserted. Lancelot found a bathtub in one of the rooms nearby, and set the water on the fire to heat.

We did not speak. So much had passed so fast, and after so long he was back with me, and yet I did not know where we stood. He had come for me, and he had saved me, but now that he had, I was beginning to remember everything else. Everything painful. The way he had turned to me and said, *Marriage is sacred, Guinevere*, and all the things he had said about sin and shame. I remembered, too, that he had not wanted me anymore. That I had not thought him as brave as I was. He had taken me into his arms with relief when he had seen that I was alive, but that was a moment's relief. What if nothing had changed? What if he still wanted to talk about sin and regret? Now we were alone and he knew I was well and alive, we still had to work out where we stood. I was not sure if I could survive one more time offering my love to him, and having him turn it away.

When the water was hot and he poured it into the bath, he kissed me softly on the cheek and left. I was sorry for it, but I thought too late to ask him to stay. I peeled off the ruined Maying dress and threw it into the fire, and then the underdress I laid aside at the last minute. I almost threw that into the fire as well, but then I remembered that that would mean I had nothing to wear. I did not want to ride back to Camelot naked.

I rubbed the blood away from my hands in the hot water, and leaned back to let the water soak through my hair. I looked around the room as I sat in the bath. I did not see any evidence of a woman, not a comb or a dress. I hoped that a man as awful as he did not have a wife somewhere. It was a strange castle, half ruined, half filled with this slightly sickly richness.

When I was clean, I got out of the bath and, having nothing clean to wear, wrapped one of the silk sheets from the bed around me. The water had washed away the blood, and now I saw against my pale skin the dark marks of bruises. But I had survived, and he had not touched me, and now he was dead for trying, as he deserved. I stood at the window and looked out at the stars, bright in the clear spring night.

Somewhere not far from here, Arthur was wondering where I was.

I heard the door behind me and jumped around, still on edge, but it was Lancelot returning. He had washed, too; I could see his hair was damp and his face clean, and in his hand was a set of men's clothes.

"This was all I could find," he said, setting them down on a chair beside the bed. He, too, had worked out that I would have nothing to wear for the ride home.

He stood by the door, unsure as I was, it seemed, as to what would happen now. I did not dare move forward. Not yet. I did not think I could stand to hear him talk of sin, which seemed so far removed from the purity of the love I felt for him. He took a step towards me, and I took a step towards him. I felt the old flutter of excitement quicken within me, the old desperate longing for him. We came closer to each other, as though drawn by gravity. I stopped still when we stood close, close enough that I could have reached out, and laid my fingertips against his chest where it showed at the open neck of his shirt. I could have felt his skin against mine. We had not stood this close, not alone, not like this, for six long years. I could feel the electric thrill of it in my veins, but also the fear – the lingering, tentative fear that nothing had changed since we last spoke, and he would turn me away.

Slowly, I looked up at him, and he leaned down a little towards me, tentative too. I had been angry, so angry, when I sent him away. He leaned closer, a little more, and brushed his nose down against mine. I felt my breath catch, my heart race. He put a hand to my cheek, and he brushed his thumb across my jaw, over my lips, and whispered,

"You were all I thought about, when I was looking for the Grail, and all this last long year. You."

I closed my eyes, turning up towards him. I heard him sigh my name, and I felt myself weaken deliciously with it as our lips met. It was soft at first, but then more passionate, and my lips opened under his, and he slid his hand into my hair, pulling me closer. I sighed against him, letting go of the sheet around me to reach up and wind my arms around his neck. It fell to the ground, leaving me naked in his arms. He gave a soft sigh of desire, and I felt his hand at the small of my back, then running up my body, pressing me tight against him, and his other hand brush, light, down the side of my breast, tantalising. I was wild with longing already, my head swimming, filled with it, with him, the closeness. How many times had I dreamed of this moment? Of feeling his hands on my body again, of his kisses, his touch. I had never forgotten them. If anything, they had only become more vivid with longing as the years had dragged by. I pushed his shirt up over his head and threw it aside, and the feel of his skin against my own sent a rush of dizzying desire to my head.

No question now stood between us of anything other than our coming together, anything other than the need of our hearts and bodies to be as one. His hands tangled, pleasantly rough, deeper into my hair as his lips fluttered against my neck, my shoulder, my nipples and then, as we sank to the floor where we stood, down all over my body, until he reached with his tongue that place which longed for it, and I moaned softly, arching my back with delight, feeling the rub of the rug beneath me against the skin of my back, and the soft hot steam still rising from the bath whisper against my face. The heat within me rose strong and fast, and as I felt the blissful rapture break over me, white-hot, I cried out for Lancelot, and pulled him up into my arms, tearing away his breeches. I cried out again at the feeling of him inside me, so longed-for, and he looked into my eyes, holding me fast against him. I felt him all around me, all through me; the brush of his fingers against my cheek, my throat, and then, rough with passion, gripping me at the thigh. Still full with delicious heat from his tongue, the pleasure of our coming together was overwhelming, deliciously unbearable, and I moaned for him, throwing my head back, and feeling his lips press hungry against my neck. I felt as if I were made of light and fire, and the white heat of pleasure was fast on me again, and I felt it run through him as well as he moaned deep and sank onto me, our mouths meeting in a long slow kiss.

After six years of living like a ghost, it felt as though, once again, I was whole.

Chapter Forty-Two

When I woke, for a moment I didn't remember where I was, but I knew that Lancelot was beside me, and I settled back into his arms, the morning sleepiness still close about me. He murmured, waking, and pulled me closer against him, kissing softly at my ear. I smiled and my eyelids fluttered against the morning sun, still low in the sky. Through the window I could smell the fresh grass of spring. I felt Lancelot's hand stroke my stomach, and then, slowly, my breasts, and then down between my legs, until I sighed softly for him, and he turned me gently onto my back, moving over me to meet my eager mouth with his own, grasping the sheet that covered us and throwing it aside. The wildness and urgency of the night before, when we had been so long parted, was gone, and I felt a delicious slowness hang about me. I stretched out under his touch, all over my body, slow and relishing. His eyes roved softly over me, too, and the hungry look in them stirred the heat within me. I pulled him to me in a kiss, soft and sensual, feeling it thrill through me as his grip on me grew firmer, more hungry, and I turned us over, rolling on to him, running my hands over his chest, up his arms, feeling the muscle strong and dangerous underneath as I held his arms over his head and interlaced my fingers with his, feeling the roughness of his hands from the sword against my own. Then, wanting to taste with my touch everything I had missed so long, I let my hands slide back down his arms, lightly over the dark lush hair beneath them, across his chest, feeling the small ridges of scars, and the smoothness and softness of the untouched skin over the hardness of muscle, and down to take him in my hand. He groaned with pleasure as I guided him inside me, and we moved slowly together, my hands against his chest, Lancelot holding me at the thighs. The gentle slowness of it was an intoxicating luxury, as if we had all the time in the world, and when he felt that I was close to that point of iridescent bliss, he turned us over, and the pause and change made the heat gather more richly within me, so that when at last it came it overwhelmed me in a dizzying rush, and I sighed deeper than I had ever done before, and sank back, my body filled with the sensation of sparkling light; and soon after he sighed as well, and we gathered each other up in our arms. I felt the morning air against my back, like a lovely kiss. I could not have been more happy, more full of the bright sweetness of my bliss. Yet, in the back of my mind, I knew I would soon have to go back. I was sorry the thought had come to me so soon, and yet there was no denying that the dawn of that day had brought with it my return to Camelot. Perhaps if Kay had not been injured, we could have stayed another day, or two, but I would always, eventually, have to be returned to the man to whom I belonged.

In the end it was Lancelot who rose first, with a sigh, slipping from the bed and pulling his shirt over his head. I sat up to gaze out of the window, to feel the breeze on my skin in one last heady moment of freedom.

The men's clothes felt harsh and scratchy against my skin, and fitted poorly, but the underdress was ruined and stained with blood, and the little that was left clean of it we tore into bandages for Kay. I wrapped one around Lancelot's hand, too, though the wound was small and already beginning to heal. I thought the friction of the reins in his hands as we rode back might hurt him otherwise.

We went down together to Kay, through the empty half-ruined castle. He was sleeping still, and as Lancelot leaned over him to listen for his breath – which mercifully I could see moving his chest up and down still – I heard Kay murmur my name.

"Guinevere, Guinevere... is she...?" His hand reached up and grasped the front of Lancelot's shirt. "Did he... were you here in time?"

"She's here," Lancelot said gently, picking Kay up in his arms as though Kay were light as a child, though Kay was taller than him, and broader. "And she's unhurt."

"Kay." I ran over and took his hand, and he looked at me blearily from Lancelot's arms.

"You were right after all, then," Kay mumbled, "that Lancelot would come."

I did not remember saying that, nor feeling secure in it, but when I saw the look of deep contentment to hear it spread over Lancelot's face, I decided not to say so.

When we reached the courtyard, there was only one horse to be seen. My horse.

"They killed Kay's horse," I told Lancelot.

"Mine, too, when I met some of them on the road," Lancelot said, gazing around for any more horses. They must have taken them all when they fled.

"How did you get here so quickly without a horse?" Kay mumbled.

Lancelot didn't seem to hear him.

"We will have to all three fit on yours."

We held Kay between us, fearful that in front or behind he would not have enough strength to hold on, and I sat in front with Lancelot behind. As we held the reins together, he let his hands rest lightly on top of mine. It was delicious, like a secret, the touch a memory of touches before, and touches to come. We had given ourselves back to the power of our love – I was sure of that after the night we had spent together – and I knew, and he knew, that this time it was for good.

When we at last arrived back in Camelot, dusk was falling. The great gates were open, and in the courtyard, Arthur and Gawain were standing armed, preparing to mount their horses. When Arthur saw me he froze, and stepped forward towards us slowly, as though in a dream.

I slipped from the horse, running forwards into his arms instinctively. I felt the cold metal of his armour against my cheek, and his arms were awkward around me in the platemail, but the sight of him made me feel I had come home, safely home. Arthur pulled off his leather gauntlets and took my face in his hands, looking down at me, breathless.

"You're alive." He kissed me in ardent relief. "You're unhurt."

He would later see the bruises under my strange clothes, the marks on my body from another man's violence. Right now, all he saw was that I was home. He looked up past me at Kay, slumped in the saddle against Lancelot.

"Kay..." He ran forward to Kay, and lifted him down into his arms. Kay groaned against him.

"I'm well enough," Kay said, wincing as he walked leaning on Arthur.

"You're alive," Arthur said, worried. "And that's what matters."

Behind them Lancelot jumped lightly from the horse, and handed it to one of the stableboys standing by. He nodded a greeting to Gawain, but warily and curtly, and came and guided me along with Arthur and Kay, his hand lightly against the small of my back.

We followed Arthur and Kay as Arthur took him to Marie's room, for Marie to see to his wounds. It was only when we had shut the door behind us, leaving Kay to rest, that Arthur seemed to fully notice Lancelot was there. He greeted him cheerfully and clapped him on the back, pulling him into an embrace.

"You come back, you bring my queen home safely and you seem to have saved the life of my foster brother. I have never been more glad to see you, Lancelot," he told him earnestly. "Do not leave us again."

Lancelot gave a little obedient bow.

"I will not."

Lancelot took his leave with a bow to us both, going to find lodging somewhere in the castle, and I let Arthur lead me upstairs to my room. Arthur took off his armour and sat in the chair by the window, and rubbed his face in his hands. He drew in a deep breath and sighed. I stood before him in the strange clothes and waited for him to speak. He reached out a hand to take mine and drew me to him, looking up at me with eyes full of concern.

"What happened? Why are you wearing those clothes? Did someone... hurt you?"

I told him what had happened, the traitor knight who had come upon me and Kay, whose knights had shamefully killed Kay's horse and injured him. When it was time to tell him how the man had locked me in the room, and come to me as his prisoner, I found I could not say the words for what he had tried to do to me, so I pulled off the man's shirt and took off the boots and breeches and stood naked before Arthur, holding out my bruised wrists towards him.

"But he didn't *touch* me, and I killed him," I whispered.

Arthur held me by the hips, looking up at me, his face serious.

"Truly, I have a very brave queen."

"It's the bravery of an animal, Arthur, to kill to save yourself. I didn't manage to protect Kay."

Arthur jumped to his feet and took me in his arms, hushing me as it all rushed back to me and I found myself shaking. I held tight to him, pressing my face against his shirt. The smell of Arthur's skin was the smell of safety and home. I couldn't stop thinking about Margery, how terrified she must have been the day by the pool in the woods, where she had felt Gawain's violent strength against her. Gawain was a strong knight, brave in battle if nothing else, and had the shrewdness of a natural predator; the man who had hurt me had been weak, and cowardly and foolish. Margery had had no chance of defending herself. I had been afraid. I could only imagine what she must have felt.

Arthur stroked my hair and kissed the top of my head.

"No one expected you to protect Kay. No one could have known this would happen."

He put his hand gently under my chin and tilted my face up towards his, to kiss me softly. I leaned into him, taking his face in my hands. He had been coming to look for me too. That was what he and Gawain had been armed to ride out for. I had these two wonderful loves, these two men who would look for me, and bring me home. I wished I lived in a world where I could love them both in the open, but this had to be enough. *This is the way of it*, Kay's voice floated through my mind.

Arthur lifted me lightly in his arms and carried me over to the bed, lying me down gently and pulling off his shirt to lie beside me. I curled up against him, and we lay a long time quiet, and still. I didn't mind. I was home. I was safe and Arthur and Lancelot were here with me. I wanted to hold tight to the moment. I wanted to think of *that*, rather than that awful man with one hand over my mouth and the other tearing at my clothes.

Arthur must have worried much about where I was, for he held me tight against him. I think, too, he was frightened by the thought that another man had tried to do me harm, and he wanted to feel that I was safely in his protection. He began to look over me once more, trailed his fingers lightly across my body, where the bruises were, and to my surprise lightly across my cheek, his gaze sad. I must have had a mark there from where the man struck me, but I had not seen it, nor felt it. When I pressed my own hand against the spot I felt the telltale throb of a bruise. Arthur leaned down to kiss my shoulder softly.

"I am so glad you are back safe. I was afraid," he paused for a moment, letting his hand trace lightly, forgetting the bruises quickly, down my body, over the swell of my breast, down my stomach, "that I would never see you again." I supposed that was easier to say than *that you were dead*. But I had feared it too, and I nodded and murmured my agreement.

Arthur moved on to me, kissing me tenderly, gathering my body against his. I was tired, and shaken, but the familiarity of his touch filled me with comfort. He kicked away his breeches, and I sighed with gentle delight to have him inside me. It was sweet and good to be so with Arthur, and I held him tight against me as we moved together. Union with Arthur felt like union with the place of home, a deep oneness and familiarity and belonging. I did not find the bright point of bliss that I had often known as he did, but I did not care. I was filled enough with a lazy, sweet warmth from being home, from being safely back with him. He wrapped his arms around me and pulled me onto his chest, where I rested my head, and we lay as we always did until I fell asleep.

I hoped I would dream of Lancelot, or of Lancelot and Arthur together, but instead I dreamed of a man holding me down in my own bed, as I struggled and kicked, and I reached for the knife at his side and there was nothing there, and when a hand clamped over my mouth and I looked up into the face of the man on top of me, it was not the man who had taken me captive, it was Mordred. I woke in a cold sweat, trembling. I was glad Arthur did not wake with me. I knew I would not have been able to keep it from him if he had, and I did not think it would do him good to hear any more ill-omens about his bastard son.

Chapter Forty-Three

The next day, Arthur called a council in the room with the Round Table. I pushed aside thoughts of my dream as Mordred entered to take his seat beside his brothers, and the sight of Lancelot beside Arthur, my two great loves, made me feel safe and bold. I missed Kay beside me; his empty chair on my left made me feel sad. I knew, at least, that in Marie's care he was recovering. I had checked on him on the way. As I sat down, wearing the heavy crown of Logrys, since I had nothing else but the crown of Cleopatra, Lancelot leaned across Arthur to pass me back my gold circlet. So, he had not only found it, he had kept it safe. I thanked him with a gentle, secret smile and set it on the table before me. I wanted to put it on, but it seemed wrong to take off Arthur's crown before them all.

"Does anyone know who the knight was who treasonously captured my queen?" Arthur demanded.

Quietly beside him, Lancelot said, "It was Meleagant, my lord."

A murmur went around the table. I saw Gaheris blanch. Arthur noticed as well.

"What is it, Gaheris?" he demanded impatiently.

Gaheris looked uneasily around the others at the table, Lamerocke lounging in his seat, one hand smoothing his shining hair, Dinadan keen-eyed and watchful, Gareth wide-eyed, never quite losing the naivety he had come to Camelot with.

"My lord Arthur, Meleagant did say sometimes ... that he intended to do such a thing. He often said he loved the queen. But... my lord, we called him Mad Melly, and we laughed at him. None of us thought he would ever do it –"

Arthur banged his fist on the table, and it shook. His voice thundered with rage. It was the terrifying anger of a king that was rarely seen on Arthur's mild face, but when it was it shook through the room.

"You did not see fit to tell me?"

"We thought he was a madman," Gaheris answered in a small, apologetic voice.

"We have one of his knights," Gawain declared. Behind him I saw Aggravain holding an armoured man, his helm torn off, pinned at the arms. The man's face was a picture of fear, stained with blood and sweat. He was trembling. There had been eight knights with Meleagant. I suspected the brothers, fierce and bloodthirsty in their loyalty to Arthur, had killed the rest.

Arthur looked expectantly at the knight, as though waiting for him to explain himself.

"The queen lay treasonously with your foster-brother Sir Kay, my lord," he blurted, as though desperate to excuse himself by throwing the blame on me.

Arthur shook his head, waving the accusation away.

"Because of your cowardly attack on my brother Sir Kay he is in such a state that he can barely move. Your accusation hardly has any credibility in such a circumstance."

I noticed that, beside him, Lancelot's hand had gone to the hilt of his sword.

"He will be hanged for treason," Arthur declared, gesturing for Aggravain to take the man away. He turned to Gawain. "He is the last of them?"

Gawain nodded.

"You did well," Arthur told him.

The council proceeded with unrelated business. I was glad. I did not want it to be spoken of any more than it had to. Nimue was returning to court soon, which I was pleased to hear. I somewhat hoped she would bring me another armoured dress. I was aware of Lancelot close by me, and I enjoyed the little thrill of knowing he was near, and that we had shared a secret happiness. Yet, I could feel all the time Mordred's eyes on me. Something about his look seemed to brush against my skin, clammy and unpleasant. I was pleased when council business was complete, and I could go.

Somehow, Mordred had reached my room before I got there, and sat in the chair by my window, one heel on the edge of the seat and one arm casually resting on his drawn-up knee. I jumped to see him there, expecting to find myself alone, but gathered myself quickly, crossing my arms in front of my chest and standing in the doorway, meeting his smug stare with a cold and queenly gaze.

"Are you here to threaten me again, Mordred?" I asked, dryly. He grinned.

"Oh no, good lady. I come only out of concern for your wellbeing. I thought you might be anxious after seeing how sternly my lord father – or as he would prefer my dear uncle – deals with traitors. I thought you might require some... especial comfort."

I was pleased that that day I was wearing the green armoured dress. Besides, the fresh memory of Lancelot in my arms was something no one could touch – not him, not anyone – and the warm brightness of it inside of me made me feel strong, and bold, and safe.

I was not afraid of Mordred, not today. He would not touch me. That had been nothing but a dream.

"You should be careful what you say, Mordred. You don't know what you're talking about. I think even you are afraid to come sword-to-sword with Lancelot, so unless you intend to make your accusations good, I would keep them to yourself, for the sake of your life."

Mordred stood slowly and walked towards me. I held my ground, even until he was standing right before me.

"Careful, Morded. Did you not hear what I did to the last man who touched me without my permission?" I said, low and threatening. Right then, I felt as though I did have it in me to kill him. The strength of daring was in me, and Lancelot's return was making me braver than, perhaps, I should have been.

Mordred raised an eyebrow and put out his hand, palm flat against the platemail bodice of my dress, and with the smallest gesture, pushed me back against the wall. It was just the smallest distance, but I felt the power of his strength through it, the violent potential in his body. It was nothing more to him than a reminder that he was strong and I was weak and as long as we were alone he would do as he liked with me. But that was not so, no matter how he believed it, and I would not show fear on my face. I met his look with a proud stare.

"I'm more interested," he whispered, leaning close, "in what you did to the last man who touched you *with* your permission."

"You should not speak to me like that. I am your queen. I ought to have you punished for believing and repeating Aggravain's disgusting rumours. But you're not even brave enough for anything other than covert threats and bullying women. There is no truth in what you're saying and Arthur will not believe it. You are a coward to come to me like this expecting – what exactly? What exactly do you expect from me?"

Mordred did not answer, but pressed a little harder against the plate bodice. I showed no pain, no fear. He knew nothing, he had seen nothing. If I was not afraid of him then he had no power over me at all. He leaned in closer, as though he was going to try and kiss me, and I slapped him hard across the face. He stepped back, laughing under his breath, and raised his hand to touch his already reddening cheek. I expected him to say something, to make another threat as he had done before, but none came, and he left. It made me wary, though, that I should not be alone with Lancelot, not now I knew Mordred was watching me.

Spring ripened into summer, and the summer grew hot and heavy, the days long and feverish, warm as the hot May weather had predicted. I was often with Lancelot, either with Kay and Marie reading in the garden, or riding out hunting with him and Gareth, or sitting with him to watch the knights fighting and training. It was a sweet, secret joy to sit side by side, talking about nothing, but remembering our closeness, relishing in the secret love. I spent my nights with Arthur, and any time I found myself alone, I did not send for Lancelot. I felt Mordred and Aggravain watching me. Gawain seemed to have forgotten it. A man of simple thoughts and pleasures, interested in hunting and women, full of momentary anger that passed quickly, or so I thought. Still, I had not forgiven him. Arthur thought my dislike of Gawain was on Margery's behalf, and silly. He told me Gawain was a rough man with a good heart, and a brave and true knight, and I should like him for his loyalty to his king. I did not think I had to like any man for another man's sake.

Still, I longed for an opportunity to come when Lancelot and I could be safely alone. Any time a momentary opportunity came, we might steal a kiss, but we dared nothing more. Not after what had happened before the Grail quest. But it was enough to have him close and know that we both wanted the same thing: to be together.

Nimue came back to court with a husband. Arthur was stunned. I did not know the man well, only remembered his name from a quarrel that he had with Gawain over another woman entirely, for whom he had asked Gawain's help to win as his wife, but who – according to him – Gawain had simply lain with himself and abandoned. I wondered if the real story was even as savoury as that, but this knight seemed to have forgotten his former love, and seemed happy enough with Nimue. I wondered what that was like, to forget love. It must have not been love, really.

When I asked Nimue about it, she said in a small, even voice, "Oh no, he still loved her. But I wanted him, so I put a spell on him, and now he loves me."

I was not sure if she was joking or not. I thought about Merlin, shut under a rock.

One late afternoon, I thought I would go and lie on the Round Table and make a wish on it. I thought perhaps I would wish for peace for Christine. Or for a moment alone, properly alone, with Lancelot. But, as I approached the door, I heard voices inside, and my own name. Arthur had not called a council, but I could hear *his* voice. I pressed myself against the door.

"It's plain to see, Arthur, and it's no good. I don't know how you can stand the shame of it. You have to do something about it. Everyone is talking about it, saying they are lovers, and it's dangerous for you." It was Aggravain speaking, and I could guess already what it is about.

"Aggravain, I can't give out justice based on rumour. There are tales all around that are not true. Her and Kay, at Meleagant's castle. Isolde and Palomides. You don't see me rushing to have Kay's head, for the sake of a bit of gossip. If you stop talking, others will stop talking." Arthur sounded brusque and annoyed. The voices were quiet for a bit, but then I heard Mordred's voice, low and dark.

"Yet, my lord, the rumours about Isolde and Tristan *were* true. And Lancelot harboured them at Joyous Guard. He's obviously not a man who has a problem with adultery. Don't you think it is suspicious that she goes missing overnight and he brings her back without any of her clothes?"

"You're being ridiculous." It was Kay. *Kay* was there, too. Who else was in that room? I expected Nimue was there, too. Perhaps Gawain as well.

"My lord, they are *always together*. Always talking together and walking together, always *whispering* together. It's plain to see from the way he looks at her that he has had her," Aggravain began again.

"*Enough*," Arthur's voice boomed, and even if I had not had my ear to the thick door, I would have heard it. "I won't tolerate any more accusations based on gossip. I don't want to hear any more about it; nor do I want to hear that any of you have spoken of it. Do you understand?"

I moved away then, slipping down the stairs out into the courtyard. Under the midsummer sun, the packed mud floor radiated heat, and I felt the sweat bead against my skin. Lancelot and Gareth were fighting casually in the courtyard; just playing, really. I smiled absently over at them, but I was not going to interrupt with this. I didn't know what to make of it. Arthur still did not believe it, but they were still talking, and danger was closer. I had tried to forget him, and we had tried to live without it. It was not to be borne, for either of us. He and I were careful now, older and wiser than we had been. We had waited, and we could wait again until we could love in safety.

That night we ate, Arthur, his knights, Nimue and I, around the Round Table. Arthur had taken to wanting to eat like that, with just his small band of companions, unless it was a great holiday feast. I liked it better, anyway. I liked to be close to the table and lay my hands on its smooth wood. I liked to be aware of Lancelot close by. But it meant I was close, also, to Mordred, and I could feel him watching me. I had worn my armoured dress again, wanting to feel just a little stronger and safer. But the talk was light-hearted and merry, Gareth talking about his daughter, Gaheris about the marriage he was soon to make with Lynesse's sister. I wondered if he had told Marie, and if she would be sad. Of course, she was a servant and he could not have married her, but I hoped he had at least been kind to her about it.

When we had finished eating, and the men began to move around the table, Lancelot slipped into Kay's seat beside me as Kay went over to join in some story Gawain was telling. I wished I had had time to warn him about what Aggravain had said, but it seemed more suspicious to behave suddenly differently with him. Besides, I was pleased to have him beside me. We talked about the food – it had been good, finishing with sweet little cakes filled with late summer blackberries – but it was just to talk to one another. I could not help smiling as I looked at him, and I knew I was getting lost in the closeness of him, as I always did, and he with me. I could see a flash of chest through his open shirt, and the sight of his skin made me think of it against my own. I was sure I could have closed my eyes and imagined the feel of it against my lips, but I held myself back. *Soon*, I told myself. He was telling me now about some time when he had been lost looking for the Grail, but I was not listening, not to his words anyway. I was listening to the low, delicious sound of his voice. I needed only the sound of his voice to remember all of the things he had whispered to me when we were alone, to imagine his lips against my neck, to slip back into the heady heart of my memories of him. I was leaning with one arm on the table, over towards him, the back of my hand resting against the old, smooth wood, and as he spoke, he reached out and lightly, half-consciously brushed his fingertips across the upturned palm of my hand, and I felt the brightness of his touch go through me, the warmth rise slightly in my cheeks. It was nothing, almost nothing, and still I felt it flicker in the centre of me. Perhaps I ought to have been more careful even then, but we were always like this together now, wrapped in the safety of other people around. If we would be thus around others, then surely there was nothing suspicious in it? It had protected us for the past few months.

But, then I glanced up for a second, and across the room I met Arthur's eye. It was just for a second, but I felt the blood drain out of my face, the heat leave my limbs, and I heard my heart thud in my ears. *He was watching us.* I looked away fast, as though I had not noticed, not noticed his quiet, watchful stare. I felt my cheeks flush. I was already giving myself away. Lancelot had noticed and fallen quiet. I was doing nothing wrong, nothing different. Arthur had seen us like this countless times since Lancelot had brought me back from Meleagant's castle. It was clear, to me at least, that he was seeing something different now.

That night, Arthur was quiet. He took me in his arms as he always did, but without speaking, and I dared not speak either, in case he asked me about it. I was not sure if I had the strength in me right then to lie.

The next day, I stood side by side with Arthur to watch the knights training in the courtyard. He seemed better this morning, happy even, as though the night had erased his worries, and having me beside him had put his cares about it to rest. Lancelot came to join the training, but he had his eye on a particular partner to practice with. He called Mordred forward, and Mordred came, his practice sword drawn.

"This should be interesting," Arthur said, in a strange tone that I could not place. It could have been nothing more than casual interest, but it sounded to me like something more, though I told myself that I might just have been more sensitive to it because of what I had heard.

Mordred seemed to have the upper hand initially, pushing Lancelot back with his blows, but Lancelot was only testing his strength, and after allowing the younger man to drive him back, Lancelot came against him with his full strength. Mordred, caught off guard, stumbled back, surprised at the sudden display of power. It was easy then for Lancelot to knock his sword from his hand and, catching him hard across the shoulder with the flat of his own sword, knock Mordred from his feet. I should have suspected this would happen since, that morning in the garden, I had leaned over to Lancelot while Marie was reading, and told him in a whisper how Mordred had come into my room, made his accusations and tried to kiss me, how I felt him watching me, how I was sure now of what he must have said to Arthur. Lancelot was defending me again, as he had done with Aggravain. It was too clear a message for Mordred to miss, although I was worried that it was a message that he would be eager to respond to in kind.

Arthur laughed, and seemed pleased at the skill of the fighting. But, then, he took off his crown and handed it to me, taking up Mordred's fallen sword and squaring up to Lancelot. *What was happening?* Arthur was unarmoured, in a light silk surcoat for the summer, unbuttoned in the heat of the afternoon sun, and Lancelot threw off the little armour he had on to match him, weighing his sword in his hand.

"Come on, Lancelot," Arthur suggested, his tone easy and friendly; "no one ever wants to spar with me, but I'm sure you'll take the challenge."

Lancelot hesitated, but Arthur struck a blow against his sword fast, and they came together. They were an even match; Lancelot lithe and skilful, Arthur powerful yet graceful. Unlike Gawain and his huge brothers who moved in their vast strength like bulls, Arthur's huge muscular frame gave him a fluid grace, the easy elegance of a man who is sure of his own strength. Still, it seemed to me that Lancelot did not go at him with his whole strength, and let Arthur knock his sword from his hands quickly, lifting his arms in the air to yield. Perhaps another message had been given, then. I did not know, but Arthur said no more about it over the next few days and it seemed to me that everything might go back to normal.

Chapter Forty-Four

Things seemed to calm down, but the matter had left me feeling uneasy, and I thought for the sake of safety I ought to warn Lancelot, and he ought to go back to his castle, until things quietened down. He could make some excuse to leave, just for a month or so. I would be sorry to see him go, and I would miss him, but better to be safe. Now we both knew that we would love this way forever, I could wait. Arthur seemed to have forgotten, but I was sure he would forget faster with Lancelot gone. It need only be a short while.

I waited for my opportunity to speak to him alone, and it came fast. Arthur had gone out hunting in the morning, and sent back a message that he and the others would camp, and stay out overnight. That was usual enough for him, when he was out with Gawain. Neither of them ever seemed to get their fill of hunting. I sometimes wondered if they spent so long in those woods because they were still looking for the white hart. Or perhaps it was the drinking afterwards, roasting what they had caught over the fire, all men together. It must have reminded them of their early days of war. Arthur still missed those, deep down, even while he understood that nothing was more valuable than peace.

I sent Marie to ask Lancelot to come to me. It was a lovely, mild evening that seemed to be the first of autumn, full of the smells of harvest time: hay drying, sweet berries, plenty. I did not know who else was still about the castle, but since we would only be talking I half hoped someone would come upon us in our innocence, and Arthur's fears would be abated. I did not know who that would be, though; almost all the knights had gone on the hunt.

But Lancelot did not come, nor did Marie return. He must have been busy, or with Arthur hunting, unable to slip away, or perhaps Marie had been snatched up by Gaheris on the way. His new wife did not seem to have cooled his ardency for Marie, nor hers for him. I could not say I blamed either of them.

So, standing and watching the sun set slowly out of the window, I slowly unwound and brushed out my hair, thinking of Carhais in the autumn, the huge bonfires and the dancing. They would be doing that in the villages, but not here in Camelot, under the sad eyes of Christ. There were times, even now, when I still missed my old home. I undressed slowly, clumsily, finding it difficult to get out of the overdress on my own, and then got out of the underdress more easily, and put on my nightdress. It was pleasantly loose and the autumn breeze brushed against my skin beneath it. I wished I had someone to send for a bath. The hot water would have soothed me to sleep. I wondered if Arthur would come. Sometimes, if the day's hunting had been bad and he could make it back before nightfall, he made his plans to stay out overnight, but sometimes would change them, would ride back for me as the sun was setting, to take me in his arms, fired from the hunt and warm with wine. I did not think he would tonight, though. He was probably drunk with Gawain already, listening and laughing along to some old story. Besides, it would be sunset soon.

It was dark at the edges of the sky, the stars small silver specks against a dark velvety blue, when I heard the door behind me and turned in my seat. It was Lancelot. I stood slowly, as though in a trance.

"I didn't think you'd come," I breathed.

He pushed the door shut behind him, and stepped into the room.

"Are you well?" he asked, his face crinkling in concern. He looked worried, too. He had come in his shirt and breeches, without his sword, as though Marie had found him preparing for bed. Perhaps he had ridden back from the hunt like that, in urgency and without his armour. The thought that he would have done so, just to see me, made me feel the spark of yearning for him catch within me. But I had to be prudent. For once in my life, I had to be careful. I shook my head.

"I think we are in danger," I replied, quietly.

Lancelot shook his head, as though he already knew it. Arthur would not come back, I was sure of it by now, and I could not resist his closeness, to have him alone with me, and I moved into his arms in a few swift steps, and he gathered me up against him. I held his face in my hands and whispered close.

"I think you should go back to Joyous Guard. Just for a while. Mordred and Aggravain are always watching us, and I heard them talking with Arthur."

Lancelot nodded, but one of his hands was already tangled in my hair. I felt my body lean towards his; I felt the longing cloud my mind. I could feel the warmth of his touch as his other hand ran up from the small of my back, through the thin silk of the nightdress. We had not been together since we had been in Melegeant's castle. We had been so careful, and we had waited so long. The air smelled thickly wonderful with the late autumn night; I felt suddenly unbearably lonely – lonely for his touch, lonely in a way only he could ease.

"I know. I know this is foolish; I know this is not safe. But I will come back. I can't forget you." He kissed me, deep and urgent. "I can't forget you," he whispered.

I wrapped my arms around his neck, and lost myself in his kiss, the heady soft sensation of our mouths together, our tongues brushing against each other. I felt the madness for him rise in me, it was so long since I had held him alone. *One last time*, I thought. *I don't know when we will be together again.* But I was struck by a sudden fear, and pulled away.

"What if someone comes?" I breathed.

"No one will," Lancelot murmured, and I felt his lips against my neck. "Arthur's still out with the hunt, and the others with him. They're all there: Arthur, Gawain and all his brothers. They won't come."

He reached a hand behind him, not drawing his kiss away, but pushing shut the bolt clumsily. I opened my mouth to say, *wait*, to say, *are you sure we are safe?* But he kissed me, and the fear began to dissolve away, replaced with the rushing delight of being close with him again after so long. When we were young, we had made love on the stairs, in the walled garden, reckless and never afraid. And we had not been found. He was leaving, he was going once again. How could I know if it would be six more long years before I saw him again? And I could feel Lancelot's hand at the small of my back, pulling me tight against him, and his lips against mine, and the warm skin of his chest under my hand, through his shirt, and I knew I would not, I knew I *could* not send him away without our coming together one last time.

There were no candles lit, but the light of the autumn moon rising slowly flowed into the window, pale and lovely; and Lancelot was kicking off his boots already, and I could feel his hands move to the ties of the nightdress, pulling them slowly undone, and I felt his hand against the skin of my stomach, and though we were desperate, both, for the moment to last, we were both wild already with it. I stumbled back towards the bed, pulling him with me by the front of his breeches, where my fingers caught on the laces, clumsy with haste, and he pushed the nightdress lightly off my shoulders, and I felt it tangle around my feet as I stepped back, and it fell to the ground. I pushed his breeches away and stepped back again, and we fell together onto the bed. I could feel the excitement quivering through me already, but I held back, wanting as much as I could of him before he was lost from me again. I slid my hands up under his shirt, pushing it over his head, savouring the feel of his skin under my hands, but even as I tried to be slow, the feel of his naked body against mine was clouding my mind, filling me with the heat that would not be denied, and as I took his face in my hands and kissed him hard, we suddenly came together, gasping, and I felt the wonderful, almost unbearable satisfaction of my longing fill me. I wound my hands into his hair, trying to be slow, to make our passion last, but I wanted it as much as he did, the wildness of it. I needed it. I felt his lips against my ear, heard him whisper my name, felt the brightness catch within me. *Not already*, I thought, and as though he knew my thoughts, he turned over beneath me, moving me onto him with his gentle, powerful touch. I spread out my hands against his chest, and our eyes met. With the touch of that lovely moonlight upon him, I was sure I would never see anything more perfect, more painful again. His hands, firm against my thighs, moved me with him, and he was slow and savouring as he could be, but as I saw the pleasure rise in him, I felt it come upon me, white-hot, strong and overwhelming. I sighed out his name, and he sighed for me, and I sank down upon him, and he wrapped his arms around me, gathering me close against his chest. I kissed the skin of it, softly, closing my eyes. Was this the last taste of it? Even so, this was a moment I could replay over and over in my dreams.

Suddenly, Lancelot sat up, as though listening for something.

"What is it?" I whispered. He put up a hand as though for quiet, as though he was listening.

I heard, awful and unmistakable in the night, the clink of someone in platemail moving, just outside the door. I sat up fast, too. No, no not so soon. Whatever horror it was, I wished it could have waited for one more moment of savouring, one moment when the lazy warmth of satisfaction could have hung about me, but it was cold and awful, and it had shattered through it.

Lancelot was already out of the bed, and threw my nightdress to me. I pulled it back on and, with fumbling clumsy fingers, tied the strings back together. Lancelot was already dressed and pulling on his boots, already prepared though I did not know what was happening, all I knew was that I felt danger, and my skin prickled into goosebumps all over me.

There was a loud bang on the door, the bang of iron against wood.

"Come out, Lancelot." Mordred's voice burned through the thick door. My heart thudded within me, and I moved fast off the bed, over to Lancelot. "We know you're in there with the queen."

How long had they been outside?

"Come out, your treasonous coward. You will face our hard justice for this." Aggravain's voice joined the shouts. More men shouted in agreement. I heard men drawing their swords. My blood ran cold in my veins and I felt my stomach clench to nothing with me. Lancelot looked at me, the same empty dread on his face. There were *many* of them out there. The banging on the door resumed, hard and insistent, with the cries of "Come out!" and "Traitor!"

I turned to Lancelot.

"So, my love. It seems that this is the end," I said softly. I did not see any other way that this could finish, but that we would be parted, by Arthur, or by death. Lancelot took my face gently in his hands, and kissed me, unbearably brief. He grasped one of the curtains from the bed and tore it down, wrapping his left arm in the thick brocade, a kind of makeshift shield. It would be nothing against even one man with a sword. He looked to me again, raising his hand again to cup my cheek against his palm.

"It seems so. Well, I will sell my life as dearly as I can." I shook my head, feeling the tears prick my eyes, but chasing them away. Tears would not help me now.

"No, Lancelot. Run if you can; go to Joyous Guard. Save yourself, if you can. I don't care if they take me, I only care that you – just run, Lancelot. Be safe." I was filled with a sense of guilt for what I had taken from him. He could have had a safer woman, a love that would not have brought him into danger. It was all the same for me. I would not survive without him, and if Aggravain and Mordred did not kill me, I would be put to the fire.

He kissed me again, this time hard, rough, almost defiant. I was glad of it, though I knew if he was to go out now, and die, it would be for me, and that I could not bear.

"I will come back for you. If I survive. If I do not, my kinsmen will come to rescue you." I nodded. *"I will come back for you,"* he whispered forcefully, and this time he did not say, *If I survive.*

"I will not live without you," I whispered back, and he kissed me one last time. As his lips moved away from mine, it was the most awful parting I could imagine. Snatched from absolute happiness into this hell. I was still warm from his touch, still slightly dizzy with it, and suddenly we were both waiting for our death.

Outside, the banging was louder and louder. It seemed that men were shoving hard again and again at the door. Lancelot walked to the door, braced himself with his makeshift shield. I saw him take one deep breath in, pull back the bolt, and plunge out, out unarmed and unarmoured into the awful sea of armoured knights standing against him.

In a moment, he was back through, dragging a man, limp in his armour, and bolting the door behind him. I kneeled down to help him strip the platemail from the man. Lancelot already had the man's sword in his hand, and it was already covered in blood. I did not look too long at the man's face; he was a man I knew. Not well, but I had seen him often with Arthur's band of knights, around my Round Table. My hands shaking, I helped Lancelot to dress in his armour, and Lancelot took the sword in his hand again, kissed me briskly, and opened the door to plunge back out into the corridor.

I shut the door fast behind him, and leaned my back against it. I was gasping for breath, shaking. I could hear outside shouting, the clashing of swords. At least it was not over fast, with Lancelot slain at once. It was unbearably loud, seemed painfully close, the scrape of iron and steel, the clashing jarring through me, as though it was happening inside my own head, and I felt the shocks of the blows go through my body as though I was out there, under them.

Eventually I heard the noise in the corridor go silent. I slowly turned and put my trembling hand on the bolt, waiting. Still silent. What would I do if I opened the door to find Lancelot had been killed for my sake? No, they would have taken him alive. They would have wanted to take him alive to Arthur, for a traitor's death. I did not think Mordred would waste the chance to relish his revenge; nor would he want Lancelot to have an honourable man's death in battle.

Then, the silence meant that he had escaped, and all the others were dead. Or, that they were all dead, Lancelot and the others alike. I supposed I ought to stay in the room, stay safe, until Arthur came, claim I knew nothing. But how would I explain the curtain of my bed, torn away, and the dead man lying in my room? Besides, the thought struck me suddenly that the longer I waited the further away Lancelot would get, when I could slip away now, before anyone heard, and ride to Joyous Guard, avoid the explanations and accusations. Avoid the death of a treasonous queen. I could not pretend that I did not want to live. If Lancelot were alive, and I could go with him, I did not care at all that it would be a life of shame. I pressed my ear against the door, and heard silence; nothing but the tense beating of my heart.

I slipped back the bolt and opened the door a hand's breadth. For a moment I saw a hallway strewn with bodies. I did not want to look too closely at whose they were. But then, into my narrow field of view, came the grinning face of Mordred, smeared with blood, like some half-dead creature crawled from the barrow-lands. I tried to slam the door shut, but he was too strong and too fast and he pushed the door so hard back open that it rattled on its hinges. I tried to slip past him, but he grabbed me easily, one hand tight in my hair, pulling my head back, the other twisting my arm behind me until I gasped in pain, and he began to drag me down the stairs.

He took me to Arthur's council chamber, where Arthur was waiting with Ector and Gawain. He had known about this, then. He had not really been out hunting. It burned inside me, that he had known about – perhaps himself set – the trap. But I was pleased to see the table. To have it there made me feel calmer. There were things Arthur and the others did not understand. I did understand.

But when Arthur saw Mordred push me forwards before him, holding both my arms behind me now with a single hand, and pulling my head back by the hair, I saw sorrow and pain flash across his face, and for a moment, he rested his forehead in his hand. I noticed that though Mordred and Gawain were armoured, Arthur and Ector looked as though they had just been called from their beds, dressed only in their shirts and breeches. It was deep in the night, and a single brazier burned at the back of the room, filling it with an ominous half-light, and Arthur's face was obscured in the shadow of his hand.

"My lord," said Mordred, "it is done. It was as I said."

Arthur looked up slowly, at Mordred, not at me.

"Bringing my wife here in her bedclothes is proof of nothing, Mordred." He sighed, rubbing his brow with the heel of his hand, but he did not sound as though he believed his own words.

"You want to see proof?"

Before I knew what was happening, Mordred had let go of my hair to pull up the skirt of my nightgown and run a hand up the inside of my thigh. I twisted away and kicked but he held me fast.

"No," Arthur, shouted, holding up a hand for Mordred to stop, and he lifted his hand away letting the skirt fall. I was shaking, too stunned to speak, too desperate to defend myself, too full of racing hopes that Lancelot had slipped away to safety. He was not there. He was not, too, a prisoner. If he was alive, he would come back for me. He had only left me then because he had thought all the others were dead. "Mordred, there is no need for that. She is still my queen and you will treat her gently. She will have the chance to defend herself. Send for Lancelot, and he may fight with you for a chance to prove her innocence."

To this, Ector nodded in agreement. I felt a wave of relief wash over me. Arthur would bring Lancelot back, and he would kill Mordred, and things could be as they had been. But then Gawain stepped forward from where he had stood, just behind Arthur's chair.

"No, sire." He fixed me with a cold stare, and I felt my blood freeze in my veins. "A queen she may be, in name at least, but in this *she shall have the law.*"

His voice echoed around the room. Arthur sighed again, pressing his hands against the table and leaning against them, bracing against it. He still did not look at me. I wished I too could touch the table, feel the smooth old wood, wish away what had happened. Wish myself back to safety. How could we have been so foolish? How could we have thought we could love in secret forever and hurt no one?

"It is no justice to let Lancelot fight," Mordred agreed, "and kings and queens too must abide by the law."

Arthur waved a hand in resignation.

"Very well. And Lancelot – If I can get my hands on him, he too will die a traitor's death." Arthur's voice was full of a cold, hard anger that I had not heard in it before. I could see, in the half-light, that he was shaking with that anger slightly, and with something else, something deeper yet empty.

I could not see Mordred behind me, but I knew he would be grinning with perverse pleasure.

"I will take her to the dungeons." He jerked me back with him, moving towards the door already.

"There is no need for that," Arthur said, shaking his head. "Take her up to my chamber. She isn't going to run."

At last he looked at me as he said this. Anger, I had expected. I had not expected sorrow, or surprise. Or regret. Regret that he had to hand me over to the law. Or regret that he had ever taken me as his wife. Even now this good man who I had loved almost my whole life was sorry for me, for what I had done, or perhaps for what I had become. I felt the guilt turn my stomach and I closed my eyes away from the look.

Mordred dragged me on again, up to Arthur's room. He shoved me roughly in through the door, and after casting a narrow look on me for a second, hit me across the face with the back of his hand so hard that I stumbled and tasted blood in my mouth, feeling my lip tear. Before I could step away, he was on me, pushing me to the ground, forcing his hand up my skirt again as I struggled and kicked, trying to push him off. The heavy weight of his body on top of me crushed the breath from my lungs. I felt the cold panic within me, flashed back of half-forgotten dreams, and Meleagant holding me down, but he stopped at the top of my thigh and pulled back his hand, only to hold it in front of my face. On his fingers, in the light from the fire, I could see the slick moisture.

"Liar," he whispered, close and dangerous; then, shoving me hard against the floor again, he got up and left. I pushed myself slowly up from the floor.

I felt oddly calm, now that the worst had happened, and I knew my fate was coming. The thought that Lancelot might have escaped hung about me, a thin veil of comfort. But calm as I felt, my limbs shook as I tried to move. I was shaking too hard to stand, so I sat where I had fallen, before the fire, too hot on the autumn night. I pressed the back of my hand against my lip and it came away bloody. Drops of it fell on the white nightdress, spreading and darkening into the cloth.

I heard my name and looked up to see Arthur standing in the doorway. He shut the door and knelt down beside me. He gently took my face in his hands, looking at the broken lip, and the bruise already throbbing against my jaw and sighed again.

"Mordred should not have been so rough with you." He stood up and walked towards the window. I heard him pour out a cup of wine. He came to sit on the edge of his bed, close by me. He drank, tipping the cup right up, then put the cup down beside him on the floor, and rubbed his face with his hands. I sat at his feet on the floor. I began to speak – I didn't know why, because I had no words to give either of us any comfort or relief – but he cut me off. "Stop. I don't want to hear you deny it." He gazed at me with eyes full of sadness – sadness and weariness and defeat. "You know what this means?"

I nodded.

"I'm sorry it has to be this way, but I have no choice," he told me, his voice dull.

He was apologising to *me*. I was filled with the heavy feeling that I did not deserve him, that I never had. We were never meant to be together, never made for each other. If I could not love a man this good with all my heart, I must *be* no good, but even then, *even then* I could only think of Lancelot. I did not care that they would burn me; all I could think was, *I do not know if he is alive*. Mordred had dragged me by too fast to look for him among the bodies in the corridor. Arthur had suggested sending for him, but he might not know if Mordred had cut him down.

I could not tell what Arthur was thinking. He seemed filled with some feeling, some anger, too great, too complex, to be expressed, paralysingly unbearable, and yet he was gentle with me. Sad. It was as though his anger was so great that it wasn't hot any more, but cold and heavy and hard. I supposed that there was no good, anyway, in him being angry with me now. It was already done, and I would be burned.

I moved over to him and rested my head against his knee, closing my eyes. He put a hand gently on my head. I felt the heat of the fire on the other side of my face and wondered if I could bear being burned to death, or if I would never feel anything again; if the pain in my heart was so great that it would block out the pain of my body.

"How did we come to this?" Arthur asked quietly, thoughtfully, as though he were asking himself, or asking his god. "We loved each other, once. Not just like man and wife, but *truly*. I know we did. And now you have done *this*, and I have to give you to them, to burn. And I will kill Lancelot as well. I am more sorry for his loss than yours. I could have chosen any queen, but there will never be a knight like Lancelot again."

There was a soft knock at the door, and it opened before Arthur could answer, before the coldness of Arthur's words could sink in enough to cut me to the bone.

It was Ector, his sweet old face heavy with care. It made the lines seem deeper.

"Arthur, Lancelot is gone." *Dead gone?*

"Gone?" Arthur asked.

"Ridden to his fortress at Joyous Guard." *Alive*. I was ashamed of my relief. I was sure I did not hide it. Ector drew in a deep breath, as though it pained him. "Arthur, Kay has ridden with him." Arthur nodded slowly, his face unreadable.

"Anyone else?"

"Bors. In the morning we may find that more are gone." Ector hovered at the door as the silence stretched out. I knew what Arthur was thinking. Ector's brothers and his son had ridden out of Camelot, and Ector was still here.

"Kay," Arthur murmured under his breath. He rubbed his face, as though he was trying to wake from an unpleasant dream.

"Arthur," Ector spoke, soft but firm, "I am staying here. I will not go to my kin; I know my place is here with you, but don't ask me to ride out against them in battle."

Arthur nodded.

"No, of course, Ector. Of course."

When Ector had left and we were alone again, Arthur spoke again, quietly,

"This is the beginning of the end. I can feel it."

Chapter Forty-Five

When Ector came back with dawn, we were still sat as we were, Arthur at the end of the bed, me with my head against his knee. Neither of us had slept. Neither of us had spoken. Neither of us could have borne it to get into the bed and lie side by side where we had been together in happiness so often. Not now. The dawn felt clammy against my skin. I had been afraid to sleep, and wake again only to have to remember what had happened.

Arthur looked up at him, and I followed his look.

"Truly, Arthur?" Ector asked. I could hear the deep sadness in his voice, and his sweet gentle face drooped under the weight of it. I felt horribly responsible for good kind Ector's suffering. I felt awful, too, that I had cost him a brother and a son and he had still come to plead for my life with Arthur.

Arthur stood, rubbing his face and pushing his hair back from his forehead. Overnight, stubble had gathered on his face and he looked tired and haggard.

"There is no other way," he replied flatly. "But I cannot watch. Let her girl come in and dress her, and find knights to take her to the pyre."

Ector nodded. Arthur stood slowly, moved to the door, leaving me to lean back against the end of the bed. As he got there, he turned back for a moment as if to say something to me, but whatever it was passed away before it was spoken, and he left. Ector, with a weak smile of little comfort left after him, and the door shut heavily behind him.

I leaned back against the bed and sat in an empty, stunned stupor until Marie at last rushed in. In her arms was the green dress sewn with gold crosses. I wished I had had one of the armoured dresses, but this is what it would have to be. At least I would go to my death looking like a good Christian queen.

Marie fell against me, into my arms, sobbing and babbling in Breton. Through her panicked tears, she gasped out.

"I'm sorry, I'm sorry."

I took her face in my hands and smoothed the hair, torn loose in her frenzy, back from her face.

"Marie, what for?"

She shook her head as she gathered her breath, trying to calm herself enough to speak.

"Gaheris – Gaheris – he said they were all talking about it, all of the brothers. He didn't believe them, that they would really do it, but Aggravain and Mordred – I'm sorry, I'm so sorry. I should have warned you. But I didn't think it was true. I thought it was just *rumours*."

I hushed her gently.

"Marie, this is not your fault."

She collapsed down onto me sobbing, and I wrapped my arms around her, holding her close and smoothing her hair until she calmed down, moving away and rubbing the tears from her red and puffy cheeks with the back of her hand. I stood and pulled off the nightgown, and Marie helped me into the underdress, lacing and tying it slowly, as if this would give us – or me – any more time. Joyous Guard was more than a day's ride from Camelot. Obviously they had decided that I must face the law at once, before Lancelot and those who had gone with him had the chance to come back and rescue me. Or perhaps before Arthur had a chance to change his mind. I pulled on the green dress, and Marie laced it up, all quiet. It was strange to have her with me without her chirping chatter and I missed it, though I was not sure what I would be able to say in response to it, now. The only gossip worth talking about was about me, and it was leading me to my death.

When Marie was plaiting my hair and slowly winding it up into a bun she stared crying again.

"I've done it wrong," she said.

I gave a soft, resigned little laugh. "Oh Marie, it hardly matters now," I told her.

She pinned it up in the gold net, but I could feel her hands were shaking. As soon as she was done she rushed to throw her arms around me again. I held her tight. It might be the last kind touch I would ever feel. I buried my face against her neck, against the sweet familiar smell of her hair that smelled of straw and flowers and Carhais and home, and that I associated with laughter and the long friendship that had carried us across the sea, through years at Camelot, to now. When I finally released her from my embrace she rushed away to the bundle of things she had brought as though she had suddenly remembered something. It was my circlet. I was glad to see it. At least when I walked through the crowd to the pyre, I would have something from my home, and people would see me go proud and like a queen. Even after everything, that was important to me. She set it lightly on my head, and kissed me on both cheeks. I took her face in my hands and pressed my forehead against hers.

"Get out of here if you can, Marie," I told her quietly, still in Breton. I knew she would not want to. She would want to stay with Gaheris, but I did not think it would be safe for her. Soon, people would start asking her questions about how much she knew, and the accusations would begin to fall on her. I didn't want that. Still, she nodded. "I could not have survived this long without you," I added, softly.

"Marie." I heard Ector's voice from the door, stern. I could hear in it that he was annoyed to hear us speaking in a language he did not understand. I felt that kind Ector was hiding his sorrow with this sudden strange sternness, and that made me sadder still. "It's time you left the queen, now." So, he could not even bear to call me by my name. After all the years of his kindness. Still, he did not seem unkind, or angry, just tense and terse, straining under what had happened.

I was sorry that they took Marie away, and even more sorry that they sent the priest from the chapel to me. I did not need the sad-eyed Christ's curses for my sins, as Arthur had had them. I did not want to go to my death hearing a god was angry with me, whoever it was. The anger of men was enough. But the priest came nonetheless, and I sat on the end of Arthur's bed with my arms crossed protectively in front of me as the old man in his white and gold brocade cassock came shuffling in, with his face so wrinkled and slack that it looked like wax melting. He would have known nothing in his life of the passions of the body, the undeniable force of nature that was real love, between a man and a woman. All he would have for me was platitudes about sin.

He stood before me, his huge leather-bound bible, the cross embossed in gold on the front, clasped in his arms. I think he expected me to kneel, but I would not.

"Would you like to confess your sins before you go to the fire?" he asked, his papery voice wavering with age.

My sins. I thought hard about that. I supposed I had one sin to confess.

"I am sorry for the hurt I have done to Arthur," I replied. I felt it. I felt sorry at the very heart of me that he had suffered for it. I had hoped he would never know, that I would never hurt him.

The priest frowned.

"And what about the sin that caused that hurt?"

No, I would not wish it away. That would be the greatest sin, I felt, to sit there facing my death and wish that I had never loved Lancelot. It was a sin to deny to love, a sin against me and him, against the self, against all the earthly beauties of the world. I would *never* regret that love. Not all the gods in the world could make me say I repented of it.

I shook my head. "I could not have done anything other than what I did. But still, I am sorry for the suffering it has caused," I replied evenly.

The priest scowled, his lined and folded face crinkling in displeasure. I was not the repentant sinner he had hoped for, but I might as well have repented the sun rising, or the waning of the moon, for all the power I had to stop myself loving Lancelot, or him loving me. The winter kills the weak with its cold when it comes, and we are sorry for their loss, but we are never sorry for the coming of the winter, because that cannot be changed. To repent Lancelot now would be to betray everything, and that I would not do.

"Will you take the sacrament, and say the lord's prayer?" he asked me.

I nodded. I would. And if I had time, or freedom, I would lie on the Round Table and pray to the ancient gods of my own people. I said the Latin words, though they were meaningless on my tongue, and only spilled from my memory without much thought, and I ate the bread and drank the wine without tasting them. I was glad when the priest left, though sorry that, as he shut the door behind him, I saw that I was guarded and I could not go down to the Round Table. I felt that right now that was the only thing with the power to save me. Or Lancelot, or Marie. For others I cared about were in danger because of me. Perhaps even Arthur as well. Mordred, after all, still lived.

I sat at the window, gazing out onto the fields that now stood empty behind Camelot. I could not see anything that might be a pyre there. Perhaps they would burn me in the centre of the courtyard. That did not seem very likely. Mordred, at least, would want to make a spectacle of it, encourage the peasants to come from nearby. It was approaching midday by now, but it was overcast, a dull autumn day heavy with coming rain. I should have liked to feel the sun on my skin once more, but memory would have to be enough.

I heard someone come through the door and looked up. I thought for a moment it was Arthur, returned to say goodbye. I recognised the red and gold surcoat as his. But it was not him, it was Mordred, dressed in his father's clothes, a coil of rope hanging from one hand. So, Mordred had at last earned Arthur's trust, and I had been the price.

"Stand up," Mordred ordered, roughly. I could see that he had a fine cut down across his face, from the forehead to the cheek. That must have been from his fight with Lancelot the night before. Also, he moved slightly awkwardly, as though his left leg was hurt. Only he, from what I could tell, had faced Lancelot last night and lived, though Lancelot had left my room unarmed.

I stood up, and he seized hold of me, turning me away from him and pulling my arms roughly behind me to tie behind my back. I didn't care now. I felt numb, and hollow, and there was nothing more that he could do to me. He was deliberately rough binding my hands, but I barely felt it. I was already leaving my body behind.

When he was finished, he pulled me hard against him, and I felt his breath against my neck and he leaned close to whisper in my ear.

"I thought I might have you once, at least." His lips brushed against my neck. I might have been disgusted before, but I felt empty and absent now. "But I think I will get as much satisfaction," he reached round and, putting one hand on my stomach, held me closer against him, "from watching you burn."

I stared out at the empty fields, thinking of Lancelot far away, and hopefully safe, as Mordred, bored with my lack of response, moved away. Lancelot would not think this could happen so soon. He might not even yet be at Joyous Guard for the news to reach him. But perhaps that was better, for when I was gone, he would be safe.

"It is time, now." I heard Ector's voice from the door, and turned back to see him. No, he was not angry with me. He was only sad, and tense. I did not blame him. But I was hit suddenly hard by the thought that Arthur was not coming back to see me, to say goodbye, before they took me to the pyre.

"Arthur... Arthur is not coming to say goodbye?" I asked Ector in a small, quavering voice. He shook his head sadly, and I nodded, gathering myself. So that was the way it would be, then.

Mordred grabbed me by the arm and led me down the stairs. I went with him limply, the only thoughts in my head being that after I was gone, at least Lancelot might go to France and live far away and in peace, and Arthur might forget. They might both find other women and live happy lives. They still had time. And for me, the pain that numbed me through would be gone, and I would dissolve into blissful nothingness.

When we came out of the tower, it was clear that men had been hard at work all morning. At the mouth of Camelot's great gates, a small wooden platform had been set up, and before it, outside the castle walls, a crowd was gathered, eagerly waiting. I could see the pyre, and men beside it holding torches, in the distance. The light breeze brought to me the acrid smell of burning pitch. Soon, it would be close enough to sear in my nostrils. Perhaps I would choke quickly on the smoke, and it would all be over fast.

The crowd was made up of people from within the castle – some knights and ladies, some servants – and people from the surrounding villages. Peasants who had come to stare at one of those above them brought low. They loved that, I was sure, above all things.

Mordred led me up to the platform where Gareth and Gaheris stood, unarmed, waiting to lead me to the pyre. I caught Gareth's eye as I climbed the few wooden steps up to stand beside him, and saw disappointment there that cut me to the heart, even now I thought that I could feel nothing. But I had never asked Gareth to trust me, or think that I was good. And Gaheris, he was no different from me in what *he* did, only he was a man and not the queen. Though, when I caught *his* eye, I saw no judgement there, at least. I wondered if Marie was in the crowd beneath us. I glanced through it for her, but saw nothing. I did, far at the back, see a flash of white hair, and blue beneath that might have been patterns of woad. I could not be sure, but I thought it was Nimue.

Mordred pushed me roughly to the front of the platform, and began to shout.

"People of Camelot, we have before you a traitor queen, brought to the fire for her crimes."

People cheered; some threw things, though all of them missed. I heard the shouts I had expected of *traitor, whore* and *witch*. A gentle breeze brushed my face and lifted the strands of my hair that were free about my face, and I closed my eyes, shutting out the shouts and the sight of the pyre to feel the lovely breeze against my skin one last time. A gentle drizzle was beginning to fall. That was a shame, for it would dull the heat of the fire a little, and make the burning longer, but it was pleasant, like the brush of a kiss, against my face. I breathed in the air, fresh and heady with autumn smells: the new-cut hay, the leaves composting on the ground. It was lovely. I thought also of Lancelot, of the wonderful rapture we had had together in each other's arms only the night before: the moonlight on his skin, his lips against my own, his hands on me, his eyes. Our love was so great that when our bodies came together I could scarcely bear the ecstasy of it, the perfectness of our union. We belonged utterly to each other, and the love between us to the whole world, the earth, and the stars, and the power of the seasons. It was everything. I thought, too, of Arthur, of the hungry roughness of his touch that I loved, the safe and powerful feeling of being in his arms. I had loved him truly, too, in all his wildness, in all our overwhelming passion for one another. From the ugly anger and hate I had brought with me over the sea, his touch and his goodness had made love, a deep and steady love that felt like a part of my bones. I would go to the fire knowing I had had two great loves, and I had given them both everything I could give to each of them, and had them both fully in my two hearts. I could go regretting nothing.

As the shouting died down I opened my eyes again. Mordred was shouting again, gesturing to the crowd to part so that I could be led out to the fire. The men, far away, readied their torches, weighing them in their hands, ready to touch them to the base of the pyre. The flames of the torches against the grey sky glowed orange, and then red. Gareth and Gaheris came either side of me, and each held one of my arms. I thought we were about to step down the steps into the crowd when Mordred stepped down in front of us, his back to the crowd. His eyes caught mine with a flash of sadistic enjoyment, as he reached forward and grasped the front of the green dress with both hands, and tore. Under his hands, the thick fabric shredded like paper, and the crowd behind him cheered. I could see the angry faces of those at the front, all unfamiliar to me, all come to enjoy the spectacle, hungry for blood. Mordred tore open the arms as well, and pulled the dress away in pieces, tossing them to the crowd who bayed with appreciation. I felt the drizzle and the cool autumn air against my skin through the thin underdress, and I saw even now Mordred's eyes roving over my body, its shape half-visible through the thin white fabric. He reached out again for the underdress, but Gareth beside me said softly,

"Mordred, don't."

Mordred satisfied himself instead with pulling loose my hair; I did not want to react, but the painful pricking against my scalp as he tore free my hair brought tears to my eyes against my will. Then he spotted the circlet. He snatched it from my head, and crushed the thin gold flat in his hand, twisting it together into a shapeless lump of warped metal, and throwing it into the crowd where the peasants below us scrabbled after it. It would be a rich prize for whoever got it. If I had thought I was going to live, I would have been sorry for its loss, but it was late for suffering or regret now.

At last Mordred stepped away, and slowly Gareth and Gaheris began to lead me wordlessly through the crowd. The shouting of the people close by pressed around me, but I barely heard it. Gareth whispered beside me, and that one quiet voice, wrought with blistering emotion, cut through to me.

"I thought you were perfect. You don't know how many times I defended you, saying you'd never –"

He couldn't finish. He didn't have the courage. I had never asked him to believe anything about me. I had never asked *any* of them to think anything about me. I had never even asked Arthur to believe I was faithful. It struck me suddenly that Arthur had never asked *me* if it were true or not. I supposed that he thought that since I had come to him little more than a prisoner, and he had won me round from hating him that I was *his* and that was the end of it. I supposed that he had assumed that I was always happy with him. *He never asked me.* Perhaps I would have told him, if he had. It was easy to lie with silence, but I might have given up my secrets if he had ever just asked. Might have. Still, I felt sorry for what I had done to Arthur, and it hurt me, too, to have hurt Gareth, who as a boy had been something like a child of my own, even if it was only for a short while. I kept my eyes on the fire, or the bundle of dampening wood. It would catch still; some of the logs were black with tar and pitch.

I began to wonder if Arthur and Gawain had ridden out early to try to catch Lancelot on the road, on his way to Joyous Guard. Perhaps he was dead already. I was glad I did not know. I was happier going to my death thinking that those I had left behind might be able to be happy after I was gone.

Suddenly, I heard screaming, and I looked up. Gareth and Gaheris stopped either side of me. I looked around and I couldn't see anything apart from the crowd, rushing now against itself, but I could hear the sound of horses' hooves. As I looked around for where the noises were coming from, Gareth suddenly shouted out to Gaheris, letting go of me to step out in front of his brother. I looked up to see a horse rearing over us, the crowd scattering behind it, and a flash of steel. I felt blood spatter across me. I did not know whose. A hand reached down from the horse, and I took it, jumping up into the saddle in front of the rider. It was Lancelot. He pulled off his cloak and wrapped it around me, tearing the rope from around my wrists, and holding me to him. He dug his heels into his horse, turning it away from the crowd already, and it galloped off, hard. His eyes were wild and unfocussed, but he still held me firm against him, and kissed me on the cheek, rough with relief.

"You're safe," he breathed into my ear. I didn't know if he was comforting me more, or himself.

I leaned back against him and closed my eyes, feeling the horse move fast beneath us, and the wind rush past me. He had come back, as he had always said that he would. I didn't know how he had come in time, but he had. Sitting against him, saved from death, made me think of a time a long, long time ago, when he had snatched me from beneath my horse on the battlefield, when it had all begun. I had an unsettling feeling deep within me that this was both a new beginning, and an ending.

Chapter Forty-Six

It was almost dawn again by the time we arrived at Joyous Guard. I did not know how Lancelot had ridden there so fast. I had thought Camelot was a castle built for siege, but Joyous Guard was truly a fortress. Tall, narrow and warlike, with sheer walls around it and a barbican gate, it stood against the lightening sky like a quiet monolith, stern and impregnable.

There must have been men waiting for our arrival, because the portcullis was raised as Lancelot rode towards it, letting us into the small courtyard. It was dark still, but in the courtyard were men waiting with torches. At the front of the group I recognised Kay, dressed in his black armour, his face grim in the flickering light of the torch he held before him. Lancelot slid from his horse as he was through the gate and I followed. The horse, foaming with sweat and exhausted, sank slowly to its knees. I gathered the cloak more tightly around me under the gaze of so many men, aware suddenly that my hair was loose and tangled, and I was spattered with blood. Lancelot stood beside me and put an arm around me, gathering me to him in front of the band of men who had ridden from Camelot for his sake. I saw to my surprise that it must have been almost half of the knights – all of those who were kin to Lancelot, and a few others, Lamerocke among them, whom I recognised, as well as young men, new-made knights who Lancelot himself had trained.

We all stood in silence. Words could not encompass how much had changed, what line had been crossed to bring so many men from Camelot to Lancelot's fortress. What line had been crossed when he brought *me* here. It could only mean war, and war in part for my sake, though I knew some of it was caused by Mordred's hard ambition.

Kay wordlessly walked past us, to look at Lancelot's exhausted horse, and the men with torches began to dissipate. I was surprised to hear approving murmurs among them, as though they thought Lancelot had done the right thing to bring me from the fire to here. So, Camelot's truth was not the only truth, and not everyone thought I was a traitoress, a witch and a whore. I was glad of that at least.

Lancelot drew me closer, and kissed me softly. "I will get you a bath," he said tenderly, stroking my cheek. His face flickered with anger as he noticed my split lip, the bruise swelling against my jaw, but he said nothing, just brushed them with his fingertips.

"Lancelot," Kay called out behind us, and we turned around. In his hand Lancelot's sword, drawn from its scabbard on the saddle of his horse, shone in the torchlight. It was dark red with blood. "Who?" he asked.

Lancelot shook his head, his face blank, his eyes wide and stunned.

"I don't know," he admitted. In the thick of the crowd, his wild, desperate eyes had seen only me.

As it came back to me, the moment when he had rescued me, I realised that I knew. Gareth stepping in front of Gaheris, the flash of the sword. I knew, but I could not bear to say. Not then. But I could see from Kay's face that Kay was afraid it was Arthur. Still, I did not have the strength in me, not then, to say.

Joyous Guard was readying itself for siege. As Lancelot led me up the stairs in one of its great towers I could not fail to notice all the armour and weapons lying by, the food in barrels, the lack of women and children. Joyous Guard had emptied out its vulnerable and had only soldiers left. I was sure I was the only woman. Isolde, sadly, was long gone. I was not sure, anyway, that her dull presence would have been a comfort to me now.

A lot of the rooms we passed were bare, and empty. Joyous Guard was not a large castle, but still was built to hold more than the small band of knights it housed now. Still, small as they were, there was no telling if the castle's stores would last them through a winter of siege. We came to a room at the top of one of the corner towers that had a fire burning low in the fireplace, and a richly laid bed strewn with silks of purple and gold, with thick brocade curtains, and a fur rug beside the fireplace of some dark, exotic animal. There was a dress draped over the back of the chair by the bed that must have been Isolde's. I assumed this had been her room, since in all my time at Camelot I had not heard of any other woman living at Joyous Guard. It was not a castle built for family life, after all.

Lancelot left me in the room for a moment to fetch a bathtub and a copper pot of water to heat on the fire and I stood in the centre of this room, this other woman's room, with her things still on the table beside the window, on the chair beside the bed. I wondered if the sheets had been changed since she had slept in them with Tristan. I wondered if I would feel her ghost against my skin as I slept. A circlet of pale gold, almost white, sat on the table. Isolde's crown, I recognised that, set with a single pale sapphire in the shape of a teardrop surrounded on either side by a row of pearls. A beautiful thing, far finer than my circlet. Still, I missed my own already. It was probably already trampled into the dirt, lost forever in the fervency of the peasants to get at it. I had lost Marie as well, left behind at Camelot. Those last two memories of my home gone now, perhaps forever. And Gareth and Gaheris dead. I wonder if Marie knew yet. I did not cry for them, not yet. I was too stunned. I felt their deaths lodge within me, low down. I was numb to them now, but when I was ready I would cry. Those sorrows were waiting for me, deep below the surface.

Lancelot was soon back and set the copper pot on the fire. He closed the door behind him, and at last we were alone together, no longer rushing toward life or safety. I realised then that all day I had been tense, holding my breath. I sighed it out as he came to me, taking my face in his hands. His thumb brushed my split lip.

"Did... Arthur do that to you?" he asked in a whisper. I shook my head, and I saw the relief pass over his face. But then, after the relief, his expression hardened to anger. "Still, he should not have put you to the fire."

"He was angry," I found myself saying. "Besides, it was Mordred and Gawain who pushed him to do it." I did not know why I was defending him. He had agreed to it; he had refused to say goodbye. He would have had me go to my death without even a word for all the years we were happy together, and all that we had suffered together, or for the child. I felt the anger burn in me, too, to think of it.

"So Mordred lived," Lancelot said, thoughtfully, his thumb stroking across my cut and swollen lip again. Mordred must have played dead, then, when Lancelot escaped. Hidden like a coward, waiting for me to be vulnerable and alone. "This is his work, then." I nodded. "I will kill him for this, for everything."

Lancelot kissed me lightly, moving away to pour the water, steaming on the fire, into the bathtub before I could sink against him, into his arms as I longed to.

"I did not think you would come in time. How did you get back so fast?" I asked softly.

He poured the water into the tub, his back to me. The light from the fire in the pre-dawn darkness lit his shirt through with orange, and through the shirt I could see the silhouette in black of his body underneath, powerful and strong. I just wanted to feel his arms around me, and close my eyes and know that I had survived.

"I never made it to Joyous Guard last night," he answered, turning over his shoulder to meet my gaze when the water was poured. "I made it into the woods, and then I couldn't stop thinking about you there alone, wondering what had happened to you. I decided to ride back, and I was glad I did, because by the time I reached the edge of the woods again they were already building the pyre."

I nodded again. I could feel that the shock of it all was reaching me; my hands were beginning to shake, and my voice did not feel safe to speak with. Lancelot ran a hand through his hair, pushing it back from his face.

"It's ready," he said, gesturing at the bath.

My shaking hands fumbled on the laces of the underdress and I could not get them undone. He came over and gently loosened them, and lifted the dress lightly over my head. I did not realise how cold I had been until I stepped into the water and felt its heat seep through into my bones. I had ridden, I supposed, through the depths of a sharp autumn night in my underdress, so it was no wonder, but I had not felt the cold until now. I shivered in the steaming water.

Lancelot pulled off his boots and sat cross-legged beside the bath, dipping his hand into the water and rubbing the blood gently from my face. I watched him, his face close but his expression distant with concentration. I did not know whose blood it was, and I pushed the thought from my mind. I reached out and lightly touched his cheek and our eyes met. There was relief there, and a complex sadness. I wished that I had something to say, but nothing seemed right. He kissed me softly and stood to pull off his shirt and breeches and get into the bath behind me. I leaned back against him, closing my eyes, feeling his skin against mine, warm and delicious, filling me with a pleasant slow, hazy desire for him, tired and sore as I was. He ran his hands slowly down my arms and back up again, slowly through my hair, stroking my shoulders, down my body, over my thighs. In the hot water his touch was gentle and warming; it felt as though it was bringing me back to life. I turned over my shoulder and our noses brushed, and then our mouths came together in a passionate meeting that for me was filled, too, with all the relief of being alive. As we kissed, I felt his hand stroke lightly between my legs and the hunger for him lit fast within me, although I was exhausted. I reached my hands into his hair, pulling him closer, and I felt his other hand stroke lightly against my breast and I moaned in soft delight at his touch. He stood, stepping from the bath and offering me his hand to help me from it, too, and we lay side by side on the rug beside the fire. I felt its warmth on my skin, this fire safe and low. It was a strange thought, the comfort of this fire, when the last fire I had looked on was one meant to consume me into nothingness. Lancelot moved over me to kiss me, and I ran my hands up his back, feeling the muscles ripple underneath, drawing him over me, our bodies still damp from the bath, and hot with it. I arched my back, pressing my body against his, and he gave a low groan of desire, pressing back against me. But then he stopped, his hand brushing my cheek, his face close over me.

"Are you sure?" he whispered.

I was stunned for a moment. Arthur had never asked me if I had *wanted* it. Never. Not even when I had stood before him with Meleagant's bruises all over my body, when I had stood there telling him that another man had tried to force himself on me, had Arthur ever asked me what I wanted. I did not blame him for it. That was the kind of love that we had had; that was the kind of man he was. That was the only comfort he had known how to offer me. And I had not *not* wanted it. Suddenly I saw myself as Lancelot must have seen me – trembling and broken, my lip swollen, my wrists burned and rubbed raw by the rope, bruised and vulnerable. No wonder he hesitated.

"I thought I would be dead by now, yesterday morning," I whispered back. "I just want to feel alive."

He understood. The closeness of his body filled my own with heat and life, made my heart race, my skin flush with desire. I had not expected it, either. Not expected to be filled with desire from the edge of death, but here it was, anchoring me to life, and to him. His touch filled me with a sparkling electricity, and a yearning that was vivid and powerful. There was no life as intense and overwhelming as what I felt with him. It was the beating heart of the entire universe. I wound my hands into his damp hair and kissed him hard. He moved slowly into me, and I gasped with pleasure. I felt the softness of the fur rug beneath my back, the warmth of the fire against my face, the headiness of our bodies coming together all around me as we moved together, the heat and life filling me, his lips against mine, against my neck, his hands against my hips, moving me with him, slow and tender, until I sighed for him, and he for me and he wrapped me in his arms, both of us breathing hard with relief. And I thought, *I'm alive.*

Chapter Forty-Seven

I must have slept for a whole day, or more, because when I woke it was dawn again. I slept deep and dreamlessly, and woke disorientated, not knowing where I was, only half-remembering why I was not in my own bed. The last piece of it to come back to me was Gareth and Gaheris. I would have to tell Lancelot today. He had gone already, though he had slept beside me, his arms around me, through most of the night.

I got up and looked around the room. My underdress lay against the chair, but it was stained with blood and dirty from the ride. I found some dresses of Isolde's in a wardrobe, but I did not think any of them would fit me, or suit me, and besides I did not want to wear another woman's clothes. There were some men's clothes as well, which must have been Tristan's. Tristan was small and slight for a man, and the clothes fitted me well enough. Besides, now the castle was preparing for siege it did not seem that sensible to dress in women's clothes. If I could have brought anything from Camelot I would have brought the hunting leathers or the light suit of armour I had worn to Rome, but men's clothes would have to do. I plaited my hair, but had nothing to tie it with, and in Isolde's things there were only little pins and fine gold nets, nothing I knew how to tie my own hair with, nothing that seemed strong enough to hold back the wild curls of it, so I left it untied. It seemed a little late to care for appearances now. I tied Lancelot's black wool cloak that he had wrapped around me when he had saved me from the fire around my shoulders and walked down to the courtyard.

Lancelot was there with Kay and Bors, standing by the barbican gate. It looked as though they were arguing about something. The courtyard was full of knights who looked as though they were waiting for battle already, dressed in their armour, sharpening their swords, their faces full of wary waiting. I caught Lamerocke's eye as I walked past, and he gave me a respectful nod of greeting once he recognised me, after a moment of confusion at my strange clothes.

As I got closer, I could hear what they were arguing about.

"My father is still in Camelot," Kay was saying, holding his voice just below a shout. Clearly, they did not want the other knights to know that they were arguing. "I'm sure that Arthur will protect him for now, but if Gawain is calling out for blood, for *all* our blood, then we need to listen to Arthur's terms. Life is more important than honour, Bors."

"So you want us to wait here for a siege? We should take the queen and go to France and –"

Bors fell silent when he saw me approaching. He shifted awkwardly on his feet, as though he would rather that I did not even know what was happening, but was simply passed around like a bargaining token. Perhaps that would have made it easier. Though I thought at this point it was greater than a matter of politics and honour. Especially since if they were talking about Gawain and blood then that meant that news had come to Joyous Guard that Lancelot had killed Gareth and Gaheris. Three of Gawain's brothers dead by his sword. No, I did not think that Gawain would ever forget that.

"If we run," Lancelot replied evenly, "that is an admission of guilt. We stay here, and when Arthur – if Arthur – sends terms for peace then we can tell him the truth; that we only have the queen here for her protection." He glanced at me, warily. Kay and Bors exchanged a look that suggested that they did not think this was the *whole* truth any more than Arthur would think so. "Is that alright?" Lancelot asked me, and I nodded. I did not see what choice I had.

"Arthur *will* send terms for peace," Kay reassured him. "His anger tires itself out quickly. It's Gawain I would worry about."

Lancelot nodded thoughtfully.

After a moment, Kay added hesitantly, "Lancelot... Arthur will want Guinevere back."

Lancelot nodded and pressed the heel of his hand to his forehead. There was still the real possibility that once he had me back, he would put me to the fire, and succeed this time.

Kay sighed. "Well, we don't have to think about that now. Now, we wait."

He left with Bors, back into the crowd of knights preparing themselves for battle. Lancelot turned to me, and a little smile grew on his face when he saw what I was wearing.

"No, I can't say I can picture you in Isolde's clothes, either." He smiled gently, and kissed me softly.

It was easier than I had thought it would be. My life had changed in an instant, and now he and I were here together and it was *our* life together, and Arthur was outside of that, a distant threat that we could not see. I was still angry that he had sent me to my death, so I felt no guilt. No one in Joyous Guard seemed to think anything of it. I wondered if Bors might not be right; if it might not be better for me to ride to Lancelot's lands in France with him. The other option eventually led me back to the husband who had tried to burn me, and I did not want that. Still, it was to him that I still belonged, and lovely as this dream was, somewhere deep down I already knew it would end. But I pushed away that thought.

I decided to climb up onto the battlements of Joyous Guard. Camelot had had battlements, but they had always been thick with sentries guarding them, and I had never wanted to stand on them and look out at empty fields. But I wanted to now, to stand up high on Joyous Guard and look out at the land around me, see what kind of place I had come to.

When I climbed the narrow stone stairs all the way to the top and emerged into the stiff early winter breeze I felt a thrill of excitement to be up high, close to the elements. Joyous Guard was a lot taller than Camelot, which I thought I could perhaps see, a small black square on a hill that was grey-blue on the horizon. There was a fleck of rain in the air, but no drops falling, and the rough breeze lifted my loose hair around me as I stared out across the ground below me. I walked around the narrow footway atop the fortress, gazing out onto the land beneath, greyed under the heavy clouds with a wintry half-light. I saw a man ahead of me, leaning against the crenellations, gazing out into the distance, and as I came closer I saw it was Kay. The breeze lifted his hair lightly from his brow, short but dark and thick like the pelt of a wildcat. He looked up as he saw me, and gave a little nod that I could not read. I couldn't tell if he wanted me to stop and talk to him or not, but as I came closer, he pushed himself up to stand straight before me and gave me a half-smile.

"Men's clothes suit you," he told me. I couldn't tell from his tone if he was trying to be kind or making fun of me. Sometimes they were the same thing to Kay, anyway. The look he gave me was strange and narrow. I supposed he was thinking of his father, far away in Camelot.

I shrugged. "I hardly thought any of Isolde's dresses would fit me."

Kay's smile spread further across his face.

"Oh, you got them from the bedroom?" Kay said it as though there were only one in the whole place. Perhaps that was so; it was a fortress, after all, not a castle designed for comfortable living. I supposed the rest of the castle must have been equipped more like soldiers' barracks.

"Yes. I think they're Tristan's."

Kay shook his head.

"They're mine." I didn't believe him. Kay was twice the size of me. "No, they are." He laughed. "You're wearing the clothes I wore when I was twelve."

I wasn't sure if he was teasing me or not. I was not sure I believed that even he was as tall as I was as an adult when he was twelve, but if it was true of anyone it was true of Kay. I supposed it made sense that things of his would be in the castle. What did it say about Tristan that he had not left anything behind him?

Kay cast a thoughtful eye over me as I stood before him, my arms crossed around me to hold the cloak tight, keeping out the wind, my hair falling completely loose from its plait already without anything to tie it with, and blowing before my face.

"Are you alright? You're not hurt?"

I shrugged again.

"I'm well enough."

Kay turned back to the view, resting his forearms against the stone wall of the battlements and leaning over them.

"Let's hope that lasts. There will be war again soon," he said darkly.

I leaned against the wall beside him, facing the opposite way, towards the centre of Joyous Guard, the courtyard, the other wall and, beyond that, the grey-brown scraps of a forest that had already lost most of its leaves for winter.

"I wish it did not have to come to this," I said, softly.

Kay, beside me, pushed himself back up slowly.

"It didn't *have* to come to this. If you and Lancelot had managed to keep your hands off one another we would all still be in Camelot enjoying peace and plenty. And good wine." His voice was harsh and bitter. I turned to him, already flushed with anger, my mouth opened to protest, but he carried on. "It was a long time ago that you told me it was all over. And then *this*. What happened? I thought you had finished it."

"We did," I told him, shaking my head slowly and holding my hands out before me, palms up, in confused surrender to it. I didn't understand either why it had been so impossible. "But, it just *was*. Neither of us can help it."

I saw the anger harden behind Kay's eyes. He folded his arms before him and leaned back against the wall, regarding me narrowly and chewing his lip.

"Nothing is ever your fault, is it, Guinevere?"

"No, Kay –"

"No, you *listen*." The power of his sudden anger stunned the indignation out of me. He was flushed and shouting, I could see the intensity of the real anger in his eyes; it had come to him in a sudden wild flash, and it frightened me a little, though I did not show it. "You go through your life as though everything you do is something you can't *help* doing, or something someone else has done to you, but this wasn't beyond your control. What you felt was, but what you *did* wasn't. You're not just some woman in a village somewhere who can do what she pleases. You're the queen. And *you* did this. This wasn't done to you. I don't think you ever think about anyone else. You just do whatever you *feel* you *need* to do, rather than doing what is your duty. A woman like you ought never to have become a queen."

I was angry, too, now. The fear and surprise had passed quickly and I stepped forward towards him, clenching my fists at my sides. I felt my nails dig hard into my palms, but the heat of it was high in me and I felt no pain. How *dare* he suggest I had not made a good queen. But I was sure I knew what made him so particularly angry with me.

"Don't talk to me like you wouldn't have done exactly as Lancelot did, if I had offered you the opportunity."

Kay laughed, and it was harsh and cruel, leaning forward over me, to meet my anger with his own.

"Well, I suppose that wasn't your fault either, was it? It wasn't your fault when you led me up to your bedroom, and pressed yourself against me, only to change your mind at the last moment."

"That's not how it happened, Kay." I felt the instinct in me rise to lift my hand and slap him across the face but for the moment I restrained it.

"Isn't it? That's how *I* remember it." He sighed in frustration, and the anger drained out of him as fast as it had come. He turned away from me and ran a hand through his hair, gazing back across the courtyard. "I've left Arthur behind. Arthur who will always be my brother, even if we don't have any blood in common." He glanced at me, his eyes flashing. "But don't think I came for your sake." He glanced back away. "I came because Lancelot asked me to. And because I don't trust Mordred and Gawain. I left my father in Camelot. Gawain will be after his blood. How many of Lancelot's half-brothers, nephews and cousins do you think he will be satisfied with as blood-payment for Gareth? I wouldn't put my money on anything less than all of us." Kay sighed again, deeply, shaking his head. "It would have been easier if Lancelot had killed Arthur rather than Gawain's brothers. Then, Lancelot and Mordred would have fought for the throne, and the winner would have married you and it would be over fast." Kay stood up straight, shrugging his cloak closer around his shoulders. He turned to me and fixed me with a look that rooted me to the spot. "Don't fool yourself that you had no control over this. No one else is fooled."

He turned and left. I wished that I had slapped him. I had been too stunned to respond. I had not thought that Kay would think those things about me. I felt the cold more intensely after he had gone, and I went down from the battlements quickly, but as fast as I went, I could not chase Kay's words from my head where they went round and round like a curse.

Chapter Forty-Eight

Life at Joyous Guard took on a strange normality, a kind of surreal domesticity. Lancelot and I walked the battlements together, watched the men training together, ate our meals together, sometimes with Kay – who had been kind and gently remorseful after what he had said to me on the battlements, though he never apologised – and Bors, sometimes alone, and we slept in each other's arms every night. But while Arthur had always wanted to bury his worries and his troubles in me, and our coming together had held for both of us a touch of delicious oblivion where we lost ourselves, Lancelot was quiet and thoughtful about his troubles, and the love of our bodies did not seem to offer him the same kind of erasure. He worried about his men, about what would become of me, and he felt guilty about his broken promises to Arthur, though he went about the castle and spoke as though no such thing had taken place and I was there being guarded for Arthur until he could be sure my return would be safe. No one questioned this, though everyone knew we slept in the same bedroom, and he kissed me openly in front of his men. I was happy, with him, but I knew that it could not be for ever, or even for long.

I was also surprised to realise that I missed Arthur. Once the anger that he had sent me to my death faded, I found I felt my guilt as a hard lump in my stomach. I missed Arthur's simplicity, his rough and easy needs, his moods that passed quickly. Lancelot was quiet and complex, and I could not offer him the simple comfort that Arthur had taken from the closeness of my body. It was better, and it was worse, but most of all it was different. I did not feel that I lacked anything with Lancelot, only that, just as I had not been whole without him, I lacked in a different way without Arthur. Still, I knew if I was honest with myself, I would have been happier living the rest of my life without Arthur than I would without Lancelot. Lancelot shared his thoughtful worries with me, whispering to me in the night as we lay together, and encouraged me to take the sword in my hand again, even having a few gentle training fights with me himself. I could tell that he came against me as though I were a child, and even then I felt behind every little tap the power of his body, and the control he had over it. I knew I was still strong and my childhood skills had not been wholly forgotten, but I knew that I would not ride out to battle. It was comforting, to feel the sword again, to feel my own strength, that it had not entirely left me, but I knew it was nothing but a gesture. I would not ride out against Arthur. I could not bear the thought that I might meet him on the battlefield. I would not face him there. We were not enemies. For once I was glad that I was a woman, and no one could make me fight.

Still, it made me wonder what kind of queen I would have been if Arthur had never asked for me as his wife. I would have stayed in my home, among my people and their ways. I would have dressed in armour, rather than silks. I would have ridden at the head of my army. I would have been a queen like my mother, like my ancestor Maev. No, that was a fantasy. An illusion. That way was gone. Arthur's knights with their heavy armour and their broadswords had torn my mother's Breton army to pieces. Our ways were gone. The world had changed. I could not lift the heavy weapons the British smiths made for the men to bear, and the light Breton weapons I had borne as a young girl would not even have dented the armour of the knights, nor was I broad enough in the shoulders to carry on my back such thick, heavy iron armour as they wore. So I had changed. I had adapted to survive. There had been no place in Arthur's new world for warrior queens, though he had liked it enough when I was an exotic thing to be looked upon in my hunting leathers. I had become a different kind of queen. A queen of secrets. I had hidden away my warrior's blood, and been a lady of graces, and politics, and the new way of war, the shows of strength, the pageantry, the terse false politeness of Arthur's civilized world. I had strangled with it. I had wanted to be free. Now I was sure that there was no way to go back, and in my yearning for the freedom I had lost, I had destroyed everything that I had.

I had dreamed once of spending all my days and nights with Lancelot like this, and now I had it, it was both beautiful and awful. I was aware how fragile a thing I had, and how it could not last. I knew this, I *knew*, and yet even after Lancelot and I stood each day on the battlements and saw more and more pavilions rise up on the fields surrounding Joyous Guard, I could not bear to think too hard about how all this was just an illusion. When Arthur's pavilion was raised among them, it felt painfully unexpected, and far too soon.

I recognised his pavilion among the others, the white and blue dragon banner flapping high above the others, and beside it Gawain's with the colours of Lothian and Orkney. Men within Joyous Guard began to talk of siege and shame, of wanting to ride out into the open field and fight. Men had come to Joyous Guard to fight for Lancelot, and the castle was full of knights and noblemen, but it was nothing to the number that had gathered with Arthur and Gawain. Palomides had come to us, and a knight called Urry, whose limbs were marked with huge scars that twisted across them, and who seemed to owe his life to Lancelot, came with a large party; but Lamerocke had ridden out with a few men to try and bring people from the village of Joyous Guard to safety within the castle, and Gawain and his knights from Lothian had killed them all. At night, sometimes the shouting of the men camped outside Joyous Guard reached us, shouting for Lancelot's blood, calling him coward and traitor, and daring him to come out of his castle with his knights and make open war with Arthur.

The stores were dwindling already. The influx of knights wanting to fight for Lancelot's cause – and mine as well, I supposed – brought not only their swords for battle but their hungry stomachs, and bodies that needed warmth now that we were in the depths of winter. One night, we heard a soft knocking at a back door low down in the store rooms and opened it to find it was Ector. Lancelot said nothing, but wordlessly took his ageing half-brother in his arms. Ector, too, had heard the call of blood. It seemed, then, as though this was a war that was going to call people back to their kin. I thought of Marie, the closest thing I had to family from Carhais. I hoped that she was safe in Camelot.

Kay was almost back to his old self when he knew that his father was safe within the walls of Joyous Guard, not surrendered by Arthur into Gawain's vengeful hands. I think enmity with Arthur still played on his mind, but he seemed as if a weight had been lifted from him. But talk rose and rose around us of the men eager to ride out and face the armies gathered outside. There were many who had reason to hate Gawain, and were eager for their own personal revenge, and Lancelot's kin wanted to refute Arthur's charge of treason against him, since it was shame to them as well. The time came when it could no longer be delayed and put aside, and in the depths of winter when the ground was hard and the blades of grass white with frost every morning, and my breath rose beside Lancelot's on the battlements in thick clouds of steam, he looked out at the men gathered beneath his fortress, and thought of the food stores below us growing less and less, and he turned to Kay, Bors and Ector who stood there with us and he said,

"Prepare the men for war. Tomorrow we can ride out."

That night, we ate in the bedroom with Kay, Bors and Ector. There was not all that much firewood left, and it was freezing cold outside, so we often ate like that, all huddled in one room around a fire. Lancelot only wanted to heat the one room. Outside, it grew dark early, and against the shut window the heat of our breath and the fire inside steamed the pane. The five of us sat on the floor to eat, Lancelot and I on the rug, Bors, Ector and Kay on cushions from the bed. There wasn't much food to be had, and what we ate was a simple stew of potatoes and vegetables, but even that seemed dangerously too much when I had gazed down into the barrel at how little was left. Bors wanted to talk of battle and war – he was eager for it, I could see that – but I didn't want to listen. Kay had found some wine somewhere in the cellars and the wine made up for the lack of food a little. He kept everyone's cup full, but he and I drank faster than the others. I think we two were the most anxious about what the next day's battle would bring. I did not want to think of Lancelot riding out to clash with Arthur. Either way, I would lose one of them, and though Kay seemed sorry for what he had said I could not stop thinking that whatever happened would be my fault, entirely. So, I drank until I felt the heat of the fire glow like a warm touch against my face and the guilt recede at the edge of my thoughts, and my body grow light and fuzzy.

Ector and Bors left early, Ector tired, his old bones aching with the cold, and Bors eager to sleep and wake ready for war the next day. As soon as he left, Lancelot groaned and drained his cup of wine. He, clearly, was not looking forward to it any more than Kay or I were. Kay leaned over and filled his cup from the jug in his hand. He glanced at mine as he leaned back, and sloshed a little more in for good measure. I did not mind. I did not know how else I would sleep through the night. I leaned back against Lancelot, and he put his arm around me, letting me rest against his shoulder and turning towards me to kiss me tenderly. I put down my cup of wine to stroke his cheek. I wished Kay would leave. The wine had made me feel hot and ready with desire.

"Do you know what day it is?" Kay asked loudly, his words slurring a little.

Lancelot and I turned back to him, and Lancelot shook his head. I could see that he was flushed a little from the wine, too. Bors' talk of battle had unsettled him, or at least made him think of what he might have to do tomorrow. I was sure that as angry as he had been, Lancelot would not want to fight Arthur.

"It's Christmas day," Kay declared, taking a deep drink from his cup.

I had not realised. The days had become meaningless to me. Still, I was surprised that so much time had slipped past me. Lancelot shrugged and made a little noise of nonchalant half-surprise, drinking from his cup again. I leaned against him, warm with desire for him. I didn't care it was Christmas. I wanted Kay to go so that we could be alone.

But Kay stretched his legs out before him before the fire, like a cat, and leaned back on the heels of his hands.

"Do you remember," he asked me lazily, "that Christmas we almost... when you..." he waved his hand vaguely at Lancelot, half-unbalancing himself by lifting a hand, "you were looking for the Grail. She was so drunk, I think she thought I was you."

I kicked Kay with my bare foot, angry and embarrassed, blushing harder. I was afraid Lancelot would be angry or upset, but he laughed beside me and kissed the top of my head lightly.

"Oh Kay," he laughed, and I felt the wonderful familiar caress of his voice against me, deep and sweet with its tones of French. He did not seem to mind, and it seemed that Kay had said it more for Lancelot's sake than mine. "You were ever the same at Christmas time. Ever drunk, and in the mood for love. Yes, I remember something similar, from a long, long time ago."

I supposed if I had not been pleasantly dull with wine I would have thought more of it, perhaps been bothered by it. It just reminded me vaguely of something Arthur had said to me years and years before, that had just gone into my consciousness as a simple truth. I was surprised to see that Kay looked uncomfortable, and glanced at me with an anxiousness that I did not think someone who had drunk so much wine could muster. I poked him again with my bare toe, though more gently this time.

"Oh foolish Kay," I said softly, playfully. "Did you think I didn't know? No, I heard. Someone told me." I shied away from saying Arthur's name, from calling his ghost there into the room among us. Somehow it did not seem right. "I don't care," I added boldly. I wondered if I would care in the morning.

A wicked smile flashed across Kay's face, and he drained another cup of wine.

"Oh, you don't?"

He threw his cup aside, empty already, and it clattered across the floor. He moved over towards us on his hands and knees. Lancelot was laughing and I felt warm and silly as though some great game of Kay's was going to begin. I was hungry for any kind of distraction. By tomorrow evening we might all be dead. That was what hung unspoken between us all that night, and I was glad that no one said it. Kay kissed Lancelot lightly on the lips, and we all laughed, Lancelot lightly ruffling his hair and playfully pushing him away. But then their eyes caught on one another and Lancelot stopped laughing, and Kay kissed him again, in earnest this time. I saw Kay run a hand through Lancelot's hair as though he had done it many times before, and I saw the gentle, habitual passion of the way he held him. Lancelot seemed to yield to it, slowly letting his hands run up Kay's arms. I had thought I would feel angry, or jealous, but I found to my surprise that I felt a dangerous flicker of excitement within me to see it. They were both strong and powerful as they held one another, and I felt Kay's Otherworld strength mingling with the wine running through me, mixing in my blood, intoxicating.

Kay grasped Lancelot's shirt in his hand and pulled it roughly off, over his head. Lancelot's smile flickered across his face, surprised, pleased, excited. Then his eyes fell on me, wary at first, but seeing my wide-eyed look on the pair of them, and my flushed cheeks and my own little smile of excited surprise, he reached out a hand to me. I felt Kay's eyes fall on me, then, too, as he sat back on his heels, watching for what I would do. I took the hand that was offered me, and Lancelot pulled me against him, into his lap, between him and Kay, and my mouth against his, hungry, daring. I felt him slide one hand in my hair, the other around my waist, holding me fast against him as I wrapped my legs around his waist. I tasted wine on both our lips; I felt the heat of his skin, hot from the wine and the fire as I slowly trailed my hand down his bare chest. I felt light-headed, but pleasantly so, and the touch of his skin only increased it in me. Then I felt another pair of lips, cool against the flushed skin of my neck and my ear, and I turned aside from Lancelot to look over my shoulder at Kay behind me. My eyelids hung heavy, as the haze of the wine filled me, and I leaned towards him just a little, just enough that our lips met, at first soft and light, then harder, more passionate as I felt Lancelot's hands still on me, running up my bare back beneath the shirt, and his lips against my collarbone where the shirt was falling open, Kay's hands at my shoulders, sliding the shirt down. Where Lancelot was sensual and intense, and Arthur rough and hungry, Kay was powerful yet gentle, and with the wine, and the nearness of tomorrow rushing in my blood, clouding in my mind, I gave myself to it. I was breathing fast with excitement and anticipation already, a little dizzy with it. I could not tell whose hands were on me, whose mouth, whose skin I felt against mine, but I closed my eyes and sighed into it, blissfully giving myself away. I was half-lost between them already as, as soon as Kay's lips moved from mine, Lancelot came to kiss me again and I felt hands, I did not know whose, unlace my breeches and pull them away. I felt Lancelot's skin, and the warmth of the fire, against my bare legs, or perhaps it was Kay now, and they had switched places, because it was Kay kissing me again, and his hands tangling in my hair, though I only knew him from the feel of the Otherworld, and I put out a hand to feel the bare skin of his chest, though I did not remember seeing him take off his shirt. Lancelot pulled me back against him, playfully, lightly out of Kay's arms, and pulled the shirt which was hanging open on me anyway, over my head. I giggled softly as I fell against him, feeling our bodies brush together, skin against skin, as I had spent my life longing to feel. I stretched out my legs, wriggling my toes into the soft, thick rug, and I felt Kay's hands on my ankles, running up my legs as Lancelot turned my face round to meet him in a deep and sensual kiss over my shoulder. We were all naked now, though I did not remember undressing either one of them. They must have undressed one another. In the wine and the heat of it, the fuzzy, hazy pleasure of being lost between them, a mouth met mine with hot, hungry kisses, and I felt two hands wind in my hair, although they might not have belonged to the same man, and I felt a soft and gentle touch graze the inside of my thigh, and go between my legs, and I gasped. Whoever was kissing me paused to give an appreciative, low little laugh at my surprise, before the kiss became more deep and demanding, and the hand touching me firmer and more intense, and I felt the light catch within me. At my ear I heard a soft low whisper, in French, as Lancelot's lips moved down my neck, and a hand – possibly his – slowly and at first light and gentle, then hungry, across my breasts. They moved away from me for a moment to come together in a kiss again, Kay's hands in Lancelot's lovely hair, Lancelot with a hand pressed to Kay's chest, and in my delicious sleepy desire I lay back on the rug, feeling the silky tickle of it against my bare back. I stretched my arms over my head, lost in the intoxicating, disorientating drunken whirl of it all. One of them, maybe both, I could not tell, moved on to me and took me in his arms. I felt hands all over me, and everywhere I reached out, I found the softness of bare skin, and hard, exciting muscle, and velvety, inviting hair.

I lightly pushed over the man on top of me, whose kisses I felt brush lightly against my ear, and my neck, and as I moved on to him I saw it was Kay, his face half lit orange, half in dark shade from the firelight. I felt his hands slowly run up my thighs as our eyes met and I felt the spark of daring fire within me. I traced a hand down Kay's chest slowly. It rose and fell heavily with breaths of anticipation and desire as I followed down the dark line of hair from his navel. I felt Lancelot's hands go into my hair, and I turned over my shoulder to kiss him. As our mouths met, and I felt his tongue against mine, he slid his hands down my thighs, over Kay's hands, and they pulled me on to him, and I gasped. I felt an overwhelming rush of the Otherworld all about me, ancient and powerful and raw. Lancelot's mouth was still on mine, his hands sliding up my thighs to my breasts, but it was Kay I felt move inside me. I had one hand against Kay's muscular stomach, and the small, tempting trail of hairs, the other against Lancelot's strong thigh beside my own. I leaned my forehead against Lancelot's as I gasped for my breaths, feeling the heat all around me, Kay and I moving together close and fast. When it gathered around me, the bright white point of pleasure that spread through me, it was different again, different in part because of the feel of the Otherworld that I felt running through my blood, but also because of Lancelot's hands on me as well, the feel of the bare skin of his chest against my back. I cried out softly with the almost-painful bliss of it and I heard Kay groan beneath me. As I opened my eyes, I saw that in the moment he had grasped Lancelot's hand, where it rested on my thigh. I leaned back against Lancelot, catching my breath, and he pulled me fast away, round and into his arms, throwing me down beside Kay and moving on to me with a passionate urgency. He was hot, fired and excited by what he had just seen, and he went into me fast. I was still hot and bright with it, I still felt its tingle through my limbs, dizzyingly delicious in my head, and I held Lancelot's face in my hands, our eyes locked together, my fingers winding into his hair as so soon again I felt it gather around me, white-hot and intense, rising through me, filling me with its beautiful heat, and it was not long before I cried out again, harder, as the pleasure burst over me. Lancelot fell against me, sighing out in his delight, gasping for his breaths, too. I turned my head aside to see Kay lying beside the fire, one arm lazily over his head, and a look of sleepy satisfaction on his face. Lancelot rolled off me between us, gathering me on to him for a tender, satisfied kiss, and Kay pushed himself up on one forearm to lean over and kiss first Lancelot, slow and tender, and then to slide a hand into my hair and draw me to him for a last soft, sleepy, tender kiss. We sank down either side of Lancelot, and my hand brushed Kay's as both of us went to run a hand through Lancelot's hair. Drunk and exhausted, I was falling asleep already when through my flickering eyelids I saw Lancelot turn to Kay, and their lips meet again, and Kay run a hand slowly down Lancelot's chest, all the way down to take him in his hand. I felt one of Lancelot's hands find mine, and our fingers entwined. I was curious, but drunk and exhausted, and full of a drained and sleepy satisfaction, I drifted off to sleep to the sound of their quiet groans of delight.

Chapter Forty-Nine

The winter morning sun felt sharp against my eyes when I woke, and I groaned and wrapped my arms around my head. As I faded in and out of sleep, pieces of the night before drifted back to my mind and I groaned again. I could still taste wine in my mouth. At least my head was throbbing too hard for me to be able to decide how I felt about the little pieces I could remember. I pushed my head slowly up from the pillow and peered through my eyes, sticky with sleep still. Kay lay on the far side of the bed, face down, his arms wrapped over his head, and the sheet tangled around his waist. Lancelot was gone.

I wanted to get out of bed without waking Kay. I didn't know what I would say to him, or he to me. I pushed back memories of the night before as they came floating back, of Kay's hands in my hair, his mouth hot against mine. It came back to me in a sudden, overwhelming rush, how it had felt to be loved by a man from the Otherworld, the rawness in it as if with Kay I had felt that my ancient blood and his had known one another, and I had felt part of the earth itself, and the sky and the ancientness of the world. And Kay had been tender and Lancelot intense in their love, and I had been wonderfully lost between them; four hands on me, two mouths, one swirling haze of pleasure all around me, and both Lancelot's sensual passion and Kay's primal tenderness. Overwhelming. Dizzying. I shut my mind to it. I couldn't think about it now. Lancelot was out already, perhaps had already ridden from the castle out to face Arthur on the field. I slipped out of the bed and pulled on the clothes I had worn the night before that lay strewn before the cold ashes of the fire. Since they were men's clothes, and the same as the other set discarded there which must have been Kay's, I had to pick each item up to guess by size if it was mine or not. It seemed strange, now, to wear the clothes that Kay had worn as a boy. But I didn't have anything else.

As I was about to leave, I noticed that Kay had left his armour lying by the door. He must have been wearing it when they all came up to eat, and since he had not left, he had not taken it with him. I glanced back to the bed. He seemed to be sleeping deeply. I reached down and lifted the breastplate. The sword which I had not noticed resting on it slipped away and clattered to the floor. I turned back, my heart thudding, but Kay only groaned in his sleep and rolled over, throwing an arm over his eyes in his sleep, as though to keep out the morning sun. It did not seem as though he was going to wake. The breastplate was surprisingly light in my hand, and I wondered if it came from the Otherworld, like Excalibur. It was huge, after all, and thick iron, wrought over with a distinctive pattern of vines and swirls in dark metal on its surface, and ought to have been heavy. I pulled it over my head and buckled it at the side. It felt strangely light on my body as well. I then tied on the greaves that matched on my arms and legs. They did not fit well, I was too short and small, but they did not feel heavy. Last of all, I tied up my hair and wrapped it in a strip of cotton torn from Kay's shirt that lay by the dead fire, and put his helm over my head. I didn't want any red hair peeping out of Kay's helm to give me away. I thought the noise of ripping might wake him, too, but it did not. As soon as I was on a horse, no one would notice that I was not tall enough to be Kay. I could hang back from the fighting, and watch. I would be in danger, but I was not going to give up this chance I had to not be left waiting to hear of Lancelot or Arthur's death. That was what I loathed the most: the waiting of war.

I got down to the stables and on to a horse without anyone seeing me. It was awkward moving in the platemail, and slow, but I managed it because Kay's suit of armour was preternaturally light, and I was determined. It was a pity that his huge broadsword was not made like it, because though I managed to carry it, I doubted my ability to strike a blow with it, or lift it above the height of my hips. I had seen Kay before lift it over his head with one hand, to bring down a crashing blow on an enemy. I would be doing no such thing. If I even tried to draw it in the saddle, everyone would know I was not Kay.

I took Kay's horse, because I imagined taking any other would invite question, but it was a huge and stubborn warhorse that seemed disdainful that its usual rider was no longer tall or nimble enough to leap into its saddle at first attempt; but once I was up it seemed content enough to trot out into the yard.

I was not too late. Lancelot's knights were gathered, about to depart, by the first of the barbican gates. I could hear the sound of the portcullis drawing open: an ominous scraping of iron on stone. Lancelot was mounted at the head of the group, his helm in his hand and in the other, his sword drawn and raised. He was shouting in French to his men and they were cheering. I hoped that Kay did not understand French and that he would not try to speak to me in it. He saw me and gave a nod. I rode up to him as the cheering died down and the men fell quiet, adjusting their grip on their swords, bracing themselves to charge out at the enemy. In the winter morning the air was thick with the fog of their eager breaths, and those of their horses, stamping in the cold.

"Kay," Lancelot said quietly as I reached him, thankfully in English, his helm held out ready in his hand to slide over his head. "I did not expect you to be up." An uncomfortable look passed across his face. I did not say anything. There was no way I could imitate Kay's voice. "Is Guinevere alright?" I inclined my helmed head in a nod. "Asleep?" I nodded again. Lancelot gazed off through the rising portcullis in the second gate at the enemy gathered beyond, thoughtful for a moment, then he turned back. "Kay, last night was – but it can't, it *won't* happen again."

I nodded again, as best I could. I didn't want to dislodge the helm or the fabric around my hair from my head and spill out the red hair wound tight beneath. I did not want to give myself away.

Lancelot gave a terse smile and, sliding his helm over his head said wryly, "Death or glory, Kay. Death or glory."

He had not meant it earnestly, but some men behind picked up the shout and soon behind us they were all chanting. I could hear men pounding their swords against their shields. *I do not have a shield.* There hadn't been one in the pile of armour and I hadn't thought to pick Kay's up. Everyone else seemed to have a shield. I even knew what Kay's looked like – dark blue and marked with the great grey keys of his office – but I had not thought to look for it. It was too late now. Too late to turn back, as the crowd of men around me surged forward and Kay's horse, knowing its duty, rushed with them. I drew Kay's sword and tried to lift it with both hands, but I could only hold it level with the horse's neck and if one of Arthur or Gawain's men got that close to me, that would be the end. I felt on the saddle for any other weapon. There was an axe, which I could hold easily, and that would have to do. My only choice, really, would be to stay out of the thick of the fighting. Perhaps it would turn out to be a mercy that I had forgotten Kay's shield. Gawain's men would have been looking for it out on the field, after all. It would be only Gawain himself who would recognise the suit of armour. Or Arthur. I did not think that Arthur would be seeking out Kay for revenge.

I pulled back slightly, and let the other men rush around me, Lancelot at their head. Hidden by the crowd I had a chance to look, and I saw Gawain at the head of the other party. I recognised him from his shield, marked with Lot's two-headed gryphon in gold. I could not see Arthur.

The fighting was fierce, fast and bloody. Gawain tore through the ranks of Lancelot's men, fuelled by his anger and borne by his brutish strength. His men, too, were wild northern men like him, and roared with him on the battlefield. They had not been trained at Arthur's court though, and they had no skill. Whatever else Gawain was, he was a fearsome fighter, and I saw brave men turn their horses aside from his path. I, too, stayed as far from him as possible. It was clear as the sun passed midday that Lancelot would not win, but his men seemed unwilling to draw back into Joyous Guard. These were not men used to waiting out a siege, nor men who saw any value or honour in anything that was not open war on the battlefield. They had been longing for this all through the autumn and into the depths of winter. I kept moving, and mostly men kept out of my way. They all wanted Lancelot, and the honour and advantage that would come to them from Arthur from bringing him as prisoner. No one was particularly interested in attacking the huge knight in dark armour on the massive armoured warhorse that was not attacking them, though I did have to strike out a few times with the axe to protect myself. I was not strong, but I was fast and my aim was good, and I was safe.

Lancelot was pushing forward hard, and since Gawain could not reach him as Bors and his sons and their men stood between them, he was cutting easily through the lines of men. But, though he knocked many down, he seemed reluctant to kill them. It was as though he was trying to get somewhere. I went as close as I thought I safely could. It was getting late, and the early winter dusk was beginning to fall. Soon we would have to go back inside.

Suddenly a huge shout went up as one knight was knocked from his horse. I was close enough to see why. The knight's helm rolled away as he hit the ground and I saw the flash of golden hair, the familiar face. *Arthur.* Lancelot, who had knocked him down unknowing, jumped from his own horse, his sword raised over his head. Men had backed away, leaving a small clear circle of ground around the two men, and though close by fighting still raged on, in that place an eerie silence seemed to fall. Arthur, in his heavy armour, did not try to stand. Excalibur shone in his hand, but as he was bareheaded and on the ground, Lancelot standing over him sword raised, everyone watching knew that it was no good. He would not be faster, he would not be stronger. Lancelot pulled off his own helm, and their eyes met. The chill wind moved through their hair, but apart from that, the men were deathly still except for the heaving of their tense and heavy breaths. Lancelot moved forward slightly, and I heard Bors shout out,

"Lancelot, *finish this*."

Lancelot froze, and hesitated. I felt my heart hammer in my chest, I felt a wave of dizziness pass over me. *Was this going to be the end?* I did not want Arthur to die.

But Lancelot did not strike. He reached out his hand to Arthur, who took it, and he pulled him to his feet. I could hear Bors shouting incomprehensibly in a mix of English and French as Arthur jumped back into his saddle, Excalibur still drawn, and rode away into the crowd of his own men and Lancelot slowly pulled his helm back on and climbed back onto his own horse. There was shouting and confusion all over the field, and it seemed as though at last men were preparing to ride back inside. I rushed ahead, not wanting to be caught disarming. I did not have time to take in fully what I had just seen, only to feel intense gladness and relief that neither of them was dead.

As I rode through the gates fast, the first to return, I saw Kay standing waiting for me in the centre of the courtyard, his arms crossed over his chest. He took the bridle of the horse as I brought it to a stop before him, and when I slipped from the saddle with a clatter of ill-fitting armour he pulled the helm off my head with both hands. My hair, pulled from the cloth I had wrapped it in as Kay pulled off the helm, tumbled down around my shoulders. Kay tutted, but gave a wry little smile.

"I knew it would be you, you little thief," he said, unbuckling one side of the breastplate as I did the other. We were both as eager as each other that no one knew it was I who had ridden out in his armour. "And you forgot the shield," he added, pulling the breastplate over my head as I kicked off the greaves from my legs and pulled them from my arms.

Kay sighed and shook his head at me. "What if you had got yourself killed?"

"I didn't."

"Well, you had better not have broken my sword." He pulled it from the scabbard as I unbuckled it from around me and handed it to him, and regarded it narrowly for a moment, but seemed satisfied. He slid it back into the scabbard and held it in front of him, point against the ground, to lean on it, closer towards me.

"You let me sleep through the fighting," he said quietly, raising an eyebrow at me. Alone in the courtyard together, it suddenly felt uncomfortably intimate. I gave him a little shrug.

"You didn't seem in any state to fight, to me," I told him haughtily. He gave a strange smile, gentle and slight. He seemed as though he was about to say something else when all the other men cascaded through the gates and we scooped up his armour in our arms and rushed out of the way. At the head of them rode Bors and Lancelot, shouting at one another in French. The rest of the men seemed pleased, though I could see that we had taken heavy losses. Perhaps they were just pleased to have survived. Bors jumped from his horse before us and stormed off without seeing us. Lancelot was close behind and jumped down. He looked for a moment as though he was going to follow him, but then he walked over to us, his helm in his hand. I could see the uneasiness on his face, but none of us said anything. I think each was not sure just how much any of the others remembered.

"What happened?" I asked, remembering to pretend I had not seen.

Lancelot shook his head defeatedly.

"I had my chance to kill Arthur, and I couldn't do it. He was there, in front of me," he gestured before him, as though the scene was playing itself out again in his head, "fallen from his horse, his head bare, and I had my sword in my hand; I was ready, but I couldn't do it." He looked up at me, his eyes wide with despair. "I looked into his eyes and I couldn't. He didn't even try to fight; he didn't lift his sword. It seemed like it was all over for him already. I think it must have been over that night... well..." He sighed deeply. "I could see he was still angry, but he doesn't want this fight. This is Gawain's battle, not his. And besides, after everything, the man has done me no wrong. Nothing that deserves death. But Bors is angry. He's angry that I spared Arthur while their men slaughter ours. Maybe he's right." Lancelot pressed the heel of his hand into his brow, and I laid a hand on his arm. I didn't know if he could feel it through the platemail, but he must have done because he laid a gloved hand gently on top of it.

"What now?" Kay asked quietly. Lancelot opened his eyes, and shook his head again, stunned still from his encounter with Arthur.

"I don't know," he whispered. "I don't know."

Chapter Fifty

Kay went with Lancelot to gather the leaders of his men so that they could decide what to do next. I didn't want to hear more talk of war, so I went up to the bedroom. It was still in the mess we had left it in the night before. Empty wine cups lay fallen on the floor, the empty jug of wine on its side by the fire. I picked those up and set them on the table, then scooped the ashes out of the fireplace and set and lit another fire. It had grown bitterly cold in that room without one. I thought the fire would make the room feel refreshed, but the sight of the firelight reminded me again of the night before and brought back to my mind the image of firelight on *two* naked muscular bodies next to mine, of three pairs of legs tangling lazily together, me leaning back and closing my eyes, letting the empty cup of wine tumble out of my hand. I shook the thought away. In truth, my memory of last night was hazy. I did not know exactly *what* had happened, only that it had. I had snippets, sensations, but nothing more. It had been good, I remembered that; it had been in the depths of a hazy pleasure that it had taken place, and I had wanted it. Still, it seemed in the cold light of day better to forget it. Or, at least, not to speak about it.

Once I had tidied the room and Lancelot had not returned, I decided to go and look for him. I didn't want to sit there all on my own where the memories might creep back, unbidden and tempting in the darkness.

I found him up on the battlements, staring out across the camp below. There were fires burning, and I could hear the distant sound of men singing. Out there, they were celebrating. Inside Joyous Guard, the mood was sombre. Lancelot leant on his forearms, his eyes focussed far away and the breeze that always blew this high up lifting his hair about his face, rough and icy tonight. It felt in the air as though it was about to snow, and the night was dark and starless. I pulled Lancelot's cloak more tightly around me. I wished that I had some of my fur-lined cloaks from Camelot, or really any clothing of my own; any of the useful things I had had to leave behind. Lancelot was still dressed in the clothes he had worn under his armour: the black shirt and black woollen leggings. He was not wearing a cloak; even though it was bitterly cold, he did not seem to feel it.

I went up to him and laid a hand on his shoulder, saying his name softly. He started, as though he had not seen me there, as though he had been lost in some dream, but when he saw me he smiled tenderly and pulled me into his arms. His expression, though, remained thoughtful. I rested my head against his chest, holding him close against me. He didn't know I had seen him spare Arthur on the battlefield, that I had seen how much he suffered to go against his king, for my sake. I wished that I could say something, but I could not find the right words.

I turned my face up towards his in the warm little shelter from the wind between our bodies.

"Are you well?" he asked me softly.

"We're still alive," I replied, reaching up to put my hand against his cheek. His skin was cold from the icy night wind.

"We're still alive," he agreed, though his voice sounded grim. I knew what he was thinking. *For now.* He laid his hand over mine against his cheek, and whispered, "We're losing, Guinevere."

I nodded slightly. "I know."

I had seen it. The men were still hungry for a fight now, but what would happen when there were only a hundred left? Fifty? No new men would come to Joyous Guard; not now, with Arthur camped all around it. I thought of Kay's words to me up on the battlements. Kay telling me this was my fault. All of a sudden I could not stop the tears from gathering in my eyes, but I held them back.

"I'm sorry," I whispered. "This is my fault."

"No, no," Lancelot whispered back, sliding his hands into my hair, pressing his forehead against mine. I became aware of his body against mine, the sleeping desire woken suddenly within me. "Some things cannot be helped."

Our lips came together in a kiss, slow and deep. His lips were cold against mine, his face cool under my hands, but soon I felt the heat from him, and he wrapped his arms around my waist and held me tight against him. The sensual touch of his lips on mine, his tongue, was making me warm and dizzy already. His touch erased all thoughts of anything else, and I sank into it, winding my hands into his hair with a small noise of pleasure and excitement. I wanted it; wanted to feel again the power of the love that had brought me to this place. Wanted to feel that it was worth it; wanted to be reminded of the deep, undeniable love that had brought us inexorably here. It ought not to have been the moment for it, the memory of Arthur fresh with both of us, and the tangled confusion of the night before, but I wanted it just as much as always, all the same. I needed it. He needed it. It brought us together and bound us. No, we had to come together because we were already bound, in our hearts. By the time he lifted me gently against the stone battlements, I no longer felt the icy wind, only the heat of my body, and his, the touch of his hands against my thighs where he held me, his mouth against mine, his hair wound between my fingers. Pressed tight between him and the cool, rough stone of the battlements, breathing in the hot air he breathed out, we pressed our foreheads together and both sighed as we were once again one, lost in the deliciousness of our love that dissolved everything else into nothing. I felt the wind tear through my hair, and the tiny drops of snow beginning to fall, deliciously cool against my hot skin. I felt wild and elemental, powerful. I felt once again how our love was a part of the world, a part of the wildness of winter, and the lazy heat of summer, and the moon and the stars. And my blood and my bones.

It wasn't until we were in bed, and Lancelot beside me had fallen asleep, that I thought again about Kay. I wondered how much of what Lancelot did he had learned from Kay. I was sure that, though Lancelot was a few years older, it would have been Kay who had been the leader of it all. I had expected a man as big as Kay to be rough like Arthur, but he had not been. I wondered if Lancelot had learned his gentle sensuality in part from Kay, though they were not the same.

Then I thought about Arthur, down far below us, out in his tent in the cold winds of winter. What had he come for? Not for me. Not really. Pride, probably. A sense of violated entitlement. After all, he could, as he said, have had any queen at all.

The mood in Joyous Guard as the days went on was tense and electric. Bors paced the courtyard, checking the men's equipment, the horses, clearly still set on riding out for war. He bore little resemblance to his half-brother Lancelot: shortish in comparison – though still just more than my own height – and stocky, with short-cut brown hair. Still, he had skill at arms and was a brave fighter. He must have had the looks of the mother he shared with Ector, who in his youth must have been more like Lancelot, and who had passed those dark, handsome looks to his son. Ector now was tired and grey, sick of a life of wars, and he and Lancelot stood side by side at the edge of the courtyard talking in hushed tones. I knew that they would be talking about terms for peace, and I did not want to go over. If I were there, then Lancelot wouldn't be thinking of the safety of his men, he would be thinking about me, and I could not shake off the memory of Kay's words that this was all my fault.

Feeling restless, I wandered around the castle, and then up around the battlements. The sky was heavy with clouds that seemed almost close enough to touch, as I stood up there. Snow was coming, or sleet and rain. It would not be good conditions for a fight. The men would be more likely to agree on a peace. I would have to go back. I knew that the time would come, that this life with Lancelot in Joyous Guard was nothing but a dream. I couldn't imagine it anymore, being in Camelot with Arthur. It seemed like another life, someone else's life; it all seemed as though it had happened so long ago, though I had only been in Joyous Guard a few months. I could see why Isolde had waited here so long alone, and not wanted to leave. It was a little patch of glorious freedom. Escape. But I couldn't escape from who I was forever. Far below, I could see Arthur's tent. If it were ruled by the heart I would belong to Lancelot more than I did to Arthur, but it was ruled by the law, and in the eyes of the law I was Arthur's property, and wrongfully stolen. I wondered if I would even fight if I had the strength to, if I could ask men to lay down their lives so that I could choose the life I wanted. Many good men were dead already.

I wandered down again, finding I could no longer look at the gathering of tents beneath me, threateningly close. Especially Gawain's. I wondered, too, if Mordred was there, sharing Arthur's tent, finally taking the place he had coveted at his father's side.

As I descended the stairs, I heard floating through an open door before me, Lancelot's voice. Hearing my name, I hung back to listen, afraid I knew all too well what it was about.

"No," I heard Kay reply. "Don't send for her yet."

"Give it to me," I heard Bors demanding gruffly, and the sound of paper snatched from someone's hand. After a moment, he gave a low grunt of dissatisfaction.

"We can't agree to this," Lancelot protested softly; "he tried to have her killed, and there are the same accusations in this letter. It's not right. I'm not going to just hand her back over to him."

I heard a sigh I recognised as Ector's, deep and weary. So they were all there.

"Lancelot... You've been living here with her like man and wife and it's not *right*. She's still Arthur's wife, whatever he has done. Besides, he would have been within his rights and the law to kill her with his bare hands if he had wanted to. She's not yours to keep here. She has to go back."

"I won't do it," Lancelot objected, more forcefully.

"She might *want* to go back to Arthur," Kay said sharply; more sharply than was necessary, I thought. "Have you thought about what she might want? They've been man and wife for nearly twenty years, and they have been through a lot together. Lost a child together."

There was a pause.

"I didn't know that," Lancelot replied quietly.

"No," Kay said bitterly. "You didn't."

"None of that's important," Bors interjected, obviously annoyed. It was a political issue, clearly, for Bors. That, and an issue of family honour. "What's important is that if we keep the queen here, that's an admission of guilt. We have to yield her up to Arthur, saying we kept her here for her protection, no one touched her, and we were just protecting her from Gawain. Lancelot, you have to go out before them and publicly swear that none of these accusations in the letter are true. Give her back. It will be like it never happened. Then, we retreat to France and brace ourselves for whatever Gawain is going to do to avenge his brothers. You have to think about the honour of this family, Lancelot. If you don't give her back now he asks for her, then that's treason. And rape."

There was the sound of scuffling, as though Lancelot had lunged towards Bors, and I heard Kay shout out to Lancelot. I stepped through the door and I saw them all freeze – Bors halfway through lunging forwards, Kay with a hand on Lancelot's arm, holding him back – when they realised that I had been listening. But I was not going to stand there while they decided what to do with me. I was not an object to be traded back and forth between Lancelot and Arthur to suit the political desires of Bors and Gawain. Bors and Lancelot shrank back from one another, and I looked around at them all, standing staring at me.

"I'll go," I said, breathlessly.

"No." Lancelot stepped towards me, and I laid my hand gently on his arm. He fell still under my touch, and looked sad.

"No one will harm me," I told him, sounding more sure than I felt. "I don't want anyone else to die. Not here. Not for me."

"I'll send back to Arthur then," Bors said, his tone business-like. "Peace agreed on the terms that you will go to him and return the queen, whom you only held for safekeeping, without threat to your person. Once she is returned, you and your kin will leave Logrys, also without threat to our persons."

"He'll agree to that," Ector said quietly.

Kay, standing back in the corner behind Lancelot, his dark eyes trained on Bors, said nothing. He had a strange, terse look on his face, but he did not speak.

Agreement to the terms came fast, and the next day was set for my return. That night, when Lancelot took me in his arms, neither of us said a word about how it was the last night. We came together with a silent intensity, relishing each moment of sensation, desperate to make it last. We lay by the fire, on the soft rug. I felt the warmth of the flames against my skin, as I had on the first night we spent together in Surluse, and he pulled me into his lap and I wrapped my arms around his neck and my legs around his waist and we tumbled back together, falling into it, into each other. I wanted his hands, his lips, his tongue on every inch of my skin, and mine on his. I waited until the last moment, until I could not bear it but that we would become one, and I leaned down to kiss him, running my hands down his hard, muscular chest; and the joy I felt at closeness, at oneness with him was so intense that it felt like pain in the centre of my heart, to know that this was the last time, the last time we would be together like this. So many times before I had thought that, and so many times I had been wrong, but I did not see how this could not truly be the end. I tried to gather away into my memory the feel of his lips against my neck, my collarbone, my nipples as we moved together, and my lips on his, hot with the tingling pleasure of his touch. Every moment of that night was exquisite, and awfully fleeting. I did not want the end to come, but it did, hot and bright within me, and after the slow intensity of our love, overwhelming, and I cried out with it, feeling it wash over me, through me, filling me with light; and then for him too, it was over, and we lay by the fire, our legs tangled together, in each other's arms, and I rested my head on his chest and prayed I would not fall asleep; but I was exhausted, and sleep came on me fast, bringing an end to the dream I had dreamed of my life with Lancelot for so long, and so painfully brief a time.

Chapter Fifty-One

It was early the next morning that Lancelot and I rode out for Arthur's camp from Joyous Guard. From far away, I could see already the fluttering white banners with Arthur's blue dragon spread across them, and the blue-green pavilion beneath. From the walls of Joyous Guard the tents had looked so close beneath us, but the camp was more than a mile away. My heart sank within me, and I felt a cold lump of dread in the pit of my stomach, but I knew that it had to be done. Lancelot and I rode in silence. There were no more words, no words enough for what we had to do now. We had already said goodbye so many times before now. The fact that neither of us had tried to say it this time, even now, gave me the awful, gaping feeling that this was finally the end.

As we drew near I saw Arthur sat in a gilded chair on top of a raised wood dais outside the pavilion, and at his shoulder stood Gawain, dressed in platemail with his huge broadsword drawn, both hands resting on the hilt and the point at his feet. Arthur was unarmed, except for Excalibur at his side, but dressed in his red and gold surcoat, rich white furs around his shoulders, and the big gold crown of Logrys on his head, its sapphires and rubies glinting in the winter sun. A small group of armoured, visored knights stood around him, among whom I recognised the shields of Mordred and Dinadan. The others were unfamiliar. So Mordred *had* come. And, he had survived so far. I could not say I was not sorry to see that.

I wished I had not worn one of Isolde's dresses, though I had had nothing else, and Bors had come to insist that I be taken back in women's clothes. Though I had been stripped of them for the pyre, they thought it was best that I was returned to Arthur in the clothes of a queen. But Isolde's dress suited me far worse than Kay's old clothes. The ivory silk seemed wrong for the occasion, too maidenish, and I too old for the dress. It fitted poorly, too, gaping slightly at the neck, and tight across the shoulders, and the delicate little pattern of pink flowers around the neck and sleeves altogether unlike something

I would ever have worn, and ugly against the red of my hair. Yet it was the most queenly thing in Joyous Guard, and it would have to serve. My head was bare. I had tried on Isolde's crown, but then I had remembered what I had said to Galahalt about Helen of Troy and the bad luck in a fallen queen's crown, and I had put it away.

Kay had come to say goodbye when I was stood staring at the pretty little circlet, wondering where Isolde was now, if she had survived Mark's anger. We did not say much, but he put his arms around me, and I laid my head against his shoulder and wrapped my arms around his neck. I prayed to all the gods I knew that I would see Kay again. That Arthur might welcome Kay back to Camelot. I had heard some of the men say that Kay's office of Seneschal had been given now to Mordred, though Kay still possessed the Seneschal's shield. But I hoped that Arthur's anger would not last, and he might return. Kay had put his hand against my hair, gentle and soothing, and kissed the top of my head.

"Take care of Lancelot," I had whispered to him, and above me, I had felt him nod. It had been hard, truly, to say goodbye to Kay.

Lancelot stopped his horse a little way off, and slid off, holding out his hand to help me from mine. I slipped down to join him, drawing in a deep breath. He had come without armour, wanting to appear submissive and peaceful, but the magnificence of his body was all the more plain as he stood there in his shirt and breeches, his shoulders wrapped in a black and silver woollen cloak edged with dark fur. I shivered in my dress. Isolde had not left any winter clothes, or they were nowhere to be found, and no one had thought it was a good idea for me to be wrapped in one of Lancelot's cloaks. The winter wind blew right through the thin silk and cut me to the bone.

As Lancelot took my hand and began to lead me up to the dais, he leaned down beside me and whispered softly.

"*Courage*, my love."

I could have cried, but I did not.

We stopped before Arthur, and Lancelot bowed.

"My lord Arthur, I am loath to do such battle with the noble king who made me knight," he said.

Arthur's steel-grey eyes locked on him, cold, with a harshness unfamiliar to me. I supposed that this was how Arthur had always looked on his enemies.

"It is late for fine words, Lancelot, when you have been with another man's wife." Arthur's reply was quiet, but powerful enough to cut through the air between us. There was real, cold anger there, and danger. He had been more sad than angry before he had put me to the fire; the deepness of his anger shocked me. I had, I did not know why, expected him to be calm and kind.

"There are some that might say a man relinquishes his right to a woman when he puts her to the fire." Lancelot half-stepped forward, and I could see the rage had fired quick within him, his voice raised, his face lightly flushed. I was afraid for a moment that Arthur would rise from his makeshift throne and another fight would start, but Lancelot checked himself, drawing the anger back inside. "But I say there is no truth in the accusations against your queen and me, and any man here is welcome to step forward and make it good upon my body that I was ever a traitor to you. My lady queen has held me in her favour as her champion, as is right, and she is a true woman. I think you pay me poorly for the service I have done to you, for often, my lord, I have saved her from danger you yourself let her fall into, and then you thanked me for my service to you both. It would have been poor service for me to suffer you to burn her for the sake of these slanders against me. But, my lord, take your queen again. I swear here now that she is true and good."

It was so strange to hear them speak to one another like this, so cold, so formal, when not long ago they had spoken easily and intimately as friends. But I could see the ghost of Arthur relenting. Lancelot had made the public declaration as he should, and no one stepped forward to challenge it. I was surprised to discover that I was disappointed; this meant that I would definitely be taken back. I could feel my hand trembling where Lancelot held it, and I closed my eyes for a moment, trying to hold myself calm. I could feel the tears creeping up to my eyes, and I held them back.

Gawain spat at his feet, and spoke before Arthur could reply, his voice dripping with venom.

"You false coward knight. The queen is not yours to return, and Arthur could kill you both if he so chose. It is within his rights. And his strength." Lancelot's hand went to the hilt of his sword, but what Gawain said next stilled him. "But, why, Lancelot, why did you kill Gareth, who loved you like a brother? He trusted you with all his heart, as the man who made him a knight. Why did he deserve to die for this?"

Lancelot reeled back from the question. I, too, was shocked by Gawain's suddenly trembling tone. The loss of his youngest brother had broken him, I could see that. Even this huge brute of a man had been brought low by loss.

"It was – an accident," Lancelot replied, his voice small, choked.

"No." Gawain stepped forward, his foot thudding loud against the dais. He looked ready to raise his sword and strike. "You did it for hate of me. And my kin. But we shall *never* be reconciled while you and your kin are living. You traitorously slew my brothers, and blood will be paid with blood. Return the queen, and leave. And prepare yourself for war."

Arthur raised a hand for quiet, and Gawain fell back. I could see that he would have started his war of revenge right then if Arthur had not been there. Arthur's stern eyes fell on me, then, and I saw a slight sigh go through him.

"You have nothing to say for yourself, for once," he said quietly. He did not expect a reply. I drew myself up proudly and met his look with one of level calm. I had wronged him, but he had put me to the fire. In my eyes, it was he who should make reparation.

"My lady," Lancelot began beside me, and I turned from Arthur to him. Our eyes met, and I felt the tears I had held back gather in my eyes and begin to fall. He took both of my hands in his. The breath gasped out of me, and I was trembling. "Now we must part, and I from my lord Arthur's noble court forever." I nodded. We should have said goodbye alone. We should not have to do it like this, painfully formal, in front of Arthur and his knights. We had missed the chance to say goodbye for the last time. *I want to go back. I want to go back. Take me back to Joyous Guard.* I did not say it. I could not say it. I would have given anything for the strength to say it then. "Pray for me, my lady, and I shall pray for you. But send for me, if anyone says you were untrue unto my lord Arthur, and I shall come and defend you."

He laid a hand against my cheek, and I closed my eyes against it, feeling his skin on mine for the last time, and there, right before Arthur, he kissed me. I tasted the salt of my tears there, as I felt for the last time the sensual softness of his lips against mine. It was the kiss of a moment, but it would have to last me the rest of my life.

He led me, then, up the steps of the dais, and Arthur stood to take my hand from him as Lancelot knelt to one knee before him, and swiftly turned away. Arthur's hand on mine was cold and still, and I did not look at him, but turned to watch Lancelot climb back on his horse, and ride away.

Arthur took me back to his tent in silence. The pale sunlight through the blue tent made it seem cloyingly as though it was underwater, and chill with it. I stood at the opening, nervous but still defiant, as Arthur took off his crown and furs. My tears had dried on my cheeks, and no more had come. I was angry now, resistant. I was ready for a fight with Arthur. My heart was beating fast and nervous within me. It was a long time since I had even seen him last. He looked well enough, uninjured from the fighting. But I could see that he was trembling with rage. He leaned for a moment against the small table set up there for his food, as though he was bracing himself, or perhaps calming himself. He stood straight, suddenly, running his hands through his hair and turning to me. I froze where I stood under his gaze, my heart thudding in my chest. I thought it was so loud that he would be able to hear it.

He strode over to me fast, and seized me by the wrist, pulling me to him.

"Is it true, then? *Did* you lie with him? You did, didn't you, at Joyous Guard?" he hissed. I tried to push him away with my other hand, but he did not move, nor did he loosen his grip. I tilted my head back proudly.

"Arthur, *you put me to the fire*," I replied, loud and stern and cold.

Arthur grabbed the front of the dress hard, pulling me up towards him. I had felt his roughness before, but not like this. Now, for the first time, I was afraid.

"No matter, he should *not* have taken you to his castle, he should have returned you to me, you are *my wife,* you are *mine.*" He was shouting now, close and terrifying. I tried to hold my eyes cold, my body stiff and aloof, but the power of his voice, of his anger so close to me shook me to the core. His hand tightened on the dress, and under his grip the fine silk tore. He released my wrist to grab me by the hair, pulling my head back, and leaned down as though he was going to kiss me.

"Would that make you feel like I was *yours*, Arthur, if you forced yourself on me?" I asked, deadly soft. I did not want him to touch me. I was still angry.

He pushed me away from him, hard, and I stumbled back. My scalp ached, and my wrist. He paced away from me, but the anger was hot in me already and I stepped towards him.

"You put me to death, Arthur. You wanted me dead, and now you've demanded me back. You wanted me *dead.*" My voice cracked on the last word, but it was under the power of my anger rather than tears.

"Well, is it true?" Arthur rounded on me.

I drew myself back, gathering in a steely calm.

"Which would make you feel better, Arthur? To hear that I have loved another man, or to hear that you sent me to the fire for the sake of rumours and you have waged your war against an innocent man? Does it even matter if it's true or not, now? Gareth is dead, and Aggravain and Gaheris. Blood will be paid with blood. And you have your *thing* back in your possession."

Someone take her back to Britain.

Arthur grabbed at me again and I jumped away as his hand closed around the torn neck of the dress where it flapped open and it ripped to the ground. I shrugged the ripped overdress off me and tossed it aside in anger. I stood my ground, crossing my arms in front of my chest. I could see his shoulders rising and falling with his anger, his eyes watchful on me. He pulled off his surcoat and threw it aside. He, too, was bracing for a fight. I stepped back. For a moment, we paused, our eyes on one another, waiting for the other to make a move. But he was quicker than I was, and stronger, and he darted forward before I moved away and grabbed me by the arms, twisting them behind my back. I realised then that I had not felt his full strength before, the savage raw power of it. I was sore everywhere he had grasped hold of me. He had always been rough, but he had never hurt me before. Not like this. I struggled against him as, holding my arms in one hand, in the other he grasped a handful of my hair and tried to pull me into a violent kiss. It was meant to hurt me. To show me I was his. I held back as much as I could, feeling my neck strain away from him, and fixed him with a cold, angry look.

"Arthur, you're hurting me. *Look at yourself.*" I had meant to be calm, but it came out of me like a scream. Arthur loosened his grip on my hair, but did not let go of my arms. The strength of his body pressed against mine was threatening in a way that it had never been before, and I was truly afraid, but I was not going to show it. "Arthur," I forced my voice to be even, and calm, "the matter is settled. Lancelot swore in public it was not true, and he was not challenged. It's over. You have me back. I'm not going to talk about it anymore."

Arthur leaned in closer so that our noses brushed and our lips almost touched as he hissed, low, "That was a matter of politics. This is between *us*." With the arm holding my wrists he pulled me tighter against him. I could feel his chest rising and falling against me, and in the cold of the tent, the heat of his breath on my face. I was surprised to feel that I wanted to kiss him; I was so used to kissing him if ever we were this close. It had changed now, and his closeness was dangerous. "Now tell me, *is it true?*"

I shook my head, refusing to speak, but he was not satisfied, and I could feel the dangerous closeness of my tears, the smallness of my body in his grip, that I was alone now, only among enemies. His hand tightened in my hair, and the wild anger of his voice struck against me as he shouted once more, "*Is it true, Guinevere?*"

In his grip, under the stare of his eyes, tired and afraid and hopeless, I broke, and the tears came from me in gasping sobs and through them I whispered, "It's true."

Arthur shook me hard. "Don't cry," he shouted. "You can't cry your way out of this." But now I had let the tears out, they could not be stopped. I could barely breathe through them, couldn't speak, and they were taking the little strength I had. Arthur pulled me over towards the bed. I resisted as much as I could but I was small and weak and tired and he had all the power of his anger coursing through his massive body. As he dragged me across the tent, one hand in my hair, the other pulling me by the wrist, he spoke in my ear in a voice trembling with rage, forced down from a shout into something worse: an awful quiet anger. "I never taught you to obey me. There were many men who said I was wrong in that, who said I gave you too much freedom. Some of them were the ones that told me you were fucking Lancelot. The others told me you were *fucking Kay*." Arthur shouted the last two words, throwing me down roughly on the bed. I shouted out for him to stop, but through his anger he didn't seem to hear me, and he climbed on top of me, pinning me down, still shouting. "Is that true? Is that true as well? You were always with him. How many others were there? How many?"

"You had others," I shouted back at him, still angry, still fuming with it through my tears. I hated them, too. I was not sad, I was not weak, but they came anyway. I wanted to be cold and calm; I wanted the strength to push him off me. I had not come back to submit to his punishment, or his violence. But, to my surprise, Arthur froze, and the anger fell away from his face to be replaced with a look of sorrowful confusion, and I felt his grip around my wrists slacken as he fell still.

"I didn't," he said, softly. I felt that hit me with a sharp pang of guilt that went right through me. I almost said, *but Morgan said*, but then I realised that I had been stupid to believe her; Morgan had always been a liar. Now we were still, and Arthur's anger had left him, I was aware of how hard we were both breathing, the closeness of our bodies, on the bed, and I had an unbearable sense of how recently we might have been like this in happiness and love.

"Never?" I asked in a whisper.

"Not after we married. There was only you. I – you... Of course, there were many women who tried, especially when they realised there was not going to be a child. But I didn't want them. I only wanted you."

The tears came back to me, hard. *What have I done? What have I done to both of them?* Arthur released his grip and sank bank, rubbing his face, shaking his head. I raised my hands to my face, burying my tears in them, trying to get myself back under control. Arthur was right; crying was not going to get me out of this. Eventually, my breathing slowed, and the tears stopped as Arthur moved slowly to sit on the edge of the bed, and rested his head in his hands.

Very, very quiet he said, "I thought you loved me, once."

And very, very quiet I replied, moving my hands from my face and sitting up behind him. "I *do* love you."

"But you love him, as well." I could feel the vibration of grim anger in those words.

I did not reply, because there was nothing I could say. There was no point, now, in lying. I moved forward on the bed on my knees and gently rested my head on his shoulder. He didn't push me away. The anger had left both of us quickly, left us weak and empty, and tired.

"It was just him?" Arthur asked softly.

"Just him," I answered.

"How many times?"

"Arthur," I sighed. "Arthur, please, you don't want to –"

"*How many?*" he insisted.

"I don't know. Just a few." I knew that wasn't really true, but right then it seemed desperately, desperately too few.

"When?"

"Arthur." I leaned around him and took his face in my hands. His eyes were so sad, so lost. I had done this to him. I felt hollowed out with regret. "Please. Stop. This won't help you."

I kissed him lightly, tentatively, testing for the response now his anger had burned away. He did not respond to my first kiss, but at the second, I could feel him beginning to relent. He put his arms around me and pulled me gently into his lap, his hands finding my hair and teasing it loose so it tumbled free down my back. This was Arthur's simple way – any feeling could be resolved or at least forgotten by our coming together, and soon he would begin to forget. I wondered then if I would have been satisfied with the love Lancelot had offered me when he returned from the Grail were it not that this was the only kind of love I had learned from Arthur, who had always shown me how he felt by taking me to his bed: when we were happy, when I was sad and needed comfort, when we were worried. I had never known anything else. But I hoped that it would ease his pain, and help a little in bringing us back together now. I lifted Arthur's shirt over his head as his kisses became more rough and demanding, and he rolled us over onto the bed, moving on to me, his hands running up my thighs under the thin underdress, gently moving them apart. I ran my hands through his hair, returning his hungry kisses as he tore open the lacing of the underdress and pulled it away. He stopped for a moment, looking me over and tracing a hand lightly down my body. I sighed lightly against it, feeling the old hunger for him slowly coming back to life within me. I drew him to me, kissing him hard again, desperate to help him forget, to help me forget what I had done. What he had done. What we had done to one another. I had missed him; I had missed the rough pleasure of his body. I reached down to his breeches to take him in my hand, but to my surprise, as I touched him, he jumped away. But I had already felt what I had feared – that there was no stirring there, not for me. Arthur leapt from the bed and turned away from me, and I sat up drawing my knees up to my chest and wrapping my arms around them, hot and embarrassed and ashamed.

"I can't do it," Arthur said, thickly, his back still turned to me. "I keep picturing you with *him*. I can't do it."

"Arthur –" I called after him, but he had already pulled on his shirt and strode out of the tent, even though it was almost night and the snow was beginning to fall.

Chapter Fifty-Two

The next day the camp packed up at last and we rode back to Camelot. I forced myself not to turn over my shoulder and look back at Joyous Guard. I did not want Arthur to see, and besides, Mordred and Gawain rode side-by-side close behind us. I would not yield anything to them. I could bide my time to have my revenge on them both, if I could. For now I was powerless without Arthur's trust, but I had time enough and I was good at waiting.

Isolde's dress torn to pieces, I was pleased to find that someone had had the mind to bring some of mine, remembering perhaps that Mordred had stripped me for the stake, though among them was neither armoured dress. I chose one of dark purple, edged with white fur. I was sick of being cold. I missed my little gold circlet, crushed away in Mordred's hand. There had been no crown brought for me.

Perhaps it was because they were, as I was, not sure if they were taking me to the pyre again.

We seemed to ride painfully slowly as we went in a long column across the fields and low hills between Joyous Guard and Camelot, and Arthur was quiet at my side, his eyes fixed on the distance. Behind us, Mordred and Gawain were laughing and joking, re-telling stories from the battle. Gawain was boasting about killing Lamerocke, who according to his story had been caught in bed with his mother Morgawse. I was surprised, but not unduly. Morgawse was much older, but still beautiful and oddly compelling with it. As much as I had been resolved not to like her, I found that I very much did. It was painful to listen to them, their laughing and joking, the ease with which they had both withstood it. I was sure that deep inside himself, Gawain still nursed his angry pain, but it was to my chagrin that he didn't show it. I suffered, Arthur suffered, Lancelot suffered, and Gawain laughed. And Mordred. But I would have Mordred brought low. Mordred who had hurt me and humiliated me and hidden like a coward from Lancelot's sword. If I could make him suffer, then I would.

As Camelot at last came into view, Arthur moved closer to me on his horse and spoke in low tones, obviously not wanting Gawain or Mordred to hear.

"Did Ector reach Joyous Guard safely?" he asked.

I was surprised. I thought that those who had left would be dead to him. Perhaps there was hope that I would see Kay again. *Kay.* I had forgotten about Kay in everything that had happened, so fast, afterwards. I pushed the thought back.

"Yes. Did you know he had come?" I asked, evenly.

Arthur nodded. "I sent him. It seemed the safest place for him. Gawain wants a blood feud, and I did not want Ector within his reach. That man is the only father I ever knew, and I have sent him away."

Arthur was quiet for a moment. I wished I could say something comforting, but all I had in my head were Kay's words, that this was all my fault.

"Tell me about Kay," he said softly. That startled me, as though he had caught me at my thoughts, and I turned to him in surprise. His face was crinkled at the brow in quiet concern. My heart was racing, but he did not know, or suspect. I gathered myself in my saddle, holding tight to the control I had mustered, like a hard lump, at the centre of me. He asked again. "Kay... is he alive?"

"Kay is well. Unhurt. He misses you."

"And yet he was the first to ride off with Lancelot," Arthur replied, bitterly.

Perhaps my hopes of seeing Kay again were in vain. After that Arthur fell quiet again until we reached Camelot. It felt like coming home, and not coming home. The sight of the glorious castle on the horizon filled me with hope, but as we got closer and closer I realised that Camelot looked the same, but everything had changed. It was no longer how it had been before I left, full of knights play-fighting. It was how it had been while Arthur was in Rome. It was the castle of a realm at war. Even though we arrived from the long ride in the depths of night, in the light of torches burning in the courtyard I could see men were sharpening swords. There was no singing, no drinking, no feasting. It looked empty. As we went through the courtyard, I looked out for Marie, but I did not see her. I hoped that no one had harmed her for my sake.

I slid from my horse and went to go to my rooms. I wanted to be alone, to look down at the garden covered in snow, but as I went Arthur reached out and took me by the arm.

"Where are you going?" he asked, darkly.

"To my room," I told him, half-turning back to go, but he did not loosen his grip on my arm.

"No you're not."

I pulled my arm roughly from his grip. He could have held me if he was determined to, but he was surprised enough that I dared, even now, that I was able to wrench my arm away.

"What do you mean, *no you're not?*" I demanded, drawing myself up, giving him an even stare.

Gawain beside him squared up to me, but he could not do anything to me. Arthur wouldn't let another man strike his queen, and, anyway, I wasn't afraid of Gawain's violence. His broad, brutish face was even more scarred than before, his eyes more wild and angry. I was sure he hated me, but he had done the first wrong. He had raped Margery. I would not back down before him. If I backed down now, I was lost. I was coming back a disgraced queen; they might all have to speak well about me in public for fear of Arthur's punishment or Lancelot's sword, but they would talk in private. I did not care so long as I got the respect I deserved in public.

"The blood, my lady." Mordred, who I had not realised had crept up beside me, said, his voice slick and unpleasant. His voice, his presence, made me feel queasy. I would have killed him if I had had any weapon to hand. "No one has cleaned away the blood."

I turned to him, my gaze steely. "I don't care about that. I'm not afraid of blood."

"Nonetheless," Arthur stepped forward, interrupting the cold stare that held me locked to Mordred and leading me, more gently, towards his own rooms, "I would prefer you to stay in my rooms until they are cleaned."

All of my things were in those rooms. My clothes, my books, my jewellery, my letters from Isolde, my writing materials. Marie.

"So I'm a prisoner now?" I hissed at Arthur as he led me up the stairs, shutting the door to his bedroom behind us and bolting it, not releasing his hold on my arm.

"You're not a prisoner," he said, tersely.

"No?" I crossed my arms in front of my chest as he at last let go of me. "So I can see Marie? And I can go to my garden?"

"Guinevere, it's snowing."

"Fetch Marie. I want Marie."

"Not now, Guinevere."

I turned away from him, fuming with anger already. So he had brought me to Camelot to lock me up like a naughty child. He did intend to punish me, then. There was a fire burning and I was hot in the fur-lined dress, and hot with the anger. I pulled off the belt and threw it aside, and then wrenched the dress over my head.

"What are you doing?" Arthur asked, his tone annoyed. I turned to him and threw the dress at him. He caught it in both arms.

"That dress is too hot. I need my dresses. Send for Marie and tell her to get them."

Arthur looked at me, the dress limp in his arms, his face slack with disappointment. He shook his head slowly, letting the dress fall from his arms to the floor.

"You're not even sorry, are you?" he said coldly.

"For what?" I snapped.

"You know what," he shouted. I reeled back from it, but only slightly. I crossed my arms over my chest and met his stare. "The chaplain told me that when he came to take your confession, you wouldn't confess to any sin. You really believe you've done nothing wrong, don't you?"

I stood there, in my underdress, my arms folded, and I met his look. I didn't know what to say; I was sorry that people had suffered for it, but I did not believe that what I had done came under right or wrong. It was just something that had to be. I knew he wouldn't understand that. I wasn't prepared to lie, or apologise for it, so I said nothing. Arthur shook his head again and left.

I shouted after him, "Fetch Marie!"

After a while a girl came with a different dress, but it was not Marie. It was some young slip of a thing with mousey hair wrapped round her head in a plait. She brought a green silk dress, good and thick for the winter, and one that I liked, but I was not pleased to see her.

"Where is Marie?" I demanded, when I saw her.

"I don't know, my lady."

"Yes you do. I don't want you. I want Marie."

"Please, my lady," the girl said. I could see she was nervous and trembling, that I was frightening her with my shouting, but I didn't hold back. I *needed* Marie. "I can't bring her."

Then I heard, low and awful, from the corridor behind her, the voice of Gawain. I was angry enough that I did not care that the door was half-open and he stared right at me, in my underclothes. He was the lowest kind of creature to me, and I would not care.

"Gaheris is dead because of you. Marie doesn't want to see you."

"I don't believe you," I said, but I felt his words hit me hard, taking the air from my lungs, and the uncertainty was obvious in my voice.

"Just leave the dress," he said gruffly to the girl. She put it in my hands and hurried out and he shut the door. So I was a prisoner, after all.

I didn't bother to put the dress on. It was already late into the night from the long journey we had taken from Joyous Guard. I didn't want it really. All I wanted was Marie. I wanted to hear her chirping in Breton, I wanted to feel her deft little hands plaiting my hair, to close my eyes and listen to her chattering pass over me, sweetly silly. Instead, I pulled off the underdress and stood naked before the fire, letting the heat warm through me. That was when I noticed, on the chair beside the table, folded neatly was the nightdress that I had been wearing when Mordred dragged me before Arthur. Someone – it must have been Arthur – had folded it and placed it there. The gesture was unbearably tender somehow, that he had picked up my nightdress from the floor and folded it, even as he knew I was being taken to the fire. I leaned down and laid my fingertips against the soft silk, imagining Arthur's hand as he laid the nightdress down, thinking I would soon be dead. The last time I stood in this room, I was waiting for my death. That must have been almost half a year ago now. It seemed a world away. A lifetime away. I picked up the nightdress and pulled it over my head, not bothering to untie the laces. It fell loosely around me. I was thinner now, from the siege at Joyous Guard. I had not felt the hunger. Last time I had worn it I had been lovely and slightly plump with the plenty of Camelot. I was not sure I would see such a time as that again.

I slipped into the bed and closed my eyes to wait for Arthur. It was a long time later that he got into bed beside me, and I was already half asleep, but I moved instinctively into his arms and to my surprise he wrapped me up in them, holding me against him.

"I'm sorry," I whispered, my voice thick with sleep. I was. I was. I loved Arthur, and I had hurt him. I was sorry for that. I was more sorry than I could ever express.

Arthur kissed me softly on the forehead. I let my hand trail down his bare chest, down his body, but he gently pushed it away.

"Just, go to sleep," he whispered.

So it seemed that Arthur was coming back to me slowly, piece by piece, and I could not have him all at once. I could wait for that, too.

The days passed slowly. I wandered around Camelot a little, and stood in my garden as the snow began to thaw, but there was no one to read with me, nor was anyone permitted to go into my tower, so I could not even send a servant to get my books. I sat in Arthur's room a lot, and I was glad to be close to the Round Table; but that room was rarely empty and I longed to be alone so that I could climb on top of it. I avoided Mordred, but everywhere I went I felt his eyes on me. Gawain was simpler; he wore his anger on the outside as spring approached, stomping around always dressed in his armour, shouting boasts across the courtyard of what he would do when he finally met Lancelot in battle. His posturing didn't bother me, but Mordred's dark watchful eyes did, and I was acutely aware of my isolation, that I had left behind my two protectors at Joyous Guard, and hard as I looked in Camelot I could not find my last dear friend.

Arthur slept by my side at night, but he did not often come before I was asleep, and if he did he was quiet, and though he would wrap me in his arms and let me rest my head on his chest he could not bear, it seemed, to touch me as he had or to let me touch him. I had a feeling in the pit of my stomach that if we could come together as we had done, as man and wife, then Arthur would begin to heal from what I had done to him. But I did not see how it could be done if he would not even try.

It was finally breaking into spring, and my garden was growing greener, and my heart more hopeless that war might be averted and I might see any of the people I had left behind at Joyous Guard again, when the news came. Arthur called a council in the room with the Round Table, and I went, dressed in the green armoured dress that Nimue had had made for me. I wished that she had been there. I felt safer with her at my side, with another woman nearby. It was early evening and the room was filled with a dimming sunlight, just slightly more orange than in the daytime. I was not called to attend in person, but I heard them talking about it and I decided I would not be barred from it. Arthur would *not* keep me as a prisoner queen. I had been absolved of my crimes in public and I refused to live in disgrace.

So I was there waiting when Arthur arrived with Gawain, in my usual place at the table, dressed in the armoured dress with the heavy crown of Logrys on my head. I had had a servant find it for me, and I was glad to have it. It would remind the men that I was still queen, and that they owed me the same respect they showed their lord. Arthur didn't look surprised, but a look of resignation passed briefly across his face, as though he was not entirely happy but had known I would do this eventually. Mordred, as he entered, twisted his face into an amused smile to see me, but Gawain expressed outright displeasure, refusing to sit in his seat.

"She shouldn't be here," he protested to Arthur, gesturing at me. Arthur raised an authoritative hand.

"She is my queen, Gawain. She has a right to be here, and you will show her respect."

Gawain was unhappy, and grumbled under his breath, but he took his place beside Mordred. There was Dinadan, and a few other young knights that I did not recognise, but the room looked awfully empty. Kay's place at my side unoccupied, and Lancelot, Ector, Lamerocke and Perceval gone. It was a paltry gathering of knights, and they all knew it.

"My lord father," Mordred began smoothly, leaning forward across the table towards Arthur, "it is well enough for you to take the queen back into your bed – that is a matter between a man and his wife – but into your counsel? It's not wise, my lord."

Arthur was shaking his head, but Gawain was already speaking again.

"Arthur, she engaged in treason with Lancelot –"

A young man beside Gawain agreed with him enthusiastically, and Mordred leaned back in his seat with a self-satisfied smile on his face. I could see Arthur darkening with anger, but I was there first.

"*Silence.*" I stood, banging my fist against the table. The armoured greaves of the dress clashed against the hard wood and the sound of that along with my harsh, powerful voice cutting through their male grumbling chatter silenced them, even Gawain. "I find it interesting, *brave knights*, that none of you felt like stepping forward with these accusations when Lancelot was before you with his sword in his hand. You prefer to conduct your justices against unarmed men, or bound women." I turned my eyes to Mordred. He was enjoying this, I could tell. He was enjoying seeing me fight against him. He would not enjoy it for long. "Lancelot has declared his innocence and mine in public and no one challenged him. To speak thus in front of my lord Arthur is to question his judgement and authority. *Which is treasonous.* So, I suggest you *control your tongues*, noble sirs."

The knights who had not heard me speak before looked between one another, shocked. Those that I knew, Dinadan among them, seemed unsurprised. I supposed that to men who had not grown up around Breton women it must have been strange, but I was not going to sit there and be slandered to my face. I sat down slowly. The silence hung around me, and I was pleased. There were enough men there who were afraid of me, then. I was not a broken queen.

Arthur, exasperated, thumped a flat palm against the table.

"What was the news, Gawain?" he asked. I laid my palms flat on the table, too, feeling the wonderful grain of the wood against my hands. I had missed this table. I had not realised how much, until I had seen it again.

Gawain fixed me with a narrow look, but with my hands against the table I felt safe, protected from his aggression.

"Carhais has sided with Lancelot, and Brittany with it."

I felt my heart do a little leap of joy to hear it, but I hid it. It was enough to hear the name of my home, more joy to hear that it was resisting Gawain, even if that meant it was resisting Arthur as well.

"How can that be?" Arthur asked, his voice weary. "Guinevere is with us, and she's still the queen of Carhais."

Gawain pulled a letter from his pocket. I suspected that he could not read it from the way he peered at it, and that he had had it read to him and was reciting from memory. Many of the knights did this, I had noticed.

"This letter comes from a boy who calls himself the Prince of Carhais. He says the Breton people were appalled to hear that Queen Guinevere was being put to the fire, and they have put their might behind her protector."

I knew who that was. When I had left to marry Arthur the heir to Carhais had been nothing more than a babe in arms. He wasn't a boy, though, not anymore. He was a nephew of mine, and now he must have come of age and decided he did not like a foreign king threatening a Breton queen. I was pleased about this, too. Pleased that new fire had sprung up in Carhais, and the strong, proud people I came from were exerting their power once more. Arthur was slowly rubbing his forehead. He looked tired of it all, desperate for an end.

"The Breton people are proud," I declared. "And you have insulted them by *falsely* calling their queen a whore."

"Carhais is small and feeble," Mordred drawled, bored, it seemed with the discussion. "Carhais is nothing. Let this boy side with Lancelot. It makes little difference. We will walk right past Carhais straight down to Benwick castle, and tear it to the ground. This Prince of Carhais won't have the power to stop us."

He was saying it to provoke me, but he was not going to succeed. I wanted Arthur to forget about Carhais. I wanted them to think nothing of it. I wanted it to remain untouched by war, and survive.

"No." Arthur banged his fist on the table. Mordred was looking more and more pleased. So, it was not me he wanted to provoke. It was his father. "I will not be losing territory already. Whom did I charge with keeping Carhais?"

An uncomfortable murmur went around the table. I heard the name under everyone's breath. They were cowards that they did not dare to say it. At last, Dinadan spoke.

"It was the Seneschal, my lord."

Arthur rubbed his face and ran his hands through his hair. Only I, at his side, heard the weary sigh he gave.

"Very well." He stood, and pointed at Mordred. "Then it is your responsibility now to get that territory back."

So it was true. Mordred was Seneschal now. And men were afraid to say Kay's name in front of Arthur, the name of the absent brother that had ridden out in the night with the man who was now Arthur's enemy.

That night, Arthur did not come to bed. I wished that Nimue would come from Avalon, but I also had the uneasy sense that it was the malignant presence of Mordred that held her away. I still remembered the sudden and overpowering sense of the dark part of the Otherworld I had got from him. I never sensed it now, but that made it seem worse; he hid it within him, like an awful, poisonous secret.

Chapter Fifty-Three

I had not realised, from inside Joyous Guard, how badly the war had gone for Arthur, who had seemed to be winning. I learned as the days passed that although Arthur still held Logrys and Scotland, Cornwall and North Wales had gone with Lancelot, along with all the French kingdoms and Brittany. Rome was still Arthur's, but Rome had no power or armies anymore. Arthur had destroyed those long ago. Lancelot had many brothers and half-brothers, and besides, everyone knew his strength and the shrewd move was to side with the stronger party. Still, people remembered Arthur's days warring at Rome, and many men still supported him, and Lothian's armies alone were stronger than all of the territories in Britain that had gone with Lancelot. It felt as though Camelot was bracing itself for a long and awful war. I dreaded its beginning, but more I dreaded its end, where I would be given into the hands of the winner, whoever they were. If Gawain were the only survivor, at least I could expect a quick death. It was Mordred I was wary of; he had started this war, so he could only have done so with his own gain in mind.

I looked and looked for Marie, but she was nowhere to be found. I hoped that she had gone to Lothian, perhaps, seeking protection after Gaheris' death. I thought she might have gone with Morgawse, and that made me feel glad, until I heard that Morgawse was dead, killed by one of her own sons when they caught Lamerocke in her bed. I supposed I had at least escaped that fate, though I was sorry to hear that she had been killed. If Marie was in Lothian, then, it would be all alone.

Spring was at last fully on Camelot, and I found it strange that it was only a year ago that I had ridden out, side by side with Kay, in the green dress. That carefree day had darkened fast, and really it was what had led me eventually to this. I walked down into my garden. I wanted to be alone, away from Arthur, away from his silence, his reluctance for me to touch him. Whenever I tried he held me away. Last night he had been in bed already when I came up, from reading some awful boring history in the room with the Round Table, and I had pulled off my dress and pushed back the covers and climbed into bed on top of him. At first he had been responsive to my kisses, my touch, but then as I had reached down to move him inside me, he went limp in my hand and threw me off him, angry and embarrassed, shouting, "Don't think I don't know where you learned to do *that.*" He had then pulled on his clothes and left. He could not seem to bear me anymore, or at least the thought that I had been someone else's.

Arthur's withdrawal from me completed my loneliness at Camelot. Margery long gone, Christine dead, Marie beyond my reach, Kay and Lancelot far away and at war with Logrys, Morgawse and Igraine dead and Nimue absent, I was finally alone. Even Lynesse, who I had never had much interest in, kept far from me. I had seen Mordred drag her into his lap a few times in the courtyard, and I suspected this had something to do with it. I did not see the little girl, Anna, Gareth's daughter, around, nor did I see Lynesse's sister who had married Gaheris. I was disappointed in Lynesse, for going so soon from Gareth to Mordred, though I suspected he had not given her much of a choice. Still, it was quite a fall for her; Mordred was recognised as Arthur's son now, and would want a virgin princess, not a widowed gentlewoman for a wife. No one spoke to me much. They were respectful and deferential, but also without trust. I suspected that those who still held affection for me kept it hidden, too, under Mordred's heavy gaze.

I stood in the middle of the garden, smelling the growing honeysuckle, tasting the freshness of the air. I closed my eyes and remembered the night that I had been in the garden with Lancelot, the cool grass against the bare skin of my back, the stars over us, his face close to mine, the feel of our bodies coming together. The memory was vivid and overwhelming: delicious. But we had been foolish then, and careless. We had thought nothing of danger, or other people, but we had loved wildly and freely as though we would never be caught. That was so long ago, and I had been so young, though I had not thought myself young. I had thought myself old and wise, shrewd enough to keep my secret. I had thought no one would get hurt.

I was so deep in thought that I did not notice that someone else had come into the garden until I felt a man's hands take me by the hips. I thought for a moment it was Arthur, come to apologise for shouting at me and treating me roughly the night before, perhaps at last come to finally reconcile with me, so I leant back into him and sighed,

"Arthur..."

I recognised the touch as his, and I longed for us to be together again as we had been. I felt his lips brush against my bare neck and I closed my eyes into it, leaning my head back.

"Not so, my lady." The voice at my ear spoke softly, and I felt my skin crawl. It was Mordred. I jumped away, turning round to face him. I wished that I still had my dagger. I could have stabbed him in the garden and I would have taken the consequences, even if they were death. I felt the blood rise in my face, in embarrassment and disgust, but Mordred was laughing.

"What do you want, Mordred?" I demanded, backing away from him. I was unsettled, panicked, and it was the wrong thing to do because it gave him ground, and he moved towards me. I would have given anything to have Lancelot or Kay at Camelot then.

"I came to seek your advice. How should I deal with this boy, the Prince of Carhais? Shall I send his head to Lancelot when I have killed him, or to you? He is a nephew of yours? Ha! He's just a boy. Though he is only a little younger than me. Still, people stopped calling *me* a boy long ago."

I had no space left to back into. In my panic, I had thoughtlessly backed myself onto the foot of my tower, and Mordred leaned over me, slowly closer and closer. I put my hand against his chest, against the red and gold of one of Arthur's fine surcoats, and pushed him back. He moved back a little, but I felt the dangerous power of his strength; he made me aware that he would not have moved if he did not want to.

"You're still a boy," I told him, haughty and proud. I was gathering myself now, feeling stronger. He would never see that he frightened me.

"My lord father was a boy of sixteen when he conquered Britain. By the time he was twenty, he was Emperor of Rome. I think I'm lagging behind," he smirked, leaning closer again, one arm resting over my head against the stone of the tower. I felt around me for anything I could use for my defence, but there was nothing except the smooth rounded stone.

"You will never be a man like Arthur," I spat. I noticed, then, his sword at his side, and I darted out my hand for it, but he had followed my look and caught me by the wrist as I went for it, slamming it against the stone tower over my head. I burned with anger at myself; I had lost it now. I couldn't get away from him, or get my revenge on him, now. He had me where he wanted me, and I would not get away unless I was released. I cursed the weakness of my body, then. I wished I had been born a man.

"Easy, Guinevere," he said, his smirk deepening even further. "Haven't you committed enough treasons? Still, I don't blame a woman for being angry when I know she is so terribly, *terribly* lonely." He pushed one of his legs between mine. I pushed at him with my free hand and he swatted it away as though he barely felt it. As much as I pushed against him, he did not move back. He brought his face down close towards mine and I felt his breath against my neck as he whispered in my ear. I felt my skin prickle in revulsion as his breath touched it, and the nausea rising within me. "Do you dream of Joyous Guard, my lady, all those nights you spend alone? Oh yes, I saw my lord father leave his pavilion outside Joyous Guard, and I have seen him wander through Camelot alone at night, often. Now you are without the duties of a husband or a lover. You must long for a man in your bed."

He tried to kiss me and I turned my face away.

"Don't embarrass yourself, Mordred," I said, coldly.

He laughed again, low and joyless, but to my surprise he moved away, releasing his hold on my arm, and stepping away. I moved to leave, rubbing my wrist, when he seized me again as I tried to pass him, one arm around my waist pulling me tight against him.

"You will not refuse me a third time," he hissed, close. I pushed him away again.

"I will refuse you until the day I die," I hissed back.

I rushed from the garden, hot with anger – anger at my own vulnerability. I was alone. I had only a woman's strength and no friends in this country anymore. I supposed I could run, but where would I go? To Cornwall, to Isolde? I doubted her husband would be pleased to see me, or if he was he would be *too* pleased, from the tales I had heard of him. I was not willing to seek safety in a man's bed. I still had my pride. No, the only way I could make myself safe was to get Arthur back to me. Back to me, and away from Mordred. He trusted the boy too much.

I was sorry, but not surprised, that Arthur did not come to me that night, either. I stood and waited in my nightdress, slowly combing through my hair, until it was long past dark and the stars came out in the clear spring night. He did not come. I told myself that he was caught in talks of the war, which I knew they would have to leave for soon, to avoid travelling across France in the dry heat of summer, but I knew that was not really what kept him from me.

I decided at last to go down and wish for him to come back to me on the Round Table. The room was empty, as I had hoped, and dark. I lit a few candles and set them on the shelves so that there would be room for me to lie across the table. I shut the door and slowly climbed up on to the table and lay down across it, closing my eyes. It felt like coming home. It felt like all the times I had lain on the table as a little girl and wished and wished. I felt that small and hopeless. But I had the table, and I was not lost. I ran the backs of my hands across the smooth-worn grain of the wood and breathed in deeply, smelling the lovely old smell of the table, and I wished, *Let things be with Arthur how they were. Please let him forget.* It was a sad, desperate wish. Arthur's love was the only thing that could save me now. I held my eyes closed, holding tight to the wish, as I sat up, wrapping my arms around my knees and looking around me at the empty chairs. Once they would have been hopeful chairs, waiting for knights to return from their travels; now they were the chairs of ghosts, long gone.

I slipped down from the table and went over to take the candles down, but before I reached them the door opened behind me and, as if called by my wish, it was Arthur, dressed only in his shirt and breeches. He shut the door behind himself and bolted it, clumsily. He was drunk. I could smell the wine on him and his eyes were slightly wild with it.

"Guinevere," he breathed when he saw me, coming towards me slowly, as though in a dream. "I... I have been thinking about you. I have been looking for you." He reached for me and drew me into his arms, cupping the back of my head in his hand as I turned my face up towards his. "I have been thinking about that day you rode into the stables, and I was there." He kissed me, already hot with passion and memory; "and we were together in the straw," he added, kissing me again, wrapping his other arm around my waist and drawing me to him. His lips tasted of wine, his tongue, too. He held me tight against him and I pressed back, the passion waking in me for him, the relief. I felt my body begin to grow bright all over with excitement that we would at last come together again, with the raw relief of it. I slid my hands up under his shirt, across his body and then lifted it over his head. I wanted him to undress me, to feel my skin against his, but the wine and our long time apart had made him even more urgent than he usually was and he picked me up and set me lightly on the table. I wrapped my arms around his neck as he stood between my legs and kissed him hard and eagerly, and as my hand went down to his breeches I was relieved to find him hard, at last. He groaned low with pleasure and desire as I slid my hand inside, pulling the laces open. With a sudden moan of passion, he threw me back onto the table, pushing my nightdress up to my waist, grasping me by the hips and pulling me hard onto him. I gasped as he entered me, letting my arms trail across the table, over my head. I liked the feel of his hands, rough and powerful against my hips, I liked the urgency of his rough love, the hotness of his desire for me. I hoped it would burn everything else away, and leave us how we had been. I felt the heat light within me, at my centre, and wrapped my legs around him, pulling him tighter against me, but Arthur was already finished, sighing down over me, climbing onto the table on top of me to take me in his arms and kiss me softly. I was still full of heat and energy, and I pressed myself against him, murmuring his name. Arthur understood, and moved down to put his tongue on me. It was not long before the hot white light of it seared through me, and I cried out his name. Then Arthur came to lie beside me on the table and I rolled over into his arms, resting my head on his chest. He kissed me tenderly and slow, and I sighed with the sweetness of it against him. This was the happy beginning, I felt, of Arthur's return to me. I had missed it; I had missed him. The Table had brought him back to me.

"I love you," I whispered, and he kissed my nose lightly.

"I know," he replied, slowly stroking down my back. I closed my eyes and spread out my hand on his bare chest, feeling the softness of his skin against mine.

"I still remember the first time I saw you," he said quietly beside me, his voice thoughtful, staring upwards at the ceiling above us. "Down at Dover. You were a wild creature, all red hair and this angry frown. I couldn't keep my eyes off you. You thought *I* was a brute, and you looked to me like some kind of ancient barbarian princess, the way you swung yourself up onto Kay's horse in that dress. You were a savage, and I was pleased. Ector warned me, the night before we got married, that you wouldn't be like the girls I'd had before. You wouldn't know what you were doing; you might cry, or not respond at all. You would go to it as your duty. You were a princess, he said, so you might be shy." Arthur laughed softly. "Well, he was wrong about that. You were angry and rude, and you thought I was beneath you, and you were neither shy nor dutiful. I liked it." He laughed again, with a gentle fondness, and took my hand in his, entwining our fingers together. "I think it was when you told me you would kill me if I tried to force you that I began falling in love with you. Do you remember that?"

"I remember," I replied softly. I had meant it. Or I thought I had.

"I didn't want a girl who would just lie down for me and do her duty. I had dreamed of a queen like you: fierce and wild. I wanted to earn you, your respect *and* your love."

"You did," I told him quietly. He rolled onto his side to face me and leaned down to kiss me softly. I reached up and stroked his cheek. I had loved him so long, but I had never truly deserved him as he had deserved me. I had never tried to be worthy of his love. Perhaps it wasn't too late. I still saw the old love there, in his eyes. I wanted to be worth all the goodness, and the patience, and the forgiveness in him, and all these years I had loved him truly.

"We will try again," he said, pressing little kisses lightly against my forehead, my cheeks, my lips, coming to kiss me soft and tender for a moment, "when I return. Maybe when this is all over, we can go back to how we were."

I knew what that meant. *When Lancelot is dead.* The thought chilled me, but I didn't show it. I could never have Lancelot now, and I had to try to be happy – wholly happy – with the life I had with Arthur. I nodded and took his face in my hands to draw him into a kiss, deep and loving. *Just come back alive*, I thought. *Just come back alive.*

Chapter Fifty-Four

It was painfully too soon when Arthur told me the next morning that they were riding out for war that day. I was not surprised that no one had told me exactly when – there were men who still suspected I was passing messages to Lancelot about Arthur's plans, though they would not say it in public – but I was sad for it. I wished I had been more prepared to say goodbye to Arthur when we had only just found our way back to one another. He was up early, too, and out of bed, and only returned to tell me when he was already dressed in his armour.

"I'm sorry," he said, taking my face in his hands. "But the sooner I go, the sooner this is all over. I will come back to you soon."

I nodded, and he gave me one last, loving kiss, gentle yet passionate. I didn't want to watch men ride off to war again, so I stayed in his room. At least Mordred and Gawain were gone with him. I did not like the waiting, but it was better than the watching.

I passed a few long days wandering around Camelot, but since I could neither find Marie nor convince Lynesse to speak to me after I had berated her for taking Mordred into her bed in a fit of anger I now deeply regretted, there was not much for me to do. Now the castle was mostly empty there was no one to stop me going up to my rooms, but I could see, then, why Arthur had not wanted me to see them. My public room below was bare and empty. Someone had taken my books and my cushions and there was a long stain of blood on the floorboards, as though a wounded man had dragged himself in there to die. Further up, there was dried blood and gore, dark brown against the dark grey stone, and when I opened the door to my room and saw the bed, with the covers still tangled and thrown back and one of the curtains torn from it and lying in a bloodied heap in the corner, I found it too unbearable to look at, and I left.

As the days went on, I became intensely bored. It was a long, wet spring and I did not in any case feel like riding out hunting on my own. My encounter with Meleagant made me feel less inclined to ride about without a band of knights, and I doubted that any here would help me with my leisure. I didn't like the servant girl Arthur had left me with. She was slow-witted and she was not Marie. But she was slow witted enough to bring me all the wine I asked for, and in the evenings I would sit at the window with the fire beside me, warming my bare feet, and drink the wine until I forgot how bored, and sad, and lonely I was, and then I would get into bed where I would think of Arthur, or Lancelot, and slide my hand between my legs until the thoughts became a delicious warmth that spread through me, and I would fall asleep and dream of them, and sometimes, even, of Kay.

One evening it rained particularly heavily, and I opened the window wide to let the fresh wet smell of spring rain come in. I breathed it in, deep and delicious. It reminded me of Surluse, and Lancelot. If I closed my eyes, I was back there, all those years ago, sitting in my pavilion with a book on my lap, almost having given up on the hope of us ever being together. Then he had stepped through the pavilion door; and when I had seen him there, rain running down his face, I had known then that I would never go back. I held tight to the memory of that night, of his skin cool and wet from the rain against mine in the light of the brazier, of his hands on my body, of his hair damp still in my hands, the delight we had taken in one another, the way he had whispered close to me, *don't rush*. How painfully wonderful it had felt to come together with him at last. It felt unbearably close, the memory of him, when I knew I would probably never see him again. But I would hug that memory of our night together close to my soul, and it would carry me through eternity.

As night fell and it got colder, I moved to the fire, reluctant to close the window and lose the freshness outside. I sat for a long time by the fire, hugging my knees to me, staring into the flames, wondering what Arthur was doing. He had not written to me, nor sent any messengers to tell me what he was doing. I thought he was afraid I might write to Lancelot, or perhaps he was reconciling with Lancelot and he did not want me to know; he wanted to keep us apart. Perhaps he had reconciled with Lancelot, and Lancelot would come back with him to Camelot. If Gawain was dead, then it could happen. If I feared for Lancelot against anyone it was Gawain, though the raw and savage anger that filled Gawain would give him strength, but not skill, and Lancelot was by far the better knight. It was too much to hope, I thought, that Arthur would return with Lancelot. Even if they reconciled, I did not think Arthur would want Lancelot near me. I should try not to hope for it. I should accept things as they were.

Food came for me, and I was glad of it, because I had forgotten to ask for it. I hoped it would be Marie, now that Arthur was gone and someone else was in charge of the castle, though I always hoped and it was never her. It was a girl I did not know, who looked at me with big, brown reproachful eyes. Most of the serving women did. I suspected that several of them were the women Arthur had declined to take into his bed for my sake, who resented me now they had heard that I did not consider my marriage-bed as sacred as Arthur did. Well, they did not know anything about it, and in any case they were all too afraid to say anything in front of me. The meat, whatever it was, tasted of nothing in my mouth, and I left the rest. The girl had brought wine as well, as I had asked, in a little jug, and I was grateful for that. I poured a full cup and swallowed deeply. It must have been a different barrel from what I had had before; it tasted different. Stronger, and I was glad of it. I did not want to sit there alone running over in my head everything that had happened, or that could happen, or that might already be happening between Lancelot and Arthur. I wished Arthur would come back. He had said it would not be long. I did not know, really, how long it had been. A month? Two? If they were just going over so that Gawain and Lancelot could fight, then they ought to be on their way back by now. I was struck with the fear, again, of Arthur being killed. I wished he would come back. I didn't need him to have forgiven me; I just wanted him to hold me. I wanted to feel he was alive. I did not think I could bear it if they killed one another. What if Lancelot had killed Gawain and Arthur had taken up his cause? What if Arthur was still angry with Lancelot? The thought of them fighting made me feel anxious, and I drank more deeply from the wine. Lancelot would be safe, but Arthur... No, I was not sure of Arthur.

The wine was strong and it made me feel sleepy. I finished the cup and poured another, and drained it; I wanted sleep to come to me fast. I stretched out on the sheepskin rug by the fire, feeling the heat of it against one side of my face, down my side. I felt light as a feather all over my body, as though I was floating outside myself, my limbs heavy in their movement. It was pleasant. That wine *was* strong. Mercifully strong.

I dozed peacefully until I heard the door open and shut behind me. I sat up sleepily, feeling slow and fuzzy as a dream. I couldn't tell what time it was, but it was deeply dark outside.

"Arthur," I murmured. I had been dreaming of him.

I felt his hand gently lift the loose hair away from my neck and he kissed me there, winding his hand through my hair. I sighed into it, closing my eyes, my eyelids deliciously heavy. It had happened again; I had wished for him, and he had come to me. His touch raised a sleepy heat in me, and I sank back against him as I felt one of his hands move down, out of my hair and over my nightdress, first brushing lightly across my breast and then taking hold of it with the pleasant roughness I knew so well. I felt flushed already; I wanted his hands on me, wanted us to love together as we had when we were young. He gently laid me back on the rug and climbed on top of me. I let my heavy legs fall slightly apart as he lay between them and wrapped my arms around him as he came to kiss me. My eyelids flickered and I saw the golden hair, the strong body that I knew. I was in such a haze, I did not know if it was still a dream. I hoped it was not a dream, and Arthur had come back to me. Dimly, I realised that this must mean that Lancelot was dead, but the thought passed me by like a ghost. Perhaps I would feel it hit me in the morning, but in the lovely night-time I was just glad to have Arthur in my arms again.

I felt his hands untying the strings that held the front of my nightdress together, lifting it open. Arthur made a small, low noise of appreciation as it fell open, as he had done on our first night together. I was glad he still desired me as much as he had done then, after everything, and the knowledge of this made me feel warm and eager for him. I felt his hand against the bare skin of my breast, with its heady familiarity, the touch I had known so long returning to me memories of the happy nights we had spent together, and the familiar strength of his body around me, too, awaking the desire in me, and I gave a soft, happy gasp. He had not touched me like this in a long time, not since I had been returned to him, not with such hungry tenderness, such powerful desire. I pressed back against him, and he slid a hand under my back to hold me fast against him. I stretched my arms over my head, luxuriating in his soft kisses as they touched my breasts, my nipples, and I whispered his name. Perhaps it could be like this again, always. He moved away for a second, and it must have been to pull off his shirt, because then I felt the bare skin of his chest against my own, and gave a slow murmur of delight. Our mouths met with hungry, passionate kisses and I reached lazily down, filled with a tingling sleepiness still, but a sleepiness that had become a languorous desire, and pulled open his breeches. He groaned above me, and thrust into me with all the urgent passion of our past love, of the times of our youth. His breath was hot against my neck and he ran his hands down my body, moving down to grasp me by the thighs and pull me harder against him. He was rough and urgent, and I had longed for it. I felt the pleasure spread through my body, through my hazy mind, and sighed his name, running my hands up his arms to feel the hard muscle there, my fingers tightening their grasp as we moved together and I felt the bright ecstasy gathering within me. It was so good to feel the power of his love again, and his body on top of mine, the way we used to be. After so long, the heat rose quick within me, and as I felt the wave of rapture break over me, I cried out for him, softly. Arthur pressed his face into my neck as he, too, sighed with relief, and, full of warmth and joy, and relief to be back thus with Arthur, I slipped off into sleep.

Chapter Fifty-Five

I woke to the cold feeling of the fresh morning air against my bare back. My head was pounding. Around me hung the delicious memory of Arthur's return. I hoped that I had not dreamed it. I put my hands over my eyes and groaned. I was in bed, I could feel that, so I had not slept beside the fire. The sheet was wrapped down around my hips, tangled in my sleep, leaving my back open to the chill.

"Good morning," I heard Arthur say. I pushed my head up from the pillow and through my blurry morning vision as I blinked awake I could see that he was already dressed and sitting up in the bed beside me. That seemed strange. And then as I blinked again I saw it was *not* Arthur. It was Morded. I felt all the heat drain out of my body. I sat up sharply, pulling the sheet around myself, my heart thudding painfully hard in my chest. *No.* Mordred reached out and grabbed a handful of the sheet, under where I clasped it in my hand.

"It is a little late for modesty, my lady."

'Where is Arthur?" I demanded.

"Arthur is in France." He grinned.

An awful silence stretched between us for a moment, in which I only heard my own heart thud.

"And you are not." The words came from me, quiet with dread. I had thought he was going to France with them. This could not be happening. This could not.

"No, my lady, I am not. Arthur left me here to hold Logrys from Winchester in his absence. I had it in my mind to come back to Camelot, but Arthur – Arthur is still in France." He smiled more deeply, more cruelly, to see the panic and dread on my face as I realised there was no way it could have been Arthur I was with last night. And it had not been a dream. "Oh yes, my lady. I'm afraid so." He tugged at the sheet, in malicious playfulness, but I kept a hold of it. "But I don't think it was so awful for you. After all, you moaned like a whore when I took you."

I slapped him across the face. "*Get out.*"

He laughed. I wished that Arthur had not taken Excalibur. I would have killed him. Arthur had left me alone in Camelot, without any friends, without telling me that Mordred was still in Logrys. Arthur had not even written to tell me where he was. Arthur hadn't told me anything.

"Don't worry, my lady. When I return from battle, I will make you my wife." He ran a finger across my jaw, down under my chin, turning my face up towards him so that I had to meet his gaze. I would have pushed him off, but I wanted to keep hold of the sheet. "When I have killed Arthur. And Lancelot. I would have spared *him*, had you not repelled me so rudely." He leaned closer to whisper, "I told you, didn't I, that I would punish you?"

As if he had not punished me enough already. He gave the sheet one last tug and laughed to see me struggle against him, then shoved me back against the bed. My head smacked hard against the wood of the headboard. I felt the tears prick at the back of my eyes, but I held them back. He would not see that he had won.

When the door slammed shut behind him and I heard the lock I felt all the hope drain out of me and an awful cold settle against my heart. So, I was Mordred's prisoner now. But I would not cry. Crying was not going to help me.

I slipped from the bed slowly and, my head throbbing, dressed in the dress I had worn the day before. I wished that I had been wearing the armoured dress, but this one was nothing more substantial than plain blue wool, dark and simple, but warm at least, with a thick thread border in gold around the neck and waist. That gold wouldn't do me any good now. I needed a weapon. I saw the nightdress lying by the fire, which had burned out to black, dead lumps, and I felt sick. I sat by the window, slowly, hoping the cold morning air would clear my head and settle my stomach, but it was nothing that the clean air could heal. The thought of Mordred inside me made my stomach churn, made me feel sick at myself. I wanted to absent myself from my own body. I wanted to go back to sleep and wake up again and find it was a dream. It had half-felt like a dream. I leant my arms on the edge of the open window and laid my forehead against them. *I thought he was Arthur.* And Arthur was fighting Lancelot in France, and he had not forgiven me, would not forgive me until Lancelot was dead. I would never truly feel him with me again. And now, if Lancelot's forces did not kill him, Mordred would. I could only hope that Lancelot somehow managed to kill Mordred first. But if anyone could hurt Lancelot, it would be Mordred. He had the unstoppable power of being a man without honour.

Perhaps I should kill myself. I looked down out of the window. The rain had stopped overnight, and it was a clear morning. The ground beneath was far away, but it would be soft. I couldn't be sure of it, and I did not want to be shut in Camelot as Mordred's prisoner, too injured to run if I got the chance. Still, at the moment death seemed like the kindest option. I was alone, and broken. Better to die a brave death than live on defeated by Mordred. The thought of his hands on me again made me feel sick. I leaned out a little further, feeling my balance waver. I closed my eyes.

Then, I heard a woman's voice say my name softly. I looked round, stepping back from the window, startled from my thoughts of death. Sat on the bed, cross-legged, was Morgan. It was unmistakably her, her face painted in woad, in the dress she always wore that glistened with dark gems like the scales of a dragon, her dark hair lying over her shoulder in a long plait.

"I've come to help you," she said softly.

"Why?" I asked in disbelief.

"Why?" She looked genuinely confused.

"You hate me," I explained evenly.

"*Hate* you?" Then understanding dawned over her face. "Guinevere." She slid from the bed and came over and took my hands in hers. They were papery, soft and dry. I realised that she had never seemed to look right at me before. The cold, unfocussed eyes I had assumed glossed over me in disdain were intelligent and attentive. She must, I supposed, have not thought me worthy of her attention before. "We were rivals for a man's love, once, and we both did everything we could to win him. I never hated you." She smiled a little mischievous smile, but not unkindly. "I know I play a little rough. True, I have no love for Arthur. His father raped my mother, and he got that monster on my sister, and he married me to that disgusting old man against my wishes. But you? No you're an innocent really in all this, aren't you?" She smiled kindly and stroked my cheek as though I was a child. Did I look that frail? That vulnerable? "Oh, Mordred was cruel to you," she said softly, thoughtfully. She seemed to drift away with the thought for a moment, then come back to herself and began to speak with a sort of brisk purposefulness which I imagined she had learned from the nuns who had raised her. "We are women together, and I have come to protect you from Mordred. Agree to be his wife, until you can get to somewhere safe, and I will come to you again. Just pretend to give in. He will show his weakness when he thinks he has won." She pressed my hands in hers again and said softly, "I will come to you again."

She pressed a hand on my head, like a blessing, and as I had seen her do before, she melted from the room, disappearing into dust. I didn't quite trust her yet, nor did I understand why she would want to help me now, but I suddenly felt less alone. I also felt ashamed of my hopelessness. My fight with Mordred was not over, not lost, not yet. I just had to pull myself together.

I tried the door again, but I was, as I had suspected, locked in. But it was not long before one of the anonymous serving-women came with something for me to eat, and I was waiting for her. I grabbed her by the arm before she could get away down the stairs. I could see the wild fear in her eyes, and I was pleased. She was more likely to do as I said if she was afraid of me.

"Tell Mordred I want to see him."

She looked back blankly for a second, then began to babble about him being angry and punishment. I shook her by the arm hard.

"I may be your captive, but I am still your *queen*, and you *will* do as I say. Especially if you want me to forget that you knew I was being held here and did nothing to help me when Arthur returns. *Which he will.*"

The girl nodded furiously and I let her go, stepping back into the room. She closed the door fast and locked it hastily. She was perhaps a halfwit, but I thought I had impressed on her the importance of my message. I looked at the food she had left: some porridge. I wasn't hungry.

I did not have to wait long for Mordred. When he came, he was dressed in his platemail for battle. He must have been about to ride out to war. Though he was a young man, the iron was already heavily dented from battles. I had made an effort to look more powerful, more like a queen. I was wearing the heavy crown of Logrys. Arthur had left it in its place beside his in the bedroom when he rode out for war. His had been gone since he left. I hoped that Mordred had not stolen it. I had tied up my hair as best as I could on my own. I only had the single dress, and it was not so grand, but this would have to be enough. I had, at least, one of my gold and emerald necklaces. It was hardly what I would have wished for; I wanted nothing more than Excalibur and my armoured dress, but I supposed these women's things were a different kind of armour.

"What do you want?" he demanded rudely, pushing the door shut behind him. He did not bother to lock it. He trusted well enough in his own strength.

I drew myself up to my full height. He still towered over me, and he had come with his sword at his side, but it made me feel a little stronger, a little braver. But I *was* brave. I had the stone-cold bravery inside me of a woman who has nothing left to lose. With that in my mind I did not have to see myself as the one of the two of us who was in the more vulnerable position.

"I have reconsidered my position," I told him.

He shrugged in annoyance.

"What do you mean?"

I stepped towards him. It felt like gaining territory; already I was gaining ground.

"I have decided that I should like you to take me as your wife, and I will go willingly, and I believe I will be useful to your cause."

He looked suspicious, but he didn't look as though he was keen to hurry away anymore, and he rested his hand thoughtfully on the hilt of his sword.

"Why would you do that?" he asked evenly, his dark eyes watchful.

I gave a little shrug and fixed him with an even gaze. The years had made me good at lying, good at pretence, and I was glad of it. I had lied to Arthur, whom I loved, for years. I found it easy to lie to a man I hated. He disgusted me, and being in the same room as him again made my stomach turn, but it did not show. I would wait; I would bide my time. If I had to go to bed with him again in order to kill him in his sleep, I would do it. He thought he had broken me, but what he had done to me had given me the strength of a deep and slow-burning hate. I gave him a sly little smile, and stepped closer again.

"Because I want to survive this. Arthur is in a weak position, and you will probably defeat him, but you will *for sure* with my help. I don't want to hazard my life when I can be sure of it. Arthur has already agreed to have me put to the fire for what I have done, and I doubt that I will be safe if he wins. Besides, I doubt he would have me in his bed again. I don't want to die, nor do I wish to take sanctuary in a nunnery and never again feel the touch of a man."

Mordred seized me by the front of my dress and slammed me against the wall, pulling me paces across the room in a single swipe of his powerful arm. The crown bit hard into the back of my head, but I held in the little cry of pain. I thought he was angry, I thought that he knew that I was trying to manipulate him, but when I looked at his face I saw that he was *enjoying* it. He was aroused. He did not release his grip, but held me still against the wall, leaning down to me with a leering grin. I met his gaze fiercely.

"Oh yes," he growled softly. "You do seem to me like the kind of woman who *particularly* enjoys the touch of a man."

He released his grip on the fabric, but kept his hand there, pressed flat against me, the heel of his hand against the bottom of my ribs, spreading his fingers across the middle of my breasts. I could feel my heart hammering against his hand. Perhaps he thought I was excited, too. I was repulsed.

Then a thought crossed his mind, and narrowing his eyes he leaned away a little.

"What of Lancelot?"

"Even if he lived, he would never want to see me again. I'm the woman who drove him against his king, and will be the cause of his king's death. He would not want me, and I'm not interested in a man who doesn't want me."

"Hmmm." Mordred considered it, pushing his hand harder against me. It was becoming hard to breathe against it, but I did not want to appear weak. I did not want his casual cruelty to appear to affect me at all. He moved around beside me, to lean against the wall next to me, to speak softly in my ear. "I must say, my lady, I *am* surprised. After this morning I thought I had found you a Helen of Troy, weeping with regret at having destroyed a great kingdom with her tragic love." He laughed to himself quietly at his own cleverness. His lips brushed my ear, he was so close, and the sensation, the *thought* of him so close turned my stomach. I swallowed hard, pushing away everything I felt; I knew I had to, to survive. "A hopeless simpering thing. But no, instead I find you a shrewd little Cleopatra, offering herself to whichever man seems to be the likely victor. Well, you have chosen wisely, this time. Much more wisely than you did with that fool, Lancelot, who doesn't know how to finish a man in battle."

He took hold of one of my breasts, squeezing at the nipple through the fabric, and though his touch made my skin crawl, I was relieved to breathe freely again. He was lost, now, in his own imagining of himself as a great conqueror, with the proud, mistaken thought that he had seduced me. I could hear in the distance men calling for him. They must be eager to ride out, because the day was already getting late. He ignored them. He pressed himself against me, and whispered close, lightly taking the top of my ear in his teeth.

"You know I am the King of Britain now; I had letters made that said Arthur had met his death in France at Lancelot's hand, and they have crowned me King." I could hear him get more and more excited as he spoke, more filled with lust, though it was more for himself than for me, I suspected. "And you will make me a fine queen, I think."

He reached down and took hold of the skirts of my dress, but I put my hand on his to stop him.

"No, sir," I said firmly, turning to look him in the eye. He looked so like Arthur. He was so like Arthur had been. It made me ache to see Arthur again. Staring into this husk of a man who bore his face was unbearable; what a pale shade of Arthur he truly was. Where Arthur was kind and noble, he was weak-minded and cruel; where Arthur was dutiful, he was greedy and selfish. He was proud and easily flattered and this had made it very easy for me. "Come to me again when you have defeated Arthur, and we will love together as King and Queen."

He reluctantly released his hand and moved away. The voices calling his name grew louder.

"Very well. I must ride out before nightfall, so I will leave you *for now*. But you will ride and join me on the battlefield tomorrow. Arthur is coming back from France to try to reclaim his kingdoms and I must ride out to meet him. I want Arthur to see you by my side." He took my chin in his hand and held my face turned up to his. I looked into his empty eyes and felt only the desire for revenge against him. "I want you to tell him how you have chosen me. I want to see that on his face before I kill him."

"I would be pleased," I told him evenly. "I was raised to ride out to battle."

"Good."

He kissed me roughly, and I forced myself to respond, to block out the raging desire within me to tear his hands from my body. Thankfully it was brief, and he left. He did not lock the door behind him. In his victory, he had forgotten to mistrust me. After I heard the sound of his footsteps recede into nothingness I allowed myself to relax. I was shaking with repulsion, with hate, with the nearness of my victory. I had been holding in my disgust so hard that now I was finally alone, I retched with it, and ran over to the window to breathe in the cool clean air.

But I was free.

Chapter Fifty-Six

I planned my next move carefully. I needed to be sure that Mordred and his men had left Camelot. I waited until the sun was dipping towards the horizon and I could no longer hear the soft clanking of men moving in armour far away in the courtyard. I pulled the door open boldly. If I looked as though I did not expect to be caught at anything, and if I walked about with the crown on my head – which was already making my neck ache, and the back of my head throb where Mordred had slammed me against the wall – then people would not question me.

I went slowly down to the armoury. I knew what I was looking for, and I was pleased that it was still there: the suit of armour I had worn when I rode with Arthur to Rome. There was no one else in there, so I stripped off my dress and pulled it on. The chainmail was well enough, but the leather plated jerkin didn't seem enough protection, and I was surprised that I had been happy to ride out into battle with it; but I supposed I had been a young woman, and thought myself beyond harm. I thought about taking one of the men's breastplates, but I thought it would impede my ability to move my arms. My bow and arrow wasn't there, and I couldn't pull the men's bows back, but I took a squire's sword, light enough for me to lift, though only with both hands, and buckled it around my waist. Last, I put on my mail cap and set the crown on top. I was as ready for battle as I would ever be.

I found a serving woman and ordered her to fetch my armoured dresses, and some food, and gather some horses. Seeing me armed and wearing the crown, this girl obeyed without question. I walked out into the courtyard. Lynesse was standing out there, her daughter beside her, holding her hand. The girl had Gareth's looks, and I supposed she would look like Morgawse when she was older. She had the same bold, broad features and russet hair. She wasn't a pretty child, but she would make a striking woman, like her grandmother. When Lynesse saw me, she gathered the girl against her legs protectively and gave me a wary look. I saw that her lip was swollen and she had a small bruise at the side of her neck. That could not have been anyone but Mordred. I was sorry that he had taken out his excitement at his victory on her, since I had refused him. I walked over to her.

"Lynesse," I said softly, "I am riding for London today. I will take you and little Anna with me, if you want."

"Is... Mordred in London?" she asked, her voice quavering.

I shook my head, and she nodded her acceptance.

"Get everything you need," I told her.

I turned around to begin gathering some others – I had seen about Camelot a few knights I knew would be loyal to me – and I turned right into Marie. For a moment, I did not recognise her, she was so hugely pregnant, but as I realised it was her, I cried out with joy and threw my arms around her. I was relieved that she did not push me away. I hoped she did not blame me for Gaheris' death. I held her out from me at arm's length, speechless with relief to see her. She had been at Camelot all along, and Arthur had kept her from me. I felt a little stab of anger towards him for that.

"You're alive," Marie gasped in Breton. "I was afraid, because they wouldn't let me see you. Arthur hates it, you know, when we talk in Breton. He has had it in his head that when we talk in Breton, we're talking about Lancelot. That's what the lady who they left me with when they brought you back said. I thought it was a lie, though. I thought they might have killed you. When I heard that Mordred was back in Camelot, I slipped away, because I had to know. I was so afraid. But you're alive."

Marie threw her arms around me again and I held her tight to me. I felt her huge belly press against me. I realised that it was strange that this had not happened before, since Marie and Gaheris had been lovers for so long, and Marie was not young any more. Five or so years younger than me, but certainly she ought to have been in more danger of this ten years ago, or whenever it had begun. Though I had some dim awareness that Christine had known how to deal with things like that. *Christine.* I missed her. Still, Marie was back with me, and if it was a boy, and Lancelot killed Gawain, that little bastard in her belly would be King of Lothian.

"Marie," I spoke fast, hushed, even though I was sure no one else around us spoke Breton, "get your things. We're going to London."

"Mordred says Arthur is dead, and he's going to marry you," Marie said, worried.

"Arthur's alive, and coming back to Britain. Mordred *thinks* he will. If anyone asks you where we're going, say we're going to London to talk to the bishop and arrange things for the wedding."

Marie nodded and I kissed her on both cheeks and she hurried off.

I found a horse in the stables that seemed good enough and harnessed and saddled it, leading it out into the courtyard. Word had spread, and a small party of women who wanted to get away from Mordred, and knights who were still loyal to me, or Arthur, had gathered. It was as well that the word passed in secret; it would pass fast enough, and perhaps as we travelled people would join us. I sent a messenger out to Joyous Guard to tell anyone there still loyal to me to wait for me in London, in the tower.

Night was falling when the small party of us rode out of Camelot, me at the head with Marie at my side, and Lynesse behind us. We had about fifty knights with us. Enough to defend us if we met someone on the road; not enough if we met Mordred's army. It was a paltry gathering of knights, really. Those older knights whose loyalty to Arthur was set in their bones, from their promises to his father, the very youngest who had come to be made his knights in the last year, the weak and afraid, the strays who were afraid of Mordred, and the few who still believed that my name as queen meant something. But since we were few we could ride swiftly enough, and we reached London before dawn, in the secret depths of the night. I slid from my horse, sore and tired, but not yet able to rest. We were not yet in the tower. I had not told the people following me my plans. I didn't want anyone to balk and ride off to Mordred, telling him what I was doing.

There were men in the tower when we reached it. I could see them moving around inside. I hoped that they were mine, come from Joyous Guard. London smelled acrid with sewage and poverty, far indeed from Camelot's smells of rural freshness, but I needed somewhere small enough for me to hold it on my own, and I did not think I could have borne it, to go back to Joyous Guard alone. Besides, Mordred would find it hard to wage war against me in the middle of a city.

The party I had brought with me waited behind me as I walked forward to the tower's great door. They were tired, and afraid, and I was their leader. I had brought them here. It was my duty to them to show no fear. I let my hand rest on the hilt of my sword. If an armoured knight opened the door then I did not stand much of a chance, but I needed to *look* as though I stood a chance. I drew myself up to my full height and banged on the door.

"Open the door. It is Guinevere, Queen of Britain," I shouted. It was well enough to sound grand. It would please the men who followed me.

The door opened slowly, and my heart pounded with every second, but when I saw who opened it, I could have sunk to my knees with joy and relief.

It was Kay. He stood in the doorway, a torch in his hand throwing dark shadows across his face. He looked tense and grim, but gave me a nod of greeting, and stepped aside. I walked past him with Marie and Lynesse beside me, and the men came in after me.

"Is this everyone?" Kay asked me. He spoke to me as if we were two men at war, and I was pleased. I had come to him as a queen at the head of her army – albeit a small one – and he spoke to me like an ally. Later, I hoped, we would talk as friends.

I nodded.

"Bar the doors," Kay shouted, and some of Kay's men – I supposed they were the men of Joyous Guard – stepped forward and barricaded the big door with huge timbers. I moved further into the tower and my party followed.

"Guinevere, what's going on?" Lynesse asked breathlessly, running up to me, her daughter in her arms, though the girl was far too old for it.

"We're preparing for a siege," I told her. "It won't be long before Mordred comes for us."

He did not seem to me like a man who would let this insult go. I had tricked him, and he would want revenge for it. I was prepared. He would only lay hands on me again if it was on my cold, dead corpse.

Kay led me up and into the main part of the tower, showed my knights where they could take off their armour and rest, and gestured Lynesse towards a room I could see had a few ladies in it, though most were old and some looked like peasants to me. Kay seemed to expect Marie to follow her, but I wanted Marie with me. He led me around, showing me the defences. They had come from Joyous Guard with the remains of its siege stores, too. It was fortunate that I had not planned to go there. After Lancelot had left, the armies of Lothian had burned the village and tried to burn the castle. The small garrison there had held it, but the losses had been heavy. It would have been no place for me. The tower had enough food for both our parties to survive through until the autumn, the winter at a push. Kay warned me that the smell of London was worse in the summer. I looked over everything with a thoughtful eye, hoping the tower would hold and Arthur would return quickly from France. We shouldn't have to wait that long, but if the battle between Arthur and Mordred reached a deadlock and we were unlucky, then it might be years. It wouldn't be long if Lancelot joined Arthur's side. I had no doubts in me that if he joined the battle, it would not be for Mordred.

After I had looked over and approved all of Kay's preparations, he led me up to the top of the tower, to a small room that looked like an old library, its walls lined with dusty books. A small fire burned in the grate and there was a low bed beside it that looked as though it had been made up of things that lay around. There were a few old-looking chairs in a circle, and in one of them was Ector.

To see his old, kind face was a blissful relief, and I rushed to embrace him as he stood to greet me. He seemed surprised, that funny formal old man, but not displeased. I put the heavy crown from my head and placed it on one of the bookshelves, and slid off the mail cap, letting my hair fall loose around my shoulders, and sat down. Marie sat awkwardly beside me, lowering her heavy body carefully into the chair. She looked even more hugely pregnant than she was because her body was so small. I saw Kay's eyes move over her in concern, trace the vast swell of her belly. It would be soon.

Kay offered around a jug of wine. I shook my head at it, not wanting to even smell it again. Not after last night. Kay looked surprised, but didn't ask. When we were finally settled in our chairs, Kay leaned forward to me, his forearms resting on his thighs, his look confused, concerned.

"What happened, Guinevere?"

"Arthur left with Gawain to ride to Benwick, and when he had gone Mordred forged letters to say he was dead, and he's made himself king."

I didn't mention anything about me. I didn't want to talk about it, and I was afraid that if I mentioned even the beginning, it would all come tumbling out of me. I didn't want to seem weak, because that would make me feel weak. I somehow felt that if I admitted it had happened, Mordred would have another victory over me.

"So Arthur lives," Kay murmured thoughtfully, sitting back up in his chair. "That's good. And Lancelot, too. We can only hope that Gawain can put aside his anger and call Lancelot from France to help Arthur. It looks bad for him, Guinevere. Most of the men who were with Lancelot when we fought at Joyous Guard have gone over to Mordred; that's Cornwall and some of the kingdoms of Wales. A few lords are resisting him, and perhaps it will be more when people hear that Arthur is alive and has returned."

"We can only hope," Ector added grimly. His hair was almost all grey now, and he sounded so tired. I was tired, and he had lived half as long as me again. He stood slowly, as though his joints pained him.

It was cold and damp in the tower, even though it was getting late into spring, and the years had not been kind to Ector. "Truly, my lady, I am glad to see you so well. But you must excuse me. I am going to retire."

Marie nodded. "Me too."

She looked exhausted. It must have been hideously uncomfortable for her to ride so far, through the night, so pregnant. Ector offered her his hand, and she took it. Ector lingered in the door a moment, looking at Kay expectantly. An awkward silence fell, and I could not tell what it meant, but after a moment Kay waved his hand dismissively at his father.

"I'll follow you soon."

Ector left with Marie reluctantly. I had the sense Ector had not wanted to leave me and Kay alone, though I could not understand why. He had not worried about it at Joyous Guard. I groaned and stretched out, my body aching from the travel, from the heavy armour and the heavy crown. I stood to pull the greaves from my legs and slide off the chainmail beneath. Underneath I had some light woollen leggings which were stained with rust from the greaves. I had not had time to stop and clean them, and they had rusted a little in Camelot's armoury. Kay stepped forward to help me unbuckle the plated jerkin and I pulled it over my head. I was too hot and uncomfortable from wearing it to think too hard about standing before Kay in the little cotton vest and leggings. He did not seem bothered.

"How was Arthur?" he asked quietly.

"Still angry," I admitted.

Kay nodded, and wrapped his arms around me, pulling me into a tight embrace. I rested my head against his chest, closing my eyes and wrapping my arms around his neck. I was so glad to see him again, so glad to have a friend by my side. His familiar smell and the gentle sense of the Otherworld that came from him made me realise just how much I had missed him. Kay rested his chin lightly on the top of my head.

"How is Lancelot?" I asked quietly, into his chest. If it was bad, I was not sure I wanted to hear.

"Well. He fought with Gawain outside Benwick, and he has wounded Gawain. I heard it's bad and Gawain is not going to survive. But if Arthur is bringing him back to Logrys it will be against his will, because the last I heard he was clamouring for Lancelot to fight him again, so they can finish it."

I was so relieved, I could not speak. Lancelot would come back. Arthur would ask him back, and Arthur and Lancelot would defeat Mordred, and – well, Lancelot would have to go back to France, I expected, but it would be in peace, and perhaps I would see him again, and I would go back to my life with Arthur. All we had to do was hold in the tower until Arthur forced Mordred to come out of London to meet him.

Kay loosened his arms around me to lean back and look down at me.

"We were afraid when Mordred declared himself king that he might have you killed. Though you know he has declared his intention to marry you."

I nodded, looking away from him. I felt exposed under Kay's look, and I did not want him to see that I was weak, that I had been hurt by Mordred. "Yes, he told me." Luckily, Kay was too interested in his own story of Mordred to ask, or notice.

"The bishop tried to stop him, you know. Told him he couldn't marry the wife of a man who was both his father and his uncle, and Mordred threatened to kill him, and he's run away. No one knows where he is. It won't be long before Mordred comes looking for you. I'm surprised he didn't have you guarded."

I laid my head back against Kay's chest and he stroked my hair. I didn't want to explain, didn't want to tell him how I had got myself here, safely away. If I began to explain I might begin to cry, and I was not going to cry anymore.

"Guinevere," Kay said softly, "you're shaking. What is it?"

I hadn't realised. I shook my head.

"I'm just exhausted," I lied. Kay nodded and grabbed his cloak from the back of a chair.

"I'll show you where you can sleep. You'd better wear this."

I wrapped it around myself and followed Kay down to a little room. Someone had lit a fire, and there was a proper bed, though it was small and without curtains. As I stepped in, Kay put his hand on my arm and I turned back to face him.

"Guinevere," he said warily, "we don't have anyone for Marie. When the time comes."

I nodded, taking it in. I had seen it done, but I had never done it, and Marie was old to be having a first child, and she so small and the child so large. If only we had not lost Christine. Kay leaned down and kissed me gently on the cheek and I leaned my head against his for a second. I thought for a moment of asking him not to go. I didn't want to be alone; I was afraid I would dream of Mordred. But I thought he might think I meant something else if I asked him to stay, and it would not look good when Arthur returned, so I said nothing, and Kay left, closing the door softly behind him. I would, still, have felt so much better with him in the bed beside me.

It took me a long time to get to sleep. I was afraid that I would wake up back in Camelot with Mordred beside me, that I had dreamed my escape. When I finally did sleep, I dreamed of Mordred holding me down with his hand over my mouth and I woke up screaming. I was glad, then, that I had not asked Kay to stay with me.

Chapter Fifty-Seven

It was not long before word reached Mordred that I had left Camelot, and his men began to gather around the tower. I was sitting with Marie, her arms wrapped around her huge belly, and Lynesse, in the little library that seemed to also be Kay's bedchamber, reading to keep away the boredom of siege, when I first heard them banging against the door, and a young knight ran up in his armour to tell me that Mordred had come to the gates of the tower and was demanding to be let in.

I turned to Lynesse.

"Bring my armoured dress," I told her. Marie helped me unlace the dress I was wearing and when Lynesse returned with the green armoured dress I slipped it on, and buckled the sword I had brought from Camelot around my waist. I set the crown I had left on the bookshelf on my head. I climbed up to the top of the tower. I would speak to him. I wanted to look him in the eye, so that he could see that he had not beaten me.

I stood on the battlements, my arms crossed over my chest, and looked down at Mordred throwing his shoulder against the barred door. It rattled a little, but it didn't budge. I had to squint down to see him in the bright early summer sun, but he was unmistakable. I watched him for a moment, enjoying myself already.

"Good morning, Mordred," I called down, unable to keep a smile from my face. He had not been expecting this. He looked up, and I saw the rage and shock on his face. Good. I was glad he was angry. He had thought he had convinced me, that I had been easily won, and I had caught him in his own self-confidence.

"Guinevere," he shouted up. "What are you doing? It's me. Let me in." He slammed his palms against the door in impotent anger.

The knights behind him held back. I wasn't sure if they were doing so because they were afraid of him, or because they were embarrassed.

Mordred wasn't dressed for battle as they were; he was wearing Arthur's red and gold surcoat and Arthur's crown, which the sun glinted off, brightly. So he *had* stolen it. He had a sword at his side, but it wouldn't do him any good against the door.

"I'm not going to do that, Mordred," I called down. He glared up at me narrowly. "I'm very busy making plans for our wedding."

"What?" he roared. He was still confused, still unable to believe that I had outwitted him so easily, and shut myself away, out of his reach.

"Yes, well, I'm afraid I've rather changed my mind about it," I told him. I leaned down over the battlements, to look him in the eye. He fell still for a moment, and I spoke quietly, but it carried well enough down to him below. "I would rather cut my own throat than ever marry you, and if you ever get your hands on me again it will only be on my lifeless body."

Mordred seemed at last to be absorbing the fact that he had finally lost a fight against me. He beat against the door again, but he was beginning to realise that it was useless. He stopped, his chest heaving with the effort of beating at the door, and snarled up at me.

"Come out now, and I'll be merciful. If I have to tear down the tower to get you, I won't be so lenient. I'll let my men rape you in the street. You won't last long in there."

"Goodbye Mordred," I called down, moving away from the edge. It wasn't much of a victory after everything he had done to me, but it was sweet enough.

Mordred would be left with the choice of whether to bring siege weapons to London to get me out of the tower or to turn his strength against Arthur, who we had heard had landed at Dover and was marching his army towards Mordred's, which was camped on Salisbury Plain. There was still no word on whether Gawain had relented and they would send for Lancelot's help from France. We sat in the tower and waited, and I listened to Mordred's men outside, their swords and armour clanking, and Mordred's shouting, sometimes flattering and entreating, other times threatening. I would not go out to him again. I had said everything I wanted to say. I was just a piece of territory that he had failed to win from his father, another loss in the war. I sat with Marie in my room, leaning my head back against the wall, my eyes closed, and listened to the shouting and banging so close outside, and I prayed for it to stop, because if it stopped that meant that Mordred and his army had left London.

Then, the time came, as I knew it would, that Marie turned to me, her eyes wide with fear, and she said,

"It's happening."

We were sat in my room, on my bed side by side talking about Christine, laughing to remember all her sweet, stern ways, when she felt the rush of water down her legs. I called all the women to me, but none of us really knew what we were doing. Kay, too, stood in the doorway, watching, his arms folded, his face clouded with concern. He did not have any help to offer, but I was glad of having him there. I took off my dress and knelt between Marie's legs in my underdress as she screamed and screamed. Lynesse behind me was just coughing and coughing, and I had to shout at her to leave because she was upsetting Marie, who was afraid she would make the baby sick. Anna, the little girl, did not leave with her mother, but stood staring open-mouthed and wide-eyed at me, my arms slick with blood to the elbow, struggling in my ignorance.

The baby was a little boy who seemed strong and cried loud, and at first Marie seemed to have made it through; but I could not stop her bleeding. I tore all the spare cotton underdresses I could find into bandages, but I couldn't find where it was coming from, and Marie got paler and paler, and weaker and weaker until, late in the evening the day after the birth, she wouldn't wake up when I shook her to get her to feed her little son, and I screamed at her to wake up until Kay came in and put his hand on my shoulder, and I stopped screaming and started sobbing. I hadn't slept since it had begun and I was exhausted. Kay took the baby from me and handed it to someone else, picking me up in his arms and taking me up to his room and putting me gently in the bed, wrapping the covers around me. I didn't have the strength to protest.

When I woke, it was because Kay was standing over me with the boy in his arms. The baby was screaming and screaming. I felt groggy as though I had slept for a long time, and it was bright outside. It must have been past midday.

"I don't know what to do," Kay said, grimly. "There's no one who can feed him."

I took the baby from him and bounced him in my arms. He was quiet for a moment, but then he started crying again.

"He doesn't have a name," Kay added, hopelessly.

I sent for warm water and honey and tried to get the little boy to suck it off my finger, but he only had a little before he cried and cried again. He knew his mother was gone. I had wished and wished for a child, and now I had this little orphan in my arms, and I already knew I could not save him. I kept him with me until the end. I felt I owed his mother that much, though his screaming was worse than the shouting of Mordred's men outside the tower. I tried again and again to get him to eat something, but we had nothing he would take, and less than a week after his mother, he was dead, too. He could have been a great man. He had been born strong, and he had fought hard for his little life. He would have looked like his father; he was born large, and with a slick of dark hair. He would have made a worthy prince of Lothian.

It was only after he was gone, and Marie and Kay had helped me wrap their bodies and burn them on the battlements of the tower at night, saying the old prayers with me, that I heard that Lynesse had died of her sickness, leaving the little girl Anna an orphan, too. It did not look as though the siege would end soon, and summer shaded into autumn without any respite, though I did not hear Mordred's voice, nor see him among the men that stood in wait outside the tower. As we watched the smoke rise from the bodies, I leaned back against Kay, and I thanked all the gods I knew that they had kept him alive, and I was not yet utterly alone.

I did not sleep well in my room with the ghost of Marie and the memory of Mordred there beside me. I thought of Lancelot, far away, and I wished he would come, but I knew he could not; and I thought of Arthur, and I wished that he would come, but the longer battle went on, the more and more I feared that Arthur would not win. Still no word had come from France. The stores of food were running low, and the mood in the tower turned from a bored complacency to a mild panic. I was facing my death once again, for I would never surrender to Mordred.

Late one evening, I drew my sword and looked at it in the moonlight. I was sure I could do it. I would die like the great queens who had gone before me, like Dido of Carthage, or Cleopatra: by my own hand. I would not be taken as a prisoner. But it sickened me, the thought that Mordred would be the last man that I had known. I would have given anything for a last night with Lancelot. I thought of him every day, and if I dreamed of him at night I woke aching for him; but more often I dreamed of Mordred on top of me, his hand over my mouth, suffocating me, and I woke gasping for breath.

But then I thought of Kay. I would go to Kay before I died. I did not think he would turn me away. Then I could go to my death knowing Mordred had not been the last, and with the fresh memory of a man who I loved, even if it was just the love of a friend. It would be better, anything would be better, than Mordred's hate. And besides, it would remind me of Lancelot.

Kay was still awake in his room when I came up. He was stood in his shirt and breeches at the bookcase, with a book open in his hands when I came in. As I shut the door behind myself, I felt a flutter of nervousness in my stomach. Kay shut the book and slid it back onto the shelf when he saw me. The room was filled with a red glow from the dying embers of his fire and shadows loomed big around us.

"Guinevere, are you alright?" he asked me. He moved towards me and I moved into his arms, which he wrapped around me in gentle concern.

I laid my hands on his chest, and slowly looked up to meet his eyes.

"I didn't want to be alone," I said softly.

"Guinevere," he began in a whisper, as though he was going to say something else, but as I tilted up my face towards his, he stopped, leaning down towards me slowly. Our lips brushed first, and I felt the softness of his lower lip tingling against my own and I gave a little unconscious murmur of longing. Kay, hearing it, slid his hands up my back, drawing me to him, kissing me tenderly, and then more and more passionately as we pressed our bodies together and I felt the heat of him, and deep below it the feel of the Otherworld, close against me. The memories came back to me of the night we had spent with Lancelot, and with my eyes closed I could imagine Lancelot just behind me, that I was about to feel his hands in my hair, his lips against my neck, and I would be wrapped in the intoxicating closeness of them both again. I felt my head grow light with anticipation and excitement, but as I slid my hands down Kay's body, he suddenly pushed me away. I could see, to my surprise, that he was angry, his dark eyes flashing in the low firelight. It was sudden, and disorientating, and I was too shocked to speak.

"What, so you think I am your *creature*, and you're just going to come to me now that there's no one else?" he shouted. He was flushed, indignant.

"Kay, no –"

Perhaps if I had had it in me to explain what Mordred had done to me, he would understand, but I did not.

"You know you're not such a great beauty, now. You're not a young woman anymore. You can't just have any man you want at any time." Kay leaned back away from me, crossing his arms, an unkind, disdainful look spreading across his face in his anger. "Perhaps I would have had you ten years ago. Five if I were drunk." I did not know why he was being so cruel. I stepped away from him, feeling his words strike me hard at my chest, pushing the breath from me. I couldn't take it in, I couldn't keep up with what was happening. I had come to him for comfort.

"Kay, it was not so long ago that we did –"

"Oh, you remember *now*," he cried out in frustration, running his hands through his hair, and stepping towards me so forcefully that I unconsciously jumped back. "You never *said* anything about it. You know your problem, it's that you don't understand love. The pair of you, you're as bad as one another; neither you nor Lancelot ever see anyone, see any*thing* apart from each other. This mystical perfect love you have with Lancelot – it isn't made of anything. There's no substance to it. You don't know *anything* about one another." I could not even tell if his jealousy was directed at me or Lancelot. I suspected it was both of us. "And the love that Arthur gave you for years and years, it means nothing, *nothing* to you in comparison with this *special* love. And me. I never asked anything from you, Guinevere. And now you're going to come to me like it's nothing because you're lonely, and I'm the closest thing to Lancelot you can find. You just take what you want from everyone, and you don't care who you hurt."

I drew myself back, folding my arms over my chest. I was not going to argue with him. I could not believe he would say those things to me. I could not believe that he *thought* those things of me. It was he, though, who did not understand love. Not love as powerful as what was between me and Lancelot. We would always love each other; it was part of the cycles of the earth, part of the fabric of nature. I knew him more deeply than knowing *about* him. But Kay would not understand that. He had not felt that kind of love. It hurt even more that I had come to him for comfort and he was saying these things to me. He stood, watching me for my response, his chest rising and falling hard in anger that was turning quickly to despair, to exasperation. When he saw I was not going to speak he began again, his tone appealing now.

"Guinevere, don't you see this isn't fair? You know that I – how I... Guinevere, Arthur is my *brother*, and I lied for you for years to protect you and Lancelot. How can you come to me now, knowing... just because you're lonely? I would be betraying *everyone* if I – and how can you be doing this now? You only just escaped one charge of treason alive. Why are you so reckless? Why are you always *so careless*?" He was shouting again now, and the loudness of his voice and the rough, caustic truth of what he was saying shook me right to the core, and suddenly, before I even had the chance to try and hold it in, the tears sprang out of me, and I turned to leave, my hands fumbling against the door; but Kay had caught me up in his arms again, pulling me back from the door as I struggled to leave. I didn't want him to see me cry, to see how hard his words had hit me. I didn't know why he had to be so cruel. He pulled me back around so that I was facing him and held me fast by the shoulders. I turned my face away from him, down towards the floor, but he had already seen. He put his hand gently against my cheek and turned my face up so that I had to meet his eye. All the anger had gone, and he looked sad, and lost.

"Guinevere," he said gently, "I'm sorry. But, Guinevere, you don't make doing the right thing easy for me."

I tried to get away from him again – I wanted to be alone, and I felt as though his dark eyes were seeing into me, and would see what had brought me to him; I was ashamed that I had lost to Mordred, and been so easily tricked – but he held me fast.

"Kay, let me go," I mumbled, through the tears falling down my face. I was ashamed of those, too. Kay did not let me go. His sadness had changed to concern. He could tell something was wrong, that something other than the selfish desire that he had seen in me earlier had brought me to him. I could see him repenting his cruel words, but he had said them anyway, which meant that he had thought them about me at one time or another. I felt horribly raw from his words, from the harsh truth of them. Kay grasped my face in his hands and held my head so that I had to look at him.

"Guinevere," he said, his voice low with concern. "What brought you here, really? What is this about? I know we lost Marie, and her baby, and Lynesse, but that's not all of it, is it? I know there is something you are keeping from me. *Tell me.*" I shook my head, the tears blocking my throat. Kay rubbed away a tear with his thumb. "Guinevere, *please.*" I couldn't speak, I couldn't force the words out of me, but I could see the thoughts flashing fast behind his dark eyes. He was adding up the pieces. "What happened when you left Camelot? You never told me how you got away from Mordred. What happened? What did you do?"

I shook my head again, but as he was asking, he was already realising. Kay wasn't stupid, and he had heard what I had shouted down at Mordred from the battlements, seen that Mordred had been sure I would marry him, heard what Mordred and his men had shouted while we feigned ignoring them, that the others had assumed were empty taunts, and lies. I could see the realisation come on him gradually. I hoped I would be spared the saying of it.

"Guinevere, *no*," Kay whispered, his voice thick with dread. I was choking, holding back my tears, struggling for my breath. I would not cry thinking about Mordred. The more I suffered, the greater his horrible victory became. I had not truly escaped from him if I could not keep him out of my head. I had come to Kay to wipe it away, and now I felt the wrench of Kay getting the truth of it out of me.

"You went... willingly?" Kay asked, almost beneath his breath. I could see what he was hoping. That I had planned it as some sly trick to slip away. But I could not lie, not now Kay had brought me to this point, and I shook my head.

Kay's hands fell limp away from me, by his side, and I saw the surprise drain the colour from his face. He understood, and he had not suspected that that would be it. I felt an awful relief, and the wrench of speaking it aloud, half-spoken as it was, only made it more painfully real. I covered my face, hot with tears, with my hands, and fell back against the door, trying to gather in my breaths. I could hear Kay pacing away from me, and back. Then, as though he had only just noticed I was crying, he gathered me into his arms again and held my damp face against his chest, his hand on the back of my head. I let myself lie limp against him.

"I pretended that I wanted him, afterwards," I said softly, into Kay's chest. "And he thought enough of his own greatness that he believed me. So I got away."

Kay was silent for a moment, his hand stroking lightly against my hair. He seemed to be elsewhere with his thoughts, lost with taking it in.

"It would not have made you feel better," he whispered gently after a while, kissing the top of my head. "You would have regretted it, with me. It won't undo it." I shook my head against him, but I knew that he was right. Wordlessly, he began to untie my hair, shaking it loose, then he wiped my face with the sleeve of his shirt until it was dry. I felt swollen and raw. Kay unlaced my overdress at the back and pulled it over my head, but it was more in the manner one might use towards a child, as he had when he had put me in the bath after he had taken me from Lancelot. He led me gently to his bed, and, kicking off his boots, lay down beside me as I lay down, drawing me into his arms. The sense of his Otherworld close about me made me feel calmer, more comforted. I closed my eyes. Having him close by made me feel safer, made me feel that the dreams I had that woke me in the night were further away. Kay, who always understood, had understood everything, and I slept in his arms better than I had the whole time I had been in the tower. I just wanted to feel that he was close. And Kay was right: he was everything to me as my friend, almost like a brother of my own. I would have regretted it, but as it was, I at last felt a presence by my side that chased the ghost of Mordred away from me.

Chapter Fifty-Eight

I only woke the next day when Kay shook me. I was disorientated from being out of the bed I was used to, but I woke quick enough when I remembered. Kay, already dressed, had my dress in his hand, and I quickly pulled it on as I got up from the little makeshift bed. Though we had lain there in all innocence, it would not look well for either of us if anyone found me in there in my underclothes. Kay laced me up fast, pulling slightly too tight in his haste, while I wound my hair back into a plait. As we rushed to dress me, I asked him breathlessly what was going on, what the hurry was.

"There's a messenger at the gates. We need to get up on the battlements," he told me, handing me my crown. I set it on my head and gave a curt nod. My face still felt puffy from the night before, but whoever it was would not be able to tell that from the ground. I raced up, ahead of Kay, who followed behind, heavy and clanking in the suit of mail he had pulled on as we rushed from the room. It was not, I noticed, his set of Otherworld mail. That, too, must have been lost at Joyous Guard. I only had a moment to gather myself before I stepped to the edge of the battlements and looked down. A man mounted on a horse was waiting patiently at the door. As Kay came up behind me, I shouted down.

"What news, sir?"

"My lady, Queen Guinevere," the man shouted back, leaning back on his horse to squint up at me against the bright sun, "Mordred is dead."

The relief that washed over me was dizzying, and I was glad to feel Kay's hand on my shoulder. *Mordred is dead. It is over. Arthur has won.* But something about the man's tone, and the way Kay stood so close behind me made me feel uneasy, uncertain. Why had this man come alone? Why hadn't Arthur come to take back London and reclaim his queen for a second time? Why wasn't Kay saying anything? Why wasn't Kay cheering? No one was cheering. There was a crowd gathered around the man on the horse, and they were all sombre and still.

"Where is Arthur?" I shouted.

I felt Kay's arm around my waist, and I shook him off. I would be told the truth.

"*Where is Arthur?*" I shouted again.

"Let the man in," Kay called down, and, putting his arm around me, he led me down the stairs, down through the tower. Those who had seen through the siege with us had gathered there, and I could hear the same panic among them that I felt in my heart. They gathered about us and followed behind us as we went to unbar and open the door that we had kept fast so long. But I did not feel relief as the doors were drawn wide, only dread. Kay kept his arm around me. What did Kay know? What had Kay sensed already from that man's strange tone, and London cheerless in our victory? What was he not telling me?

The messenger rode in slowly on his horse and leaped down before me, falling to one knee.

"My lady, Queen Guinevere," he said again.

"Tell me," I demanded, my voice harsh with desperation, and rage. "Where is my lord Arthur?"

"My lady." The messenger got slowly to his feet, his face grave. *No.* I stepped back with one foot, steadying myself, feeling myself reel already, under the possibility of it. It couldn't be.

He was a young man, barely more than a boy. I could see, also, that he was wounded, probably from the battle Arthur and Mordred had fought, and dressed in old and battered armour that must have been a father's or an older brother's. "When my lord King Arthur met with Mordred in the field, he smote him through with his spear. Sir Mordred, seeing that he had his death's wound, pushed himself all the way up my lord King Arthur's spear, to strike his father with his sword. My lady, it was a mortal wound that Mordred gave him, and they have taken him to Avalon."

I could hear people saying my name, among them Kay close by, but there was an awful rushing noise drowning them out, and my chest felt tight. I couldn't see anything before me. I did not know if I had closed my eyes, or if the world had just passed away before me. Through it all, I whispered,

"Lancelot, then, did not come?"

"He did not come, my lady. They say he has gathered his armies to ride to Arthur's aid, but he has not come. Not in time."

I could feel hands tight against my arms, and I tried to move away from them, until I realised that they were holding me up. The dreadful roaring still rushed in my ears, and my heart fluttered faintly within me. The darkness that obscured my vision deepened. Arthur was gone. Arthur was gone.

"Arthur," I called out into the darkness as it closed in tighter around me. "*Arthur.*"

But I knew I could not call him back from where he had gone.

I came to my senses, lying down in the bed in the room I had occupied, but which had never truly been *my* room, for all of our time at siege. Someone held a cold cloth against my forehead. For a moment I wondered if I had been ill, and then it rushed back to me. Arthur was dead. It knocked the air out of my lungs, and the strength out of my limbs. I did not know what the world meant without Arthur in it. And he had died far away from me, so painfully close to reconciliation with me. Mordred had stolen that last moment from us. Arthur had left me with a promise of the love we had known together before, and now I would never know it, and he would never know it, again. I felt the rawness of the pain tear through me. It was beyond tears. I felt hollow, right down to the depths of me.

Through my bleary eyes, blinking back to consciousness, I could see Kay standing against the far wall, watching me on the bed, his arms crossed over his chest, one foot resting against the wall as he leaned there. Ector stood beside him, his face grim and drawn. I peered up to see who was holding the cold cloth against my brow and I was shocked to see a face tattooed with swirls of woad, proud and aquiline, gazing down at me with concern. Morgan. Behind her stood Nimue, her long white-blonde hair loose around her shoulders, dressed in the black of mourning. I was surprised to see her so; I had not expected such things to touch the witches of Avalon. Morgan took my clammy hand between her cool dry palms.

"Do you want us to take you to him?" she asked softly.

Kay stepped forward to protest, but Ector put out a hand to hold him back, and he fell back.

I nodded. Morgan twined her fingers with mine on one hand, and Nimue stepped forward to take the other. My eyes met Kay's with sudden realisation and fear that they were not asking me to *ride* with them to Avalon, but I already felt rising over me a sensation of deep drunkenness, dizziness, my limbs light, my head reeling, and the room in the tower dissolved around me, and Kay and Ector with it.

Around me, and Morgan and Nimue, a landscape came into focus and solidified. I felt soft, fresh grass beneath my bare feet – someone must have taken off my shoes when I fainted – and saw before me a beautiful, clear lake spreading out, glassy and perfect, before a tall tor covered on its lower slopes by woodland, and stony and grand at its head. If this was Avalon, I had been wrong about it all along. It was not a barrow-land, but some beautiful place at the heart of the Otherworld, for I felt the Otherworld all around me. A land between life and death surely enough, but nothing how I imagined it would be. If this was where they were taking Arthur for his death, I was glad of it, because it would be as though he was being welcomed into the heart of somewhere that I also belonged. Morgan and Nimue did not let go of my hands, but led me gently towards the lake. As we got closer, I could see a barge moored at the edge of it, and beneath a tree beside it, the figure of a man, slumped, with three women kneeling before him, mourning. I recognised Arthur from far away, and ran towards him, slipping from Morgan and Nimue's hands. The other women stepped away as I came. As I got closer I could see that their faces, too, were painted with the woad of Avalon. I fell to my knees before Arthur and took his face in my hands, whispering his name. His skin felt hot and feverish under my touch, and though his eyelids flickered at my voice, he did not seem to know me. I pressed my lips against his, feeling the tears shake through me at last, and I let them come. I felt my hand grow sticky with blood as I held him. The wound Mordred had given him to the head was still bleeding. I kissed him once more, harder. If love had the power to bring a man back to life, I could have done it then, but it did not have that power and I knew, really, that he was gone.

Gentle arms lifted me away from him and I went with them, limp with grief. Nimue and Morgan stepped forward and stripped him of his armour. I noticed Morgan reach down and unbuckle Excalibur from his waist, and fasten the sword about herself, but I had neither the strength nor the will to stop her. Nimue had his red and gold surcoat and they dressed him carefully in it, and the women holding me let go to lift him into the barge. I ran forward, desperate to touch him one last time, but the three women and Nimue got into the barge and pushed it off, and just as I reached out my hand to touch his, it glided just out of reach. I called out after him, but I knew he could not hear me anymore.

I fell to my knees by the side of the lake, the tears falling from me silently as I watched the little barge move across the glassy lake and disappear out of sight. Arthur was gone from me forever, the man who had given me his love, wholly, for all our lives together, and my heart with him, the one that was his, lost forever, across the lake to the misty Avalon. And I had never had the chance to be worthy of the greatness of his love, which had been pure and whole for me, always, though I had never tried to deserve it.

Chapter Fifty-Nine

Morgan stood by my side to watch the barge go out of sight, but her eyes were dry. Her long, dark, glossy hair was loose, too, in mourning, though her dress was the same, black and glistening with dark stones from the neck to the waist. The wind moved the long tips of her hair lightly, but apart from that she was still beside me until Arthur had finally gone, out of sight.

I felt a sudden flash of anger towards her, remembering her words to me about how she hated Arthur, and the sight of her wearing his sword seemed somehow insulting. I turned to her and tried to snatch it, but she was faster than me and jumped away, drawing Excalibur between us. I noticed that she held it easily in one hand, as I did. But she did not hold it out in aggression. She held it out between us as though she was showing it to me.

"Do you know for whom Excalibur was forged?" she asked me, evenly. He was her brother. How could she be so cold now? *He was gone.*

"For Arthur," I answered stubbornly, stepping forward to take it again, even though I knew I did not stand a chance against her. She moved it lightly out of my reach.

"You know that isn't true. Arthur can barely lift it without both hands. Excalibur was forged *for me*, but Merlin tricked me, and took it from me. Said it was Arthur's destiny. Like you, I suppose."

And before I could answer, she turned and hurled the sword into the lake. It vanished into the low mist that gathered far out across it, that seemed to be gathering more thickly and moving across the lake towards us now that Arthur had passed across it, as though Avalon in the distance was melting away.

Arthur's destiny. I had lain on that table, a stubborn teenage girl, determined not to be wed to her conqueror, and I had wished for his death. Now I had my wish, and I would have given anything not to have it. Had Arthur sealed his fate when he conceived Mordred? When he took the sword? When he sent for me to be his wife? Had I done this with my wish? What if Mordred had not been born full of hate, but my wish for Arthur's death had put it into him? What if *I* was Arthur's bad destiny? Truly, I had loved him with all the ability I had, but it had not been nearly so much as all the goodness of Arthur's heart, and the greatness of his love.

I felt Morgan's hand on my shoulder, and heard the pounding of horses' hooves behind us, and turned to see Kay and Ector ride up together and leap from their horses to run towards us. Both were breathless and flushed from the ride, and Kay's eyes were tinged with red.

"You're too late," Morgan told them, impassively. Kay ignored her to rush to me and pull me into a rough embrace. I buried my head against his shoulder. So, after I was gone and he did not have to be strong anymore, Kay had let himself cry for his foster-brother.

"Say your goodbyes," Morgan snapped at Kay. "And fast. I am taking the queen with me, to the abbey at Amesbury."

Kay ignored her, holding me tight against him. I felt his shoulders shake a little, but he held it in. He did not need to. I would not have thought less of him. Behind us, Ector and Morgan were talking in hushed but friendly tones. I was surprised that the kind old man liked her.

At last Kay's desperate grip fell away from me, and we stood side by side and stared out across the water, and I leaned gently against him. I had cried myself dry, and though my eyes stung and my heart was wracked with pain and sorrow, I stood still as a statue and gazed out at the place where Arthur had gone.

"Guinevere," Morgan called to me, sternly, "it's time."

I turned to Kay and took his hands in mine. I was going to say goodbye, but it did not seem like enough after everything.

"Come and see me, Kay," I said softly, "when I am at Amesbury."

Kay nodded. He did not trust himself to speak either. I leaned up and kissed him on the cheek, and he clasped me in his arms one last time.

I did not want to leave Kay, but I wanted to go to Amesbury. If the world did not have Arthur in it, I did not want to be a part of it. I wanted quiet, anonymity, a world without men, and that was what Amesbury would give me. Kay would come; I knew he would.

Slowly and reluctantly I turned from Kay to take Morgan's hands, and I saw the landscape dissolve around me again, and felt the wave of drunken dizziness, and then I was with her in Amesbury. She told me that it was the place where she had grown up as a girl, and as she led me through its quiet cloister, all calm old stone and lovely arches with the trees and flowers of the little garden winding through them, and we passed the chapel where I heard the nuns singing, I realised that she had brought me away to her own place of safety, and I was grateful.

I took the nun's veil and habit, though I never did fully forget my old gods. Though I thought that could not have mattered much, since this was the abbey that Morgan had been raised in. Besides, now I felt a peculiar affinity with the sad-faced Christ; we had both had a part in sealing Arthur's fate. Morgan came and went, and I was pleased for her visits, though I always found her strange and cold. Once she took me to Arthur's great marble tomb. It was carved in Latin with an inscription that I could not read, but I recognised the word *rex* and Arthur's name. I ran my hand over the smooth marble, but I could not reconcile that cold, dead box with the man I had known, the man I had loved, whose life and strength I had always felt so vividly about me in our time together.

Kay came, too, and I was more pleased of these visits. We would sit in the cloister garden and he would read to me. He told me how he had taken a wife, and it made me happy to hear of the quiet life he had made on his father's small but plentiful lands, and that he had had a child. He came with news, too, of Britain. After Arthur's death the countries had split up again, each king setting out the bounds of his realm and guarding it jealously. Gawain had only given up his anger on his deathbed, finally writing to Lancelot for aid against Mordred. Arthur and Mordred had drawn up a truce, which Arthur had hoped would buy them time for Lancelot's armies to arrive from France, but when the two armies had met to agree the terms of the truce, fighting had broken out anyway, and Arthur and Morded had killed one another. There was fighting still, Kay said, all over the land. No one had suspected that Morgawse of Lothian, who had borne five sons, would leave the kingdom without an heir. Whoever married Gareth's daughter Anna would hold Lothian and Orkney. She was in Kay's keeping, but he did not know how long he could keep her hidden. He had heard that Mark wanted her, now that Isolde was dead. They said that Isolde had died of sorrow when she heard of Tristan's death, but I did not think it was beyond the work of Mark to have done it himself. There was little news of Lancelot. I was sure that he would come to look for me, that he would need to know if I had lived, and where I was, but I was not sure I could bear to see him again, or if it would destroy me.

I thought always of Arthur, and of Lancelot. Sometimes it was of the two great loves I had had with them, and the wonderful rapture of the different passions I had shared with them, but sometimes it was guilt I felt when I remembered them. Guilt at what I had done to Arthur with my lies, and at my inability to let Lancelot go, to free him from my love so that he could have loved another woman freely, and without danger.

Life was quiet, and life was simple, and I was left to my thoughts. I looked forward to my visits from Kay, and I read often, sitting in the cloister garden when it was warm and pleasant, or by my fire when it was cold. I missed them the most at night, when it was cold and dark, and in that half-sleep, half-wake time I would re-live my former life of passion in my heart and my mind, and I would hold a warm and secret gladness to my heart that I had felt such love as theirs.

Chapter Sixty

It came sooner than I thought, the moment I both longed for and dreaded, when Lancelot found me. It was early spring, fresh and green all about the abbey, and I sat in my room with the window open, a book open on my lap. I wasn't reading; I was staring out of the window across the fields around. There were rabbits, and little birds, and everything was full of serenity and new life. I felt more and more, in those days, the knot of pain where Merlin had closed my womb. Morgan had told me it was as I feared, and Arthur had stopped Merlin from finishing his spell entirely, and as I was growing older, what was left of my womb, still inside, was beginning to grow hard and heavy, draining the strength from me.

"My lady." One of the young nuns ran into my room without knocking, her eyes wild with panic, her voice shrill and breathless. "My lady, there is an armoured knight in the abbey."

I set down the book and stood slowly from my chair, forcing myself to breathe calmly. I was prepared for this moment. I had imagined it over and over again in my head so many times.

"It's alright," I told her, gently. "He has come for me."

The girl still looked worried. Of course, to her, an armoured knight meant danger. She had not spent her life around these huge men clad in iron. She associated them with blood and death and war.

"Take me to him," I said quietly.

Lancelot stood in the courtyard garden, dressed in his armour, his sword at his side and his helm in his hand. He did not recognise me at first as I came, but from far off I knew it was him from the powerful, graceful way that he stood. As we got closer I could see what the years had done to him; grey had begun to thread through his hair at the temples, and his face was dark with stubble. He looked dirty and weary from travel, as though he had not stopped searching for me since he left France. I knew I, too, had aged, my lovely red hair paling at last to light copper with the years, and I was pleased it was hidden from him. I wanted him to remember me how I had been, how we had been together, when we were young.

The young girl ran away as soon as she was sure I had seen him. I was glad of it. I did not think I could bear to say goodbye to him any other way than alone.

I stepped out under a stone archway into the garden. I was trembling slightly already. For a moment Lancelot's eyes lighted on me without recognition, but then he saw it was me, and he dropped his helm to the ground and threw off his leather gauntlets, coming warily towards me. I had meant to hold back, but the magnetism of his presence pulled me towards him, too. I was glad of my nun's clothes; they made me feel a little stronger, a little more detached. I did not want to give in again; our love had been so great that it had destroyed Britain, and brought Arthur's death. It would have been unbearable to go back to it, as though it were some ordinary kind of love, something domestic. It had been raging and dangerous, and I knew if I felt it again one more time, I would be lost forever. It had cost too much, our love.

Lancelot reached out to touch my face, and as I felt his skin brush mine I sighed and my knees gave way beneath me as all the memory and joy and pleasure and regret washed over me. Lancelot stepped forward to catch me and we both fell to our knees. I reached up and took his face in my hands, and he held me the same, and I looked into those dark blue eyes that had drawn me in so long ago, that I had loved with a power that was beyond words. We were both breathing in gasps, both trembling. Lancelot pressed his forehead against mine, and I felt the closeness, the presence of his body stir the heat within me. I could smell the blood and sweat and metal on him, and beneath that the soft familiar scent of his skin that I had felt so often and so blissfully next to mine. His breath brushed my face, and my heart pounded in me. I turned my face up, a little closer towards his, drawn by the delicious memories of our love together, and he leaned down towards me, his nose brushing mine. I remembered the first kiss, when he had brushed his lips against mine as I gave him my gold token, and I remembered the kiss after that, when he had lifted me on to the table and I thought we were about to come together, and I remembered Surluse – him stepping into my pavilion dripping with water, the touch I had longed for on my body, his hands cold from the rain, his mouth hot against mine, the light from the brazier on his naked body – and after that, when we had made drunk, rough love on the stairs at Christmas, and the morning after he had come to rescue me from Meleagant when we had loved together slowly, safe from the eyes of others, far from Camelot, and the last time, when we had met in desperation, knowing that it was the end. My body remembered the touch of his hands and his lips, and it pressed me towards him in longing, in need. I remembered strong about me the intoxicating pleasure of his love, the feel of our bodies together.

But, as I felt his lips touch mine, and the threat of sensual drunkenness at their touch filled me, I shied away, gently shaking my head. It would be too much. To give in once, just a little, would have been to give in forever.

"Guinevere," he whispered, his face still close, our foreheads still touching. I could feel the roughness of his stubble under my hands, and the heat of his skin. "Come back with me to my kingdom. As my wife."

I shook my head again, feeling the tears falling from my eyes, dropping onto his hands, onto my lap. We could never live like that, and I was old and barren and dying. Lancelot was handsome, still. I loved him enough to do him a last, painful kindness, and release him from me.

"No, Lancelot. We have destroyed everything with our love. What would we do?" I gave a dark laugh. "Go to your kingdom, and grow old together, telling each other stories of Arthur, and our times together? How between us, with our love, we brought his death? No, Lancelot. Find a young wife. Have a child. Be happy."

I felt his tears, then, against my hands, and they shook through me as my own did.

"I won't. I can't. There's no one but you," he said thickly, struggling through his own tears, through mine. They mingled between us, on our hands, and both of us caught our breath gasping, shaking. "If I can't have you as my wife, I will take to a religious life, as you have."

"Lancelot," I gathered as much breath into me as I could manage, "do not forget the beauty of the world."

I did not want to have destroyed him, to have made it so that he, like me, was a hollow shade filled with memory and longing and guilt. He was still full of life, still strong, and could go out and be happy. But he shook his head.

"There is no world," he said, his voice dark and grating through his tears, "without you in it."

We held each other as we were, our faces in each other's hands, both sobbing, shaking, but we both knew it was the end. We could not go back, not when we had killed Arthur and torn up Britain with our love. At last, Lancelot nodded slowly.

"Just kiss me," he breathed, leaning down towards me again, "once." But I laid my fingers gently against his lips and shook my head. Even that, the feel of his lips against my fingertips, was almost beyond what I could endure to resist. I could not speak. The tears had filled my throat, and I could not; but if I kissed him I would give in, I would lose myself in him, and we would both be destroyed. It was too hard, too powerful, the love I had for him. I wanted him to have one last chance at life, at happiness, without me.

Slowly, he stood and left, and I sat there on my knees, letting the sobs wrack through me until the young nun came back with some others and they carried me gently to my room where I sobbed until at last I fell asleep. When I dreamed, it was of him, and the sound of the rain on my pavilion, and the glorious earth-shattering feeling of his arms around me, and our bodies together.

When I woke, Morgan sat beside me, and beside her on the table sat my little French book of Ovid. I wondered if she had had it all along, or if it had somehow come back when I had said goodbye to Lancelot, as though it had been something I had exchanged for him.

"It is time to go," Morgan told me softly.

"Where?" I asked.

"To Avalon."

And she held out her hand to me, and I took it.

Guinevere is also available on kindle:

www.amazon.com/dp/B00QJFVCI4

To discover more great books like Guinevere by Lavinia Collins visit:

thebookfolks.com

Printed in Great Britain
by Amazon

40468965R00219